THE CLINIC

RAY CAROLE

Ray left school with a black eye, someone else's coat and his virginity intact to join the Royal Marines in 1996. Four years later, he was the youngest then serving member in 22 SAS. For over a decade he toured the world helping everyone to like each other again, with the odd bomb and bullet accelerating the process of reconciliation, before leaving as a Sgt at age 31.

Filling the void of elitism, he raced 500 miles to the Magnetic North Pole, then set off to be the first person to walk 1430 miles solo to the South Pole and back, with no support, or any tangible reason as to why he was doing it. In between, he's been a billionaire's bag carrier, an ultra-athlete, mentor and a social liability.

In the last few years, Ray has written *The Clinic*, and its screenplay adaptation; the first in a new trilogy. He is currently writing book two, *The Trace* and a TV series called *Cell Zero* about a disillusioned SAS operator who conspires to defraud the CIA and land a $25 million bounty on the world's most wanted terrorist.

Ray is fascinated with how random thoughts, self-doubt and catastrophic thinking prevent people daring to reach full potential. Turning this on its head, Ray has also created his Project 8: Who Thinks Wins pocket journal series. It's a simple and concise 15-minutes-a-day action guide to empower anyone to develop a healthy and fulfilling mindset.

For more information about Ray, and Project 8, visit

www.raycarole.com

THE CLINIC

RAY CAROLE

Matador
9 Priory Business Park,
Wistow Road, Kibworth Beauchamp,
Leicestershire. LE8 0RX
Tel: 0116 279 2299
Email: books@troubador.co.uk
Web: www.troubador.co.uk/matador
Twitter: @matadorbooks

ISBN 978 1838593 933

British Library Cataloguing in Publication Data.
A catalogue record for this book is available from the British Library.

Printed and bound by CPI Group (UK) Ltd, Croydon, CR0 4YY
Typeset in 11pt Aldine401 BT by Troubador Publishing Ltd, Leicester, UK

Matador is an imprint of Troubador Publishing Ltd

In loving memory of Mum

My family
For never doubting me

ACKNOWLEDGEMENTS

To all my dearest friends and family who have never grasped the concept of fiction, like I have never grasped the concept of reality, but have spent five years hounding me to publish my novel as that's what writers do apparently!

As I have mentioned before, you are not in this book as it's made up; just like my name Ray Carole, it's fiction. But if you come across characters who are twice as smart, twice as hard, half the size of you, making love to hot girls, then tell your friends, that it's you.

With great thanks to Cherry Martin, my editor who has patiently honed my writing skills over the past few years. Your own record-breaking shortest marriage in history, coupled with my natural ability to lose myself in alcohol-fuelled weekends on occasions, delayed this book's release. To Billy Allinson who created the cover design and branding from a weak, back of a beer mat brief from myself.

For some reason the odd mad character asks me if I had a ghost writer. The answer is in the history of past achievements. Never a fraud, or one to take short cuts, I wrote it myself, inspired by 41 days of solitude in Antarctica where questioning my motives triggered this trilogy. It's another new journey to personal literacy excellence that demands hard work, commitment, with no fear of the consequences of exploration in life.

THE CLINIC INCEPTION

This novel's inception is inspired by my 1430-mile solo expedition to the South Pole and Back when a psychological concept was borne in my mind that would scare women away, and even hardened killers.

At the time I wanted to create history, search for the elitism I craved, and refine my mental masterclass during 85 days of hell. To my despair, I only had a 64-day window instead of a planned 85 due to the weather. This iconic trip was doomed, and I was advised to abort and attempt to beat the one-way world record of 39 days instead.

The founding father of the British SAS, Sir David Stirling, said that 'Nothing is impossible to a few determined men'. I was one of these SAS men years ago, and I have seen first hand how feats of huge daring, through extreme planning and elite skill can bring about seemingly impossible results. In my mind I had to *prove* the South Pole expedition impossible, not predict it like everyone else. So, I set off as planned powering the first 715 miles in 41 days to the Pole, pulling over 150kg with no support or assistance.

Ironically this monumental effort convinced everyone it was now possible, for me to turn around and ski back in 23 days. I knew it was impossible, I needed 30 days plus, so abandoned my efforts and focused on paying back 50K of debt, drowning my sorrows for a few weeks, and crying about getting a normal job again. My expedition went unnoticed by the public, but certainly let the experts know that with the right window, and the right amount of suffering, this feat was now possible. My new mission was to pen the novel that had become burnt into my mind during those days on the ice.

This isn't a true story of former SAS men's daring. I have ultimate respect for the privacy of the organisation that once gave me the privilege to serve with them. My decision to remain as discreet as possible and to write under the pseudonym Ray Carole is based on principles that still honour the spirit and legacy of the SAS, that is to leave and live life as quietly as you joined and served.

Some character's names are true from the Polar Expedition world. All the other names who inflict serious pain with pleasure, or deliver calculated misfortune effortlessly are fictional in every sense.

All events that are military in nature, are scripted by my imagination and not based on real events.

CHAPTER 1

He watched the dejected man make his journey to the doorway which once closed will never be reopened. Keeping his eyes on the man's painfully slow footsteps he almost had the minor urge to jump up and shout 'stop'. However, his intuition borne from years of experience, told him that people like the figure reaching for the handle would never look back for sympathy or one last chance. He knew the door would be closed weakly by the man who was shutting out a past that had tortured his mind, and destroyed the resolve to carry on the fight he had been so used to winning, once upon a time, now that fight had dissolved in to nothing.

He remained seated, completing his report that pretty much amounted to yet another tragic case of a killer going full circle.

The footsteps stopped and he paused to look up. He was still met with the man's wilted frame. 'Jesus,' he mused. Ten years previously, that man had crashed through the door, almost forgetting to use the handle, knowing that he was surrendering his life to a cause he would never question, that the cause would be brutal on the body, terrorising on his mind, and maybe the man even predicted that this day would come. He, like so many others before him, probably realised they wouldn't recognise themselves one day.

He stopped punching at his keyboard. It hadn't just been hatred he'd seen staring at him moments earlier. It was humiliation, even embarrassment as the man's stale alcoholic breath floated across his desk like an invisible fog, almost making him choke on the fumes. Bloodshot eyes that could barely meet his former Commander's.

Silently, the man had simply placed his ID card down on the desk and spun around to head to the door that he was now pausing at.

A turn of the handle and the man disappeared.

Still seated and not getting the look back that he had half expected, he pushed back hard into his seat, rocking backwards, his hands interlocked behind his head he surveyed the empty room. He could almost see the vapour trail of alcohol the man had left behind him. He watched the door, Would it swing open again he thought? He held his breath for ten seconds.

The door stayed closed.

He sighed, knowing full well that that was the last time he would ever see him again.

'And I couldn't give a shit.' Just another super star operator that had become weak, and finally broken under the immense pressure of deniable operations. The world could ill afford mentally unstable operators cutting about with lethal hardware on their person.

Knowing the man would end up in the gutter within months he began typing away on his keyboard again, formally sealing the man's existence in cyber space. Normal out-processing stuff - security and threat assessments for departing members of the elite organisation was standard. Always susceptible to possible defection, or selling secrets to the outside world, this particular final section was the easiest he had filled to date.

SUBVERSION LEVEL LOW, requires no further monitoring or follow up activity.

ADDITIONAL INFORMATION, life expectancy possibly 3-6 months, threat to self.

He paused, double checking the lines, before pressing the final key marked 'done'.

CHAPTER 2

White frozen ice and zero visibility to his front forced him to stop. Slumping down on his sled, he rested his head in his hands. Closing his eyes the white turned to black, driving him back to the darkness of the past, re-triggering the memories that he had fought so hard to run away from. Unable to fight, he found himself years ago, back in Central Baghdad.

As he checked the canopy above his head, he realised it was almost pitch-black, just the fluttering of the end cells in his parachute caught his eyes.

'Ideal,' he muttered, knowing that these were perfect conditions to ensure an unexpected visit by not alerting any local lookouts who would surely be on high alert to notify their bosses of any unusual activity, suspects or military operations in the area. Just innocent kids or unsuspecting old men cowering in the streets were often only an arm's length away from a radio to inform the terrorists that soldiers were coming.

Looking through his night-vision goggles 10,000ft above a city that was descending into chaos every day, he saw battered buildings interspersed with blocked roads and territorial enclaves. Daily life in the rabble of war under a corrupt government meant he would be back for sure, even though he knew this would be his last operation of his current tour, his fourth to date.

'Got it.' He recognised the DZ, the Drop Zone that would be their landing area. It was a field south of a prominent disused water tower that was glowing white, courtesy of a few street lamps still flickering slightly due to the abused circuitry; all they had to do was head north-west and hit it without breaking anything.

'Zero, this is Tango 1, check,' Decker checked in to Zero, the Commanding Officer in the operations room, against a strong wind that was distorting his voice but was crystal-clear to the experienced operator listening to him.

'Tango 1 that's good to us but a little broken. All jumpers are good and tracking in sequence towards DZ.'

'Roger that, visual DZ, give me target update,' Decker asked for any new activity on the target. The operations centre had a live feed so could see exactly what was happening on the target the eight men were heading for to conduct a potentially brutal hostage rescue.

It was an Al Qaeda (AQ) suicide bombing network holding construction workers hostage. Decker had dealt with these cells before and knew that not everyone would be left alive; they blew themselves up, were killed or blown up by close air support delivering a kinetic bombs strike.

'Tango 1, that's two terrorists on the roof of target, carrying weapons, all other aspects quiet, DZ clear,' this informed the team, who were all listening, that there were two enemies on the roof with weapons, everywhere else was quiet, and where they were about to land had no activity. From Intelligence and experience, Decker knew at least another three or so terrorists would be in the building awaiting his team's arrival, with suicide vests donned, more AK-47s and a huge bomb to bring the whole building down if they were overrun.

'Copy that, wind speed is up, we're tracking at 15 knots so have the legs to make DZ,' this transmission was a critical one that put everyone at ease, especially the Prime Minister who had given it the go-ahead 60 minutes previously. It meant they would not drop short of the target and land in an urban area full of lunatics who wanted nothing more than to dance in the streets celebrating a British or American soldier's head on a stake.

When the boss had given Decker the go-ahead for the hostage rescue, Decker had walked into the orders room eight feet tall, this was instantly met with John's comical impersonation of the PM's decision.

'Negotiations have ceased, there are no alternatives, gentleman, send in the Black Death, please, Brigadier.' This magnified the sick humour and lack of real concern of death by suicide bombers within the regiment.

Decker had thought about the consequences of landing short, and he wasn't bothered about crashing into a hell hole full of rag heads, but he was bothered about the fucking embarrassment it would cause the SAS.

'Zero, copy, will update any changes on target or LZ. Out.' With about two minutes left until he hit the deck, he took one last long look at the city that had been his second home for almost five years. Whether he was blowing into buildings and killing terrorists, driving a car around undercover following terrorists, he took a moment to absorb the sheer pleasure it had brought him. His five long years had given him the skills and knowledge to kill any high-grade terrorist, anywhere in the world, but above all here, he had mastered his instinct that had kept him alive in the face of impending death.

Within 90 seconds, all eight guys were on the ground, had quickly rolled their chutes in and dumped them. There was no need to hide them as this operation would be live in ten minutes and the whole area would descend into chaos as the other assault teams and helicopters landed. The team listened in as Decker whispered his confirmation set of orders.

'Right guys, this is it,' looking towards the target building 500 metres away.

All the while, everyone could hear Zero in their earpieces informing them that two bad guys were still on the roof but everything else was quiet.

'Perfect,' all of them thought. They almost had the upper hand and could now move covertly to the entry point on the west wall.

'Okay, as planned, Dave, you lead the breach team straight to the breach point, no messing about. We've done this a hundred times. Give me the thumbs up when the charge is set. I will call forward the helicopters with the rest of the teams. When they are a few hundred metres out, we blow in. The rest, we know. Happy guys?'

Stupid question really – this team had done over a hundred odd jobs in their six-month tour. Even so, no plan ever survives first contact with the enemy, or as Decker used to say in his younger fighting days, 'Everyone has a plan till they get punched in the face.'

Decker ran again the tape of action he'd imagined filmed in his head: *Unlike most buildings in this region, it doesn't have a compound wall surrounding it, maybe this is part of the disguise or deception so will make things easier for us.*

Having to blow through a compound wall then move 20-odd metres to blow the building wall in makes us susceptible as the moment of surprise is always lost but tonight is different.

The breach is straight into the target building hallway with the hostages all in the first room on the left. This is only the case if the undercover agent, who was arranging the transport that would drive the hostages to their next holding area at first light, was right when he had seen them six hours earlier. It made sense: the curfew made it too dangerous to transport at night as no vehicles except police and military were permitted to move.

The hostages had only arrived 12 hours earlier, the agent reckoned, and their end destination was rumoured to be across the border.

His thoughts were interrupted as a bead of sweat stung his right eye. That musty stench he had always associated with the Middle East was as ripe as ever tonight. Wiping his brow with his brown leather gloves he looked over at Dave, who was moving with complete confidence, knowing his team of the SAS's most elite were covering his arse.

As he placed the explosive wall charge on the breach point, they watched knowing that it would not only put a great hole in the wall but take out any terrorists behind it, too. Decker held his breath. They had put a lot of faith into their agent's sketched out map of the house. He knew he couldn't afford to blow direct into the hostages' room, that would be messy, embarrassing and result in mission failure.

Wall charge all set, he started reeling out the shock tube to the end of the team, who were all stacked up in a line ready to assault the building. This was a vulnerable time without hard cover, but standard. Unlike the recommended safety distance of twenty metres from the charge when it blew, the team were five metres away, bracing for the explosion.

Zero quickly came on the network with complete urgency.

'Terrorists on the roof, apporaching the team...'

Before Zero could finish his sentence, the silhouette of a man popped his head over the roof wall, shouted something in Arabic to the other terrorist, then drilled half a magazine of bullets at the guys. Instantly, Mike reacted in the covering team ten metres from the building, engaged and clipped his shoulder, spinning him around and to the roof floor.

'Go, go, go!' Decker shouted across the gravel yard to the breach team.

Not even in position, Dave hit the detonation switch only a few metres from the charge, knowing a delay of seconds to save his own skin could mean death to the hostages. A huge explosion penetrated the wall as the shockwaves and after blast ruptured their eardrums. This was the norm, bleeding ears and noses were a given.

The vital second it took to absorb the back blast was met with another hail of bullets from the roof wall as the terrorist did a classic Lebanese unload, the cowardly act of pointing an AK-47 over a wall, not even looking where he was firing and not stopping till 30 bullets had been discharged.

Andy took a round straight through the head and dropped instantly;

Sean next to him caught up four rounds but luckily to his right thigh and lower left leg, the other two landed in the chest plate of his body armour.

The breach team didn't hang about and were through the hole like rats up a drainpipe.

'Frag on the roof. Frag on the roof,' Decker screamed as he threw a high-explosive grenade over the roof wall, knowing they were in serious trouble, big style, and as soon as his first was over, he prepped a second.

A huge explosion was followed instantly by a second.

'He's let himself off,' Decker concluded, imagining that the terrorist had detonated his vest, but with no time to think further, his second grenade was airborne as he aimed his weapon with Johnny at the roof wall in case another terrorist popped up.

Even though Andy was dead and Sean wounded, it didn't matter, they were here to rescue the hostages, and Decker needed to get in behind the team as quickly as he could to give support.

Sean, bleeding heavily, was already crawling to the wall to get out of the firing line, knowing Decker and Johnny needed to get in the building fast and not worry about him.

'Johnny, let's go!' Decker screamed as he heard gunfire erupting inside. He automatically knew it was going south when he realised he hadn't heard the strip charge take the hostages' door down yet. A gun battle was going on and there still may be one left on the roof, vested up.

'Sean, get your grenades on the roof and keep covering.'

Sean could just about manage it – he was an ox and would fight on, even with holes in his body.

Inside, Dave had been placing an explosive strip charge on the reinforced door, hearing the hostages shouting when the familiar sight of an AK-47 barrel came pointing around the end corridor wall, letting rip. With three men all lined up behind Dave waiting for the door to be blown, Dave was hit and dropped instantly. It was a fatal blow.

Fuck, Dave was dead.

Decker had just seen this happen and forced himself, with Johnny, past the team on his left and straight towards the hidden gunman who had just killed Dave. This would give the team time to breach the door and get the hostages before anyone else got killed in this tight corridor.

'On me, Johnny, on me,' Decker screamed on the move with his

7

weapon up, firing at the corner wall, closing down the dead space to come face to face with the threat.

Rob took the shock tube and detonating switch from Dave's dead clenched hand, left him there and hit the plunger. The other two men knew what to do once the door was breached. Another spine-shattering explosion told Decker they had blown the door in. In such a confined space, this fully ruptured anyone's ears that still needed rupturing and kicked up a dust cloud that instantly blinded everyone in the corridor.

No hesitation. Jack and Rob punched forward hard into the room for rapid room domination with Mike covering over their shoulders, and they started to clear the room.

Immediately Jack saw the threat: a terrorist, looking shocked by the explosion, with a weapon and holding something else. Behind him, Jack saw the hostages, tied up in a huddle.

Enemy, weapon seen, shoot, was how Jack and every other soldier's thought process worked. The boy dropped with two bullets to the head and a couple to the body. What dropped just after him switched the room into slow-motion.

Except for Rob, the last man to enter the room, had played this scenario out in his head a thousand times before but never thought he'd ever have to actually do it.

A quick step and dive saw his body launch through the air and land on top of the grenade as it rolled out of the terrorist's limp hand. Silence. Everyone dived to the floor, holding their heads, crunched up in the foetal position, eyes closed, bracing for death. Rob could feel the grenade digging in underneath his body armour as he braced for his final few moments. Two seconds, still nothing. Then three, then four.

Knowing full well how old their grenades could be, Rob held tight, waiting for it to explode, resisting the burning temptation to move off it. Everyone else was thinking the same and started to nervously twitch and move.

Boom!

A blunt explosion, deadened by Rob's body and body armour hunched over it, absorbed and contained the blast's devastating blow, throwing his body a foot off the ground.

Decker and Johnny heard it but knew not to react and probed forward to the stairs. They both knew momentum is everything – going back wasn't an option when a load more terrorists may be in the next room. Rounding the corner, Decker, from an acute angle, identified the hoodlum causing trouble and drilled him on the move, kept closing, kept shooting, while Johnny covered the rest of the corridor and stairs. The roof shook under the pressure of what could only be Sean throwing a grenade from outside on to the roof.

In all of the confusion, no one heard Zero transmit the other bad guy was coming down to join the party and about to bump into Johnny and Decker.

'Open door!' Johnny shouted as he was missed by a couple of bullets that screamed past him, hitting the wall behind him. Leaping across the room to the side of the open doorway, Decker was behind him. Johnny knew they were ready when he caught the small projectile fly past his right eye with the call 'Frag in, Frag in'; Decker had thrown in the grenade and they both tensed up, ready for the explosion.

Boom!

Weapon on aim, Johnny was in, engaging the horrible piece of scum lying on the deck with his hands up and a million and one pieces of frag in him. Shooting straight through his hands and into his face, Johnny got the job done, whilst Decker discovered he had company of his own.

Popping out from behind a small recess, another terrorist, still disorientated, stepped into the fray, hiding from the grenade that just smoked his mate. A little too slow to raise his weapon even though he was firing in blind panic into the floor, he was no match for Decker, who unleashed a lightning-quick five bullets and put him down. As he smashed the floor, they both realised he was vested up, and instinct drove Decker to put two more bullets in his head. A slight second of disbelief was met with the realisation they had got away with it yet again. They knew instantly the guy must've been in shock from the grenade and failed to act quickly enough to detonate the vest. It was time to get out the room.

Decker shouted to the hostage room.

'Jack, Mike, Sit-Rep.'

As Mike got to his feet he checked Rob's body out of habit for a pulse. He was lifeless. The four others were crimping on the floor, blood around their heads, but luckily from the overpressure of the charge and not fragments from the lethal grenade.

Pointing his weapon at them, he confirmed they were westerners and there was not another terrorist in the mix. All four were alive. It was only now he smelt human excrement and urine, with an overpowering scent of body odour. Weeks of no washing, zero urinals and constant beating's were now visible as the dust settled, and the moans of elation rose. He saw Jack wretch at the pile of human faesis in one corner.

Before he replied he noted the battered and bruised victims on the floor. This didn't compensate for Rob, who had just sacrificed his life for theirs.

Jack turned to the hostages, all gazing up at them with relief in their eyes. 'You bunch of complete selfish money driven pricks. I would execute you now if I could.'

Decker nodded, they shared a mutual hatred of contract workers in Iraq who yet again had cost British SAS lives. Yet still they had orders.

'Jack, Mike, give us an update,' Decker kept shouting.

Jack replied 'Rob and Dave are dead, four hostages alive, four hostages alive', repeating himself as this was the mission objective and it had been achieved thus far. Counting the cost of dead operators on the ground was not the priority at that moment in time.

With no time to lose, Decker knew he didn't have to push further – they had the hostages, alive. The job was done and it was time to consolidate and wait for the other teams to push through in a few minutes.

One problem was that three of his team were dead, one injured and Decker didn't like to be made to look like a bastard or to leave a job half finished. As Decker covered the stairs, Johnny pushed back to the hostages' room, checking Dave's pulse as he passed outside the door but nothing.

'Tango 1, this is Zero, what's happening?' The Commander desperately wanted an update on the line as the explosions he saw on the live feed back in the comfort of the operation centre made him twitch. Decker finally heard him at the same time he heard the distinct sounds of the little birds approaching the target with fresh teams to neutralise the remaining terrorists.

'Hold off, hold off, still a possible terrorist vested up; we haven't cleared the first floor yet.'

'Zero roger, the helicopters will pull off and cover the area for runners, you have the other two teams landing now west of the building to push through and clear the rest.'

'Roger that, I'm going to get the hostages out of the building in case the remaining terrorists blow themselves up or this place is rigged to blow.'

'Zero roger.'

'We have three fatalities, and one critical: one lower-limb flesh wounds but stable.'

'Zero copy, just hold them all till the backup is there in 90 seconds,' said the commander, reassuring them the ordeal was almost over.

'Got it,' Decker confirmed.

As Decker quickly ran a battle appreciation through his mind, it was already made up and Johnny knew what was coming too.

'Let's finish this, Johnny, we haven't time to wait around for backup.'

Without question, Johnny did a quick magazine change, Decker followed suit. Both checked they had a few grenades left and that they hadn't been shot. From experience, they knew the adrenaline coursing through their veins could genuinely hide this obvious fact, until afterwards when they finally stopped charging around and realised they were bleeding heavily.

No brief was needed. Simple, they both knew they were heading up the stairs and about to come face to face with at least one suicide bomber and they weren't leaving till he was flat-packed, dead on the floor.

'Okay, let's do it, mate,' Decker signalled to Johnny to take the stairs. Both working the short 2-tier staircase, they hit the first floor without incident. Holding on for a moment to listen as a strange silence had fallen over the dusty broken house, they used just hand signals as they quickly looked for an open door off the landing, but they were all closed. With only two grenades between them, that made it tricky. With the threat of a suicide bomber, it was always preferable to chuck a grenade in first before entering.

Decker gave Johnny the nod; grenade was in and four seconds later it detonated.

'Here we go, control, control, control,' Decker thought before punching into the room his weapon ready to engage with anything that posed a threat. Nothing.

'Room clear,' letting Johnny, who was already covering the next room door, know. Immediately pushing the door in, another grenade spun its way in. Johnny waited for the explosion then followed it in.

'Room clear,' was the call that came back out. Then it started getting tricky: no grenades and no surprise, just speed and aggression.

As Decker nodded towards the next door on their left in the tight hallway, the opposite door flung open; they swung their heads around to face the maniac screaming 'Allahu Akbar, Allahu Akbar' literally only a metre away. Decker swung his weapon around, but it was too late, the man was already in their faces. But nothing happened. Time stood still as all three men froze with saucepan eyes, wondering why they weren't spread across the hallway.

Knowing full well that hesitation costs lives, Decker threw a headbutt straight into the maniac's face, quickly followed up with a few more. The ceramic Kevlar helmet he was wearing connected with the maniac's face, busting it wide open, and Decker violently pushed him back into the room he came out of.

Johnny covered the door. The suicide vest didn't detonate, not that Decker gave a toss that it still might. Slinging his weapon behind his back and letting the maniac drop to the floor, Decker was straight on him, jumping on his head, driving the sole of his right boot hard, repeatedly into his nose.

Johnny looked over his shoulder to see the bloodbath behind. 'Not again,' he said, 'just shoot the rag head; this isn't the time or place,' but he heard Decker shouting his head off uncontrollably with each stamp on his head.

Having completely defaced the dead man, Decker was covered in blood whilst giving Johnny the nod. The space around them was now noisy with other teams entering below, helicopters hovering around and spotlights on the building. Time was running out to close this one down Decker thought.

'Okay, Johnny, last room, you know what to expect?'

No reply. Johnny was already moving to the last door, their last door of the tour, probably their last together.

As Decker aimed his weapon at the closed door, waiting for Johnny to throw it open, Johnny gave him the nod then slung the door open. On rapidly stepping into the room, the threat was clear to see. Though the darkened room hid all facial features, a figure was standing there in a stance that signified defeat, weapon in hand hanging down by their side, their body language clear that they were not going to put up a fight, almost willing the two armed men to quickly end the hell they had been living in.

'Terrorist, weapon by side, that's a green light, engage,' was all that Decker had running through his mind and his finger started to slowly squeeze the trigger. He was about to deliver the final blow to this terrorist's existence. The face that he was about to shoot through wasn't one with a beard, a dark tan ingrained with hardened lines of terror indoctrinated throughout the years. Instead the face was one of extreme beauty, a spotless complexion with piercing brown eyes that looked unblinkingly straight into Decker's. The woman didn't flinch, didn't even attempt to raise her weapon. She simply dropped it.

As her weapon crashed into the floor Johnny suddenly smashed into Decker's side knocking him off balance. Decker in slight shock quickly looked at Johnny who was shouting 'STOPPAGE, STOPPAGE' like a mad man as he dropped to his knee. Stoppage meant his weapon had jammed or malfunctioned and couldn't deliver the killer blow. The immediate action was to drop to your knee and draw your pistol that was holstered on your chest.

The female was bending down to pick up her weapon, spotting the threat he fired two bullets. They bounced off the AK-47 assault rifle that made her dive away and cower in a curled up ball.

Seeing Johnny stand up with his pistol Decker stepped across him instantly preventing him firing his pistol at the lady.

Johnny looked confused. 'What the fuck are you doing?'
Breathing out, Decker looked towards the body still cowered on the floor. She slowly sat up, correcting her shamag that was a mess due the previous seconds of panic.

Johnny shook his head then walked out the room and started clearing his M4 carbine assault rifle.

As Decker stared deeply into the gaze of her eyes, he was instantly met with the freezing cold ice that was plastered around his face. Every time he saw her eyes, he woke up in a state of panic.

Always that image.

Killing her might have been the easier option as the pain ripped through his mind again, instant knots cramped up his stomach.

He ripped his mask off and rubbed his eyes.

'My dearest Larnaka,' he whispered into the Antarctic wind.

CHAPTER 3

A black dictaphone held court in the centre of a conference table. Though small and fragile it was achieving the intended aim. Two highly trained operatives, experts in their previous fields, were quick to note it was a showpiece to stimulate wild assumptions. The third man was closer to a boy than a man, looking like he had just finished sixth form and was still battling outbreaks of acne, it was clear he was aware of the calibre of the two strangers sat across the table from him. A certain unease was detected by his constant fidgeting and determination to keep looking at his iPad that was concealed by its black cover.

A visible plastic dome on the back right ceiling was housing a camera unit that recorded all meetings. It was currently relaying these real-time images to Sully. Like all government agencies these days it was all about accountability; evidence of all discussions that provided decision-making capability and final sign-off had to be recorded. The flashing red LED light within the dome's plastic outer was picked up by the guys, they knew it was filming, and they knew that someone was watching. Standard.

Two floors above Sully was picking up the minor idiosyncrasies, he noted Bob's eyes were as deadpan as ever. Knowing this was the last time this camera would ever film live again, he couldn't help but detect an atmosphere of anticipation was present looking at his iPad downlink.

He knew from experience that whilst they would each know that their body shapes couldn't be further apart, they were all in the same game and intrigued how they would all come together; different parts of the chain, but all intricate to whatever this whole thing was. He grinned, knowing that their minds would be on the classic question as to whether this upcoming job was connected to something they had been working on before. For men that didn't really vocalise too many questions, their minds would be teeming with them, not knowing when the man who

14

had organised this would rock up. Sully smiled as he watched them all remain silent. They were professionals, they knew it was senseless making small talk – it was London, the weather had been shit all week, each one had endured running the gauntlet of the Underground and grazing though the freebie newspaper, whilst absorbing conversation around them. Just the odd clearing of a throat, or a few minor readjustments to their body postures slightly broke the silence. He noted it was only Alex, the less experienced member of the trio, that seemed to twitch in an uncomfortable and slightly nervous manner.

The other two, a pair of seasoned professionals not shy on intellect or personality, didn't speak a word to each other. Both older gentlemen wise enough in their game not to give the watchers any material to analyse, or was it simply a matter of pride and not being the one to break their personal Mexican stand-off?

'A few more minutes,' Sully whispered, as they took another glance at their watches.

Looking at Bob's steadfast mountainous frame, even in his seat he towered over the boy sitting opposite him, whose breathing had now quickened in pace under Bob's continuous stare.

Unlike Gerry who had a honed frame who was sat on Bob's right shoulder, with his right foot perched on his left knee clearly not giving a damn. No surprise there, Sully smirked. Knowing that Gerry would be wrapped up in his own thinking process, picking up the clues if any, pegging the acne clad boffin across the table was an intelligence officer or a subject matter expert in something.

Switching back to Bob he had a moment of reflection. Both guys had worked with him before in differing capacities. Bob was the 'brawn', he smiled. Having led numerous strike squadrons right up to the front door of the most wanted terrorists in the world, Bob's teams never used the doorbell, rarely walked out with prisoners, and as he'd noted previously, his eyes still looked as though he didn't take any.

Gerry was the polar opposite to balance his team out. His quiet unassuming manner brought the brains to any given operation. He was the guy behind the scenes working painstakingly to bring strike options into fruition. Gerry always got the intelligence needed to confirm what needed confirming. Whatever it took and whoever he had to meet, his only two personal demands had ever been to never, ever question his intelligence or ask him where he got it from. Sully nodded his head as he remembered Gerry telling him this the first time they met.

Gerry would know that it was obvious that at least one other person would fill the empty seat opposite him next to the young boffin guy, but he wouldn't be sure who it would be to brief them. Gerry watched the dictaphone intently, Sully knew his thought process would be flitting between the urge to hit the play button and find out if it was a grid reference, a voice he might recognise before instantly dismissing all notions of doing so as being pure crap and just waiting.

Bob's slight eye move to the camera earlier indicated to Sully that he'd clocked the red flashing light, it wasn't covert, it was just flashing innocently and he could tell he wasn't bothered in the slightest; he just relaxed his body into his chair even more, just like all the times he'd done it before under harsh questioning in a foreign land with a false identity and a false agenda. Calmly and easily does it.

Sully's eyes flicked back to his youngest attendee – on the far side of the table, obviously still a little twitchy about Bob being sat opposite him, the younger guy rolled back his chair a few metres and reached out with an extended arm, his right hand grabbing the air-con remote controller and quickly adjusted the unit without looking away once from the table. A few beeps later the air-con fans started spinning faster, the loudest the room had been for five minutes. He replaced the controller. 'I hope that's fine gentlemen, it was a little humid I thought.'

'No that's fine,' Gerry replied looking at Bob, raising his eyebrows a fraction. Between them they both now knew for sure that he was not a field operative. He had been in this room before. He had felt hot in that chair before. He was in the know, even though the dictaphone had drawn a few vacant looks from him too.

As Sully glimpsed once more at the live footage from his chair he too saw that Alex had compromised his knowledge of the room.

'Right, enough is enough,' Sully said to himself decisively, knowing from the increased deadpan faces on both of the other men's faces and the fact that their breathing had slowed down as if to counteract the excitement of having found out a tidbit of knowledge. 'This game could go on forever.' It was time for him to take control. His fingers moved quickly over a few icons on his iPad to deactivate the live feed and quickly deleted the footage forever.

'Okay let's do this,' he whispered to himself.

Taking a last swig of his double whiskey he polished it off in one gulp, savouring the sharp bite on his throat, he stood up straight and tall and gave a succession of coughs to purposely clear his throat. He knew that his next play had to be immaculate. From the moment he'd walk through the door to break the silence, he needed to shake any doubt of his future actions from his mind and focus on his objective. He slammed the empty tumbler down on the solid-oak desk and rose to initiate the proceedings.

He entered the long hallway with its plainly painted grey walls and wooden floorboards. The style was a recurring theme throughout the entire converted warehouse, that was yet in its infancy, still brandishing the freshly painted smell and sawdust in the air. Silent, it had a vacant feel about it, almost sterile.

Whilst not being at the peak of his physical fitness, he still boasted a frame that was still light and agile, showing evidence of former strength and endurance. This was matched by what the common man would assume to be heavily engrained laughter lines. Not laughter lines really. These grooves were etched in place as a result of his irreversible habit of scrunching his eyes; he did it every time his mind processed strategies and outcomes within fractions of a second. Never a person to classify anything as a problem, as a potential problem meant a potential crisis, which made politicians panic, instead everything was viewed as a challenge, an opportunity to win and profile his greatness. His eighties bouffant was proud evidence of this fact with no receding hairline in sight. He'd consciously made a point of never nervously scratching his head whilst noting that when others around him did so, it conveyed an aura of uncertainty about them. Appearing flustered was not on Sully's radar.

Avoiding the lift, he skipped down the stairs, taking them two at a time as he had done his whole life, always eager to get from point A to point B in the shortest time possible.

Bursting through the doors he entered the holding room. All three heads turned immediately to the left whilst all three men simultaneously rose to their feet courteously the instant the door started to move.

'Evening gents, far too gracious for me,' Sully said noting their standing positions as he quickly scanned the room. Bob was working hard to conceal his instant look of amazement on his face; Sully quickly worked his way around the table, after shaking hands like he was on a presidential campaign and acknowledging their whispers of 'evening boss,' they all sat back down again. He was happy that his two more experienced operatives didn't sport a Masonic handshake indicating a crossover to the dark side. He hated those lot; they infected the military and government in his view and he had declined the offer on many occasions, even the 'Knights Templar' old boy networks were out, unless they needed something of course.

Standing tall and rubbing his hands together with schoolboy glee he began. 'Well the intrigue is over, well not quite,' correcting himself whilst pointing to the dictaphone. 'So I've no doubt that thing has caused a few assumptions to arise. I'm surprised you didn't hit the play button Gerry?'

'Twenty years ago I would have. In fact it's been 20 years since I used a dictaphone and a good 10 since I've seen one,' Gerry retorted being completely truthful.

'Indeed. Well we do have a challenge. In fact it's a severe challenge and that thing will show us to what extent later.' His comment was met with complete silence and concentration, all men sensing correctly that the build-up was beginning.

'That's why I have you two here,' acknowledging Gerry and Bob with a nod. 'Thanks for answering the call, especially you Bob. I hope seeing me again doesn't evoke feelings of anxiety and terror.' Bob laughed at the comment, recalling images of past encounters and hoping the dictaphone wasn't a recording of one of them.

'Don't worry there is nothing that incriminates anyone on that recording. But believe me when we've finished listening you'll know where this is all going. Yes. We're on and I mean we're on, big time. Something we all thought could never happen but all craved, is here. It's happening gents.'

Sully fixed his eyes on Alex, the younger gent was still battling with acne, probably due to a severe vitamin D deficiency from being locked inside this building all day. He'd clocked him rolling his eyes back, obviously already privy to the script that was being orated. Not well trained, yet.

'Excuse me for not dealing with the small chat and asking how you all are, family, kids and what cars you're driving.'

Bob interjected, 'It's all mundane Boss compared to what I think you're about to unleash on us.'

'Not really Bob, I was pretty shocked to find out you're a Fiat 500 driver, living on a barge boat in Upper Avon, with a Jack Russell cross called Harry…'

'Ha, the Fiat is a mid-life crisis, the barge I'm still trying to work out for myself and you keep my dog out of it.' Bob's eyes crinkled at the sides, loving the adrenaline-fuelled banter at the start of any brief.

He caught Gerry surveying them both, he would have already guessed that the groundwork would have been done on them. It was the type of intelligence Gerry could drum up in a matter of minutes out of instinct not curiosity.

'Tonight I am going to let you know why you are here for starters, then, who the hell we are and what exactly what we're going to be delivering. That's "delivering with devastating effect" in the future I might add.'

Another moment to keep tuned in. No one muttered a single word.

'It is optional, but I didn't bring in two key people that would turn their noses up at being part of a game changer. Walk if you wish now but don't expect refunds on your rail tickets.'

Always a trait of Sully's. Not exactly a caveat, just a small witty comment to terminate a serious proposition. Met with stillness he continued.

'For the past six months, I have been building up a capability to fight terrorism on our own doorstep, here in the UK. When I was headhunted into this position I was dubious about the intended Modus Operandi (MO). One, because it's technology driven, and I've always said technology is a great servant but a terrible master. I was then briefed about the capability of this potential new asset which is shocking stuff as you will soon hear. Remember, you are my chosen few, my right-hand men, but you will have autonomy as always. It's only us that will know about the real agenda behind this new "start-up" for want of a better term along with Beast our intelligence guru, who will join us shortly.'

He leaned back on his heels a tad, enjoying commanding his stage after reinforcing that they were the lucky ones. They bloody were.

'I met Alex a few years back, and that's Alex over there, if he was too shy to introduce himself before I got here,' Sully pointed at the man sitting to his left. 'Yes Alex may look like that square bookworm kid at school everyone bullied but he is the mastermind behind this project's new capability. Together we have given it a new agenda. One he still struggles with,' Sully added looking at Alex with a menacing grin, 'but that's why we,' gesturing to Bob and Gerry, 'are here to deliver it.'

Alex had a small frame, greasy black hair that was entangled around the stems of his thick brown glasses, which looked like the ones he'd had at school, broken from bullying as suggested. His pale pallor which had screamed of a man who'd been confined, at will, behind a desk in a basement for two thirds of his life had backed up Gerry and Bob's assumptions. As the guys had guessed, he had never been an operator.

Obviously used to Sully's banter he barely batted an eyelid, instead he formally nodded to his new colleagues who courteously nodded briefly back before Sully continued.

'When Alex fully briefed me about this new capability it was lacking direction. My question to him was: how exactly could we implement it within a world full of terror? Alex isn't a ruthless killer, he and his boffins have never had to think like terrorists to outmanoeuvre them. Whilst we're on the subject of terrorists Alex, do you remember me telling you about that guy who I deemed to be the only sane functioning psychopath I knew?'

Alex sat up, linked his hands and started darting his eyes in a quick attempt to retrieve the conversation. 'Is this the guy you said was born to be a terrorist, but chose to bat for the right side?'

'That's the guy,' Sully nodded over at Bob, 'this is him in the flesh.'

Alex pushed back hard into his chair causing his glasses to wobble slightly. Gingerly realigning them and hoping he hadn't drawn attention to his nervous jitter, he attempted to stare at Bob with saucepan eyes. It was obvious to all that Alex had never sat opposite a serial killer before. Sully grinned inwardly as he watched Bob mess with the kid's head and stare unblinking back as if studying his next mark.

'Silicon Cyber Security Group, that's who we're not, but that's the name above the door outside. This beautifully restored warehouse is it everyone, and I will give you a tour later. When I pitched my demands I knew some would be met, others wouldn't. I was wrong. I have had no negative kickbacks thus far.'

Gerry and Bob nodded seemingly mildly impressed.

'Working in a modern world with vast intelligence networks and communities split across the pond, backed up with enough anti-terrorist squads or deniable assets to fill a football stadium, it's a crowded market. Operational autonomy is critical, yet operational security is always breached and that's within an organisation that's supposed to be secret. Agree Gerry?'

'Yeah, in part for sure. We live in a high-tech world that lends itself to external intrusion from third parties but most disappointingly the compromise is often from within,' Gerry answered, 'Christ when you designate a new area of spy HQs for only certain people to have access, everyone knows it's another feeble attempt to create yet another super cell. People talk, people drink, people listen. I agree there are major flaws especially with some of the 6 fuckers I used to run with,' said Gerry, smirking, referring to MI6.

'Spot on,' Sully agreed. 'I'm not worried about foreign informants, it's our own who compromise things and that is why we are in this building, that is why you two have been off the grid for long enough that no one knows or cares about you. No offence of course,' he winked. 'No questions about "why has Bob has suddenly left our department" or "where has Gerry gone?" You two were perfect, one living on a barge, the other doing the school run whilst the wife is in Canary Wharf funding your early retirement.'

A few grins and smiles confirmed that they had both got the point, no offence taken.

Sully's train of speech was cut into by Alex. 'Boss,' sticking his hand up like a schoolkid.

'You're not in school now,' Sully reprimanded, pissed off to be interrupted. 'What?'

'Can I grab a quick pee?'

Gerry and Bob smirked. Knowing full well now that this geek hadn't been conditioned to high level briefs. Even though Bob was bursting to go from a gallon of coffee he'd drunk at Costa before he came in, there was no way he was interrupting a briefing session. That was a schoolboy error.

Sully hissed and nodded to which Alex got up and walked out of the room.

★★★★★

Gerry gazed on not bothering to hide the amusement in his eyes at Sully's unexpected break in his speech. Alex must be crucial to whatever was at play today for him to tolerate such a misgiving. Gerry held in a sigh and used the time to study Sully in more detail, the arrogant bugger hadn't changed a bit, aside from gaining the odd pound of flesh causing him to break into using a new hole on his belt.

It had been a while since they'd worked together. During his career Sully had developed the knack of taking catastrophe after catastrophe and using each as an opportunity to shine and promote his ability to install action across tactical teams. The brain that occupied Sully's cranium vault was one that had been cultivated and groomed by years of unrelenting pressure. In that time he'd achieved spectacular yet often controversial results.

Sully had started off as a young officer in the Parachute Regiment, the elite British airborne unit, where he'd learnt fast about mental and physical resilience. As a leader, he'd been naturally exposed to all of the physical and mental pressures of a battle. He had learnt to lead his subordinates and how to make timely decisions that would potentially dictate the future lives of those serving with him. In the same amount of time he'd always been able to reshape a battlefield, form a strategy on global terrorism or simply decide what he was eating next. With his decision-making being all about dealing with the facts and not the emotions surrounding them, Sully's internal processing system, to his colleagues, appeared to be that of a high-tech computer.

His next calling was obvious. The British Special Air Service (SAS) regarded, and equally resented by foreign contemporaries as the toughest Special Forces selection in the world. Having passed the process, Sully moved fast through the ranks and won over the respect of the extraordinarily high calibre men he commanded. Earmarked for the top, Sully's capacity to strategically out-think, outmanoeuvre and forecast enemy actions was mind-blowing. Yet, like every man, Gerry mused, he had a weakness. His insatiable appetite for action on the ground became his addiction. This failing jeopardised his potential to reach the highest levels within the British Army.

Upon becoming the Commanding Officer (CO) of the SAS, his remit was to lead the organisation in a strategic fashion. He considered leading from the strategic rear as untenable, Sully could not leave the intimacy of the power-crazy world he had come to know. He craved it. The respect he once had from the men started to subside as a CO, never a pen-pusher, he found the chore of riding a desk and handling the day-to-day admin issues soul-destroying. He began to exercise his authority directly from operation centres in Baghdad and Afghanistan, instead – places he should not have been full time.

Opinions were diverse though cutting; many knew he was all about himself, hell-bent on creating his legacy at the expense of the men he commanded and treated as expendable. His compulsion to be in the thick of it set a gruelling operational tempo; he committed guys on the ground to operations that were not worth the paper they were signed off on, costing many elite lives to an enemy that was not strategically important. His credibility faded fast.

Obsessed with gathering enough information to mount numerous operations and taking personally the numbers of enemy killed, he lost direction. Gerry recalled cringing inwardly at his downfall. He became completely narrow-minded about showing off to the Americans, bragging about 'his' SAS's ability to mount sustained, unrelenting pressure on Al Qaeda Iraq (AQI) in Central Baghdad. The SAS's war on AQI had become his war, his legacy.

Sully had been living on borrowed time and he knew it; the furious glances from all ranks he received across the bar at the funeral wakes he attended solidified his belief that he did not have a future at the higher command levels of the British Special Forces community. Sully resigned, attracting national headline news, the ones that Gerry and Bob had read about.

He'd heard nothing of Sully for years until he'd received a random message from an unknown number to meet at his local Starbucks for a grande latte at 1300 hrs. He had to admit that he did feel the familiar wave of excitement rush through him when he clocked the empty table with a grande latte on it, knowing full well the instructions were on the napkin. He instantly realised it was Sully from a past personal joke and not a serious attempt at 1970s covert tradecraft. He also knew he'd probably have tapped his phone months ago and knew his life before he even breathed it, as the latte was on the table he always sat at.

The door opened somewhat tentatively breaking Gerry's thought pattern. Maybe Alex had cursed himself in the urinals. Either way he sloped back in and quietly retook his seat. Gerry grinned inwardly, Alex had a lot to learn. He turned his focus back on to Sully once more, wondering what the former CO of the SAS had up his sleeve the time.

★★★★★

Sully trained his gaze on to Gerry and Bob, giving them the respect that they deserved for not disrupting his flow.

'So let me just give you my spin on the last three years of how we're attacking this problem in the UK. That's Al Qaeda of course, Islamic State? Fuck them for now, we can't cure the cancer in one fell swoop so let's get specific.

'Asymmetric Threat? Ring a bell guys along with the New World Order? All buzzwords from post 9/11, about how terrorists operate, and how we live in a new world because of them. That's all wrong for starters. Politicians recognising terrorists change our world? Exactly the same as naming that toilet trash Jihadi John before he got smacked. Celebrity status for scum – exposing their success in papers is marketing. AQ or ISIS are companies, they are run like businesses, marketing equals recruitment and celebrity status equals idolisations. I have to have a rant about the papers and social media as this drives public opinion.' He paused for dramatic effect, looking at each of them.

'Yet in six months' time however we will be creating headlines but with a difference, there will be a story alright, lacking in facts, but exploding with theories and conspiracy that will shock these scumbags. Anyway I'm digressing…'

Gerry and Bob had both nodded at the mention of asymmetric threat. Sully liked that. Years ago it was a buzzword recognising that terrorists didn't just show up and plant a bomb, or hijack a plane and use it as one in a physical sense. They were sophisticated at every level of their organisation now and their attacks came in numerous guises at diverse targets, not just human ones.

Cyber was the new threat. How they communicated, how they recruited, how they indoctrinated from grass roots all the way up to convert people to extremism, even people they never have human contact with. It was no longer a physical war but one where the battle lines merged between online and offline activity. Intelligence communities were constantly fighting a horrific threat that was orchestrated globally, courtesy of the World Wide Web. Conventional tradecraft and guerrilla tactics were being replaced daily by a species that was always evolving and generally ahead of the game. Terrorists had to adapt and overcome with limited resources and limited equipment. Yet, as the evidence showed, they still managed to pull off what was known in the business as 'spectaculars'.

Sully snapped back into gear. 'The question I used to ask myself twenty years ago was: if we know who the IRA are, why aren't we going in and killing them all? I know my lot had a good few goes but all in the acts of carrying out terrorism. At the current moment we know who most of our key players are, where they live, what mosques they preach at or discuss operations, yet the question still remains the same: why aren't they dead? The obvious answers are the usual intelligence community classics: bigger intelligence picture, growing their network of informers, taking out individuals can compromise years of work and put lives at risk, and so forth...'

Sully noticed that Gerry's nodding was somewhat half-arsed, knowing him well enough from the past to know that yes he agreed but that didn't mean he agreed with not taking out certain known terrorists if the opportunity arose.

'The greatest obstacle we have is political backlash. The government fear a Muslim uprising on the streets of Britain if the boys are sent in to collect. It's the minority we know, and the majority condemn their actions, but the government killing them is off limits, but...'

The three heads jerked awaiting what would befall their ears after that caveat word was uttered from Sully's lips.

'...*Us* killing them isn't.'

The room was silent, even Alex was all ears for this last four-worded sentence.

Walking to the far end of the table Sully turned and faced everyone. Placing his hands on the seat in front of him he leant in, like he was about to tell a secret. Unconsciously everyone else leant in too.

'Now we're not just going to turn up and put a few holes in people's heads. It's way more complicated than that. It's way more technical than that. What we are going to do has never been attempted before because it's never been invented before. What Alex is going to talk to you about is the inception of how we are going to use a technology that was being designed for something else, however, I came across it and as usual I saw the beauty in the beast, and the agenda I talked about changing earlier is our new Modus Operandi. Basically gentlemen this organisation here is going to revolutionise the way we fight modern day terrorism and it is solely us four and my paymaster that are aware of this.'

He looked at Bob, it was clear from the spark in his eyes that he had a question.

'Boss,' Bob piped up.

'Shoot.'

'Who exactly the fuck are we then? '

All four of them chuckled at the obvious question and the blunt manner in which it was asked. The tension broken in the room, Sully squeezed the chair padding between his two hands and leant further in.

'Gents,' all three looked directly at him like excited school boys. Sully could see he had their attention 100 per cent and sensed his rhetoric had pressed the right buttons. They were ready for their first assignment. He made them wait another second before uttering:

'Gents, we're The Clinic.'

CHAPTER 4

Skiing like a man possessed, Larnaka dissipated into a distant memory as Decker squinted his eyes to try and glimpse his path through the small scratch on his frozen ice-matted ski mask. 'Christ,' he breathed stopping dead in his tracks. After skiing 600 punishing miles across a continent where the temperature was cold enough to crack teeth, he was rattled by his instinct. It had taken thirty days to finally kick in but now it was there, irking him, and with a solid urgency he noted.

Instinct he knew was designed solely for one purpose, to keep you alive. He had always acted on it without hesitation, so the fact that it was present now told him that he wasn't alone anymore. The next person he saw if any, meant that he was somehow back in the mix, his footprint live again without his knowledge, consent or enthusiasm. If they saw him first his instinctive moment wouldn't matter, his body would simply be another frozen explorer who perished on the Antarctic plateau.

Thinking someone could slide up behind him and end the psychological trauma of the past three years without him feeling a thing scared him. Not having an opportunity to ask questions or understand exactly what had happened to his life freaked him out, so much so this thought made him swing his body around to take a quick look over his shoulder, pausing, scanning hard into the distance.

'Nothing,' he muttered into his ice-covered mouth protector. 'What the hell were you expecting anyway? Nutter.'

'So much for instinct,' he grumbled.

He focussed himself back on reality. Painfully shifting his body and the 150kg sled across the barren wasteland was an absolute chore. He had had enough of this daily grind. Twelve hours a day with nothing to occupy his mind except a world of white nothing. No horizons, no backdrops, no wildlife, just plain nothingness. A black mask hid his piercing blue eyes and facial features that had landed him many an essence bird on a late or early night out. He possessed the chiselled body you would expect a man that is attempting to walk 1400 miles to have. He had never been one to hang on to a woman, he was too complex, far too smart and preferred arguing with himself than over a jealous bird that didn't understand how he fears loneliness, but craves solitude.

No one understood him, least himself but he never complained about not understanding, well not until this journey that was starting to break his balls now.

Another mentally twisted piece to this already jaded puzzle. That's the remorse and regret kicking in to his self-prescribed rehabilitation programme.

His groundbreaking expedition had seen his iPod die on day one, his DSLR camera get smashed on day three, and his first blisters appear on day four. He cursed himself, they were now the size of shark bites and bleeding more each day. His own mantra of *'you'd better make friends with pain, so you'll never be alone again'* was now deemed absolute bullshit beyond belief.

'Jesus Christ,' as his left ski twisted causing his left boot to jitter sharply. 'Fucking boots.' Laughing at pain was something he could manage only on some days, other days, like today, it was pure vindictive rage.

Uncontrolled outbursts of shouting or screaming, throwing his poles, smashing the ice with his gloved fists, after he had finished slapping his own face.

This journey wasn't disappointing him physically, world record attempts aren't handed out on plates, and this one wasn't even breaking one, it was simply creating history, a world first. The price of that was evident on every inch of his body. He had dropped two stone in weight from the exertion. Ending up with a bloodshot right eye that had got infected and was only really just beginning to clear up after he put his own ski pole in his face. Winner.

Yet he knew he could take that punishment all day long. What he was struggling with was the mental punishment this endeavour was having on his mind. It wasn't a case of how mentally battered he was, how low, depressed or lonely he was getting, that stuff was point of entry to solo expeditions. 'Suck it up' he always thought when these thoughts came to view. No. He breathed in hard, it was what was whirring behind the ski mask and balaclava that protected his head from freezing everyday that was the crux. Paradoxically he felt like freezing his brain would be the only way to calm the intensity of his over-thinking. Some days it felt like a car engine overheating, all he wanted to do was pop the bonnet and add some coolant.

Decker sighed. He'd come this far from home to search for clarity and answers in his mind. To test himself and yet he hadn't realised the huge toll, the trauma and energy it would sap from him trying to find the answers, that's if they were even there of course.

'What mettle do I still possess, what has the last three years all been about?' A mind loaded with a million and one facts and figures, theories and conspiracies, and not to mention guilt, shame and remorse.

He knew he'd either stumbled upon something unimaginable and brilliant.

Or he had lost the plot.

This was the same question that irked him.

That unexpected scene that had unfolded in the last room of the hostage rescue with Johnny, was the single point that triggered his web of suspicion. It was this piece that had borne a conspiracy that was tormenting him, his torment took him back to where he thought it all started. It had been nearly 3 years ago, roughly a year before he and Johnny had shared their moment in that last room.

Leaning on his poles he peered through the fog to his front. He blinked, moments later he was back in the room, a porta-cabin office in Balad or Camp Victory, a military installation in Baghdad.

In a small dusty corner of the huge coalition Forward Operating Base (FOB), housed the British and American covert operations offensive. Hidden behind huge blast walls, all sorts of competing agencies on the intelligence gathering front had filled it. Whether they were running Iraqi agents, eavesdropping on cellular activity or carrying out surveillance operations, their one objective being to produce targets for Special Forces from Delta Force and the SAS to assault, in order to capture wanted terrorists.

The war had now evolved into a quagmire of sectarian fuelled violence. Added to the mix was a load of foreign fighters supporting the newly designated Al Queada Iraq or AQI for short. Abu Musab al Zaqawi was the proclaimed leader of this brutal insurgency, that was demonstrating ruthless violence in the form of suicide bombings, mass killing sprees and beheading's of western contractors.

'Coalition war effort' was a futile description, the team effort had gradually eroded. Competition within inter-agencies and inter-countries had led to some not sharing, or destroying vital intelligence to aid each other's own war effort. High value terrorists like Zaqawi needed taking out fast, and everyone wanted the trophy, but the Americans wanted it desperately.

Too many recent successes from the Brits was unnerving them. The SAS didn't have huge assets but this always encouraged initiative and ingenuity, like terrorists, they made it happen with what they had.

But in their race for Zaqawi, the Brits were getting fucked over and denied access to vital agents and sources. Well, it had been Decker's opinion of the scene anyway.

Squinting his eyes and fending off the wind, Decker could see his team sat next to him, with two new members, both Iraqi who were sat on the next table a few metres away. They were all about to receive the solution to a fractured intelligence system.

Decker pictured his CO standing tall in front of them all, unshaven with a menacing grin on his face as he spoke:

Today we are going to shift up a few gears in covert operations. Firstly, men I want to introduce you to Mohammed and Larnaka your new team members. Both trained in covert ops, they have been working undercover for the last few years. Larnaka and Mohammed are also high grain informants. This is the new breed guys.'

The CO was grinning as he said this, like he had just pulled the ace card out. Which of course he had.

'Her uncle is Abu Masab al Gharadi. I won't go into the specifics of why Larnaka is working with us, but her track record and information to date has been spot on.' Looking at Mohammed, the CO nodded. 'As is Mohammed's. These guys want their country back, and their sense of duty to accept our invite into this Cell is heartfelt. Thank you.'

Decker already knew where this brief was going and he welcomed it. A Cell that had its own informants, combined with a team that could strike undercover or lead in a huge strike force was bombproof. No possibility of bad intelligence or false disinformation to throw them off the trail. Complete insulation from exterior influence.

'This new Cell is about to launch operations at an unprecedented level that will involve your current undercover work following terrorists, combined with Larnaka and Mohammed's dangerous work to identify new key players and develop existing networks. They will work on the streets with us, and only come here under darkness or meet us at out safe house in town. It's the speed and direct intelligence reporting that will require us to act by ourselves to capture individuals or lead in the strike squadron assaults.'

Decker smiled, knowing his assumption was correct. It sounded awesome, proper black ops without the white noise of dealing with multiple intelligence agency analysis or 'it's bigger picture stuff'. 'All this equipment you see here' The Boss pointed to some Pelli cases behind him. 'Are the latest phones and communications equipment to prevent any unwanted eavesdroppers intercepting any of our conversations or operations. It's not a lot, just a few special ear pieces, small jamming adaptors and the phones are modified too, in order to give us a small bubble of security.'

A blindsided blow almost knocked him completely off balance, breaking his train of thought. Bracing himself hard to fend off a screaming 75mph gust of wind that thundered across the Antarctic plateau, he focused hard to stay on his battered feet. For eleven solid days he'd been battling through a white-out with close to zero visibility, telling himself that at some point he would burst through it, imagining it to be a thin wallpaper barrier. Nearing exhaustion from skiing nonstop, his pulk, twice his own body weight, containing all his food and kit, now felt as though he was pulling a cast iron bath which was spilling over with freezing cold water.

'This place is hell,' he whispered to himself. Zero visibility, terrain underfoot that would be flat one second, then ten-foot jagged drops the next. Yet through all of the physical pains, he welcomed the fact that he was slowly starting to figure out a few things piece by piece. This journey that originally set out as a journey to find his former greatness, was now simply a matter of physical survival, with a monumental fight for sanity thrown in for good measure.

Perfect.

He paused for a moment. 'What the fuck are you doing here? What is this all about Harry? What is this really all about? Not them, forget them, you. It's you mate we are talking about?' Blowing out hard he stood in silence.

Talking to yourself isn't strange in Antarctica, especially when you are on your own. Ironically he'd been the one to tell himself that. It's exactly the same as thinking but just out loud, and when you are the only solo occupant on this 14 million square mile continent, it wasn't embarrassing, just plain acceptable behaviour. Only his thoughts were beginning to scare him, and that fact alone amused him at some moments to the point of laughter.

That really scared him.

Sharply looking up to his front, then snapping himself into a posture designed to attack, he looked on with menace. But he could see nothing, no one, just the spindrift kicking up across the jagged landscape. Slowly looking behind, the same scene was present.

Nothing.

Breathing out heavily again, moments like these were getting more common. A paranoid feeling that they would pop up out of nowhere, finally coming to collect was a feeling he couldn't shake off. Though he laughed it off because he still couldn't prove exactly what he was thinking, it always came back, always, especially when he began drinking heavily over this last year.

Thinking about drink made him furious, it was his Achilles heel, a poison that had fuelled his downfall, yet even in the evil of alcohol there had been a moment of clarity. That one moment of brilliance that could be mistaken for a madman simply looking for answers to theories that don't exist, or equally a coward creating the biggest lie in his own mind to excuse his own weaknesses and failure.

One thing that didn't lie was his Global Positioning System (GPS). Looking at the display screen he excitedly looked at how many miles he had covered. This was a daily guessing game and something he looked forward to.

'14.3 Nautical miles?' He allowed himself to acknowledge that it was actually good going for today, with hardly any visibility again and his blister being worse than normal. He was on a direct bearing of 127 degrees to Waypoint 5. Waypoint 5 was the South Pole station, not many GPSs in the world ever get to enter those coordinates. The fact he was still 189 miles away didn't faze him. He'd been telling people on his blogs that every day he was simply eating the elephant. The phrase he'd made up years ago. To eat an elephant you take one small bite a day and eventually after 85 days, 1400 miles he would have 'eaten the fat fucker' also in his words.

550 miles done. Doing the calculations in his head he knew he had

just over three degrees left, and would be approaching the 87-degree line tomorrow.

He'd been dropped off at Hercules Inlet on the coastal edge of Antarctica, a route to the South Pole which took all of 715 miles as the crow flies. A path only travelled by a handful before him.

But this wasn't a good enough test for him as he easily pissed a 500 mile challenge to the North Pole years ago. 715 miles wasn't a challenge to someone who knew nothing but elitism and daring. He needed to do what no other human in history had ever attempted. Skiing to the South Pole and back alone with no support or assistance was a 1430-mile round trip, with an estimated time frame of 85-100 days on the ice. It was all still possible too.

Even though he had lost two stone in the last month his 5'9" frame was holding out well. Gritting his teeth underneath his balaclava his square jaw matted by 30 days' growth was clenched and tucked into his chest, like he was poised to defend and strike.

★★★★★

The dark fly-eye lenses of his mask concealed a set of eyes that were full of rage again. If looks could kill, he was about to start a killing spree with no visible end, but right now, he was still contemplating… Was his current mind that of a former madman, a delusional individual or a coherent professional who had finally worked it all out, as instinct indicated. Was he in control? Or was he still the victim of a torturous three-year mental onslaught?

'Control control, you have control,' he whispered through gritted teeth.

'Switch on, stay focused,' he snarled to himself. Knowing a novice lapse of concentration could be fatal.

If his theory was true he knew that his discovery had just made him the smartest man in the room. In any room. However, as he knew from tactical experience, the smartest man in the room immediately became an asset that any company would want to retain. It made him a wanted man, even a dead man he noted, in fact definitely a dead man.

If his theory was true he must now be a walking nightmare for the people that thought his discovery would never be possible. Thinking they had got away with destroying the last three years of his life, they now had a reason to be as paranoid as he was now acting. He stared hard to his front, posturing himself to defend against an imminent threat on his life again, he felt certain that they were coming to collect.

Instinct.

That instinct took him back to an air-con room in Baghdad, listening to The Boss he recalled the woman sitting quietly at the back of the room. This did make him laugh nervously now, but he brushed it aside as he recalled him introducing the slim, pale looking brunette, sporting glasses that indicated a doctor or intelligence officer.

'Let me introduce you to Anna. With this new remit comes sacrifices, from you that is. Our work load will be 18-20 hours a day, requiring focus to deal with stress and physical strains of the onslaught. This new Cell', the Boss pointed at the two Iraqi's, 'if successful will set the tone of future operations in the Middle East. Even the CIA will want a piece of this when they see the results clock up in the next few months.'

Decker recalled again the glee in his eyes, indicating it was obviously his concept he had managed to get signed off at Whitehall, somehow.

'So Anna will make sure you are in tip-top condition to operate without ramming unprescribed drugs down you. We want to make sure you sleep on your down time, and during your up time you perform at optimal levels. Anna' The Boss introduced her as she walked forward looking nervous.

'Hello, I am Anna, an expert in Sports Science so have been working with athletes for years to enhance functions across a wide range of spectrums. I look forward to assisting you people as the strain takes hold in the next few months. That's all.'

Looking intimidated by her audience, she turned quickly and walked towards the door, clearly outside her zone of comfort. Her white cloak flailed as she turned. That whiteness turned to fog as Decker again returned to the discomfort of Antarctica, not a warm room receiving the opening brief of The new Cell.

The military had like all other organisations looked into new ways to enhance performance so did he really have a case for being suspicious back then?

As he quickly reflected on the 18 hr days they started working, he could see it was actually due care for the Cell. A few check ups, some sleeping tablets and pills that were like caffeine on steroids wasn't a conspiracy. In fact, he recalled enjoying talking to her, and Anna just didn't seem the ruthless type. He actually recalled it being the best years of his life. 'That Cell was a masterclass, Mohammed and Larnaka were amazing people' he thought to himself. 'Until we had a few tragedies on the job. With that he felt the knots grind away in his stomach. Yet again he was debating his conspiracy versus a broken mind, but it was how he had mended his broken mind that had become his biggest problem, even though the technique had saved his life. Trying to explain it to an outsider without coming across as a psychopath was the tricky part.

Closing his eyes to blank his mind, he wondered if escaping a person he had grown to hate over the previous years was working. Though he was an alpha male, crying wasn't completely off limits, but then, he did think of how it could have been different if he had used professional help instead of self-help. He wouldn't be freezing cold, exhausted and paranoid checking his back, five times a day.

Instead he clocked an unexpected break in the weather which gave him a view for once. Being able to observe the ice boulder fields as they stretched out for 4-5 km immediately released the tension from his aching body. Forgetting the physical pain he absorbed himself in the moment. It was breathtakingly beautiful. For a brief moment he appreciated how fortunate he was to be experiencing this.

Collecting his thoughts before he skied on, his theory felt tantamount to breaking the Enigma code, all the hours of thinking and scribbling away relentlessly in his diaries now held some weight.

There was another pain also, and one that he even knows took him to breaking point because the finger of blame could only point at him. This pain had no cure, no theories could solve it. It was simply dealing with the facts not wild assumptions. Because he didn't want to face these facts he never let himself release the heart-wrenching pain, protecting it always through denial, smart enough to know that one day he had to let go.

As the halo effect of the sun started to break through the lifting cloud base he had one final sobering moment.

Not giving a damn about anything was for a reason, he hadn't been born with that attitude, it was an attitude cultivated by events.

As he took in a deep breath, he thought about the image of one person.

As his eyes began to well up, he sat down and slumped against his sled.

For the man that craved solitude but couldn't bear being alone, this thought had killed and buried him long ago.

His head rocked back as he closed his eyes and reminded himself, he would never see the only person he had ever truly loved again. He took a long moment to absorb the fact, as always it travelled to every nerve ending of his body, shattering his skin with an internal agonising pain.

Upon opening his eyes he was relieved that he could still see a full five or so kilometres. That feeling of claustrophobia when you can't see anything only fuelled his chaotic mind to run riot. Looking to the edge of his visibility he sighed, 'I know you're...' pausing his sentence as he sees something he can't quite believe. Finishing with 'out... there... somewhere.' Standing up and taking a few steps to pick up the solar panel sheet laid over the top of his sled, he grabbed the cable connected to his second sat phone buried underneath the red protective cover. Charging his phones, beacons and PDA whilst skiing was normal everyday. 'What the f...'

Holding the phone in his hand the cable was hanging limply from it. Severed completely at the junction point. That wasn't normal.

He furiously pressed the green 'on' button there was nothing, no power, not even a slight murmur of previous life.

'What the fuck?' Confused and looking around. Because of the temperature he couldn't make out whether it was the sheer cold that had made a clean snap, or if someone had cut it.

On closer inspection there was no shearing of the internal wiring but this didn't count out sabotage, and the way he was thinking at the moment, sabotage would never be ruled out.

Without hesitation he reached for his primary phone in his jacket. He knew that he had to stop now for the day and report this to Steve Jones at base camp. This was a showstopper. No power, no safety network, equalled emergency extraction. He couldn't go home now. He wasn't ready by a long shot.

Slightly flustered, entering new levels of paranoia, he made the call moving his joints around slowly on the spot.

CHAPTER 5

No push backs, was a true admission from Sully earlier. The newly converted warehouse in which the four gentlemen were now ensconced, hid itself nicely from the bustling little hub that was Chiswick High Street. Surrounded by a small wasteland, wildly overgrown with foliage eating its way through the rusty perimeter fence, complimented by sycamore trees blinding the view from three aspects it had stood derelict and unnoticed for years. Completely perfect for The Clinic's operation. Back in the day the building had been used to print papers full of half decent news and not the dross of today's gossip. It was only estate agents and property developers who paid it any real attention, with one chancer actually tracking down the owner. Making a quick trip to St Tropez to buy it off the ex-pat owner, who'd actually forgotten that it was his, the papers were signed in days. It was a classic example of a place you arrived at after a few wrong turns, or where a drunken couple had stumbled upon it for a quick midnight fondle in the small alleyway to the side of it. The Ox pub was at the source of this side alley, which was no bad thing he thought when he viewed it.

Designed to provide parking spaces on the concrete ground floor and six Manhattan open-style living apartments on the upper levels. Sully captured it after taking a wrong turn on his daily commute to the station. Knowing one day they would need an isolated Operations Centre away from all the spooks at Vauxhall, and prying eyes of Whitehall, he'd naturally made enquiries. Chatting to the man sporting a tweed jacket and hard hat whilst studying plans over the bonnet of his Range Rover HSE Sport, Sully had a price. Shortly after he pitched his proposal to his one point of contact to rent the whole plot for The Clinic, he had an answer. He was left in no doubt as to the seriousness and potential funding available for the project when it was bought for over 10 million pounds.

This responsive, no-nonsense attitude gave Sully a direct insight into how powerful and highly regarded his position was. At that point he had only been working with Alex for six months on drawing up a few blueprints of probable execution of this latest technological development in his power and control. He gave them indications of the potential Modus Operandi, the manpower involved and how he would scale the new organisation first domestically, then globally. Feedback, he noted, had been minimal but the autonomy was perfect. Being left to his own devices in a new 10 million quid hangout was a bombproof indication that this project was top of the deck. It was also a quick insight into how they were doing business when the purchase went through days later.

He knew that it was likely there were only one or two decision-makers on this job and that reassured him that hardly anyone knew the real agenda at government level. It was definitely outside the Joint Intelligence Committee's (JIC) control and no doubt blind to the Home Secretary. A slush fund was hidden somewhere, probably as deeply as the initial White Paper explaining this whole creation. In fact Sully was convinced there was no evidence or paper anywhere relating to this.

Finally in a position he had craved all his career, one that was devoid of red tape and political correctness, he was determined to ensure The Clinic's operational effectiveness would make a CIA black-operations project look like a load of monkeys playing with a stack of deckchairs.

As that thought brought a smile to his face he clapped his hands together, rubbed them frantically before moving on to the more pressing part of his brief. Picking up a black indelible marker pen that was as brand new as the spotless whiteboard he stood in front of, he pulled the lid off it and faced the board.

It was like watching school kids trying not to expose their avid excitement as they all started to crane their necks sideways to get a preview of what Sully was scribbling.

They were disappointed.

One single black dot had christened the immaculate board. Unless Sully had been paralysed with a sudden onset of amnesia and forgotten to write the sentence that ended with this full stop, then they knew his Psy-Ops were off the charts as usual.

Turning round, replacing the lid and throwing the pen on the table it was met with three grown men smiling, knowing that the dot was for mental stimulation.

'This is where we're at and it's a slight irony that I've just done that on a white board. All will become clear. This is probably the only thing I've ever learnt from an Arab Commander in my entire career, but it epitomises The Clinic's predicament right now.' Everyone nodded.

'Well, what do we see?' Sully clearly expecting audience participation.

'It's a small black dot, Boss,' Bob supplied, eager to score some easy brownie points early doors.

'Okay, piss off Bob you solid twat,' Sully laughed at Bob for having the balls to state the bloody obvious, although looking over to Gerry he could see the intent look on his face as he stared at the whiteboard. Knowing that his mastermind would be whirring and already doing the maths... New organisation called The Clinic, dictaphone on table. The dot was some sort of problem. The whiteboard was the magnitude of it. Sully pushed on:

'Alex give the guys the brief.' Looking at Bob and smirking.

Alex clearly not feeling the need to stand with only an audience of three, waited for Sully to be seated, playing around with his iPad in front of him to locate the correct file. Files he didn't need to refer to as this was a brief he had given Sully when they first met, a brief Sully could tell that he still couldn't quite grasp fully. Sully took his seat, eager to see what the guys' reactions would be in the next ten minutes as was Alex, knowing how tight this inception had been kept. Unbeknownst to Alex, Sully would be even keener to gauge his reaction when the dictaphone stopped playing later. When the stop button clicked, Sully would be directing all his attention on him and finding out for the first time how he reacted under extreme questioning.

As Alex opened his mouth to speak Sully cut in.

'Oh, a quick one and not that I need to labour this glaringly obvious point, this is the highest level security brief you have ever received, and any more will be the highest I've given. I assure you what we discuss today is everything I know too. I've already heard this brief, listen up and questions at the end guys, just run with it as it's a lot to take in.'

Sully had never been the type to put endless papers in front of people with red stamp marks and 'sign here' arrows. He picked those he trusted to divulge the darkest of secrets to, with a signature that was purely a man's word, and not an unreadable scribble across a White Paper that could get you put in prison years later.

The tone had changed along with Bob and Gerry's game faces. Formalities were over, jokes aside, it was now down to business.

'Okay shoot Alex.'

'Good to meet you Gerry, Bob,' Alex said quietly to his audience who noted his right hand trembling as he placed it in his pocket. 'Okay this is a ten-minute introduction giving you the history and the inception of The Clinic.'

Alex accentuated those two words looking at Sully. It was clearly the first time he had heard the name of their new organisation too.

'Our development, current vision and future mission could not be further away from the original intentions of the brain of one mental, or incredible man, who got us here. I will not go into the whole history, but a guy called Ridley, a cognitive psychologist, was developing research on how your thought processes…'

The heavy footsteps could be heard before the door was flown open with urgency. Not even entering the room, a large chubby face sporting a scruffy beard popped through the opening.

'Sorry Boss,' acknowledging Sully, 'Alex can I borrow you for a moment?'

Sully locked his jaw. Alex looked at him awaiting his approval. Sully was immediately suspicious knowing that nobody interrupted his briefs unless it was for him.

'What's up Beast?'

'Boss, this is urgent, Alex can explain I'm sure,' nodding his head at Alex who was looking a little sheepish and pissed that Beast had just thrown him under the bus, or dropped him in it in normal English.

Sully's face had turned to stone. He rose immediately, gesturing to Alex to do the same. 'Hang five guys, chill here we'll be back shortly.'

Walking briskly, they all followed Beast down the corridor at a faster pace than normal. Hopping back up the steps to a door, Beast swiped his card, put his paw print on a security access pad, waited for the 'access granted' tone then led the guys in to a small operations centre.

Low light levels accentuated the six flat-screen TV images that were at the front of the room. The room itself was laid out like a theatre sloping from the back to front with a centre aisle dividing a number of work areas either side. Each work area was housing a few computer monitors that were manned by people with headsets on. Quiet mumblings were mixed with the tapping of keyboards, broken only by the sudden interjection of a satellite phone transmission cutting in live across the room.

'This is the live feed of the satellite phone conversation, with a few seconds' delay,' Beast looked directly at Sully and Alex.

Sully scanned the location feed on the display. He saved his questions, knowing this live feed, booming out from 10,000 miles away in Antarctica, was somehow central to the rude interruption moments earlier.

CHAPTER 6

Standing on the ice, irritated, with the sat phone to his ear, he waited for Steve Jones' response to the situation. Having explained that he had no solar panel as it was completely written off, he knew this put Steve in an awkward position. Under the safety guidelines of (ALE) Antarctic Logistical Expeditions who are responsible for his safety, they should extract him immediately.

'Hey Champ,' Steve's voice sounded clear on the sat phone. He'd never asked him why he called him champ, but whatever, he thought.

'Go ahead Steve,' Decker said, checking the horizon for the first sign of light aircraft.

If Steve had been a jobsworth and followed the rules he would have ordered a Twin Otter light aircraft to touch down on its ski wheels and pick him up by now. But Steve knew his background, knew that men like him never quit, no matter how life-threatening the odds. In fact, if the Twin Otter did touch down, it would have taken a gun in his face to get him to board leaving behind a shattered dream. What Steve didn't realise was that extracting him at that point wouldn't just deny him the chance to create history, it would have denied him the opportunity to fully figure out something he was so close to uncovering. It was just the final few pieces left to convince himself he wasn't losing the plot again and all his current actions were not delusional assumptions.

'Right you have 117,000 followers on Twitter, you're almost half way to creating history for Christ's sake.' Steve paused, and Decker closed his eyes, barely breathing. 'This means we have to lie a little, copy?'

'Copy, this sounds good Steve.'

'Okay, how much battery life is left in the phone and beacon before they go flat?' Steve asked.

'I reckon I have a few more calls on the phone and full life on the beacon but we know that ain't exactly working properly.' Squeezing a few more days of battery life out of it was ambitious. With no battery life in both satellite phones Steve recognised he would truly be on his own for the last ten days of walking to the South Pole.

'Right as far as the public are concerned your beacon is fully functioning and we can monitor you all the way to the Pole.'

Throughout this expedition the beacon had been useless, only working sporadically anyway. Ironically this was the device that had full power.

'Copy that mate.' Relieved there wasn't an imminent rescue operation and appreciating that Steve was putting his balls on the line for him, Decker was insanely grateful.

'So this is the plan,' Steve interjected. 'Do your last video upload soon, explain the situation to your followers about rationing battery life, and let them know you will update them at the Pole when we can supply you with a new panel.'

'Okay Steve, I will set up the tent now, send the last video diary upload. I will call you again when I think I have one or two calls left to give you my last known position. I will try the beacon too.' Steve wasn't normally one to break the rules so Decker knew that this would be causing a light sweat to break out on his forehead. He needed to make sure that he wasn't going to worry too much. Although they both silently acknowledged that if something were to happen to Decker now, he would be in the shit, big time.

'Cool. I will hear from you in a few days with your last position then you are unofficially on your own mate. How are things anyhow?'

He sighed, really wanting to open up to Steve about his mental state and even his wild theory, thinking that he might be the last person he ever got to talk to. He bit his lip to avoid doing this. 'I'm good mate, just the usual mental trauma of fighting this beast everyday.'

'Nobody said it would be easy. You're doing awesome and everyone here is behind you. Keep it together and keep pushing hard to the Pole. Speak in the next few days.'

'Roger that, out.'

Looking at the cable again, then into the distance noting that the blanket white landscape hadn't changed one bit since his last check, he sighed then relaxed. There were no additions to the scene, or evidence, no dark silhouettes punching their way through the frozen rubble fields.

No sound of skidoo engines contaminating the air, screaming as they penetrated solid ten-foot walls of ice in hot pursuit towards him.

Above him? Stupid question he thought, but instincts couldn't control a quick glance, occasionally the Twin Otter plane doing Base Camp to South Pole flights would purposely dive down and scare the living shit out of him, with a fly-by that shook the ice off his jacket.

It was a nice thought from Chuck the pilot as he, like everyone else on the plateau, knew how lonely he would be, and thought that a quick fly-by would boost his spirits with a little show of solidarity.

Checking his lone shadow from the sun behind him, it shone directly to his 1 o'clock position, shining brightly to his front right indicating that it was actually about 1400 hrs. Ripping back the heavy-duty Velcro fastener of his jacket clasp to view his watch, he was only a few minutes out, 1404 hrs. Becoming absorbed in the new circumstances and his exchanges with Steve, it was now time for the only 30-minute break he allowed himself all day, which was always after six hours on the go. Every other stop was normally after two hours of hardship and was for only seven minutes, the time limit of inactivity before body parts started freezing up and a short enough time to avoid thinking about stopping for the day. Instead it was just enough time to grab a quick drink and take a large bite of his flapjack bar that was roughly 250 calories. A quick sugar boost was all this was; everything he tasted now was the same, whether it was energy drink, his favourite beef Harry rations or dry skin chafing off his lips, it was a process not an occasion anymore.

After 30 days, he had been meticulous in sticking to the rules he created, but today was different.

He knew he had to get to the bottom of what was going on in his head, the thought of going home and the snapped cable had spooked him big time. He just needed to lay it all out in sequence, as opposed to having a thousand Post-it notes dotted around his brain. His conclusion scared him and being wrong petrified him even more, especially if he broadcasted it in his last diary call. If he was correct it would be a self pardoning for him, knowing he was the victim and not of his own making. Deciding now was as good a time as any to take an extra long stop, 40 minutes or whatever it took. 40 minutes? This was the absolute maximum time of being static wearing an extra-insulated jacket. Any longer meant getting the tent up and getting the stove on. That was still three hours 56 minutes away by his meticulous planning, 1800 hrs he always stopped and set up camp.

Content with his new time plan he bent down, flicked his heavy-duty outer gloves off that were attached to his wrists and clipped his skis off. Free now to move about unhindered he threw his rucksack off that doubled as a harness to pull the pulk. It was connected by a three-metre tow rope or 'trace line'. When he took up the initial strain each day he felt like an ox ploughing a dirt field, as opposed to an 85kg man pulling a pulk seemingly effortlessly behind him across the ice.

Ripping the bright red pulk cover back he grabbed the huge insulated jacket that was almost the size of a double duvet, and donned it in seconds. Next without looking came his flask, insulated water bottle and a small stuff sack that contained his Moleskine diary. Stamping the ground violently around him to create a small trench for his backside, he hunkered down using his pulk as a temporary windbreak. Moments like these were pure ecstasy as he closed his eyes, and let his body relax spreadeagled across the ice, forgetting the batterings of the last 30 days.

It only lasted 30 seconds, always a hyperactive type he knew he had some final investigative work to crack and needed to get on with it and send his diary call. He was convinced he had finally deciphered the three-year enigma that had deceived him, destroyed him, ended a glittering career and almost killed him off completely. It was just having the balls to publicly announce it.

Sitting up he reached for his thick leather-bound diary that was as battered as he was. The elastic band tightly bound all the various loose pages that had ripped out and tried to escape. But like him, they had had no such luck they were in it for long haul.

The tassel from the bookmark that stuck out of the diary flickered in the wind, but this wasn't any normal bookmark, it had history. As wide as a ruler and silver, it had the words 'NEVER, NEVER, NEVER GIVE UP' engraved upon it – one of Winston Churchill's essential quotes.

As he looked at the twisted and scratched silver bookmark that was doubling up as a mirror, it was bearing the wounds of 15 years of solid page marking in the most remote and war-torn regions of the world. It was himself he was looking at really though, the engraved quote was distant. More precisely the inch-wide improvised mirror, now gave him a clear-cut view of his eyes. This was all he needed as a reference, they were completely bloodshot, sore with his usual laughter lines buried deep into his skin. 'When was the last time I laughed?' He was not shocked at all by the new criss-cross lines that cut through the dark bags beneath his eyes. Fortunately, as dry and chafed as his skin was, he was relieved that it was without any sign of frost nip. His discipline had ensured all his extremities were intact and functioning fully. Holding the improvised mirror for a moment it took him back to the lowest moment in his life, that moment would always be a benchmark for future reference.

Mirrors always triggered two bitterly contradicting memories, he recalled looking in the mirror in his bedroom to see a superhero; fresh-faced, ambitious, funny, a true full-of-life alpha male with a fit naked blonde girl in his bed. Other days it may have been a brunette or redhead, that was standard weekend policy and was shockingly only three or so years back. He could still smell the perfume.

That sweet smell of perfume had been replaced by the stench of stale alcohol in recent years. The once fresh image in the mirror had been replaced with an alien-like character, a stranger in his own body with all the vacant features of a heroin addict, not an alpha male. Looking back at this stranger had been the hardest episode of his life to come to terms with. As he recalled the image of the man looking back at him, it made his spine shiver. That man was lost, he looked finished. That was his biggest frustration back then, he knew how to get himself out of the shit but meanwhile he just kept digging the hole deeper until he bottomed out.

Quickly looking away from the marker in disgust and cursing under his breath this second image shamed him. Never forgetting what those eyes looked like back then, it was time to see whether he was back in that delusional crackpot state, or whether he still had control. Similar to being completely drunk, he thought, you can breathe in deep, hide the physical signs of inebriation, but the eyes? Never, they can't fool anyone and you cannot control them. Once the eyes are gone, you're done. His eyes were a marker as to whether he was mentally ill or a mad genius.

Without looking at the bookmark he blew a warm breath onto it to fog it up. Next he began to rub it furiously against the inside of his jacket in a wild hope it would clear, presenting a perfect mirror.

Focusing after a last long blink he raised the bookmark up and took a nervous look.

His eyes were piercing blue, holding a stare that wasn't designed to woo women, but a stare that was designed to scare them, and everyone with them. Unwavering in the reflection, they were true, focused and fixed. He breathed out in sheer relief. Those eyes were signalling that it was time to finally piece together his once-thought-insane assumptions that had now gained authenticity in his mind.

He had waited a long time to see those piercing eyes, it reassured him. He had also promised himself in his darkest days he would only open the envelope inside when this day came, ironically it would now be the day he broadcast his concluding theory.

★★★★★

Opening his Moleskine he took a moment to pull the envelope from under the elastic band. Unsealing it, he patted it against his hand. A photo dropped out, only a few inches square.

'The dream team' he said out loud. Rubbing it as he admired the five faces forcing out uncomfortable smiles. Sitting on the bonnet of an old banger he'd nicknamed The Juke were Johnny, Larnaka, himself, Andy and Mohammed.

He studied Andy hard, noting he was happy, focused and looking well out of shape. Andy liked his weights but undercover work gave him two options, get skinny or get fat. He opted for the muscle to turn to flab, not to waste away.

Looking at Johnny he always went back to that pivotal moment in the room that night, so he skipped back to Andy looking at his fat head, smiling behind the fake aviator sunglasses he'd bought from the local souk in Baghdad.

'I should of seen it coming mate, I'm sorry, I think about you everyday. On my worst days here I believe you're pushing me when I need it the most.'

The intensity of operations after six full-on months with the new Cell hadn't disappointed. He recalled the exhilaration of being out on the ground following terrorists to meeting's, or discovering where they lived. Though the stresses were immense, bordering insane, it only took a few hours back at base to purge it out of them with a few drinks and the odd call home.

Smiling, he remembered Andy's deep conversations that seemed to pop up from nowhere and were subject to some scary theories. Thinking

47

it was the combination of work, booze and isolation, Decker just slapped him on the shoulder with the comforting words of 'you think too much mate'.

One of Andy's wild theories was that Larnaka and Mohammed were spies and that the Brits were being played by them. At one point he even reckoned they were working for the Iranian's. Decker just couldn't see it, ridiculous accusations; they both put their lives on the line everyday, there could be no way that they were the batting for the other side. His paranoia dissipated over time and he dropped his private rambling's as Decker threatened to sack him.

But it was what he started doing next that made Decker send him home for enforced rest or leave, without throwing the book at him. In the SAS you didn't shop your mates, you covered each other's asses and hid any issues from the head shed or Bosses where possible.

Decker recalled the day he'd walked prematurely back into his own room, having forgotten his phone, to find Andy looking through his private stuff. His diary had been open and Andy had his head in his laptop. He'd lost it, slapping Andy open handed across the face, knowing Andy had paranoia issues and breaking his nose wouldn't help. He felt the rage he'd felt back then.

'What the hell are you doing Andy? Why are you looking through my stuff?'

Andy in shock, was speechless. 'Answer me' Decker raised his hand again.

Andy spoke: 'You're up to something I know it. I thought it was those two Iraqi's but it's you.'

Decker could see he was vacant, on the edge, struggling to come up with a decent excuse. 'Andy you have to get a grip, I covered your ass last time. This paranoia has to stop.' Decker squeezed his hand around his neck, Andy's eyes avoided his. 'Look at me Andy, drop it, this is getting too much, you need time off.'

Andy looked at him: 'Tell me you're not up to anything Harry, tell me.'

'Of course not you crazy horse. We've been here for seven months non-stop now. No wonder your mind's wandering. This tells me we all need time off soon and you're the first mate.'

Andy looked broken and confused.

'You're out of here tomorrow for two weeks Andy, fuck off to Bali or somewhere, lose yourself in booze and women, we all need it.'

Andy had trembled as he'd loosened his grip. 'Sorry mate, this is all getting too much, you're right, I need to hit reset.'

Decker drew him into a man hug, gave him a few solid slaps on the back and told him he would be flying out tomorrow night.

Holding the photo in his hand, it had remained in pretty good condition all things considered, unlike the characters in it. Smiling at it, he began to talk to it. He knew in his heart he was like one of those drunken bums on a local park bench talking to thin air, but he was past caring. He knew they had suffered, but Decker knew he was smarter, he was in Antarctica talking about it.

'War' Decker bitterly growled out. 'War, it affected us all us didn't it? Talking to the audience of four and his former self. He was actually aware that he was acting like his local park tramp, shouting at his invisible friends in a frenzy when the cider supply runs out.

'Christ it made you a non believer Mohammad' Not expecting a reply or speech bubble to jump out the photo, he thought about the power of conflict, death and destruction. All the sectarian violence in Baghdad had seen Mohammed confide in Decker in the most bizarre circumstances.

Smirking to himself and thinking 'everyone came to me with their fucking problems? And me? Who was my sounding board? Who did I bother with my issues?

Mohammed was different.

Decker remembered being sat outside their sleeping accommodation with Mo, as he called him. Both relaxed and witnessing the usual fireworks display of tracer rounds flying high into the Baghdad skyline. Burning out into nothing. Like kids watching fireworks he thought, never get bored of watching it.

Sharing a hubbly bubbly pipe that was the closest Decker had ever been to smoking pot, they just chilled. A little lightheadedness, but just what the Doctor didn't order after 16 odd hours working.

Feeling the affects of mindfulness or escapism was what he always attributed to what Mohammed said to him next. Though he also thought Mo may be pulling his leg as he understood the dry British sense of humour the guys banded around.

Picturing Mo blow out heavily the words were crisp 'I'm a non believer Harry, I'm a non fucking believer brother'

Decker laughing at the time, almost choking, due to the context and it was the first time he heard Mo curse.

'No man, my people are killing each other, blowing each other up, chopping each other heads off. This ain't no religion. There ain't no Allah. There has to be another way'

Recognising he was wasted or serious Decker sat up. 'You serious Mo? Or just high?'

'I'm serious, pass me a beer god dam it'

Decker dipped into the cool box and pulled two cold ones out.

'Over this last few months things have changed, I see that you infidels have probably got it right. I don't even like the Middle East anymore. Once were done here if we get out alive, I'm off to the USA or even your place'

He was serious and Decker could actually believe him. His people were brutally murdering each other in almost genocidal fashion.

'Does that mean if you get killed tomorrow there is no 72 virgins waiting for big Mo?

Mo laughing 'Oh no we can still do that Harry, Ive earned it' Leaning over and toasting his beer to Decker. The clatter of the bottles was like his two ski poles tapping.

Again Decker was left with another dream team member from the photo sharing a moment from the past.

The clatter of the bottles also made him think about his downfall. As far as he can remember or recognise, it started happening after Baghdad, when he was sent back home by the Boss....

As he took another look at the photo he couldn't help but notice it was only him and Larnaka that didn't have any issues on that team at the time, maybe facing up now was the time and the place.

Like any proud soldier, especially one who had endured what he had, facing up to the fact that he was mentally weak, unstable and maybe a victim of PTSD was unthinkable. He had read about people taking years to admit they were suffering from mental health problems. It was a disease like alcoholism, and like any alcoholic, the first step was admitting you had a problem. He would never do this, even though he knew that his theory might well be his way of denial, a way of blaming something else to protect himself from the possibility he was a PTSD sufferer.

That's why he had to be right about his theory.

Carrying on with his group discussions that were one way, he felt the need to chat again to a photo that was the closest form of comfort he could muster 10,000 miles from any NHS shrink back in UK.

Looking at his former team he started to unload.

★★★★★

'You know what, I initially treated my downfall as a malfunctioning of my mind, like a few loose wires here and there, so I decided to fight back with my knowledge of Cognitive Psychology, I was still fighting what I perceived to be my own mind cracking up. Like others who fall deeper into PTSD or other types of mental illness I thought that I'd combat it with my own knowledge of the mind and fortunately I think I got there just in time.

'This evil that was driving me insane with its sick images, random voices and thoughts that came from nowhere. I decided to name the evil trigger of these memories. I know, it sounds crazy but I called it something. I named it The Fear to isolate it. To me it had become a small part of my mind that was hell-bent on destroying me…'

A constant band of tension occupied his head back then, just like walking around with an axe buried deep in your forehead. This is what had led him to his reclusive lifestyle, his paranoia. He felt safer behind four walls, well, until he trashed all his electrical equipment thinking the residual white noise was causing all his problems. A combination of paranoia that had seen him smash up phones, car radios and even his prized flat-screen TV got launched off his balcony. Just thinking back to how noisy his mind was then, made him hold then rub his head frantically.

'Over a period of months I started to mobilise my mind and started winning my war within against The Fear by confronting it. Long story short, I steadily made it back a stable state and this 1400-mile slog to create history is the final barrier I set – on my own, controlling my own mind whilst shattering myself physically every waking hour in Antarctica.'

Feeling how exhausted he was confirmed he was right about that, Antarctica had done the job of knackering him out.

'I was happy that I'd defeated my own mind by battering THE FEAR into submission by silencing it completely. It took time to recognise every stab in the back that they were giving me, but it was a good job well done. But what I've been left with is this feeling that it wasn't just me, it wasn't my mind I was defeating, it was something bigger. Something controlled and orchestrated, programmed to intrude my mind that resulted in this sickening behaviour. This is my theory. I know you would agree with me, but I just have to convince myself by backing it with credible evidence.'

It wasn't just thoughts and assumptions voiced in a pub trying to explain a conspiracy theory. He truly believed it, he just had to prove it. So much so it caused him to shift up and check behind him again.

★★★★★

Nothing.

It was these random acts that scared him sometimes. When nothing was there, self-doubt crept in again with no one to advise him.

This thing he called The Fear in his mind was the key and he knew it. Nailing it down to the specifics would take more than a few heart-to-heart conversations with a photo.

Standing up and walking around he sighed and held his head. Frustrated he yelled out, 'The Fear, The Fear, I know this is where it all lies, it's more than intuition that I called it that. If I am right and it is something bigger, then by who, and why?' After viewing the ins and outs of black ops he knew that the government would be the only people strong enough to execute something like this, with the ability to deny it later, he sniggered. Cowards. Why him though? He'd given his all to fiercely protect his country's freedoms let alone that of others in war. Had he not proven his loyalty to deserve a little more respect?

He shook his head in disbelief and placed the photo gently back in the envelope then back into his diary. He closed it and took a moment. Sitting back down and still in deep thought looking to his front he unscrewed his flask lid, a hiss of pressure released the hot steam into the cold air. As he caught a whiff of his lunch he scanned left to right over the horizon that was just about visible. 'I know you're out there, and it's time that I let other people know about you.'

CHAPTER 7

Sully held his stare at Alex and Beast, silently demanding an immediate explanation to the words that they had just been privy to between a guy named Steve and another he calls Champ.

Both jumping in at the same time to explain, Sully cut them down. 'Shut the fuck up. One of you start shooting now.'

As he predicted, Beast was the first to get talking. 'We will intercept his last video diary when he goes to post it, see what's on it then destroy it, or post it on his site if it's okay.'

'Exactly.'

'Okay I'm on it Boss,' Beast moved back to his workspace as he was talking.

Sully turned his attention to Alex, sensing an air of nervousness around him through his silence. Sully gritted his teeth. These geek sorts were sensitive and he was exercising every ounce of his patience after his brief being interrupted not to jump down his throat.

Alex took his glasses off his head and wiped the build-up of sweat off them, before replacing them. The action seemed to calm him down. Alex replaced them before rushing into his half-cocked explanation.

'Okay I started following this guy on his groundbreaking solo expedition – you know these types interest me. His blogs and previous video calls are pretty spooky. He talks about his mind-'

'Cut to the chase Alex, is he some sort of problem?'

'No, it's just he's sent a few left field blogs that highlight his paranoia, and slightly mad way of thinking that he has an entity in his mind that he does daily battle with.'

Beast standing behind Alex wasn't expecting that response. He noted too Alex's voice was raising in pitch. So did Sully.

'So what I'm thinking-'

'How long has he been down there?' Sully cut him off again.

'Over 30 days on his own and he's skied over 500 miles.'

'Well I would be slightly barking mad if I was him. So, the million dollar question coming up here is: is this something worth worrying about or can we get back to our briefing and stop fucking about with your sideline monitoring of mad men on ice?'

'Yes of course, as I said it's…'

Sully already walking away, 'Save it, let's finish this brief.'

Nodding, Alex walked past Sully to continue his brief to the guys.

Sully stood still for a moment, rubbing his chin before following Alex.

Knowing that the cameras were off them Sully walked back in to find Gerry and Bob chatting away like they had known each other years. He watched them sit back straight up again, immediately breaking their small talk. Professionals he thought. Alex had some way to go with his decorum.

'Apologies guys, just a small development we're keeping our eyes on. Crack on Alex, you were about to tell about Ridley.'

Clearing his throat, Alex picked up where he left off earlier.

'So Ridley was interested in how the mind is affected by what someone says to you. This seems all innocent enough, but what Ridley was thinking of for the future was way outside of what anyone could possibly comprehend. Cognitive psychology was his bag, and his experiment was about to revolutionise the way people will be manipulated and monitored. He wanted to embed thoughts into people's heads without them knowing it. Initially it was going to be through the cell phones that everyone is addicted to.' He paused to check that they were all still with him. They barely nodded to indicate that of course they were and he continued.

'As you know a cell phone is controlled by a network provider. This means every phone operated by that network provider could possibly be manipulated if the technology was developed to do so. Technology was already monitoring cell phones, so providers knew the exact location of a phone, what was being said, and who owned it. The systems and infrastructures were already in place to monitor worldwide networks. Now, Ridley knew that if someone said something to you on a cell phone, it could impact on your thought processes and your emotions, potentially for the rest of the day. What he started to develop was a way for a network provider to subliminally send thoughts undetected to the receiver: minus a voice. He called this 'Intra Subliminal pulsing' or 'blitzing'. The problem was how to implant thoughts in a recipient's head whilst they were on the cell phone? Ridley was dealing with a programme that focused entirely on manipulating individuals to change their thinking and the course of their behaviour at an individual level. This could enable the right individual or influencer to manipulate groups, companies or government officials thinking and behaviour. And of course, all of this would be undetected by the poor sod using the phone. In the 70s the Americans had developed something similar. People would listen to radios and Intra-Subliminal pulsing was used, radiating across the airwaves without the listeners hearing it, moving below the detection levels of conscious human hearing. It was proved that the brain picked up these messages and turned them into thoughts without the person suspecting where they came from, they were just thoughts after all.' He broke for air before continuing.

'Ridley started really working on this around 2012 with the latest technological capabilities. From what I've been told, the initial controlled testing was a little shaky but produced encouraging results. They had the breakthrough they wanted and this changed the dynamics completely. They were at the 80% stage then. What Ridley failed to realise with his creation and what was spotted instantly by our intelligence guys – that he may have created singularly the most covert type of warfare known to man. Commercially this was the end of his experiment. He was defining the new battle lines of psychological warfare that could be commanded from a single location. This location could be far from the front lines of every individual involved, without a chance of getting one's hands dirty, you could build a command centre anywhere in the world, provided you had the technology to man it.'

Alex made an obvious gesture to the floor above. Obviously manning whatever they manned.

'But Ridley was only ever focused on negative thoughts for individuals to interpret. His particular expertise and lifelong research dealt with individuals with manic depression and self-esteem disorders. Over a protracted period, his findings could isolate the key drivers to individuals suffering each condition. Behind the smile and the eloquent manner in which Jim Ridley addressed people, was nothing but a charm offensive with false mannerisms. This was a man that had had an exceptionally genius idea, of how to manipulate a mass of individuals, by infecting them with a life-threatening depressive disease. Because they would end up killing themselves such was the mental hold the technology could inflict. This disease, like any, started small with a few simple intrusions of the mind to get the ball rolling—'

'He was a lunatic, total maniac but most geniuses are,' Sully dove in.

Alex nodded with an expression of slight irony looking at Sully, which Gerry noted straight away. He'd obviously cottoned on to Sully's ego during however long they'd worked together.

'Ridley liked to identify the actual tipping point when a discontented person became a highly anxious, insecure and confused individual, profiling a downward spiral which gained uncontrollable momentum rapidly. The individual targeted would then enter the darkest realms of their life, in complete and utter desperation and depression. A lawless mind, almost, the thoughts that the brain commuted to the mind were reckless yet, of course, false.'

Sully watched his team nod their heads thoughtfully; they were obviously considering Ridley's ethics. He gestured to Alex to let him jump in.

'You're a perfectly normal person going about your business, happy as a pig in shit one moment without the slightest suspicion of anything untoward. Then you notice a slight change in your attitude and outlook – let's call this Phase 1. At first, you think maybe it's just a phase, after all, you can't be tip-top everyday of your life. As it continues to plague your daily life, chewing away at the motivation you once thought was unwavering, alarm bells start to ring. You think it could be that old cliché-style mid-life crisis, even though you're 25 years old, have a stunning girlfriend, 100K-a-year job and a penis that should be moulded in chocolate and sold at Ann Summer's stores.

'So you start feeling down, not depressed though, that's for all those losers who champion excuses of SAD syndrome, or have an uncle who suffers from it, so it's hereditary and all that crap. But bit by bit, the self-doubt creeps in. The once-confident young man now constantly starts questioning: is this what I really want in life? Do I need a new career? Why am I so deflated and not putting any effort in these days? As the crisis in your mind gathers momentum, the relationship starts falling apart, the drink starts flowing, and the personal discipline and work ethic start to slip. Now that you're on the slope, there's no point holding on and you give in. Your new world fills with a negative cycle which constantly continues to reinforce itself. The more you try and work it out, the further the answer moves away. Chasing that answer takes you past Phase 2 when the frustration turns to desperation, the desperation needs a quick fix. More alcohol, more drugs or anything else that will make this thing subside.

'You're now in the addiction cycle, Phase 3, exactly where Ridley wants you. Even if you haven't turned to some sort of drug for relief, you can hardly bear this shit anymore. What started as a simple seed of doubt planted in your brain has now matured into an addictive habit or condition of total despair being fed by our technology. However, if we take our foot off the gas now, you will survive and get back to where you used to be… eventually. If you're not on that lucky list, it will persist and hound you until we get the result he desired: you, splayed out at the bottom of a multistorey car park, or maybe found hanged or gassed in your car. Obviously just short of suicide was the point that Ridley's experiment reached its peak for him.'

His team looked aghast at what had just been described. Each of them sat in silence obviously re-running the script.

'Any questions so far?' Sully asked to break up the silence that was only interrupted by the air-con unit changing fanning planes.

Bob nodded slowly.

'Go on, Bob.'

'Where's Ridley now, Boss?'

'Ridley's dead,' Sully responded in a voice that indicated no further questioning on that front. He carried on.

'It was no surprise that the intelligence community could see instantly how the genius idea could be utilised to its absolute maximum. The whole thing was messed up beyond all belief, but what an incredible thing to watch unravel. At the Phase 3 point the person was vulnerable to a brainwashing tactic. They were broken. This is where the real targeted manipulation can happen, defining future behaviours.

'At this point the Government realised that they had begun to jump the gun and hence they brought me in to sort it all out and give it some shape. Breaking people down had become a mastered art but no one really knew what to do once Phase 3 was reached. It was no secret that the Americans had messed about with brainwashing programmes in the Sixties. These programmes were about creating fighting machines, men that ran at bullets, men that never questioned orders. But we wanted to do something far more special. Far more intricate and world-leading.'

He paused to look at Bob and Gerry, they were barely moving with each breath.

'I was headhunted to think of how, in a modern world aghast with terror on every continent, especially UK soil, we could build on this capability of manipulation.' His team nodded silently.

'So back to the whiteboard Gerry, I saw you looking at it,' Sully said, testing to see if Gerry was still sharp as a razor. Gerry was always quiet during briefs, never really contributing until the crux moment. Embarrassing for competent teams he worked with, his contributions normally discredited their assumptions and theories instantly. Out of the corner of his eye he could see that Bob didn't look at all offended that he hadn't been asked to comment, yet.

'Gerry,' Sully impatiently snapped him out of his moment of deliberation.

Gerry calmly nodded. Unflustered by Sully's tone. 'After Ridley's unfortunate departure from this world, I reckon that someone realised the potential of this technology. But this technology had to be rolled out on a proper test group to see if it delivered the goods. The test group I'm guessing would be the elites – this type of manipulation has to be stress-tested on the most mentally robust specimens I am guessing – no point targeting the weak.'

'Carry on,' Sully circling his index finger around the dot on the board.

'Probably military, government or even pro-athletes. People who were considered the most resilient in the business. I would suggest hardened murderers in prison too, but maybe not if it's run through cell phones or other mediums. Anyway, this has been done to confirm its complete viability and most importantly to see if it can be detected, and come to think of it, even defeated?'

Alex sucked in his breath, clearly impressed with Gerry's lightening speed intellect and ability to piece together a problem with minimal clues. All he had was Alex's brief and a dot on the whiteboard to go on. What represented a cold trail for most was bringing Gerry to his conclusion. Bob was nodding away at golden bollocks on his left, clearly a modern-day Columbo minus the Cuban cigar.

Gerry started his final deliberation. 'That lone single black dot I think is actually a huge dot. That is that one person that has beaten this programme or has certainly made you realise it's not foolproof before rolling it out. And I guess our next brief from you, Boss, is what we're going to do about it.'

Looking at Gerry in awe, Sully was actually ecstatic about what he had spelt out but knew he would have to rein him in a little to stop him from jumping ahead. Smiling across at him he nodded his head to reaffirm his congratulations, Gerry casually added, 'Yeah, I've been keeping my head busy with those Daily Mail cryptic crosswords of late,' before dipping his head back down. Sully remembered that Gerry was never one to accept praise, which was good because he didn't intend on giving any public displays of it.

Gerry piped up again: 'Alex, if my theory is correct and that dot has a name, what stage did he get to? Phase 3 I take it, suicidal?'

Sully jumped up not allowing Alex to answer.

'Hold on Gerry, you're running away a little here. The black dot isn't a test case or candidate. So park it for now.' With that blunt comment, the heavy footsteps of Beast were heard again. Before he popped his head through Sully caught Alex's look of confusion at his last comment about the black dot. Looking through him, Sully turned to meet Beast's huge cow head popping in.

'Boss…' Beast began.

Sully nodded his acknowledgement and without saying a word, he and Alex left the room.

Moving along the corridor Beast was eager to talk. 'Boss, we've intercepted the video diary so it's not on the public website as we're controlling it at the moment. Glad the guys ripped it off as you aren't going to like this.'

Sully didn't even respond, he just looked through Alex who, in his opinion, needed to get a serious grip on his sweat issues. The man was a streaky mess. He sighed inwardly, there was no point in light conversation until he saw whatever it was that had cropped up.

Standing around Beast's workspace, the Mac had the video up.

CHAPTER 8

'**F**ucking move,' Decker screamed out to his tent walls.

'MOVE. MOVE,' he repeated even though the bullets racing out of his Kurtz compact MP5 sub-machine gun drowned out his calls. His last bullet signalling the start of a whole new world of hurt.

This was the drill, the first 10 seconds were done.

No more drills just instinct now.

And it was the second time working undercover that he'd had to deliver lifesaving actions in order to gain the upper hand.

Shooting through the windscreen to instantly drop two policemen, before firing across Larnaka's front, who was sat in the driver's seat of their beat-up old Toyota Corolla, to kill the other policeman, who like a novice had kept his head resting up against the window still inspecting their false IDs.

Their cover was blown.

In a place that offered no protection, not even from the corrupt policeman he had just killed, the decision cycle was clear-cut.

'Go. Go. Go.' Larnaka ripped the grab bag from underneath the seat along with the short-barrelled M4 carbine, before throwing the door open.

The door met instant resistance from the dead body slouched down next to it.

'It's stuck.'

'Kick it, kick it.'

Swinging both legs up from the foot well and pounding the door the corpse was slowly pushed aside. About to exit the car they were met with a hail of bullets splashing the bonnet and windscreen.

The Corolla was a bullet magnet that four other policemen were now firing at from the next checkpoint 50 metres away.

The other traffic that had innocently boxed the Corolla in whilst queuing were all in panic mode, some just froze, others were frantically revving and smashing into each other trying to move out of the impossible situation.

Books was oblivious to all this as he exited with his own grab bag and started showering the police with accurate fire to maintain his life, unlike their wild inaccurate bursts condemning theirs.

Hearing the covering fire from Larnaka, Decker made a dash for the only cover in sight. A concrete bollard.

Peppered before with fragments from a car bomb, he judged it was about to take some more.

Laying low behind it he heard the cracks of the police bullets shooting over his head. He popped up quickly letting another few bursts go, managing to take out the policeman running towards him first before engaging the other two who dived for cover behind their own blast wall.

'I'm with you, I'm with you on your right.' Decker heard the shouts knowing his back was covered by Larnaka, who had finally got out of the car and started shooting.

Decker surveyed the scene looking for hard cover in the form of a building. 'Right, see the buildings 7 o'clock, 100 metres across the waste ground?'

'Yes.'

'We need to get there and bunker down.'

'Okay.'

'You put some fire down and we'll head over.'

'Got it.'

Just before the shit had hit the proverbial, Decker had managed to inform Zero over their comms about the imminent contact.

Zero had acknowledged moments before the bloodshed.

This was great news, in times of extreme danger this was not the norm, communications were normally down.

Now Decker knew a predator drone would be watching them and the Quick Reaction Force (QRF) would be coming. However they were 10 minutes away before their heavy armour would arrive on the scene.

'At the speeds bullets fly that's a lifetime,' he thought.

Reaching in to his bag he pulled out two grenades, the type that threw out multiple flashes and bangs with plenty of smoke. The buildings they were heading for were slightly behind them and to the left. Moving back amongst the cars was their best option. The smoke would give them some sort of cover, as the police weren't going to shoot randomly into their own people, or would they? You never knew in Baghdad.

'When I pop smoke, I will make a run for it.'

'Okay.'

'Anyone tries stopping us, shoot them you hear me? We stop now we're dead.'

'Got it.'

Quickly checking all around him for any locals that were trying to play the hero and have a go for it, Decker was happy they were alone, still surrounded by onlookers, albeit on the ground, Baghdad locals had learnt quickly to keep their heads down when the bullets started flying.

He released the grenades which followed by a few bursts from Decker's fellow operator silenced the police while the smokescreen was building up.

White smog finally covered their front, he screamed out:

'Moving, Moving,' as he listened to another burst covering his tracks from behind.

This was a standard drill practised hundreds of times on the range. Known as a hard compromise it wasn't a case of just legging it and not looking back.

Professionals don't do that.

This would be a great sight to watch from the operations room via the drone's predator downlink, but a stark difference on the ground.

Breaking out of the traffic and jumping over a gravel mound he quickly swung his body back around, on his knees, hunting for his next kill. All he could see was a white mist rolling through the line of cars.

This was good.

He couldn't make out any enemy, but peppered the checkpoint with a burst from his M4, to let his colleague know that he was covering and the police know they were still in a fierce gun battle.

They would be up for the fight, Decker thought.

He knew this seconds before he let rip at the checkpoint again.

It was an Illegal Vehicle Checkpoint or IVCP in the business. It wasn't the police but local militias, Al Qaeda flexing their muscles in the daylight waiting for a prize like Decker.

Iraqi police weren't the smartest dressed police force in the world but Decker was quick enough to notice these ill-fitting uniforms, the mismatch of footwear and poor protocol at the checkpoint. Instinct had once again saved his ass so far. Or started another fight. He almost grinned.

The idea of him wearing an orange boiler suit, suffering global media humiliation with his head getting hacked off by the AQI group of fanatics who were rampant at the moment, was in his head as the ultimate ending to avoid.

There was no fucking chance that that was going to be his conclusion.

His colleague sprinted towards him, narrowly dodging a few bullets around their feet. They were still in the fight for sure.

'Maintain cover, I'll try and make contact,' he instructed.

This was now the first opportunity that he'd had to try and communicate with two other operators in another car that had taken another route close by.

He knew they would have been informed about the situation by Zero. More importantly he also knew the other operators in the car wouldn't follow orders to hold off and stay out of the game.

'Dave, Dave it's Harry.'

'Got you Harry, you North or South side of the bus station?'

'South mate, wasteland area heading for buildings, there's a huge pylon next to them.'

'Pop some smoke Harry to give us an idea,' Dave commanded.

'I have but will pop another.'

Smoke would let the rescue team identify the exact area as they all knew every suburb of Baghdad like their childhood council estates.

'We're inbound coming from the North.' Dave shouting, adrenaline ramping.

Exactly what Decker had expected. They were coming and coming at all costs. He knew they'd enter all guns blazing mowing down anyone that crossed their paths.

'Roger, we'll try and get to hard cover,' Decker shouted.

'See you in a second we're about 500 out.'

He threw out another smoke to signal his rough position to the rescue car.

'Dave's coming, we need to get to the buildings,' Decker pointed to the exact one behind them still over 50 metres away.

'Okay, you go Harry.'

'Fucking cunt.' He let out an animal-like scream. He was down. A

7.62 short had clipped him in his calf and certainly shattered his tibia, he could feel the serrated edge of the bone dig into his jeans.

Crawling straight back to the cover he knew he was out of the game. No chance of walking and limping with the aid of his mate, he would be too slow.

Laid on his back the empty cases were landing on his chest from the covering fire getting put down by Larnaka.

Knowing it was hopeless he turned onto his front, weapon in his shoulder. 'You make the break for the building I will cover you. I can't stand up. If we stay here we're both dead. They'll close in soon.'

'No Harry. No we stay here, the guys will make it.'

'Make the break now under my fire, that may give us half a chance.'

Decker knew this three-foot mound would get torn apart shortly when the bad guys rallied some back-up, it would only take a few RPGs and a car or two to come bouncing across the wasteland in a suicide fashion.

'Time's running out go, NOW.'

She didn't even react to the words that he was now bellowing out as an order. Leaving him wasn't an option. This wasn't an all-American hero screenplay getting rolled out with the classic cliche 'you never leave a man behind.'

This was deeper.

Decker had honed her operator's skills to a level that now had strategic value. She was only just beginning what would be a prolific existence in the field of indigenous covert operations.

He knew that she was more than a mentor and colleague. He was an inspiration, an idol and the only reason that they were both still here, alive.

Together they held one more secret, known only to them, driven by the animal instinct and the lawless attitude Decker had for life. A secret not even Decker could afford anyone to know.

As he barked out his demand for her to get a move on and go he was met again with a final resistance. No reply just another burst at the enemy.

'Larnaka, you'll get us both killed.'

His ears were blown due to the over-pressures of the last magazine he had discharged, but the screech of rubber tyres and a loud clatter of a car bumper detaching was unmissable. It had to be their back-up team mounting the curb and entering the battlefield.

The situation was looking up.

'Harry, move, move,' Dave shouted giving covering fire from the driver's side of the car.

Larnaka crawled over to him, knowing that he couldn't stand on his own. Behind the mound they pulled each other up. Johnny, operator two, was 10 metres to the right of the car with a Minimi machine gun. His multiple bursts of 5-7 rounds of suppressing fire was overwhelming causing any remaining terrorists to hit the deck behind the row of traffic, knowing a burst will spilt them in half. They started to shuffle to the car under Johnny's cover.

Slowly making their way back to the car Johnny swung his weapon left pointing it towards Decker and Larnaka.

Knowing there must be another threat behind them they both kept moving ignoring Johnny's barrage of fire zip past them.

A huge explosion sprayed dirt all over the place. Naturally diving to the floor, slightly disoriented, the dust cloud was thick. Knowing it was great cover to get up and move, they forced themselves to make their last dash. Decker squinted, his eyes still blurry with fragments of debris and dust irritating them, he located Dave's car. A few muzzle flashes caught his gaze, they were close, it had to have been Johnny's weapon. It was hard to work out with his eyes focused on the open rear door of the car.

Larnaka pushed Decker into the back seat as he screamed with agony.

'Go, go, let's go!' Dave shouted getting back into the car.

With Decker seated, Larnaka headed around the back of the car as Johnny passed her to jump into the passenger seat.

Opening the door, she put down one last burst of covering fire. Decker seated pointed his weapon out of the window to do the same. As soon as his got up on aim the weapon was tossed out of his hand courtesy of a few rounds of 7.62 short from a terrorist's AK-47.

'Jesus Christ, GO, GO,GO,' Decker shouted as Larnaka slumped in the back seat next to him. The car wheel spun away doing a 180-degree turn, coughing up a dirt cloud obscuring everyone's vision. Hearing and feeling a few more 7.62 rounds bounce around the car, they headed back to the road with another huge bump.

Within ten seconds they were nearly 100 metres away, out of danger and members of the innocent population again speeding down the highway.

Decker was in agony, he gritted his teeth looking at Larnaka. She was white as a sheet and in shock. He couldn't read her expression. Looking down he saw her clenching her stomach, blood was seeping through her hands.

'MOVE, MOVE guys, she's hit bad, let's get straight to the hospital.'

'Roger that,' Dave replied.

Clasping his hands on top of hers he knew there was nothing he could physically do but reassure her.

'Stay with me sweetheart, it's going to be fine it's going to be okay.'

Looking back at him, his reassurance went unheard as tears flooded from her eyes and washed down her face.

'Larnaka, look at me baby, keep looking at me, we're nearly there, hold on.'

He noticed she had been hit a few times and immediately looked to Johnny in the front passenger seat, remembering the shots ringing out from his weapon through the smog. Tensions running high, it was past speculation. This was no accidental blue on blue in an intense cross fire.

'Johnny, Johnny!' Decker shouted at him making Dave look across at him too. Johnny remained slumped in the passenger seat.

'Christ, he's been shot Harry, through the head', Dave exclaimed.

Seeing the exit wound at the back of his head and a number of bullet holes in the passenger window, the maths was done.

'Hospital, Dave for Larnaka. Hospital, we've no time to stop'. Decker ordered desperately trying to stay focused himself.

That moment he would never forget.

In all the hype Decker didn't notice his own blood-loss from the gunshot wound to his leg. Seeing the bloodstained footwell it hit him too. In shock and as white as she was, he felt himself drifting away as both their hands were clenched tight...

'Larnaka!' he yelled. Decker awoke shouting, realising that he was back in his tent and not in central Baghdad. Fuck. How many more agonising dreams like that was he going to have? Wiping the sweat off his brow he searched for her photo in the diary. Holding it in his hand his mind raced back to the hospital, waking up to see his Commander standing at the end of his bed.

That moment he will never forget. No build-up, no explanation, just the cold hard facts. Shaking his head his Commander simply told him 'She didn't make it, I'm sorry.'

Rubbing the photo his eyes were welling up now as indeed they had the moment those words were uttered from his Commander's mouth.

He sucked in a long hard breath. Something was still amiss. What was it? Banging his head in frustration reminded him of banging on Andy's door the evening he was supposed to go on leave from Baghdad. Leave that he had ordered Andy to take after catching him ruffling through his laptop that night before.

Andy's issues were clear cut back then. He had a load of stuff going on in his head, like fifty per cent of coalition forces in Iraq fighting a war that couldn't be won.

Decker recalled getting back from the Green Zone in Central Baghdad in the evening. When someone was due to go on leave, they would be packed ready and buzzing about the place. Yet the moment he had entered the sleeping accommodation and seen Andy's door closed he had a heavy feeling in the pit of his stomach.

He even felt it now.

Andy's body was slowly twisting in mid air. Suspended by the rope around his neck that was connected to the central beam.

Looking at Andy in the photo to wipe the image of him hanging, he rolled his finger over Mohammed. His belief change conversation resonated and then Johnny.

In that last room during the hostage rescue they knew Larnaka would be in it to stay safe. She was the undercover informant that delivered the Intelligence for the rescue mission. Her uncle was the terrorist cell leader and her bravery had already delivered them some big names.

More than an informant, she had become Decker's lover too, and their relationship had evolved over a year.

Why had Johnny tried to shoot her? Decker thought. That moment of madness was looked over, put down to adrenalin, fog of war. But the gun battle at the checkpoint in Baghdad? The one he'd just been dreaming about?

'I know what I saw in the crossfire, it was his Minimi that killed her', Decker whispered to himself.

Only two of them remained in the photo that he couldn't attribute some sort of strange behaviour to.

Himself and Larnaka, although as far as he knew it was only him and Mo, who were still alive.

'I wonder where you are Mo? Not in this god forsaken place piecing it all together.'

This last year or so had seen him deteriorate to the point of destruction. He was fine for that year in Baghdad. It was only after he had come home that it had all caught up with him.

But what about Larnaka? She was fine back then too, just like me. Decker pondered to himself.

If he really thought something was going on back then, why didn't he see it sooner? His own demise confusing the issue?

'Me and her, if I could understand what was happening to us, then this will all make sense'.

Looking at the photo, the only word that came to his head was ' THE FEAR.'

CHAPTER 9

Watching the tent walls getting battered was somehow therapeutic to watch he thought. Knowing it was blowing a cool 40-50 mph and hitting lows of minus 30-40 degrees outside he took great pleasure in splaying out on his sleeping bag, warm albeit not overly comfortable.

Holding his diary above his head as he laid on his back, his read the page title that reminded him of why he wasn't in any mood to start relaxing.

'THE FEAR' was written across the opening page.

'FEAR?' he said out loud. 'FEAR? Why did I call this thing the FEAR? Why? I know the explanation lies in these words somewhere…'

He recalled the preceding morning of events that led to the beginning of his FEAR concept, over a year ago.

It had been a crisp winter morning, sun shining high in the sky as he was walking along the coastal cliffs of Studland Bay, to a local tourist spot called Old Harry Rocks. He wasn't there to take photos. Overlooking Studland Bay with a bottle of Belvedere vodka in his right hand, and the photo of her in his left, he was poised on the cliff edge like an Olympic board diver setting his position.

Earth crumbling slightly under the pressure of his signature desert boots, he remembered looking straight ahead like a diver, and not some fuck wit loser looking down for an excuse to not jump.

This point had been a long time coming, a total demise of man from local hero to local alcoholic ashamed of his predicament. Knowing he had lost his fight because he wasn't strong enough, completely heartbroken with no will to fight on and survive. No family, no friends and no future the decision was the easiest one to date.

Looking at her he placed the photo in his top pocket, gave her a tap then took a deep breath. In that brief moment he centred himself, closed his eyes and clenched his toes ready to explode off the cliff's edge.

A Union Jack flag was all he could see fluttering away in his mind. The flag then started to calm itself before settling on a coffin. A coffin being carried by six guys he recognised. Imagining how touching that would be seeing this happen, he recognised one person that made him freeze.

In full dress uniform brandishing a rack of medals the guy was cut deep. Tears filling his eyes like the other five knowing the man they were carrying had lost his life prematurely.

The back right guy he recognised was him. Distraught but strong, resolute, fresh-faced and still up for the fight regardless of having a close friend's body on his shoulder.

His eyes opened and without knowing it the bottle of vodka slipped out of his hand and over the cliff. Wiping his tears away he turned to walk back, hoping that the figure in the distance, some 300 metres away, that was probably flying the buzzing drone across the cliff face, wouldn't come running over to see if he was okay.

Snapping back into his wind-battered tent and away from the cool sea breeze above of Old Harry Rocks, Decker started his mumblings again. That was the point, it all started to change. What this invention had started off as that day, and how he now thought of it, were worlds apart.

'Is it a codeword? An operational name? Some kind of trigger mechanism?' It was these kinds of assumptions running through his mind that scared him on two fronts. One being that his thinking was that of a madman who had lost it again, or front two, if it was true, he was in deep trouble from a new outfit that he had somehow detected or been mixed up in.

He had written the concept of neural hijackings down long ago, and was now eagerly rushing to locate it. The critical question now was how he could connect the neural hijackings to the FEAR concept he'd invented, without any doubts. And critically associate it to the rest of the team's demise

'There you are,' he murmured pinning the page down with his thumb whilst licking the remains of his lunch from his stubble and reading the title, that was dated about a year ago.

NEURAL HIJACKINGS.

'Neural hijacking is the poison in my head, I've researched this and it's when a thought, phrase or image you didn't generate just pops up without conscious knowledge. Something or someone is inside my head and blurting this stuff out, showing me torturing images that were designed to humiliate

and depress me. I am being hijacked by my own mind as the rhetoric that has been intensifying over the last year is designed to do one thing – destroy me from within. I know I still have some sort of control over my thinking, and it's now or never Decker, I have to fight back before it's too late and I don't recognise what my sane behaviour and thinking look or sound like.'

He swiftly read on:

'I could also be schizophrenic for Christ's sake, all the symptoms are alarmingly present. I even researched it and shat myself when the things like false beliefs came up, confused thinking, lack of motivation, auditory hallucinations, the list goes on and I keep ticking them off. What scares me senseless is the last confirmatory observation, abnormal social behaviour and failure to recognise what is real. Umm…?

Left-side brain logic tells me to see a quack but there was no way I can see a quack with my previous experiences, he would just diagnose me with PTSD to be safe and it wasn't that. Next thing I would end up on drugs, in an institution forever donning white overalls, playing table tennis and getting belt fed drugs. This freaks me out and I wouldn't be granted a second opinion anyhow. And second opinion off who? I have ditched all my mates now, I am off the grid completely knowing I am not with it. I am a sober maniac, this is frightening, being a pissed maniac was okay.'

He remembered with pure clarity what to call 'them', even though he wasn't actually sure whether 'they' existed.

'You're now known as THE FEAR. I don't know what you are, but you're not me. You're simply trespassing through my mind and before long you will pass on by.'

THE FEAR was his constant critic. Branding them as he did the bullies of his childhood who always put him down years ago. Any horrific ideas, images or feelings he couldn't justify as his, or things that made him freak out he attributed immediately to them, THE FEAR.

Years ago all his enemies were physical and could be killed or captured. Now he had a new threat to deal with, a new enemy playing mind games, as opposed to the ones in the past that had lined him up in their telescopic sights. This was an enemy within that he couldn't see, which needed him to be smarter than ever before to recognise their actions, and even smarter to stay one step ahead. THE FEAR was a relentless adversary, unlike a modern-day army that stopped attacking when they all died or lost the will to fight, these mental intrusions never seemed to let up. Derailing him at every opportunity with negative rhetoric, hell-bent on destroying him.

'THE FEAR is a committee in my mind, around five or six people designed to torment me in every aspect of my life. Each one of them an expert in whatever area they wanted to destroy. Now it didn't take me long to get a grip on those amateurs. I began to notice their tactics, they were committing the oldest mistake in the book. Patterns, they set patterns. My techniques to figure out their moves, even pre-empting them became ridiculously complicated. Anyone would have thought I was mental if I'd explained it, yet these techniques were, and still are, ahead of the latest thinking. It was like being the grand chess master of my own mind, countering these mind intrusions. As I silenced their voices and blurred their imagery in my mind, I knew I was ready for the journey back to the elitist past that I craved, that feeling of belonging to a special fraternity, the .5 percent club.'

Decker remembered feeling like an alcoholic discharging himself from an addiction clinic, when he started turning a corner. He also knew he had to keep busy, keep momentum, knowing in order to rebuild you had to be destroyed first.

'The South Pole and back.'

Not even he knew where this mad idea came from but he didn't care and knew he had to do it alone.

Thinking about that idea and now thinking about Day 30, 500 miles later in minus 45 degrees, starting to shiver slightly. He knew his logic had worked, he was on the cusp of unlocking the key to his downfall.

'Back then my thinking was simple,' he thought. 'If I can beat these bastards in my mind whilst in the hardest, coldest, windiest continent on Earth, on my own, then they've lost.

He now knew for certain The FEAR had delivered those hijackings. It was the final theory he was shit-scared of. He clutched the camera, set it up on his flexi-tripod and hit record before he could change his mind.

His options were limited now. A few blips of power left, a confession to a camera about his conspiracy. If it was true, then he knew this may be the only recording that uncovered it.

Worst case scenario, would his theory being correct and looking behind him to see a weapon in his face, or returning home and being found dead under suspicious circumstances.

He paused. Was going for broke and telling all of his followers his conclusion a bad idea?

Looking into the camera he quickly ran a new script through his mind. The red record button went still. He was on.

'Hello Mohammed, I hope you are well and this reaches you. I don't have much time and have to explain this fast. I know why you lost your faith and belief, why you decided to leave Iraq and live like us infidels.'

Decker smirked.

'The Cell I believe was some sort of covert mind manipulation program. Not a new super cell as we thought.

'I'm not talking brainwashing or inserting chips into us like we were robots. I am talking about a longer term Program that somehow conditioned our minds to think and behave differently. I know now why you and Larnaka were chosen for The Cell. It's because the you are Arabic, and the current threat of terrorism is mainstream Arabic followers who follow Islam. It was a language, faith and mental resilience test.

Members of our Cell were systematically exposed to some kind of subliminal intrusions, to elicit a new behaviour, belief, attitude - call it whatever but look at the facts.

Andy turned against our Cell, became paranoid about all of us, then we all remember that night. The night he was supposed to be flying away for two weeks leave, we found him after kicking the door in. Hanging.'

He paused, he would never erase that image of Andy hanging there. His lifeless body slowly twisting back and forth.

'He killed himself of course, but what led him to it? Manipulation I'm sure.'

He looked straight into the camera, wanting Mo to know that he was serious.

'Johnny tried to kill Larnaka twice, succeeding the second time I believe. He was somehow made to think that he could get away with killing a member of our Cell innocently with an excuse to cover it all up. That's two people' He held two frozen fingers up to the camera.

'The next part revolves around you. And this is critical to how this mind manipulation stuff will be used in the future.

'You over time were manipulated to turn against your belief and religion. To rebel against what was going on, almost become neutral. Imagine how powerful this will be with extreme terrorism and the cells that implement it.

73

'My only remaining questions for a while related to Larnaka and me.

'One, why didn't I do anything about it when I could see the alarm bells and pattern forming? And why did Larnaka show no overt signs?

'The key piece is Larnaka was manipulated to befriend me and and extract certain things from me and she succeeded. We, or I fell in love with her and disclosed stuff I shouldn't have.

'And me?

Decker could kind of see the genius in what he was about to say next.

'They manipulated me to not see any of it. As the leader they managed to prevent me questioning it, but just rationalising it like I did back then. Then after I got sent back they continued manipulating me so I would kill myself like Andy. Which I almost did but I invented a concept I called the FEAR in my mind. I thought I was clever inventing it to isolate and cure my depressive demise. The brutal and shocking truth I realise now is the opposite. The FEAR infiltrated me, infiltrated us years ago. This FEAR is real.

'I don't know what their real name is, or what the program name is but it's a real organisation I am sure. I was a step away from these people making me commit suicide.

'You Mo? Christ I hope you are alive but I don't think they would have pursued you. You were the perfect working example. A living product that proved success and how you could transform the thought processes and beliefs of a Muslim.

'Initially I thought my concept was inconceivable but the more I thought about you and Larnaka the more it made sense.

'Imagine how this could be used to almost reverse brainwashed extremists, to de-radicalise them. Getting terrorist cell members to turn on each other, install paranoia, soften them up to become agents even...

'The most powerful form of manipulation is what they have done to you, making you think you didn't believe anymore.

'I'm running out of time and we need to meet when I return. Look up Harry Decker South Pole expedition.com. If I make it you will hear from me again. If not then you need to make sure this goes public.

'I have to go, give me the benefit of the doubt on this.

'Gods speed.

'Bye.'

CHAPTER 10

Silence ensued as the video played then ended. Sully had been staring hard at the bearded man whilst he ranted on. The eyes were familiar, he knew this man, he was sure of it.

'Alex, who is this?'

'This is P822—'

'Not his codename, I want his file now. Drag it up, Beast,' Sully ordered. Alex remained quiet. He expected Sully to piece it all together shortly so didn't bother insulting his intelligence.

Beast played about with the computer frantically moving the mouse about, entering certain passwords before dragging up a file, then hitting the photo knowing Sully would want to see his face.

The screen was full with P822's image, a head-size photo that could have jumped out at Sully and hit him hard.

Which Sully looked at and sighed inwardly as he remembered the last time he saw this man. On part of him wanted to smile, another contained his rage. Sully never made mistakes. Maybe he had overlooked something.

How ironic he thought as he turned to face Alex who was clearly expecting a first-class bollocking from his red-faced, breath-holding expression.

Times like these Sully wanted to scratch his head and even shout an expletive but now was the time for tactical thinking, not an outburst of frustration.

'Is this what you call us "never hearing from him again" Alex?' Sully barked out.

'When I saw him standing on the edge of Old Harry Rocks thinking that this Phase of the Program was complete he turned and walked away. Remember?'

'Yes I remember -'

'And do you remember what I said?'

Alex knew Sully was in flow and interrupting would only infuriate him.

'I said let's take him out, no loose ends but you said, and I fucking quote "Leave it to me Sully, I will get this all sorted so he won't recall any of it, and he can live without anymore trauma".'

An uncomfortable silence ensued. Beast was on the fence wondering who would pipe up next.

'Let me explain Sully, this is all-'

'Shut up Alex, I'm not interested in what you tried doing. What I have now is an intercepted video call to Mohammed dispensing his theory about The Cell back then. And we now have a Memory Card in Antarctica with all of it on it. And... the person it's attached to is no idiot.'

Alex took his glasses off. Always his symptom of huge stress. As he pulled his hanky out to rub them Beast noticed he was shaking.

Sully let out a sigh 'Well this changes things a little doesn't it guys. Our quiet get together tonight to formally invite Bob and Gerry into The Clinic and a few beers after, has just escalated into a manhunt.'

'Right Beast get to it'

'Yes Boss' Beast took his seat again.

Alex followed Sully out of the door.

Stopping after a few metres Sully turned to Alex whispering 'One, you ever lie to me again about some bloke on a solo expedition I will destroy you, and two, get the hell out of here for two weeks while we clean up this mess.'

Alex replaced his glasses and opened his mouth to speak. Sully silenced him by placing his index finger over his own lips. Alex took the hint.

Sully walked down the corridor aware that Alex was probably close to tears behind him.

'What was on the dictaphone?' Alex asked.

Sully didn't even flinch or break his stride.

Alex needed to understand that he was a geek and not one of the big boys who would end up getting their hands dirty.

'Sully listen to me. What I have to say might change your view on things.'
Sully ignored him.

As Alex replaced his glasses he thought 'Sod him, the arrogant prick'.

In a few moments Sully knew he would be telling Gerry and Bob that they had a problem, but he wouldn't divulge exactly how big it was. Still slightly off balance by the video he also realised this would be a brilliant run out for the Clinic's first live operation. His boss had assured him they wouldn't pry into his modus operandi, or trace his transactions around the globe. They wanted results and if they were delivered without recourse, then no questions asked. This was a great opportunity to give that trust element the acid test.

Striding up and down the corridor he was already looking at solutions to this possible problem. That was crap. He never did problems. They were blatant opportunities to show off his lateral thinking that was lightning fast, detailed and always credible.

A few more strikes to suck up the smell of fresh paint interspersed with an odour of wood shavings, he headed back to the briefing room.

Punching hard through the doors Sully cut to the chase.

'That black dot Gerry?'

Knowing an answer wasn't expected. It's a memory card and that huge white screen it's marked on is Antarctica. To finish, it's in the possession of a man who is now the biggest threat I believe we have to National Security. We ain't rolling anything out revolutionary until we have that card, camera and him'.

'So this guy has beaten the program Sully?' Gerry though modest, smiled a little smug smile which Sully was quick to wipe away.

'It's not a test candidate malfunctioning, it's a former member of my team who helped implement the project. He's managed to screw his own mind up, and worse still, about to expose the existence of this outfit.'

Sully paused as he knew that everything would be flying around Gerry and Bob's heads. Thirty minutes ago they were being introduced to a organisation called The Clinic that was going to revolutionise psychological warfare. After a few interruptions they were now facing a dangerous loose end that needed eliminating. With their experience they would both know exactly what this meant for that black dot on the board.

Erase.

Sully slapped his hands together and piped back up.

'This is our immediate problem, nothing else matters so no more questions on this project's inception or delivery systems. Everyone understand this?'

This was barked out more like an order and pretty damn arrogant on Sully's part, as both men hadn't even signed up to this yet. Sod that, Sully thought. He needed to move rapidly on this.

'Who here has heard of Harry Decker?'

CHAPTER 11

With zero response to his question about the knowledge of Harry Decker, he turned once again to the whiteboard and rubbed out the black dot. Always the showman, Sully remained silent for a few more seconds.

He started writing, the board squeaking under the pressure of the pen. Finishing with a massive circle around his work, he stepped away, placed the lid on the pen and faced the guys.

No surprises really.

'Harry Decker = CODENAME 'WHITEOUT.' Block capitals, plain to see. WHITEOUT – the name given to a target and Decker had just made himself one whether he realised it or not. A man on his own in Antarctica battling the elements, his physical endurance and sanity had just almost compromised The Clinic.

Luckily the intercepted and now destroyed video diary that Mohammed or the public would never see was the last risk that Sully could take. If the public had seen this video they would have viewed a delirious man rant about a covert mind-manipulation programme. The public and government people wouldn't take into account he had walked 500 miles over 30 days, mostly in zero visibility on his own. The fact he was exhausted, paranoid and acting deliriously due to these factors would not bother them. It was an accusation about a conspiracy, and when a former Sergeant in Her Majesty's SAS rants, people would look in and listen, in their thousands.

'An hour ago we had the initial brief on what it is we're doing here and who we are.'

He was met with curt nods.

'What is going to happen now is simple, you can either leave now or get on board. In the last thirty minutes something I had not planned for has happened, but luckily we were monitoring this particular guy. And make no bones about it, you join us today and subsequently fuck about like this guy, it's your name on the board.'

Bob was the first to speak up. 'WHITEOUT it is Boss, I don't give a flying fuck who Harry Decker is, if people like him overstep the mark, we take him down period.'

'I concur Bob,' Sully said unsurprised by Bob's reply. Just Gerry now.

'What has made this guy so fucked up if he was just monitoring the Project? I understand you don't want to talk about the past candidates in this programme losing it big time, but why has he done this?'

'Oversight on my part, after Beast has given you a full download on him shortly, you will see he was an ideal person to assist in this Project, but conversely was someone who may have let the past catch up with him. His knowledge of this project is creating a volatile cocktail in Antarctica driven by his exhaustion that is fuelling his PTSD.'

'Did you say Antarctica?'

'Yes South Pole type Antarctica Gerry, he has walked 500 miles on his own for the last month or so and has 117,000 followers.'

'Wow, wow, okay rewind, so you think his PTSD has lain dormant for years? He then works with you so knows the whole process of this project, and is now so fucked up he's not sure if he's a victim of the project, and hence a target, or has he simply lost the plot?'

'In all honesty I don't know, but we have to close him down and do it in the next 10-12 days before he goes public. Look Gerry this is a fastball for sure, unexpected. We need to move, so yes or no?'

Gerry nodded at him slowly. 'Okay Sully I am in, but expect more questions from me later.'

'Of course Gerry, I know that was ambiguous but we are going to receive a brief by the Beast who like myself has had the drop on this potential situation a few days back. He will let you know exactly where we're at with WHITEOUT, again guys WHITEOUT. That's our target's name and must be referred to always as that from now on, facts not emotions.' Sully had to hammer this home, no one likes to kill what could be regarded as an extended family member, but given the choice, they had no choice.

'Due to the time sensitivity, that walk down the corridor has already given me a few options that I think are viable but will run them by you in a bit.'

'Once we go firm on our preferred option I will then allocate your specific phases of responsibility for the OPERATIONAL PLANNING SEQUENCE (OPS) that I will give the Asset tomorrow morning at 0900 hours. We've literally got 8-10 hours guys to bang this out.'

It was a war-gaming process, essentially the who, what, where, when, and critically the how, for the Asset to take down WHITEOUT. Each person around the table had spent years of their lives perfecting every strategy from every angle.

Sully's eyes were gleaming now. He thrived on the OPS; it was the strategic art of killing your unsuspecting enemy and getting the hell out normally without being caught in the crossfire. Predicting the unpredictable, controlling the controllable bound together with psychology, intelligence reports, and external factors like weather, time zones as well as equipment and assets available. After everything was considered and thrown into the melting pot, it was down to him to decide the plan of action to be executed. This had always been where Sully had ruthlessly excelled.

In the hours to come the whole team would be imagining the whole operation, literally lived out moment by moment, infiltration till the extraction. Every single action to be taken with all its possible consequences, thrashed out in order to anticipate contingencies. Any unpredicted behaviour of WHITEOUT, as well as possible individual errors of the team executing the task. This was a part amateurs skipped over. Anticipating the human factor or more bluntly the fuck-ups from your own men. War-gaming was the full package with no shortcuts, shortcuts were for the cuff merchants and cost too many lives, with too many excuses.

Sully started his brief.

'As you know the OPS can be a highly complicated process trying to create a work or plan of genius. In reality guys, the core elements of the plan will be simple. Simplicity always withstands pressure, that's an undisputed fact of high intensity warfare, and a fact I live by.

'However the attention to detail required goes up a notch with this deniable luxury we have. Only the sharpest minds in the business can possibly execute it, and that's why we're all here.' This was the first compliment Sully had given his team. He looked as uncomfortable giving it as the team felt receiving it, he twitched and moved on.

'The plan at large I have decided, and it's driven by the strict timeline of 10-12 days, as well as location. I am already thinking of preferred options so there's no point fucking about with your input, no offence guys but you know the score.'

Sully didn't mind the notion of a Chinese parliament of everyone putting in their two pennies worth, but Chinese parliaments could quickly lead to an Irish one with each member thinking he has the master plan. When extreme timelines were involved authoritarian leadership was required.

About to carry on, one of the double doors silently opened and Beast entered, taking a seat on his left. Not interrupting his flow Sully showed no acknowledgement and pressed on.

'We know WHITEOUT is in Antarctica, we also know that you don't just book a flight to a blue ice runway there, get on a few snowmobiles with a shit load of weapons, drive up to WHITEOUT and put a few holes in his head before pissing off back home. Your latest Ridley Scott Hollywood blockbuster wouldn't find this a problem, but that's what differentiates reality against true events based on a fictitious novel by an armchair fanatic.' Sully paused for breath.

Sully, always the showman, paused for another second of silence accompanied by his schoolboy grin before cracking on with the main act.

'WHITEOUT will be taken down in Antarctica, approximately 100 nautical miles from the South Pole, going on our estimates this far.' This last statement caused raising of heads. 'That's not a joke, he will be taken down in Antarctica we have no choice. Right Beast?' Sully talking at the new arrival next to him. 'Everyone this is Beast and he's going to give everyone a rundown on WHITEOUT so we know what we're up against.' Keeping the brief moving fast would divert the team's initial shock Sully hoped as he waved the Beast to get a jog on.

Beast stood up. Nicknamed 'The Beast' due to his capacity to collect and retain huge amounts of information. Seemingly useless information for most that is, his thought process resembled that of a filtering system that resembled a recycling plant in Mumbai. How he sorted the valuable stuff from the complete rubbish was frightening and yet everyone knew that his breath did not stink of horseshit when he spoke.

'Thanks Boss, this is going to be fast and furious team. We are already playing catch-up as we know. Here is the poignant CV download on

WHITEOUT, no need to take notes, the picture you will form is pretty clear-cut.' Closing their new Moleskines they all sat back.

'OPERATION IGNITION guys is the name of this job. So WHITEOUT joined the Parachute Regiment at 17, highly effective individual. Sailed through the training and even at this stage was noted by his training staff as Special Forces potential when he passed training in Dec 1997. Three years later, true to his training staff's predictions he became the youngest member of the British SAS after passing another six months of torturous training. Getting the picture everyone? WHITEOUT does not fuck about.'

This was already clear to the room.

'2000 onwards he began his new life in the SAS which is a fucker for you guys I'm sorry to say.' Sully smiled at that one, the Beast had a knack of lightening the atmosphere when it came to dishing out serious yet disturbing facts. He was renowned for ending his briefs when he worked for the British Special Forces Group previously with 'good luck with this one team I wouldn't want to be you guys' or something similar. Everyone he worked with liked him, and this team would be no different, even though he was like a doctor diagnosing lung cancer.

Beast continued.

'WHITEOUT had a quiet first few years from 2000 really, apart from working in Bosnia hunting down those nice guys that slaughtered 8000 Muslims in Srebrenica, tailing a few diehard terrorists in Northern Ireland who just wouldn't give up the fight and, a quick hostage rescue in deepest darkest Africa where he first realised killing was fun. Lucky bastard I heard that was a good one from guys I know.'

Bob was squinting slightly clearly doing the maths. Sully knew that Bob had been away himself on another operation when that job went down and would be keen to see an image of WHITEOUT. Maybe he would recognise him.

'Yes, then Twin Towers 9/11 happened and things just went ballistic. Like the rest of the world's Special Forces, or what they deem to call Special Forces, WHITEOUT was at the forefront of initial operations in Afghanistan, *Operation Enduring Freedom*, that's the same one that is still ongoing by the way, all these years later. I hope you guys bring OP IGNITION to a close in a shorter time; otherwise the ice will have melted down there.'

The Beast's dry wit was met with another round of laughter; even Sully risked a smirk that he immediately rectified, reaffirming his authority by slapping the desk.

'Look Beast, we know WHITEOUT is a dangerous man. This room is full of people who are familiar with British SAS Operations, I used to Command it for fuck's sake and Bob had a good go as you know, so wrap this up. Give us all a quick download on his tours, any specialist skills that may concern us, and finally anything we don't know about him from post-SAS era, and we're not interested in his golf handicap.'

Beast flicked through his Moleskine.

'In a nutshell there is not really much he hasn't done. He's racked up four tours of Afghanistan in the conventional Strike Squadron deployments. He has conducted undercover work with assets all over the world, Iraq the same really and a handful of tours in Central Baghdad with Task Force Black...' The team nodded appreciatively, Task Force Black was the name given to the SAS Squadron based in Central Baghdad.

This high-intensity urban warfare had not been witnessed for decades. Breaching into strongholds under intense enemy fire, and regularly encountering terrorists blowing themselves up when the SAS entered their houses. The onslaught was addictive, costly with men being killed but ultimately successful. Their work completely wiped out the suicide bombing networks that had once dominated the whole of Baghdad.

Sully caught Gerry looking at him, probably wondering why he'd remained quiet for once instead of taking this opportunity to brag. He'd commanded Task Force Black for a few years. He knew that there had been talk that he was just a bitter bastard, knowing he'd had to watch from the sidelines courtesy of a predator drone downlink, as his lads blew holes through two-foot-thick walls before closing in, killing its occupants. But that was the price he'd paid for his success. Less action, more authority. A full career for someone like WHITEOUT in the SAS ranged from 10-15 years. Officers like him who made it to the top served a maximum of 6-8 years, spread two years apart, literally a part-timer really in a battle-hardened sense, but a critical architect when it came to strategy and operational planning. That's what he was key at and the men respected these traits, no one could deny him his ingenious flair and knack for projecting operational tempo and future hot spots. He looked through Gerry unblinking before tuning back into the Beast again.

Same thing with surveillance operations. He worked extensively following the AQI terrorist networks globally to find and fix their locations for follow up operations. All the qualifications you expect of an SAS guy with ten years' experience. Sniper, Close Quarter Combat, Surveillance, Counter-surveillance, accomplished tracker, a Counter-Terrorist expert and of course not forgetting to mention the natural ability to completely bullshit his way out of anything. As an overview he is a vastly operationally experienced guy, certainly battle-hardened with all those tours. No stranger to a firefight, and certainly no stranger to people trying to fuck him over. He's not James Bond just to put you at ease, but as we know he is an absolute liability who is not going to bend over and take it without killing as many of us as he can…'

'I will take it from here Beast. We are up against it, under the pump in every manner.'

Though the Beast could lighten any atmosphere, Sully could heighten it within a heartbeat. He rose, he meant business and needed everyone to realise what was at stake, or more importantly, this was no conventional government operation; this was virgin territory; the Asset Icarus would soon have to mobilise quickly and fluently across three continents. Undetected, or more appropriately in a non-suspecting fashion, to deliver a result that had to be successful.

Sure. Sully knew the gravity of failure but equally recognised the magnitude of success. It would officially activate The Clinic. This was the first opportunity to flex the muscles of a deniable capability not restricted by government red tape.

Sully picked up a chinagraph black marker pen off the desk and stood next to the whiteboard. The black marker pen in his fingertips was about to formally begin the OP IGNITION planning process. Old school in nature, a good old-fashioned white boarding session was priceless.

'This is where we're at,' pointing to WHITEOUT on the whiteboard.

'One fucking paranoid maniac, or totally dysfunctional character is the enemy guys. Forget the past. Our mission, objective or end state, is to take WHITEOUT down, anyone who feels nauseous or has issues with this, let it be known now.' Sully was getting darker and deeper as he began ramping up the rhetoric and narrowing his field of view. Sully had the crosshairs on WHITEOUT and from this moment on they were closing in for the kill.

The room remained motionless as the atmosphere was past being cut with a knife. Team members looked at one another digesting the question posed. Sully was effectively asking them whether they had any issues killing one of their own.

There were no replies, just the muffled sound of the Beast clearing his throat.

'So where we at?' Not expecting a reply. 'He is 30 days into a solo expedition in Antarctica just to really mess us about. Let's be absolutely clear about one thing. This is time-sensitive as I mentioned, hence taking him down on the ice. I know you have been thinking along the same lines as me, reference the geography, my guess it that some of you were thinking about taking him out in Punta Arenas, the Chilean town he flies back to afterwards. Maybe a drunken walk back to his hotel that goes wrong when he slips and smashes his skull on the pavement, or an overdose in a whorehouse, even choking on his own puke. If we're really in a hurry a bullet in the head or mugging gone wrong? Conventional thinking and wisdom isn't happening this time around, so we're playing with the cards we've been dealt. On the ice it is gents.'

Complete autonomy had been granted to Sully in this new role and he would need it. Antarctica wasn't the easiest way to break The Clinic in, especially chasing a man that had numerous followers online. Abusing this freedom was not Sully's style and his sometimes-cavalier attitude didn't reflect in his operational diligence. He had the power to really do what the hell he wanted, nothing was off limits, and if he was honest he wouldn't be passing on too much information anyway, just enough to keep the wolves away.

'So fact,' bellowing this out whilst pointing his index finger in the air. 'WHITEOUT will be taken out in "the land that time forgot," according to WHITEOUT himself in his blogs. A landscape that looks like heaven in a photo, but feels like a living hell to ski through – his words again.' He is skiing in minus 15 or even a cool minus 50 degrees temperature due to Katabatic winds reaching 70-100mph. Terrain is jagged with sastrugi or hard-packed ice that can break or shatter limbs. Not the mirror-like surface of an ice rink people tend to associate with it, visibility is a concern because it can be registered as zero for days, or even weeks as the white outs-so common in Antarctica strike without real notice. Lunatics like WHITEOUT are a unique breed of individual who choose to risk their lives in pursuit of human excellence or ironically desperate to restore sanity. Challenging their bodies beyond what could be physically, mentally and emotionally possible. Antarctica is his domain, his playground of choice the arrogant sod.

'It may also have dawned on you that we don't have an unmanned drone program currently operating out of Las Vegas. It's a shame because that means taking WHITEOUT out with a single Hellfire missile, 40km away from his position and 10000 feet above Antarctica, also isn't an option. This is going to be a job for one of our physical Assets, who will engage with WHITEOUT face to face on the ice. Kinetic strike option is not an option. This has to be clean, deniable and completely innocent in the eyes of the public. When I say public I mean it, he really does have a global following as he's trying to create history.'

Individual looks around the table moved from focused anticipation to that of a gurning competition, this task was throwing up some serious firewalls.

Infiltrating a team into a country to carry out complex operations to take someone out was a well-versed discipline to everyone present. Through Sully's contacts worldwide, they had worked up assets ready to deploy and strike within days. Known as the Emergency Response Teams (ERT) they were ready to roll out within hours if they were in the right area. Once mobile towards whatever destination, they would receive updated information developing the target for takedown. The expertise of this team was frightening. Having the capability and skill sets to think fluently and rapidly, these teams were ready and primed to execute opportune targets globally. This work was what they thrived on. But this undertaking would not be the conventional assassination as already discussed as Sully elaborated.

'Our Asset will have two enemies, Antarctica being the first, WHITEOUT the second. The team we deploy will need a short intense build-up package of training in cold weather to refresh their cold weather skills. Otherwise they will perish and inadvertently become the first victims of The Clinic.

'Due to time I have to make a decision. We will thrash out the OPS in a minute. It's the 'Who' we need to activate ASAP. We need to recall an Asset now as they will need to be flying to Norway or somewhere cold sharpish.'

Beast spoke pre-empting an order: 'I will activate and recall Verganno now Boss, as you said we need the Asset briefed tomorrow latest.'

Sully paused to think then shook his head in disagreement.

'No, activate Icarus Beast, please.'

'What boss, definitely not Verganno they are standing by?'

'Yes Icarus, Verganno can run with what they are doing.'

'Verganno are free Boss, they can be at the briefing location within six hours and with all due respect, Icarus are good but South African, Verganno are better suited and two members are experienced in cold weather climates.'

Not what you would call a Mexican stand-off but this was the first sign of tension. Beast was not trying to undermine Sully he was simply stating an obvious choice of Assets.

'Icarus can handle this, they can all ski, they're all tough guys, they'll just need a 3-4 day training camp to refresh them.'

'Any specific reason you're standing Verganno down out of interest?' Beast felt a little incensed. You always put the best people for the job, on the job. Icarus seemed like a strange decision. Sully's arrogance would never put the mission at risk. Gerry reading between the lines sensed there had to be an ulterior motive for Sully's call and one for the better good.

'Look for starters Icarus are South African, so they can do anything, just like the fucking Australians and the Americans. Secondly they have two members who are experienced on the ice, and Mick on the team knows Patagonia quite well down there. Thirdly I'm the fucking Boss so make the call.'

'Your call Boss,' Beast replied as he left the room careful not to show any intended signs of cursing once he passed through the doors.

Sully gritted his teeth, he knew this line of questioning was professional reasoning from Beast, he didn't want 'yes men' and brushed aside this difference of opinion. He knew that plenty more questions would follow with Gerry sat near him.

The atmosphere was a little off between the men still sitting around the table but they had only been together a few hours. Sully sensed it but chose to ignore it. He turned back towards the board aware that his team were exchanging confused looks and making vacant impressions behind his back. Beast came back and took his seat. 'Boss.'

Sully spun around. 'Yes?'

'Icarus activated.'

CHAPTER 12

C losing his office door behind him and turning the lock slowly so it couldn't be heard. Sully let out a long breath of air. Giving the guys a 30-minute break to digest that it all felt right, he needed one too. Despite his frustration and impatience he never slammed doors, no matter how bad it got, control and the perception that he was always in it, was key to his overall makeup. Once inside however he reached for the heavy crystal decanter, enjoying the smoothness of the glass etchings imagining that they mirrored the channels in his mind. He poured himself a tumbler of the single malt nectar. WHITEOUT was irking him somewhat, a feeling he was not used to and one that needed to be quashed as instantly as it had arisen. In terms of profiling WHITEOUT, he'd been able to predict Beast's intelligence before he was even presented with it.

He knew first hand that Decker was one of the Government's finest. When Decker had departed the SAS Sully was around. He remembered people talking of another broken man who was earmarked for the top, but couldn't handle the onslaught of pressure plus he was grieving for some bird.

Like his colleagues he didn't ask questions, they had just written Decker off as cracking under the stresses of the brutal workload, and displaying the mental weakness not acceptable to the SAS.

As a Commanding Officer of the SAS he did have compassion for the stresses the guys face. And yet sitting in his chair he could still recall Decker's promise and achievements, he knew he'd met the Queen on three different occasions to collect The Queen's Gallantry Medal, The Military Cross and finally The Conspicuous Gallantry Cross, one below the Victoria Cross. When Decker had left the SAS's gates he had left as the most highly decorated soldier for gallantry in the British Army.

Sully scratched his head, glad that he had told Beast to refrain from telling the team this, he could see that they were conflicted enough without this extra piece of information.

Wanting to kick the sense of guilt out of his mind so that he could think freely about the logistical nightmare he was about to face. He checked his watch. He still had twenty-six minutes before the updated planning and preparation process was to commence. He supped away on his small tumbler of whisky to ease the discomfort of the situation that lay ahead.

This was his greatest challenge to date. He had to deal with facts, he repeated to himself, not emotions.

Running through potential takedown options to solve this crisis, Sully sank back in to his chair, deep in thought. Forcing the neurotransmitters in his brain to play out a million war games at lightning speed, his personal hallmark of being a forward thinker, the images forming rapidly in his mind were like short films playing out all strike options to kill his target.

With each film he would rewind, readjust, pause or delete. When he paused he would zoom in and take a closer look to analyse the points that needed sharpening with his clinically concice attention to detail always present. Anything less than a blockbuster was not acceptable and like any true blockbuster, it had many different endings planned as he knew the scenes before the striking finish did not always pan out as expected.

He twitched suddenly in his seat, the tension running through his veins causing sporadic movements in his muscles. 'Fuck,' he muttered softly. He was under the pump and would have to step up and deliver a complex solution to a very complex problem. 'Two weeks to put this to bed can't go quickly enough for me,' he muttered under his breath.

He forced himself to think of the facts: The Clinic was about to go live with every covert asset and worldwide connection that it had. A deniable operation was to be launched in the frozen depths of Antarctica. When he pulled it off it would demonstrate the global reach of The Clinic, and prove it could pull all the international levers in the underworld of covert operations. The inaugural operation would probably be its toughest he mused.

Sully rose from his chair and raised his glass in honour of his next target. Even though WHITEOUT was cut from the same cloth and maybe barking mad, he had put Sully in a position where only one outcome would guarantee closure.

Fumbling around in his tight chinos pocket he felt the dictaphone.

What was on it was the sole reason he had chosen ICARUS and not the Verganno team.

It was also the reason Gerry and Bob never got to listen to it after Decker sent the intercepted video to Mohammed. If he had played it an hour before to the guys, getting them on board may have been difficult. In fact, he knew he may have had huge resistance.

Looking at his whisky he knew it may be his only true source of comfort for a few weeks. The decisions he would make wouldn't get questioned, though he knew he had already rolled the dice once tonight already.

Ironic for a man who always told his SAS men 'We are in the business of risk, high risk, but we're not in the business of gambling'. He had just broken his own rules.

Holding his glass high, 'The one thing in my control is that I can assure you Harry Decker. You will die with the respect and dignity you deserve. I owe you that much.' He cleared the tumbler, glanced at the empty base and slammed it back down on the desk with a resounding crack.

That was the signal.

It was time for business.

Time for action.

Time that they all decided how they were going to give Decker the legacy he was obviously searching for, and the activation that The Clinic was destined to live out.

CHAPTER 13

'The FEAR, The FEAR – what the hell am I missing?' He shouted at himself knowing that he had just broadcast his last video diary to Mohammed.

'The FEAR? I know it makes sense,' he repeated.

'The FEAR, what else? Come on Decker!'

Donning his jacket and soft snow boots the claustrophobic tent was suffocating him. He wanted space so he crawled outside. Antarctica, being the changeable beauty and beast that she was, had got through her mood swing and was allowing her land some time to breathe. The weather was easing off, the wind retreating to a calm light breeze. Even the mist was lifting to expose the sun's rays, sending a glimmering light, seemingly of hope, across the ice.

It was stunning. Captivating really. He'd travelled to some incredible places in his life but never had the time or inclination to stop and take it in. Decker paused now and, as he took in the overwhelming beauty of the place, a serene calmness flooded his mind. In his own quiet way, he suddenly felt at one with this vast continent.

Feeling the sun on his face, he closed his eyes and bathed in this moment of brief quiet, not letting himself contaminate the moment with thoughts and feelings.

It had been the first time in a long while that he could push aside the devil's advocate in his conscious mind and let it all flow uninterrupted.

A year or so ago he recalled himself saying 'I know you are not me, you will pass through me.' It was true. The state of mind had passed through, but not without leaving its legacy. And suddenly in the silence he knew.

He barely breathed in his silent state of shock. The silence you experience when something catastrophic has happened because there are simply no words to communicate what you have just borne witness to.

Decker started taking off his goggles, exposing his now bloodshot eyes that had just welled up in an instant. His arms hung dejectedly at his sides, letting his diary slip out from his grip. He was a broken man.

Defeat was etched into his weathered face, his bloodshot eyes started to fill with full-blown tears, which cut fresh paths down his frosting cheeks.

Ripping back his hood, inhaling what he wished was his last breath, he started his final conclusion, a conclusion that was the opposite of his last. No defiance, no promise of uncontrolled physical violence in the search for retribution, just the truth.

Decker nervously sniggered at himself, before letting out a brief burst of laughter.

'The FEAR, Jesus NO! How stupid could you be when you thought you were being so smart. Talk about out-thinking yourself. This tops them all: you are a complete train wreck.'

In all his searching for psychological mastery, and becoming a leading authority on thought control and perception, the irony was that he had completely misinterpreted perception control.

'FEAR. Why did you call it the FEAR, Harry? Why?'

He paused in his self-bollocking. 'Because FEAR is an acronym for something that you knew would protect you from the truth. FEAR would let you blame someone else as you normally do when you can't handle the truth. Your downfall and demise into the hell that is this shit life, is all you. And you thought the FEAR would cover all this up?'

His tears dripped onto his jacket uncontrollably. Taking his mitts off to rub them, he cradled his head, which felt as though it was about to explode. The last few years had been so tough. He was ready to face his truth.

'FEAR equals Fantasy Experienced As Reality.'

In his search for answers to blame people for his downfall he had subliminally chosen The FEAR to act as his adversaries. What even he had failed to see was that he had chosen 'The FEAR' because he already knew what FEAR stood for. If there is anything in life that scares you, it's all in your head. A 'FEAR' is not real, you make it real, and he'd made it real in his head to protect himself from all of his negative thoughts. Nothing in that video were true, they were just the deluded ramblings of a desperate man.

In all of his madness, he had failed to live by his own rules and lost sight of what was actually happening to him. Wiping his last tears away and sniffing, he looked across Antarctica, it was truly breathtaking, the sastrugi ice formations were glittering like diamonds and he felt the heat from the rare sun across his cheeks.

'Well, this is it then, Decker. This is your return to former greatness. This was the journey to find the truth, and you've found it. It's your fault. Everything is your doing. It's time to move on and get on with life.'

As he quietly muttered the words to himself, he knew his fight was over.

'Let's go, mate, let's get to the Pole and get back home; it's time to start over again, and it's time to stop running.'

Without warning, the beauty before him started to blur, he suddenly struggled to maintain his balance, he didn't even register what was happening behind him, as the wind started to pick up again. A weather front only a few miles away was gathering pace as the dark grey skies moved in closer, being pushed rapidly by 100mph-plus katabatic winds that were not going to take any prisoners this time around.

Instinct had long gone. He was alone in Antarctica again and knew he would never have to suddenly look behind him or ball his eyes to the horizons ahead.

He was broken not resurrected.

'You idiot,' he yelled. Thinking how foolish he had been to send the video.

Shaking his head he knew he had to stop this self-sabatoge. It was done, his fantasy world had to end here and now.

'This was the answer,' he told himself. 'It was just crazy paranoia, I'm a fucking idiot but at least I'm a sane idiot now.' He knew he was right about this. Antarctica had given him his sanity back and the key objective now wasn't breaking under this latest development, but finishing the job against all odds.

He dug the photo out to look at Larnaka. It was time to lay another fantasy to rest, she was gone, they all were except Mo, maybe. Taking a last look at the photo he smiled, recollecting the great times, but each was their own victim of war, and the war within each of them.

He always felt responsible for killing her. The short journey he had taken with her should have changed his world in the way he wanted it to, and not in the way it had panned out.

A love affair that saw her removed from insurgency to counter-insurgency, battling for the opposing side completed the circle. A full circle from a ruthless killer, maiming coalition troops in Baghdad, to killing her own, with the final irony of her own killing her. It was a story that would never be told and the love story that had never had a happy ending.

'Goodbye my love.' He touched her face once more before ripping it to shreds, tossing it into the wind as though it were her ashes. Watching the pieces fly away in to the distance he stood. Building himself back up again for the fight.

'First man to the South and back is what I'm here for. That's all I'm here for. So let's show them all that my former greatness is about to enter the big stage once again I owe it to the memory of The Cell.'

CHAPTER 14

Twelve hours had elapsed since Sully had slammed back his Whisky in respects to Harry Decker receiving a dignified departure.

Burning the midnight oil to produce a coherent plan in such a short timeframe had been excruciating.

Yet in between a few pizza drops and Starbucks take-outs, the team had joined some huge dots. From organising a surveillance team to carry out a sting operation in Punta Arenas, or booking a two day training package in Norway for ICARUS with Conrad Dickinson, Decker's mentor, the guys had dug deep and delivered.

Contingencies were now in place for team members to disguise themselves as journalists in Antarctica, a last degree or 60 mile stag do party had been organised. Ingenuity to react to what was going on in Antarctica had now been factored in.

Bribing a Russian pilot was yet to be executed, and the next few days would be interesting and critical to setting up this play immaculately.

Sully hung his head, letting his eyes rest for a while.

'Boss' Bob shouted sharply through the open door. Sully was comatose in his chair, feet on the desk with his head cranked to one side with a slight bit of dribble tracking down his chin. His left hand was flayed across the leather armrest that had previously held his glass tumbler. The tumbler was now on the floor with it's contents staining the once pristine oak floorboards.

'Boss, time for action,' Bob barked as an order this time as he walked over to his chair. No response. He adopted the old military habit of waking someone by shaking the feet. Knowing full well that if Sully was in a deep sleep and being a military professional his reaction may be mixed if he shook his shoulder. Bob remembered this novice mistake 300km behind enemy lines, after his boys had been fighting hard without sleep for 72 hours. Finally getting some shut-eye he grabbed a mate's shoulder and shook it, to let him know he was on watch. A second later Bob was on his back getting choked out on the desert floor by a delirious mate clearly still primed to react on instinct before his eyes opened. The feet it is, Bob thought as he rubbed his own neck quashing the memory. Luckily their enemy was over 10,000 miles away fighting his own demons from the confines of his sleeping bag, but Bob wasn't taking any chances of being right-hooked by Sully, especially seeing the tumbler on the deck and an empty bottle of whiskey broadside on the table.

A few more vigorous tugs at his right foot did the trick.

'Uh, oh what's the time?' Sully managed to garble out, similar to someone who had just awoken from a general anaesthetic.

'Icarus have landed, wheels down Boss and it's 0740hrs.'

Sully nodded and took the steaming black coffee from Bob to stop him slipping back into the short-term coma of the last fifty minutes.

As promised the last 12 hours had been brutal on everyone. The team had seriously burnt the midnight oil, super-charged on steroidal coffee and full to the brim with Domino's pizza. Yet the hard work had paid dividends.

Sully was content, hence he had polished off the last quarter bottle of whiskey, once he knew the masterpiece was almost tuned. The team had managed to hit the promised 90% completion OPS for the Icarus brief, the brief that would take place in 90 minutes. The last 10 per cent would develop dynamically over the course of the operation as things went wrong, or things went too well.

★★★★★

'Fucking raining, always fucking rains in this shit hole,' Sean concluded as the wheels of the Airbus 380 stopped screeching and started transiting smoothly along the waterlogged runway at London Heathrow.

'Not wrong. Bloody England or good old Blighty as this lot would say – I knew it wouldn't disappoint us,' Mick added who was sitting next to Sean knowing full well he had just committed a cardinal sin of talking about British weather, for which the UK receives worldwide recognition. Looking at each other, Sean rolled his eyes back at Mick's comment before being interrupted by a request for everyone to leave mobiles off, until the plane has stopped taxiing. This went unheeded as the familiar iPhone tunes filled the cabin with a bombardment of really popular people receiving text message alerts.

'Well we could be on that job still sat in that hole watching that prick I suppose, so it's not all bad,' Mick whispered to Sean. They both let out a quiet snigger as they recaptured a scene that struck a chord, before Sean added: 'That man will live a little longer to enjoy those coke-fuelled whore parties we enjoyed watching so much, lucky bastard.'

'Yeah,' Mick added, 'let's hope this fast move was worth it. I hate unfinished business, especially two days before we were going to take him down.'

Raising his voice to a normal level and ending the schoolboy whispering, Mick looked at Sean with a serious streak that cut through the whining phones.

'So this Sully guy, to pull us off that job so fast without a replacement team must mean we're getting teed up for something pretty urgent hey?'

'As I said before Sully is unpredictable but he must be reacting to something critical I reckon. He's not one for closing an operation down like this, but then this might just be a debrief for that job, maybe he had been given orders to back off and re-task us,' Sean reasoned.

'Saying that, maybe this is the final hurdle for us. I know Sully has been stress testing us for the last few months globally and we have always delivered. This could finally be our in to whatever he's into now.' Looking at Mick with raised eyebrows he could be right. Had Icarus achieved number one asset status in Sully's eyes?

Both men quickly digested that thought knowing the difference it would make to their lives finally entering the major league.

The final braking of the aircraft wheels, followed by the universal bing-bong tone signalling that the plane has stopped, broke their thought.

As per the standard protocol everyone rose before instructed to do so, pissing off the senior trolley dolly who probably couldn't give a shit really, as she now had a few days off to party, get laid and sightsee.

Standing and looking ten rows back to the port side of the plane Sean glanced at Robby. Not acknowledging each other the non-verbal communication was clear between them, though interrupted by a small Indian lady barging past pushing forward for a fast exit.

Who could blame her after a 12-hour flight crammed in cattle class with a bunch of loud Brits five seats back, inebriated since the departures lounge.

Mick and Robby started to retrieve their hand luggage before enduring the painfully slow process of leaving an Airbus 380. Over 500 passengers, most of them not frequent flyers have mastered the art of pissing off the frequent flying club. Their sheer slowness and natural ability to continually forget stuff just before exiting the plane, was enough to test anyone's patience, let alone Icarus, a three-man deadly assassination team, high on adrenalin, and curious to find out what the hell was next on the agenda.

★★★★★

The Clinic sat around the briefing room table once more. Summoning up the energy to pull together one last time, before Icarus were briefed. Sully rose, forcing himself to look as spritely as he could, a splash of water on the face, a few eye drops plus a couple of mints to detain the whiskey fumes. Old school.

'Well done team. Thank you for another monster session and where we have got to just short of a miracle. I am confident this…' he held a small USB drive up for all to see '…is the answer to this unique set of circumstances. The research about ALE has changed things again for us but as always, we will up our game and make it happen. Researching the Russian-owned Ilyushin airframe has been top drawer guys, this could be another game changer, our way in and out, without detection. Also the discovery of the Moon-Regan Trans-Antarctica mobility expedition is also another fast move bought to the board by you Beast. That team could solve our extraction plan tied in with Ilyushin airframe depending on how rich the Russian pilots want to be in a short period of time.'

Sully nodding his head recognising it was another great option pulled from nowhere.

'This is where it's at. Using organic infrastructures like the ones just mentioned and using them without their knowledge of what we're up to, that's the future and you're already nailing it, nice work. Our unique ability to tap into all these resources without some egotistical line manager poking his nose in saves time allowing our footprint to stay low.'

Gerry interrupts. 'Santiago is covered now Boss and just to let you know our contact at GCHQ has been superb.'

'Good to know Gerry,' Sully replied with a smile and cheesy wink.

You could tell the room were pleased by their efforts and Sully was content. If he hadn't been, then the pressure would have intensified and the game would have continued to an uncomfortable new level.

As it stood the OPS for OP IGNITION had now gone through a number of various versions. Sully now had the latest iteration.

V401 would now be the name for the OPS, simply being the idiot's guide to assassinating WHITEOUT. Icarus in 90 minutes would know the contents of V401. All timeframes and actions had been summarised and synchronised into a schematic diagram drawn up by the Beast. So even a five-year-old or Bob could follow it to the letter if everything else was sanitised or even lost. Like a cheat sheet in exams, it would get you a pass. That's all they needed.

This cheat sheet followed every element of the operation, where they would be in spatial terms of time, geographical location and what action each element would be executing to bind this operation together in total synchronisation. Contingencies were still in place for suspected grey areas or unpredictable parts of the plan. The go and no-go criteria were concrete and not subject to poetic license or mission creep, the job was done. All Icarus had to do was follow the instructions and the cheat sheet.

'Gerry and I will head off shortly to meet the Asset. Beast you can keep things in check this end. I am happy for you to draw down for now, so Bob take a few hours to sort yourself out and you Beast, you deserve a rest.'

'Okay Boss, you have V4 on the thumb-drive, itineraries and additional info will be sent to Sean's ghost email account as we continually update. This is the hard copy for him. They fly at 1720 tonight to Oslo.' Unceremoniously Beast handed Sully an envelope and the thumb-drive.

'Thanks Beast. Again this is the start everyone. Talk about tip of the iceberg. This task will bear little significance on future tasks. As I said this is the thorn in our side, once Icarus execute WHITEOUT we will truly ignite a revolutionary era in attacking every fucker in this world that thinks the UK is a soft target.'

CHAPTER 15

Passport control was always a good benchmark in the underworld of Black Ops or standard criminality. It's a conclusive measure as to actually how good you are and, most importantly, how trusted your close network of associates is.

Sean observed the green light flash then followed the instructions to exit the retinal scan cubicle. He was the last through this border control measure and headed calmly off to collect his baggage and reunite himself with his team. The cover story for any operator working in a place he shouldn't be is the lynchpin, that if not followed or executed fluently means compromise, imprisonment or a torturous death if you're mixing with some seriously bad people.

Sean knew that as a seasoned operative he only ever had to answer a few simple questions confidently at any time, any place. Who asks the question is another question in itself and another layer of intrusion to deceive. Whether you're at passport control in Munich, in the queue at Carluccio's in Downtown Dubai or booking into a hotel in Bangkok. You need to have a concise reason for that moment in time. Next layer is an entire story for that period of time after you have caught a few breaths. To really make sure you're not killed, arrested or followed again, you need another life story to melt it all together seamlessly in to the biggest pot possible, because people would start stirring vigorously.

Walking calmly down the concourse he united himself with Mick and Robby. Working as a three-man team in this alternative line of work had its downsides, though they only did a small number of jobs together to keep below the radar and reduce the footprint they created, safety in numbers was sometimes the opposite in this occupation.

Icarus had no need to be nervous. They were here visiting Sully and knew nothing, even though knowing nothing could also have catastrophic consequences as any innocent victim of torture will tell you.

If an Asset does a job properly they will have no reason to arouse suspicion, no reason to be nervous and certainly no reason to not be three guys going on a skiing trip to Norway, then onwards to Antarctica to do a last degree expedition for a surprise 40th. Icarus had a clean record, so no one was going to get lit up at this stage.

'Latte with hazelnut?' Sean asked the small eastern-European girl behind the counter.

'I will have a cappuccino. Robby will have a plain latte and two almond croissants,' Mick added to the order.

Starbucks in arrivals wasn't the standard location for any team of mass murderers to chill out and take the initial edge off their jet lag, but it was their meeting point. Here they would wait for the SMS message for the pick-up directly outside.

Right on time, Sean scrabbled for his pocket, and took his phone out. Obviously on vibrate he answered: 'Hello?' A British accent replied.

'Hi Sean, on the pick-up circuit now, inbound three minutes driving a Grey VW Transporter van with a black tinted side window.'

'Perfect, just getting our coffee, be there in three minutes' Sean confirmed. Robby and Mick stood up and assembled their bags. Mick not wanting to waste the Starbucks, got a little cardboard tray, balanced the croissants on top then followed the guys outside to meet the VW Transporter that rolled in right on cue.

The driver waved over like he had known them all his life. Sean waved back and walked the men to the van. The van was a hip modern-day affair. One window on the side door tinted black, to limit prying eyes from either an impromptu sexual liaison in a dogging car park or a deniable operation brief on the M25.

'Hello lads, great to see you again, sorry about the weather,' Jack commented.

'I'm Sean mate.' Talking quietly but directly.

'Yeah Jack.' The driver identified himself matching Sean's tone. 'Just throw your bags in the back and hop in. Sorry no food or drink mate,' Jack said to Mick.

Before Mick could threaten him, Jack quickly followed up with 'Only joking, jump in before it gets too cold guys.'

He slid the side door open. There were two rows of seats facing each other. Sully and Gerry, the reception party, were already sat on the rearmost seats. Normal protocol the guys gave a nod, brief hello but no big handshakes and bear hugs.

The van pulled away. 'Hello Sean, I bet you never expected that call, did you?' Sully said shaking Sean's hand.

'Well we were a little busy Sully. Only three weeks of wasted surveillance, sleep deprivation and a diet of Big Macs and Subways. Not to mention possible compromise when we extracted under your orders,' Sean's dryness had an edge to it that was cutting yet blunted with sarcasm.

'We have to keep you boys on your toes Sean, you are the best remember?'

The banter was fine but all could sense the apparent rivalry between the two men and this was the first time Robby and Mick had met Sully. It was evident to them both straight away Sully would be the man that called the shots, though Sean's tone indicated he was a man that had previous history with Sully who thought he had a certain amount of weight too.

"So any North Face bags on this one?" Sean says smugly.

'Luckily for you Sean, this next job may help you get rid of that fast food gut you've developed.'

'Oh really Sully? What's your excuse for that pot belly?' Sean pointed at Sully's slight overhanging paunch.

Smiling, Sully quickly hit back. 'Well, every time I fuck your misses she gives me a chocolate biscuit.'

With that everyone grinned with them both. The penis-measuring contest had come to an end. British versus South African banter was forgotten, time for business.

'You will never fucking change Sully. That's why we like working for you so much.'

'It's not mutual. Anyway this is Gerry my right-hand man,' Sean shook hands before the rest of the team introduced themselves. After that the weather was talked about along with notional concerns about each other's families that none could really give a fuck about. Only when the van was cruising steadily along the M25 northbound Sully got his game head on.

'Okay guys, brace yourselves, I am going to give you the OPS now en route to your hotels. No safe house this time, we are up against it, straight out of the gate stuff.'

He was met with silent nods.

'This job is another deniable operation. Not sure what government, but I am British and we're in London…'

Sully's usual breaking-the-ice routine got a snigger. 'OP IGNITION is the operational name. The objective: To take down WHITEOUT.'

Gerry automatically handed over his iPad to Sean to show an overview of WHITEOUT with images and a brief history in a Word document. Mick and Robby leaned in to get a glance. 'We have a few loose ends to tie up as regards a couple of former government agents that are causing problems. It will be a straight takedown of the target and retrieval of everything they possess. Okay so far?' Sully enquired.

'Did you lot miss a trick Sully? Clearing up your fucking mess again? I take it the A-Team has dropped a bollock and the real men are here to clear it all up?'

Sully did not bite at Sean's response but shared another brief smirk acknowledging the cheap shot before responding.

'Keeps you fuckers in business I suppose. Right? In fact Sean, this is actually phase two of an ongoing operation that my primary team,' Sully pronounced with a sarcastic tone, 'have just finished and, due to keeping their exposure limited, we need fresh faces to finish this one off.'

'Glad to hear it, so any information on the phase one job or is the usual "need to know" in play?' Sean asked placing the ball back in Sully's court. Sully grinned inwardly. He had taken the bait.

'No you can listen to this actually, phase one was nothing short of genius Sean, even I was envious of the mastery.'

Not expecting this reply Sean and the team sat silently waiting for Sully to disclose the operation he appeared so happy with. Sully cleared his throat.

'Okay a quick overview of the current situation. A pair of former government agents who have done something that we are not happy with. What they have is irrelevant to you guys but it is information that's critical. It is information they have in their heads, and critically on a Memory Stick too. This information is a game changer and these individuals are the only guys who have it, and effectively know how to use it. Extremely time sensitive is an understatement, when we got this tasking they wanted these guys dead months ago.'

A complete change of tone could be felt across the back seats of the van. Even Gerry had to get his poker face on as even he was wondering where Sully was going with this.

'WHITEOUT, our first target is a man who was heading towards the South Pole unsupported and unassisted, it's the sort of shit you couldn't make up guys.'

Sully expressing dramatic surprise to the men with wide saucepan eyes and hands in the air. 'This means he had no immediate support team to physically help him. The support mechanism in place was a minimum of 400 miles away at a base camp. The whole infrastructures in place were civilian, with the main components being satellite communications, a beatracking device that updates WHITEOUT's position every six hours. If he was to get into trouble they have a number of aircraft to extract him, if the weather is okay. The balloon will only go up if he does not check in for 36 hours, and most importantly his beacon update does not show movement. If the beacon shows movement they will not launch a rescue operation or overfly his position; it costs too much and beacon movement is evidence that he is okay.

'WHITEOUT is unarmed. All he has is bare essentials for this trek, mainly being food, communications equipment, and equipment to allow him to survive – tent, clothing and navigation equipment etc. That's it. WHITEOUT had around 200 miles left to get to the South Pole and this is when I was informed we have to go and track him down and assassinate him,' Sully said in a tone that made it clear that he thought the request was ridiculous. Sean let out a sigh non-verbally agreeing before Sully moved on.

'WHITEOUT needs to be assassinated I am told and we have been given the task. Immediately we crashed an asset out for a brief. Once we briefed them they flew to Norway for a three-day polar expedition workshop with Conrad Dickinson, who infact trained WHITEOUT in cold weather expeditions and is also his mentor. During these days they were refreshed on the essential skills required to execute a mini-style expedition to live and survive in extreme cold weather environments. All the kit and equipment they used was flown with them to Antarctica upon completion of the refresher course. This allowed them to tweak all of the equipment to their personal liking in Norway to save time. The team had two accomplished members who had worked in extreme cold weather on many occasions. Two members also were tasked with reading all the research on a famous Irish explorer Tom Crean to cover a filming and documentary angle. I will explain how these teams were broken down, everyone with me so far?' Sully paused for more nods to come back at him.

And they did.

'Whilst the teams were on the refresher course there were a number of other elements in motion in Punta Arenas, the main hub for all Antarctic expeditions, whilst also in the UK, the planning and research was continuing to ensure smooth transit and entry into Chile.

'A surveillance team locally sourced in South America was tasked through our contact down there who flew in to Punta Arenas. They were given some vital tasks. They watched the Russian crew that pilot the aircraft Ilyushin, this aircraft flies every expedition in and out. The team then carried out surveillance of the crew's movements and gained a pattern-of-life picture. The team then planned to set up a honeytrap in the guise of prostitutes to use as a bargaining tool later. Also weapons for the job were sourced through usual back-channel contacts we don't need to know anything about. The minimum arsenal of weapons was AK-47 or M16 variants, pistols and a stun gun, pepper spray and knives.

'In the UK, the main priority was speaking to ALE, the company that organises all logistical requirements for trips into Antarctica. We broke the Team into two. At short notice we arranged for Team 2 to fly into Union Glacier as a film crew who were filming a documentary on a legendary explorer Tom Crean. Crean was on two of Scott's expeditions and on Shackleton's, he is known as the unsung hero of Antarctica. The film crew would request that they wanted to base themselves at the base camp and also fly to the South Pole to film there too.

'We also informed ALE that Team 1, consisting of two men, wanted to use the Ilyushin flight to do a reconnaissance for an up and coming free-fall jump into the South Pole station. This has been attempted years previously but ended in disaster. The team wanted to use the aircraft for around ten hours as a conditioning flight to judge the feasibility of the attempt. They then returned direct to Punta Arenas. Simple stuff again.

Two teams, Team 1 doing a reconnaissance for a free-fall record attempt the following year. Team 2 filming a documentary. ALE gave us the thumbs up to both. Everything was set for the two teams to arrive in Punta Arenas. Proper A-team stuff so far Sean hey?' Sully commented.

'You have my attention and the teams, so carry on to the more exciting parts,' Sean fired back.

'Team 2 finished the training package and headed back to UK for a minimal period to receive a fully updated intelligence brief. Team 1 was refreshed in a few free-fall parachuting basics. This will become apparent. All their kit was placed in a transit tube used to infiltrate equipment via static line insertion. The second team was refreshed on operating the standard Canon MKIII50 field camera, they were qualified in this already from another job so it did not take them long. The brief also confirmed whether the surveillance team had been successful in Punta Arenas, and it had. Weapons had been sourced so all good to go at the sharp end.

'Next with all their expedition kit the teams then flew in two packets to Punta Arenas.

'In the previous few days, Gerry,' Sully indicating to Gerry with his thumb identifying it was him not another operator before continuing, 'and the surveillance team approached the Russian pilot. Only using the incriminating whorehouse antics as back-up if the initial bribe they proposed didn't work. The main source of co-operation was a huge fee for their services; we're talking over a million dollars cash.

'ALE organised all of the flight movements and requests so had obviously already talked to the Ilyushin crew about the reconnaissance team wanting a fly-over of the South Pole, so the initial meeting was not suspicious.

'The meeting then turned from a simple legitimate reconnaissance of the drop zone at the pole for a future record attempt, into the real operation. The operation would involve two men being dropped low-level behind WHITEOUT. With all their equipment in the drop tubes, the team would regroup on the ice. They would land a tactical bound behind WHITEOUT so he does not notice or hear Ilyushin's footprint in the area.

'The Ilyushin team would be blind to what the team is doing; they just know it's below the radar and worth a 7-figure sum, to not ask. So they have no idea they have just inserted an assassination team.

'The fee for this deviation off the intended flight plan would secure the future welfare of all the crew and families. If the Captain hadn't wanted to play ball or had freaked out when Gerry proposed this scenario then the bargaining chips would have come out. Gerry would show them the camera footage of them fucking whores and gauge the response. This tactic would definitely secure co-operation for the plan. If not it would have been be old school tactics of threatening their family's lives or simply them.

'So the Ilyushin pilot agrees to our request. Also they would be the team's exit strategy. They do a number of direct South Pole flights to drop equipment off though never take personnel back. The US C130 aircraft do this for South Pole base logistical operations but are of no use to us. The Yanks are the last people who need to know about this… As the Ilyushin can dictate its dates for dropping off equipment we could create a flexible window for the extraction from the South Pole. The beauty of the South Pole pick-up is that the manifests are loose. No one checks what gets on, or who gets off down there. It's the South Pole for fuck's sake, who gives a shit. It is not Cartagena in the epicentre of the cocaine industry.

'Team 1 infiltration and extraction was looking good. Team 2 Documentary Team plans were cool. Upon arrival they met up with ALE who arrange the insertion flight with Ilyushin into Union Glacier. This is Base Camp, the place where WHITEOUT reports to every night. The Team was given a clam shell tent to live in. They provide beds, washrooms and all dining facilities. From here the team set up all of our Electronic Counter Measures (ECM) equipment to monitor all traffic between WHITEOUT and Base Camp along with tracking WHITEOUT's beacon signal to locate his exact position when the beacon checks in. The other ECM equipment could also blanket jam ALE's communications infrastructure when needed. Communications would then be established between the teams once Team 1 infiltrated by parachute the following day behind WHITEOUT.

'Team 2 can then inform Team 1 of all WHITEOUT's positions and check in information when they monitor his Iridium traffic to base camp. If Team 1 is seen by WHITEOUT and he is suspicious then this will be highlighted in his daily sit-rep in the evening. Team 2 also has the capability to reroute WHITEOUT's daily call to base camp, straight to their satellite phone. This will be critical if Team 1 know they have definitely been compromised. This gave Team 2 direct contact with WHITEOUT to inform him the two following are a last 2-degree team, the usual lightweight adventurers turning up for the last leg of 120NM. Normally charity types, looking for a South Pole legacy to share down the pub. No threat to reassure him. It could have actually worked in our favour. We could inform him before and set it up but there were a number of risk factors involved with that.

'So Team 2 have deployed into Union Glacier bedded in and set up the communications platform and proceeded with their cover story.

'In Punta, Team 1 deployed the next day under the guise of a free-fall record reconnaissance. The insertion was successful and they are in pursuit of WHITEOUT.

'Meanwhile Team 2 monitored all the traffic at base camp, along with all WHITEOUT's blogs and personal calls back to friends and relatives.

'Once Team 1 was within a tactical bound of WHITEOUT, around 3-4 miles, they were wearing camouflage whites and moving cautiously of course. Team 2 will inform them once WHITEOUT has checked in that evening. From here WHITEOUT's routine involved a 4-hour window before he went to sleep – he's shared his routine in his blogs.

'Closing in whilst WHITEOUT was asleep. Team 1 executed him, quick, clean and concise. They knew then they had 36 hours from 1800 that night to RV with Team 2. They took his beacon and reset the pulse to 12 hours so the first location position will be away from his tent so it appears WHITEOUT was still on the move to base camp preventing any panic or concern.

'Team 2, whilst this was happening, arrived at the South Pole and continued with their cover story, of documenting Tom Crean. On a skidoo they headed out to pick up Team 1 and returned to Ilyushin aircraft. No suspicion was aroused, as it's just the crazy Russian crew out for a little jolly on the skidoos to any observers at the South Pole station.

'They liaised with Team 1 and returned safely to the Ilyushin that was waiting on the airstrip after dropping off stores. Engines were on, props were turning and burning so the extraction plan was complete back to Punta, then to the UK.

'From executing WHITEOUT to returning to Punta they took 16 hours. It was 20 hours post killing WHITEOUT before a rescue mission was launched. They went to the last beacon location and obviously found nothing bar the beacon. It took a further two days to locate WHITEOUT's body.

'Job done. Questions?' Everyone had been absorbed in the story, and what a story it was, Sully thought, hoping Sean would try and take a big bite of the cake with a typical arrogant South African macho attitude.

Sitting up straight, stroking his chin with his hand Sean made his move.

'Yeah a sound operation well done Sully, a few things I might have done differently but that's the way it is in this line of work as we well know.'

'Really Sean, so exactly what would you have done differently?'

'What's it matter now, that part of the gig is done so let's just concentrate on what you want us to do?' Sean asks.

'Well it's not as simple as that Sean.'

'Meaning?'

'You're going to get your chance to do things a little differently if you have the balls.'

'What exactly does that mean?' Gerry had realised immediately that Sully was priming Sean and could see what Sully was setting him up for so couldn't help but snigger internally at the predicament Sean had just walked himself straight into.

Enjoying his roleplay Sully continued with his dramatics. 'This USB Sean,' holding it between his thumb and finger, 'is the operation I just described.'

Sean was slightly confused but the pause from Sully purposely waiting for Sean to digest the grim reality wasn't far off. A few more seconds, Sully thought, before he gets it.

Sean let out a dismayed shot of laughter as the penny dropped. He had just listened to a blockbuster movie from hell the way Sully had described it, and now he knew his team would be the main cast.

'So is everything covered Sully, does that USB contain every possible scenario, every last planning contingency and a way to get us out if it all goes south, excuse the pun?' Sean immediately asked.

'You know me Sean no stone left unturned, this contains the fucking job lot. If I'm honest, I would want to be on this one and we have planned it that way. Everything to enable success is in play, all stops are out with every favour being pulled in. Are you ready for the next level of this game Sean?'

Look here's a quick schematic of the rough timelines we have for you. Sully showed it to him on the iPad.

INITIAL TIMELINES AND TASKS FOR OP IGNITION (APPROXIMATE)

TIMELINES TEAM ACTIVITY ON TASK	Day 1 TODAY	DAY 2	Day 3	Day 4	Day 5	Day 6	Day 7	Day 8	Day 9	Day 10	DAY 11
WHITEOUT (WO)	-200 MILES FROM SOUTH POLE	-185	-170	-155	-140	-125	-110	-95	-70	-55 MILES ICARUS TEAM PLANNED CAPTURE OF WHITEOUT	LOC: SOUTH POLE STATION EXTRACTION TBC?
ICARUS FULL TEAM SEAN MICK ROBBY	LOC: UK FLIGHT TO NORWAY		LOC: NORWAY 2-DAYS COLD WEATHER TRAINING WITH CONRAD	LOC: UK 2-DAYS PARACHUTE AND CAMERA TRAINING TEAM SPLIT	TRANS-ANTARCTICA TEAM (TRANS-ANT TEAM) HIGH ALERT WARNING A CIVILIAN TEAM WHO ARE ACTIVE WITHIN SOUTH POLE AND ANTARCTICA ON MOBILE SPEED AND DISTANCE EXPEDITION. THEY HAVE MET WHITEOUT IN PA.						LOC: SOUTH POLE EXTRACT TEAM 1 WITH SKIDOO'S THEN BOARD ILYUSHIN
TEAM 1 MICK ROBBY					TEAM 1 COMPLETE	LOC: UK MICK AND ROBBY FLY TO PA.	LOC: PA PREPARE FOR OPERATIONAL DEPLOYMENT	LOC: ANTARCTICA PARACHUTE INSERTION TIME - TBC.	LOC: ANTARCTICA PURSUIT OF WHITE-OUT LOCATE WHITEOUT's TRACKS. FOLLOW FOR 24-36HRS	LOC: WHITEOUT TENT TAKE HIM DOWN THEN EXTRACTION PLAN	
TEAM 2 GERRY SEAN	LOC: UK GERRY FLY TO PUNTA ARENAS (PA) CHILE		LOC: PA GERRY CO-ORDINATE WITH SURV TEAM MEET ALE AND ROMAN THE PILOT TO CLOSE THE BLACKMAIL DEAL. SOURCE WEAPONS.	LOC: UK SEAN FLIGHT TO JOIN GERRY	TEAM 2 COMPLETE	LOC: BOLT HOLE PA FINAL PREP FOR INSERTION TO UNION GLACIER BASE CAMP. INSERT TO UNION GLACIER BASE CAMP ANTARCTICA		LOC: UNION GLACIER SET UP JAMMING AND COMMUNICATIONS INTERCEPT ESTABLISH WHITE-OUT's POSITION	LOC: UNION GLACIER REMAIN AT UNION GLACIER AND FLY WITH ILYUSHIN TO CO-ORDINATE EXTRACTION PLAN FROM SOUTH POLE. JAM AND MONITOR ALL COMMUNICATIONS.		
PUNTA SURVEILLANCE TEAM	OPERATION TETRAS 1 SURVEILLANCE ASSET WILL ATTEMPT TO GAIN FOOTAGE OF THE ILYUSHIN PILOT FOR BLACKMAIL.				OP TETRAS 2 SOURCE WEAPONS AND CONTINUE SURVEILLANCE ON ILYUSHIN PILOT FOR ANY 3RD PARTY ACTIVITY MONITOR ALE OPS CENTRE IN PA WHILST TEAMS ARE IN ANTARCTICA FOR ANY AUTHORITIES. POLICE ETC					OP TETRAS 3 POST WHITEOUT TAKE DOWN THEY WILL MONITOR ALL ACTIVITY AT ALE HQ PA	
HQ SULLY BEAST	LOC: UK THE CLINIC HQ ORCHESTRATE ALL STRATEGIC LEVEL OPERATIONS										

PA – Punta Arenas CHILE (This is where all expeditions fly from on a Russian owned ILYUSHIN Globemaster 76 aircraft.

Union Glacier (The ALE Base Camp for all expeditions, 600+ miles from the South Pole)

ALE (Antarctic Logistics Expeditions. The company that runs all expeditions and safety infrastructure in Antarctica and from their PA HQ)

Trans-Ant Team (Moon-Regan Mobile Expedition Team with two Ice Trucks and four men. Attempting to break Trans-Antarctic speed records)

Everyone was deadpan. Whether this was a delayed shock from the other two Icarus lads contemplating the magnitude of the task just thrown out, or the stunned reaction of how they knew Sean would accept the offering without their consultation. For the first time in 20 minutes they could all actually hear the M25 traffic screaming past them. Finally the business end had been reached with the proposal on the table scripted beautifully by Sully.

'What's the go, no-go criteria?' Sean asked.

'The no-go is simple. If the Ilyushin crew refuses to cooperate then all bets are off. The beauty for you guys is this: we will know this before you leave the UK. In fact you won't leave the UK if we can't bribe the crew.'

'So what will happen to WHITEOUT if we don't get the go-ahead? When will he be taken down?' Sean follows up.

'We have a contingency for this primary option not going ahead. I am not going to disclose that until the no-go is called by myself.' Yet again Sully was not being strictly true in his disclosures, his go or no-go criteria was slightly more extreme than the Russian's saying, 'Thanks, but no thanks.'

'Will we be a part of that contingency?' Sean enquired.

'Of course, you're in the loop now and I have no reason to bring in another asset Sean.'

'Okay Sully,' Sean took a moment to glance at the team around him to gauge the level of interest. They looked convinced by Sully's perfectly pitched short story. There were no signs of skepticism or resistance in their eyes, just a blank look that was passed off as a non-emotional show of masculinity in the face of such a compelling mission.

That was good enough for Sean.

Sean nodded whilst scratching his head and pursing his lips to indicate this was a tall order. Almost like a rogue builder pricing up a simple job but indicating it would be a lot bigger than first thought that would have financial ramifications.

Looking straight at Sully he said simply: 'We're on.'

CHAPTER 16

Icarus was not the only part of OP IGNITION catching a flight out of the UK this evening. Gerry was already ensconced in the club lounge at Terminal 5 browsing through a condensed biography of Tom Crean, the iconic Irish explorer.

WHITEOUT had written extensively about Crean in his blogs and Gerry was skimming the information the book provided to further glean an insight into WHITEOUT's fascination with this man mountain. In fact it was actually a clever stroke to introduce Crean into the mix. Though he died in 1938, the spirit of his life actually embodied this whole episode that was about to unfold and similarly descend into complete chaos like Crean's life.

Crean was a man with whom Decker had a fascination, even obsession. WHITEOUT seemed to equally respect but despise the iconic British explorer Captain Scott and his leadership inadequacy, which had deprived Crean of South Pole glory in 1911 by choosing his fellow officers to capture their own historical legacies at the expense of Crean, disregarding the fact he was the most robust for the task. Though this legacy obviously never transpired, a Norwegian team beat them to be first to the South Pole.

WHITEOUT's fury was conveyed in his blogs about how he had thought that this was a typical officer trait – taking all the glory, writing themselves up for gallantry awards and screwing the other men off when it suited them. This was why he had so much compassion for Crean's story, it fuelled another bitter streak to WHITEOUT's arsenal of hate, Gerry surmised. Was this all about unsung heroes? Was this the real reason WHITEOUT was alone so no one else could steal his thunder, deprive him of the opportunity of public recognition?

As Gerry continued to read through the Crean bio on his iPad he naturally glanced above the screen that rested on his lap, legs crossed in his standard pose. Gerry's unsuspecting glances were disguised with a look that articulates a man in deep thought. Rubbing his stubble chin with his thumb and forefinger to accentuate this thought-provoking look, his eyes seemingly vacant but deadly active, curiously scan the room filtering the normal from the abnormal, the genuine from the bullshit.

The wry grin breaks the look of vacancy and highlights the deep cut laughter lines that had now spread across his cheeks in the latter years. A weathered face that was not acquired through windburn or exposure to the elements, these lines buried deep in his grey stubble were the trophies of the extreme endurance he had acquired during years of counter-espionage followed by source handling, or to be politically correct, handling spies, moles or informers.

The grin he momentarily held was triggered by the huge amount of information he had just absorbed then filtered without thought. Whether a frequent flyer in club class or a former spy, the inert vibe of complete bullshit surrounding the lounge was clear. Gerry always found this highly amusing. The art of pretending you're not showing off, and equally pretending you're not being overheard is a natural art that not even the likes of Gerry could naturally spin out. He could see and hear the offenders all around the lounge. Recognising this, and subsequently controlling your inner dialogue to not shout out was one Gerry had mastered. Secretly he thought we're all at it, a complete web of lies, deception and false promises, life's a game of bluff that everyone knows that everyone is playing. Yet the game always continued.

His phone vibrated in his pocket breaking his moment of amusement and his crossed-leg pose as he reached for his phone. He knew before looking, it was a message with news of a critical play in Punta…

★★★★★

Gerry had called in a few favours and managed to get a surveillance team down to Punta Arenas.

Their job was to set up the pilots of The Ilyshyn aircraft. The plan was to lure the two men into a honey trap that involved a full blown orgy with underage prostitutes at a hotel room fully rigged with camera equipment.

A bargaining chip if they needed it to get Roman the pilot on board.

Gerry was gutted he couldn't be on the ground orchestrating the operation, however, the South American guys running it were trained by him years ago.

He was in no doubt what the message would read…

★★★★★

Gerry swiped his phone, entered his pin and swiped the screen, which took him straight to the message feed. Reading the full message, he had a little smirk to himself, promptly deleted the message and placed the phone back in his pocket.

'Tetras completed' was all that it had read.

In 24 hours Gerry now knew that he would be able to negotiate on his own terms when he sat with Roman the pilot for the innocent free-fall parachuting reconnaissance meeting. Though he suspected he wouldn't need it with these dodgy Russian bastards, if he did, he had an Ace card up his sleeve to play.

A huge barrier had been overcome to secure the footage they wanted to get the Team inserted in to Antarctica in exactly the way that they wanted. Gerry's contact had delivered. Op Ignition was officially live. The Clinic's first job had just gone past the point of no return in a foreign land, with foreign operators. It was their first home run towards the taking down of WHITEOUT.

The Clinic was active, first operational hurdle overcome.

CHAPTER 17

Sean squinted his eyes, the dimly lit road sign was half sprayed with snow yet still signified the small Norwegian hamlet was 20km away. He was fully aware this place wouldn't give them the same exposure or brutality that Antarctica would serve up, but it would be a shock nonetheless. Conrad was the reason they had to come here, and at least Norway would be secluded enough for them all to spend vital time together to get their game heads on and focus completely on the task at hand with no distractions.

His ego had been knocked out of joint slightly due to the limited control he'd had over the events of the last ten hours, which had comprised a series of one-way conversations with Sully, with him being on the receiving end with minimal input. However, these three days in the Norwegian mountains would see this control shift back the way he liked it as he regained ownership over the task. Once they thrashed through the plan on the table, worked out and rehearsed the takedown options of WHITEOUT on the snow, he knew his team would start taking control of Op IGNITION.

Mick and Robby were both competent in cold weather, especially Mick so allowing Conrad to put them all through their paces just cemented the final prep. It was professional practice; though an old and somewhat cheesy cliché, 'failure to plan, is preparation for failure' held true. The devil was always in the detail Sean thought to himself as the road once more led into a tunnel of darkness devoid of any roadside lamp posts, Mick steered the vehicle expertly in the dark, using the two-metre-high reflective stakes marking the road edge for early morning snowploughs, to guide him. Sean rested his head against the headrest and thought hard about the last few metres of closing in on WHITEOUT and possible complications. The priority would be practising the simulated killing of

WHITEOUT in a number of different scenarios with him play-acting WHITEOUT to eradicate the unknown. This part to some he knew seemed to be the easy stretch, an exhausted unarmed man against two killers with hi-tech weaponry? No contest. But he knew from experience that just a few small variables thrown in at the last moment could propel this whole operation into chaos. In seconds, even with the hardware on their side, things could change rapidly.

As he glanced at his watch trying to figure out what time they would get to sleep tonight after meeting Conrad, he continued to etch out the potential takedown options for WHITEOUT and how to do this out of the prying eyes of WHITEOUT's mentor and world-renowned explorer Conrad Dickinson.

Entering a gravel driveway Mick breathed out and swung the vehicle next to another Land Rover Defender. The porch that it was in front of automatically lit up.

★★★★★

Conrad Dickinson placed his laptop down on the coffee table and scratched absent-mindedly at his beard, Harry Decker's daily blog post blared across the screen. He was tracking his protégé's progress with a fine toothcomb and thoroughly enjoyed his daily insight into his journey. So far Decker was surpassing what seemed to most to be impossible at first glance. Not one to boast, however Conrad knew that his words had had a profound effect on the man before his do-or-die expedition. Decker had first asked for Conrad's advice when faced with a seemingly impossible 65 days, instead of 85 days to complete the expedition. He hadn't hesitated to inform him that if he was prepared to suffer, then it could be possible. No one else encouraged him to proceed, the risk-averse professionals advised against it, totally. Conrad sighed, he'd seen in Decker's eyes a streak of what he held in his own mind. He knew he could do it. Conrad had met Decker near the North Pole during a race five months earlier. They'd immediately hit it off although only 32 years young to his 57, Conrad had respect for his SAS career. Decker had displayed a contagious attitude of a forward-thinker who possessed extreme focus and would not be shy of suffering to get what he wanted. To Conrad this was refreshing, he had seen all the young hotshots that were desperately trying to be the next

117

Ranulph Fiennes or Bear Grylls have a crack at stardom. Breaking into the Polar exploration world with a documentary team in tow and a well-crafted keynote speech was always their agenda and he found it dismally dull. He always allowed himself a big chuckle when the pompous big timers failed, and most did miserably.

But Decker was different he noticed that from the start. He seemed bitter and angry and didn't give two hoots about stardom, he just wanted success, but that success, Conrad noted, lay somewhere deep within himself. This probably explained why he despised characters like Bear Grylls and Fiennes which made Conrad chuckle so much. Knowing that the public perception had them both down as hardened SAS veterans made Decker furious and saw their fame as an absolute insult to his dead mates on the Clock Tower at the SAS's HQ in Hereford.

He knew that Decker had lost close friends who had died for the cause and felt passionately that the likes of Grylls were trading in the SAS's current reputation to making their millions under an illusion. Blatant fraud. Conrad recalled his last conversation with Decker, he'd wanted his expeditions to be disassociated from all those Walter Mittys in true clandestine fashion.

A flash of headlights and the sound of some ragged gear-shifting broke him from his reverie. He rose to greet his charge, the next stag party crew to go to Antarctica. The antithesis of Decker he sighed.

He'd been running around like a lunatic all day to source every piece of equipment in each correct size that the guys needed for their trip. A straight-talking guy who cut to the chase with an old-school attitude that made him the hardcore bastard he was, he did not like gimmicks, shortcuts or fancy technology. The basics done well, combined with a solid mentality to suffer were the only traits that Conrad would install and his face grimaced as he anticipated working with a bunch of soft city slickers minted enough to afford to do this trip at such short notice for a stag-do. He anticipated that the next three days would be painful with at least one problem child.

He forced a smile, they would of course be funding his existence so he prepared to make nice and pulled open his front doors and strode out onto the wooden porch. The doors all opened in unison from the Landy and the team jumped out and stretched their legs. Conrad focused on their breathing, sure enough they all coughed a little when the freezing night air found its way onto the backs of their throats. 'Jesus here we go,' he whispered to himself.

'Hello Gents,' he greeted them warmly, nodding as each of them returned his welcome with handshakes and gestures of how flipping cold it was. 'Let's get you boys inside.'

★★★★★

Sean surveyed Conrad as he welcomed his team. Late 50s, a tall wiry man with a Geordie accent. Like most Geordie accents, it did give the impression of being thick, but certainly a good crack and he could see Mick and Robby taking a shine to him straight away. He relaxed, this was a good thing; Icarus needed the best of both really. His expert ice knowledge would be priceless coupled with his intimate knowledge of WHITEOUT as a person and how *he* operated on the ice. His every action, routines or small idiosyncrasies may give the team an unexpected edge, or equally find a chink in his armour.

'Take a pew and I will put on a brew lads,' Conrad said as he busied himself. 'You boys don't mess around hey? Bloody stag-do present at the South Pole? At least I know you'll pay me, buying mates a trip like that.' Again he gave a hearty chortle and the guys all laughed back.

It was a warm and contagious smile and Mick and Robby kicked their shoes off and let Sean lead the conversation.

'Yeah it was a last-minute thing. Bit of a bet gone wrong really but we really appreciate you getting all the gear together Conrad. We're looking forward to a quick refresher out here.'

'Not a problem guys I love a little gem like that, glad to help, your mate won't know what hit him, apart from a few polar storms, a wee bit of frost nip and galloping knob rot if he shags a whore in Punta.'

Everyone convulsed in fits of laughter once more. Sean grinned, Conrad was a right character and had won them all over in the space of a kettle boiling.

He looked around him taking in his surroundings, The Lodge was laid out on a split-level flooring system with glass windows making it possible to see through the level below or above. It was a good standard. He nodded at Mick who grinned then watched as his face turned red and he could see him vanquish a shout. Sean's eyebrow raised immediately on full alert. What had he seen?

Mick gestured to the desk that was occupied by a huge Mac desktop, he couldn't believe his eyes when he saw WHITEOUT's website was uploaded on it. Conrad must have been tracking his progress before they turned up.

Covertly signalling to the guys and pointing to the screen they all held a unified gaze of dismay.

Sean gestured to the guys to be quiet by pressing his finger against his lips, indicating he would take the lead. Standing up and innocently walking by the computer to prime himself before Conrad walked up the split-level stairs to join them.

'Okay lads let's let that brew for a few minutes whilst I figure out what the hell you guys are up to.'

Looking at them strangely Conrad was a little bemused by the silence. This had caught them off guard and it showed, surely his first question hadn't created a fracture line in the cover story so early?

Sean and Mick literally started speaking at the same time and Mick hastily shut up not wanting to piss Sean off or put his foot in it.

'Yeah Conrad we do plant some cracking jokes on each other and this time it's Dave's turn, little does he know,' Sean said before rolling into a smooth transition involving WHITEOUT.

'Glad we're not doing what that guy is doing, says he's solo on that site? Who the hell is he?' Sean pointing to the Mac screen. 'Someone you know?'

'Old Decker boy, yeah that occupies my day checking up on that one, he's doing something ballistic, and hammering it too at the moment.' Conrad's accent was firing up thinking about it.

'What's he doing Conrad?' Sean attempted to focus him, trying to stay calm but desperate to know more.

'He's creating history at the moment is what he's doing, especially if he keeps going like that, a real fighter, makes me proud to be British, no offence guys, you sound South African right?'

'No offence taken, yeah SA but we have done a bit of cold weather stuff so don't freak out. Decker boy you said, you know him then?' Sean continued on the theme.

'Not long but I trained him over the months prior to what he's doing now and met him up North, near the Pole earlier this year doing a race.'

'That's reassuring for us, but not the same intensity of training please Conrad,' Mick added. Chuckling away Conrad answered, 'No chance of that Mick, that boy is the toughest I've come across physically and mentally, a headcase but a nice one. Really intelligent guy, deep though and focused, that's why he will succeed. He has the death-or-glory attitude, a real killer instinct, read the site later and you'll understand what I'm talking about.'

Conrad was referring to his bio on the site that mentioned he had served in the SAS. 'Okay boys get this down you, I even bought the Tetley's teabags from Carlisle the greatest town in the world.'

'Famous for teabags Conrad'? Robby questioned.

'Nope famous because I live there son.' Sean looked at Mick and Robby laughing and hoped they'd stay on guard and take any intel in. Despite the fact that arguably these few days with Conrad looked like being the most fun. Unbeknownst to Conrad he would be the second person involved in something that indirectly made him an accessory to murder. Roman the Ilyushin pilot would deliver the team to follow WHITEOUT, Conrad was about to prepare them to live on the ice before they hunted him down and killed him.

'Okay I know you guys have been on the move for the last day or so and want to get your nappers down so I've placed all your individual kit in your rooms. Check everything and let me know tomorrow if you need to change anything. All the team stores are packed ready in the pulk for training early doors, 7am breakfast, 8am ready to ski, good?'

This was just what they needed, time to chill. Sean was impressed by Conrad's style of play.

'Great stuff Conrad it has been a long one today. Show us our rooms and we'll get out of your way.'

'No bother, follow me.'

Conrad showed them to their rooms whilst pointing out that the computer was free to be used at any time for Skype or emails.

0800 hrs and the team were all kitted up, poles in hand and looking into Conrad's instructions outside the back of the lodge. All the guys could ski so Conrad didn't mess around with the basics. They were walking 60 miles to the Pole on slightly uneven ground. There was no need for theatricals or jump turns to be mastered.

Instead Sean and the guys listened as Conrad simply gave a quick brief on the pulk they would be pulling with all the kit inside it and without further ado tapped his ski poles and shouted, 'Follow me guys let's get out there.'

This was good for the team, no bullshit. Conrad had two days to fly through this and he was clearly a hands-on guy, not one who liked the sound of his own voice lecturing irrelevant facts and figures.

Over the course of the day Conrad repeatedly made them rehearse their end-of-day routine. This involved stopping pitching the tent fast getting inside to change clothes, cook food by melting snow, and send emails via satellite phone and pretending to call base camp to confirm positions.

Pausing for a breather Sean kicked off the chat. 'So Conrad that Decker guy as a soloist what's his routine? Any different to us now? And 24 hours daylight down there what hours do people travel?'

'He does exactly the same just a smaller tent, less gear and he's absolutely fucked and I mean proper trashed. You have three of you to get the tent up if it's 70mph winds remember, then one to cook, one to send emails etc., he does it all himself. He's that whacked he falls asleep typing his blog sometimes.'

'Really that bad?' Robby asks.

'Yeah I spoke to him two days ago. I told him don't write so much, just go to sleep boy.'

'I bet it's a struggle getting up in the morning for him?' Robby followed Sean's train of thought.

'Ah I don't know he's a really bad sleeper actually, he will catch a few hours but tossing and turning the rest of the time. This is what makes him special, so little sleep but massive output each day.'

These were the variables Sean had been thinking about on their road trip to Conrad's cabin.

'What's the score with shitting Conrad?' Mick asked out of the blue.

'In my experience it's the last thing we do before sleep and first thing in the morning mate, it's no different out there except you bag it up.'

Sean gave Mick a perverted look at the question but no doubt there was some reckoning behind it. It made sense he was probing whether WHITEOUT's last time outside the tent before sleeping was having a crap.

After sharing a semi-warm hot chocolate and few more non-probing questions Conrad was off again without warning.

'Okay guys let's ski back to the lodge, Mick you navigate, Robby pull the pulk as that hot chocolate was shit. Sean keeps an eye on me in case I have a heart attack after that shocking beverage. You lads won't have any problems down South. 0800 hrs tomorrow lads, for now let's go back,' he tapped his poles again and signalled for them all to start skiing.

Two hours later they reached Conrad's lodge that had now become a covert training facility you would associate with The Farm, the CIA's training facility.

With the first day out the way, they could start talking and rehearsing in detail the four options The Clinic had anticipated for killing WHITEOUT. Alongside this they would test the phones, beacons and mobile jamming devices they would use.

Sean nodded for the guys to follow him into his room and he started to power up his laptop and scratched his head as he scanned it looking for any updates from Sully after first logging into the secure email via his cell phone connection. 'Close in lads,' Sean said. Robby hunkered around him keeping their voices low. 'Okay, they have intercepted WHITEOUT's last call earlier today. No real changes except this Trans-Ant expedition team may come into play as they have sent the request to get myself and Gerry with them to possibly interview him. They're a pretty busy team so we will know more once we're out there. They are working on the beacon frequency data as this is the only way of knowing where he is now if his beacon actually works. That's good news. They must have a slick team in action or using some proper big brother technology. I take it the Ilyushin crew has literally fucked themselves into the honeytrap as he says all set for Ilyushin meeting. This is good, going to plan guys and it doesn't surprise me. I don't know Gerry but he was speaking fluent Spanish on his cell when Sully called me back to the VW. He has got that MI6 persona about him and Sully would definitely have an intelligence type, or blatant former spy as his right-hand man.'

'You reckon hey?' Mick added.

'Yeah for sure the British SAS are the guys that get their hands dirty if MI6's intelligence leads them to the bad guys. They work closely together. MI6 never get their hands dirty, people like Sully don't even need the green light off them. They provide the intelligence, Sully is used to providing the end state they didn't have the stomach to sanction.'

'How deep do you think Sully is Sean?' Robby questions.

'All the way I reckon. By all the way I mean we're working for something that the PM knows nothing about or just pretends not to know, would be my guess.'

He was met with silence.

'That's a good thing. Now let's talk through what we're going to do tomorrow when Conrad gives us three hours of playtime on our own.'

Sean opened up the OPS once more and began scrolling through the document passing through a number of headings stopping at the *Actions On* paragraph.

This was all about how they would kill WHITEOUT. There were four options. Pointing his finger at Option 1 Sean began talking. 'I think it's best to go through each option in detail, live and breathe it for tomorrow's rehearsals. Really this is your bag guys as it's you in the arena, hunting him down. I will play devil's advocate as we talk through it all.'

'Yep, so what they got planned mate?' Sean could sense that Mick just wanted to get to the nitty-gritty part of it now.

'Right at the moment Sully has not made it clear whether he wants us to interrogate WHITEOUT first or just carry out a straightforward takedown. When I say takedown, it still stands as though it's natural causes so we have to plan for both. They are looking at injection options, I stressed the job we did last year by just injecting that guy with an empty syringe of air worked a treat. It would look like he piled in then succumbed to hypothermia, exactly what they want. Obviously capturing him will cause a bit more heartache than blowing him away, but it won't be a problem for you two.'

He watched as Mick and Robby literally came alive as this was their part in the covert op, their lives at stake, their blood that he could see pulsing ferociously through the veins on their necks. 'Talking about how you're going to capture or kill someone is easy in a benign environment drinking coffee. Doing it is another story,' Sean continued. 'The gold, standard takedown option will be when he is in his tent asleep. Second option is taking him out whilst following him; this will be in bad weather. The third is an opportune encounter, i.e. bad weather, low visibility and he is just there, no real time to think, just strike. Questions so far?' A negative shake of heads from both guys kept him going.

'Before we go through one by one let's just put ourselves in WHITEOUT's position. We have to assume that this guy may have a weapon.' This was a surprise to Mick.

'What! Why the fuck would he have a weapon? North Pole maybe with polar bears roaming around, but South Pole and killer penguins, I don't think so mate.'

'It's just a thought. He is a maniac remember. At bare minimum he will have a knife, a Leatherman or Swiss Army type.'

'Don't forget his eating fork too Sean,' Mick added to emphasise the point he thought it was utter bollocks that WHITEOUT would have a weapon.

'Look we have to consider it. Yeah, highly unlikely but if we expect it, we can plan for it, especially for the first option when he's in the tent. Remember it's 24-hour daylight, if you two are closing in on his tent and he has seen you, especially with your weapons on show, he will wait until you're on top of him, just outside the tent then slot you both. He will see you through the vents. You can't see him remember so you're walking into an ambush effectively,' Sean took time to pause to make sure the severity was kicking in.

'Okay, okay I get it mate, good point,' Mick conceded, Robby, always the more silent of the two just nodded.

'So consider it in your planning. Approach from two sides, weapons concealed only on view at the last safe moment. Do you approach on skis or foot? When do you ditch the skis? Who stands where when you open the tent? You can't risk challenging him verbally from outside the tent in case he is tooled up, you getting my drift?'

Questions were coming fast and furious from Sean and they all made sense, and they all equally needed answering.

'I do get it and see your concern. I think he is harmless reference a weapon but this all makes tactical sense. It will sharpen up our final approach position-wise and not let us get complacent,' Mick was seeing the advantage of Sean's assumption of WHITEOUT being armed.

'It can do you no harm to think worst-case guys. Tomorrow we will practise all these drills. I will act as WHITEOUT. Each option we will rehearse as though WHITEOUT does not know you're on top of him and alternatively if you're seen beforehand. We'll practise every option so nothing will surprise you.'

'Sounds good Sean, how are we going to stop Conrad watching us? I mean it will be a little freaky watching us creep up on each other, or chasing each other with rugby tackles at the end.'

'Don't worry we'll shake him off us. I'll tell him we want the afternoon on our own for confidence building to do all our own routines and make a video for the stag. I'll say that we will call if we need any advice. That frozen lake we skied over today behind the wood line is perfect I reckon. If we go to the far end we can see Conrad coming from 2KM away. That way we have time to stop role playing the murder of WHITEOUT and look like we're practising putting up a tent.'

'This is definitely what we need mate, you happy with all this Robby?' Mick asked.

'Yeah more than happy now, it's not as simple as it sounds so this will give us complete confidence,' he ended to reassure Mick.

'Now with that planned you need to look here guys. Stay focussed, it's WHITEOUT's blogs,' Sean said pulling up the attachment from Sully. 'Bloody hell it's genius. It tells us exactly what he does when he stops every evening. So Thurs 10 Dec for instance, he has written this blog:

'Stopped dead on 1800 hrs again and found a flat spot. It was really windy so I pitched the tent rear into the wind, southward. I even built a snow wall behind in case it picks up tonight. Usual jump inside and get the stoves on and start melting snow while I change my clothes and place the wet ones on my washing line. Phoning base camp before the water boils I get ready for the day's highlight of eating...'

'He garbles on a bit then,' Sean scanned ahead, 'ah, here's more guys'.

'After I have sent my blog that's me ready for head down. A quick wee outside then I dive in the bag. This is about four hours after I have stopped. I'm not the best sleeper but seem to get about 5 hours a night. I set the alarm clock that kills me for 0630 ...'

'This is critical information. Once we have locked on to his beacon or Sat phone around 1800hrs we'll know where he has pitched for the night. You can work out the distance to him then do a quick time-distance appreciation. Ideally you want to close in around 1-2 am. Once you have eyes on the tent, stop and observe as per normal drills. Switch to your handheld radios with earpiece, move forward and stop short. Drop all your heavy gear and strip down to bare essentials for your final approach. Probably approach from the rear end, so south facing remember.

'Establish a release point then split up for the final approach from 90 degrees. This is the sort of drill we need to apply, I am thinking out loud obviously…'

'Carry on mate,' Mick replied.

'In my eyes this is the part you have to nail. You can't risk shouting at him to get out of the tent when you can't see him, he has an emergency distress on his beacon and worst-case he has a gun. We have to decide what the immediate action is for this. I mean if you start fucking with the zips and there are two to get through without him waking, it's a high-risk option. I think he will be spooked.'

'Damn right iced up small zips, rattling tent and the rest. If it's blowing a gale we might get away with it, although the likelihood is that if it's blowing a gale he's awake,' Mick added.

'Exactly and at minimal you might get a knife in the face, your gun taken off you and chaos inside with the bloke outside not knowing what the fuck is going on. I would suggest collapsing the tent on top of him, dive on top initially. Talk to him, even fire a warning shot, as he won't be able to see you, then clamp him down and take control. Cut him out and take it from there. Zip-tie him and that's that, he's contained. If it's a straightforward kill option this part doesn't matter but if Sully wants him to talk then this is what we have to do. What do you reckon guys?'

'Collapsing the tent for sure. We have control and still the element of shock. The tent will actually secure him. I like this option Sean.' Robby was upbeat for once, for the first time since their briefing with Sully it actually sounded like a piece of piss.

'Let's move on. What's the drill for him anticipating your arrival? Let's think he is tooled up,' Sean paused to consider it, 'I reckon he will stay in his tent. The cover man is 90 degrees to the tent. Hopefully we will have rifles so can stand off weapon trained on the target before the final approach. Exactly the same as before but let's now assume WHITEOUT makes a challenge or starts firing at us,' Sean looked at Mick, then Robby before continuing.

'If he shoots at the guy closest to the tent then it will be obvious. If he shouts a challenge of any sort then either raise your hand, or quickly fire or transmit contact on the net. Point of fire guy hoses the tent down with a mag. No messing guys, 30 rounds straight into that tent. Enough said on that. WHITEOUT if he survives, stabilise then question him if required. Then kill him.' Sean looked up at both of the guys awaiting any other comments or ideas.

'I think that's all for Option 1 until tomorrow,' Sean took a deep intake of breath.

'Okay Option 2 this time you are in pursuit without him knowing it.

In fact guys, let's sack this off. We can do this all tomorrow. It's been a long day and we'll be covering it all again. Happy?'

Mick was quick to answer 'I'm happy...'

'I am happy. We can do it all tomorrow afternoon. If we think of anything else later we can talk about it tomorrow. Robby are you good?'

'That's fine, I'm more than happy now, a few things have cleared a lot up and anything else we can sort tomorrow as the rehearsals unfold that may stimulate a few other options.'

'Sully wants us to test all the techie gear tomorrow so they know we are traceable by our phones and beacons. We will do a number of exercise scenarios for all options incorporating this element for their tracking capabilities. Let's get our heads down now. Feel free to use my computer to read over the OPS again. There's a file on WHITEOUT in there too with images, background information and this USB has a load of other shit. It's all worth reading up on.'

Mick nodded and gestured for Robby to go for it first.

Robby nodded slowly choosing to take Sean's laptop to his room with the USB.

After an hour's reading, the screen flashed to the home page with a 'Windows is shutting down' notification. 'For fuck's sake,' Robby whispered, glancing around for a power cable, a rookie mistake not to grab one earlier. There was no sign of one in Sean's laptop case and he wasn't about to disturb his boss's sleep for it.

'Always me you idiot,' he thought. Still awake and stimulated by the reading he popped down to the front room where the iMac computer was situated.

Wanting to finish up and not get rumbled by Conrad, Robby quietly stuck the USB in the computer port and hit the correct document to continue his revision. After a few minutes he felt himself begin to yawn, stretching to try and awaken his muscles he spotted a printer. 'Yes I can read in bed, perfect.' There'd also be no chance of Conrad stumbling upon him asleep, with a file containing the OPS on the desktop, he brushed that thought from his mind. The consequences of which didn't bear even considering.

Looking around him for Conrad, who seemed to have a knack for popping up out of the blue to water a plant or something, Robby right-clicked on the file, pressing print without even opening the file.

The printer jolted into life, sounding deafening in the pure silence of night, anxious to temper it he jumped to his feet and pushed the door closed. The printer kept clanking and making the same sound as if something was stuck inside it.

'Fuck,' Robby cursed himself, starting to sweat and reached to check that the paper tray was full. Nothing wrong there.

Flashing his gaze back to the Mac screen he saw the bouncing printer icon on the task bar. Hitting the icon it stated the obvious.

'Conrad you tight bastard,' Robby whispered being a tight person himself grinned as he read the three words commanding the screen: 'Replace ink cartridges.'

Shaking his head, Robby ejected the USB stick and did what he should have done three hours ago, the same as everyone else and gone to bed and got a good night's kip.

CHAPTER 18

Decker was chuffed, the last few days had really seen him pick his pace up. With the monkey of FEAR on his back now gone, he felt almost physically lighter moving forwards. Though habitually still swinging his body around without warning to potentially initiate a full-frontal assault into thin air, he was now laughing at his actions.

Larnaka wouldn't be so easy to erase, but at least he was starting the process of letting go. He wondered if the ripped photo of her was now deep in the Antarctic ocean, or stuck in a weather system, never to leave the continent.

Stopping, he pulled his GPS out from inside his jacket. '14.2 nautical'. He mumbled to himself, nodding his head in approval. Another day was flying by with impressive mileage to match. Looking forward, the view was one of the best to date due to the weather window opening up. It didn't go unnoticed that the weather had turned kind the moment he realised that the FEAR was a fantasy. This world-record attempt was possible and more importantly could change his life forever.

Tapping his ski poles together, the motion always triggered him to start skiing, he almost tried to hide the fact he was smiling. Enjoyment may be pushing it he thought, still in pain from the blisters, but the sun's heat had allowed him to expose his face for the first time in weeks. Ironically he felt it burning but welcomed the sensation. With no sunblock to hand he ignored logic to put his balaclava and mask back on. Instead he closed his eyes and lapped up more rays. He knew all too well, things could change around fast here and he needed to savour this moment.

Resisting the urge to ski on he rolled his head from side to side then back. Feeling the subtle symptoms of mental exhaustion leaking out he welcomed what he was sensing next. 'Don't fight it Harry, let go, just let it go, flush it all out.'

Eyes still shut he began opening them. Squinting into the sun tears began to roll down his cheeks slowly. Ignoring the natural instinct to wipe them. *'I'm done with instinct,'* he said under his breath. God he'd been low at Old Harry Rocks, compared to where he was now. Those two scenes are poles apart, chuckling at his 'dad' joke. It was true though. One signified near death, the other unlimited optimism for the future.

Wiping the tears away he thought of them as the final drops of poison leaving his body and mind. Laughing out loud, 'Fuck me Harry, you were inches from ending all this,' as he scanned the beautiful scene to his front. 'All because of this hyperactive thinking machine,' tapping his head as he said the words.

'Sod it let's take a break Decker .' Sliding his skis backwards he sat down on his sled for the millionth time he thought. What began as a slump turned into a full-blown lie down, as he stretched his whole body along the sled's length. No sooner had he begun to drop off he sat back up. He almost forgot about the last call to Steve Jones. Shit, so wrapped up in the elation that a new life lay ahead, he had almost overlooked the flashing low battery icon this morning on his phone. He hesitated; thinking of the video made him cringe. He would have looked idiotic and mental to all his followers if he had sent it.

Sucking in a deep breath as he always had done before doing something bold, he knew it was time to face the music.

'Let's do it. Start facing up Harry.' Pulling the phone and his notepad out of his jacket he took a few seconds to compose himself. Imagining talking to Steve and rambling on about how his mental exhaustion and confusion caused him to blurt that wild conspiracy stuff out.

Two ringtones and a familiar friendly voice answered. 'Harry, how's it going mate?' Steve shouted out.

'Yeah beautiful Steve, the weather is awesome. Look this is my last call mate so only got a few minutes.'

'Cool quickly send me your current position,' Steve requested.

'Better than that Steve, I have plotted the next 5-6 days' anticipated coordinates I will aim for.'

'Got it mate send them over.'

'Got it Harry,' Steve says as he writes down the last co-ordinate. Decker braced himself for the cringe moment but Steve interjected. 'I wasn't expecting to hear from you mate. I assumed the phone went dead when you were trying to upload the last video diary.'

'No, so did you see the video?' Decker asked closing his eyes with embarrassment, knowing he only sent it to Mohammed.

'No that's what I mean. It didn't upload Harry so I thought your phone had died in the process.'

'Wait, so no video was seen?' bluffing again.

'Nothing, but great we know where you are now, so we will update all your followers from on our website.'

'Oh, okay Steve. Strange I thought it got through.' Decker's third lie.

'Nothing, anyway I have someone here who wants to chat.' Standing next to Steve was Andrew Regan. Sporting scruffy neck-length brown hair, aviator sunglasses and a mug full of coffee and rum he grabbed Steve's phone. 'Alright asshole!' Andrew said.

Decker grinned, recognising the voice instantly. 'Alright Regan you tosser, what's going on?'

Andrew was the leader of Moon-Regan Trans-Antarctica Expedition team. A four-man, two-truck expedition team crossing Antarctica to break land speed records and gain scientific research for a university they were working with.

His mind flashed back to the scenes at the hotel in Punta where they were all delayed together for three weeks. Rich City boys partying like it was 1999, all on Andrew's corporate credit card, but then, he did own the company.

'What did I say in Punta mate? What did I say?'

He left no time for Decker to answer, 'I said we would say goodbye before we left. And we will my friend. In about 5-6 days we will head toward the co-ordinates you just gave Steve and have a quick drink, say our goodbyes before we meet in London at that dodgy bar I own.'

'Ha-ha sounds like a plan Andrew, it's great to hear from you and can't wait to see you out here on the ice.' Two great pieces of news. No video diary upload and Andrew pitching up for coffee soon. 'When do you think you will be near me?'

'Oh shit nearly forgot, another thing, did Steve mention a couple of documentary makers want to interview you on the ice? They want to hitch a lift with us but we don't know if it's possible yet.'

'Who?'

'A couple of guys doing a documentary on the famous Irish explorer Tom Crean.'

'Tom Crean hey?' Decker was impressed.

'Yes my old friend, they have been following your epic adventure. If we do pick them up then it's Hollywood for you buddy, on the big screen.' Decker rubbed his head digesting the sudden change of events. He couldn't remember if it was good or bad news that came in threes but either way that was excellent he noted with a huge grin.

'That's great news.'

'Okay I will hand you back to Steve, God speed Decker .'

'This is it Harry, you're on your own till Andrew comes thundering over for a cuppa.'

'Yeah, he'll probably fucking mow me down if it's a white-out again!'

'Ha-ha,' Steve laughing and looking at Andrew swigging his rum and coffee. 'I wouldn't discount that after all you have been through so far,' Steve added.

'Okay Steve. Is my beacon checking in at all?'

'I think we got a ping earlier mate I will check. Just make it to the Pole then we can sort out logistics there for new phones and solar panels…' Steve's voice cut off. Decker looked at his phone. Unsurprised by the blank screen he knew from that point on he had no contact with anyone. *Well maybe the beacon if it gets the pings,* he thought, not entirely convinced.

Collapsing the antenna on the phone he rose.

Thinking about Andrew's conversation he knew that in the next five days he would actually see someone after spending nearly 40 days alone. Then to polish it all off, two documentary makers were creating a film about one of his heroes and he might get to appear on it.

He knew what questions they'd be asking: *How exactly do you cope on your own out here? What do you think about each day? Have you thought of quitting? Are you going to make a TV show? What was it like in the SAS?*

Answering them in his head he let out a huge laugh. 'Christ I can't tell them the truth.' Brushing the questions aside he knew if questions were asked he would reply in a way that made good viewing. *It could lead on to a book deal.*

'No stop that right now superstar, let's keep the job in hand at the forefront of my mind, not stupid ideas about stardom. That's not why I am here.' He looked at the path ahead, pulling his pull straps back on to get walking again.

'At least I won't be remembered for being that crazy SAS man who posted a video from Antarctica thinking he had uncovered a conspiracy theory. Even though Mohammed may think I'm nuts when he hears it.'

He stopped cringing at the thought, knowing he could sort it out if necessary on his return home. He drew his head up and continued walking.

CHAPTER 19

'Cheers knobber' Sean directed to Robby as he attempted to access his emails from the black screen that was now his dead laptop.

Robby grimaced. 'Sorry Sean I was reading the OPS but the battery piled in and I didn't want to wake you to find the power cable.'

'No problems but I will be checking the user history, any Porn Hub activity and you can pay for the petrol to the airport later.'

'Ha no chance, and how do you know about Porn Hub you perverted old man?'

They moved to gather downstairs. Conrad had already brewed the steaming hot tea to kick-start their day.

'Morning Conrad,' Sean opened up with the pleasantries.

'Hey Sean how are we feeling, any soreness from yesterday's little trek?'

'All okay mate but talking of soreness how's your boy Decker doing? How far did he get yesterday?' Sean took his seat at the table as Conrad's face lit up.

'He's still powering on with 20 nautical miles covered, but he will naturally slow up when he hits the 87 degree line, the terrain is fucking horrendous for the last 3 degrees, or 180 miles in your language.'

'Meaning?' Sean asked trying to covertly gather more information on ground for the guys.

'The sastrugi can be anything from two feet to twenty feet tall, a real problematic area, hard to navigate even harder to ski on and mega-hard to keep your cool. That's why he is pushing so hard now to make up time, he knows it's coming in about five days.'

'So our last degree will be horrendous is that what you're saying?'

'Not a chance, you are coming in from a different direction, nice and easy so you will have a ball, the bearing he has come from is a real fucking bastard, I've done it before myself. Still makes me shake now.'

'As long as we're okay Conrad I'm happy.'

'You'll be fine Sean, just don't eat yellow snow, and piss with your back to the wind.' Everyone relaxed and laughed at that.

'Okay lads,' Conrad continued whilst precariously carrying three large mugs of tea to the table, spilling a fair few drops across his large battered sausage fingers and wincing. 'We'll do a few hours with me in tow so I can see what you're all up to without me babysitting you. I can see from yesterday you've done this type of stuff before so just remember to keep ventilated, check each others faces, ensure your clothing is correctly fitted around your face and don't just leave the navigation to the lead man, always check navigation with him.'

'Sounds like a plan Conrad. In fact what we would like to do is spend a few hours like you mentioned then get away on our own for a bit. It will give us the confidence to operate on our own and give us the chance to slag each other off without you noticing that we actually hate each other,' Sean purposely tried to broach the subject light-heartedly not wishing to offend Conrad.

'Hey your shout guys, I'm here and you're paying so entirely up to you.'

'We'll be fine Conrad, let's say 11am we'll go solo, we also want to make a spoof video for Dave and in all honestly it will be embarrassing you watching mate, it's all legal I assure you just a bit cringeworthy.'

'Sounds dodgy boys and I want nothing to do with it. You have my number so give us a shout later if you need me for any help that won't involve me getting arrested.'

All the guys watched as Conrad's face crinkled into a contagious smile, they had sold him a dummy and would get the precious rehearsal time they needed so badly.

After two hours of navigating point-to-point which passed painlessly and without incident Conrad drew them all round to talk about flat light levels to avoid snow blindness as well as some knowledge on cloud formations that they would see in Antarctica. Sean realised this was what WHITEOUT had talked about in his blogs as being a total white-out and prompted Conrad to elaborate.

'Ha ha lads that's what keeps Decker miles apart from the competition, he keeps the same pace and intensity no matter what. He doesn't stop when he can't see anything like most explorers fearful of crevasses or a sudden cliff drop. In fact he had walked further when he couldn't see anything for three whole days.'

'He's a machine,' Mick concluded to which they all nodded.

Eleven o'clock arrived and they stopped to get a flask out and have a break.

'Right guys good work this morning. After this hot brew I will let you get on with the soft porn version of Nancy does Norway,' it was the best comparison of *Debbie does Dallas* Conrad could summon. They all laughed knowing he would disappear now. 'Just phone us if you want anything, otherwise I am at the lodge.'

'Thanks Conrad we appreciate it,' Sean said raising his mug to toast him with his brew. After ten minutes Conrad tapped his ski poles and left. Sean swung into action straight away, the mood totally changed.

'Right guys let's make the most of this time and make it count as though it's for real. I will run each scenario as a mini-exercise to bring as much reality to it as possible.'

'You have control mate you're the boss,' Mick said seriously knowing this role-play was critical.

'First I will pitch the tent out of sight then send the grid to Sully. You will receive the grid co-ordinates over your Sat phone via Sully or Gerry. They want this run out in full, proper real-time scenario. Then carry out the full takedown option. That means checking in at the stop-short where you can see the tent, then reporting back in on completion of killing me, retrieving the Memory Card and replacing the new blank one. Sully wants the other options practised for obvious reasons with me acting as WHITEOUT on the move, so no check-in is required just pursue me then try and take me down as the OPS suggests. I know we don't have white-out conditions and can't simulate WHITEOUT on his chinstrap knackered but it will give you a clear plan of action in both your heads.'

War-gaming could only give you a slight snapshot of what the real future had in store and not everything could be practised. There were other parts to this operation the team would now have to discuss and one that Sean was never keen to discuss.

'No one likes to plan for their own death,' Sean says changing the direction of conversation. 'But it's a part of the job, and life to that matter. Things could go horribly wrong in the next six days or so,' Sean had to be frank and deliver the possible catastrophic outcomes on the ice. 'There are certain phases to this operation we can't rehearse but we can anticipate.

The next few hours witnessed the team thrash out all the procedures and scenario's that the OPS had predicted. As with all rehearsals, practising brought out a few minor changes to tweak certain areas.

The accidental death scenario had made this operation become real. Within a week any one of them could be toast.

They lounged around the table, Conrad was nowhere to be seen but he had obviously been checking on WHITEOUT again as the computer had his site page on it again.

Robby let out a huge sigh and a yawn.

The last few hours had focused completely on offensive planning. Decker was the victim of every option or plan. Only the chance encounter put them on almost level terms due to the surprise element, but quickly bearing an M16 or Glock pistol would put Icarus back on top.

Sean remained where he was sat at the table, deep in thought. His mind scratched to think what he was missing – WHITEOUT was a seasoned, though now retired, agent. He might not be working for anyone but this did not mean his brain stopped thinking the way it had been hard-wired to do for years.

Instinct, impulse and a sickening paranoia still processed his mind. What are the Actions On for when WHITEOUT attacks Icarus? This is missing. What do they do when he ambushes them from the rear with whatever hardware he has? Bang. Dead. At no point in the OPS was there any Actions On, or considerations about the lethal man potentially waging war on them. Sean surmised that Sully must have surely considered a few options that involved WHITEOUT counter-attacking. If he had a sniff someone was onto him, he would transcend in to survival mode – attack is his greatest form of defence, that was how SAS men were trained for the heat of battle. Yet why wouldn't Sully include it? He knew WHITEOUT's mindset, one of his old guard. Sully was the one who proofread everything, signed off all options and always critiqued the smallest of details, but then he was also the man who got rid of the shit that he thought was padding out a document.

Just because a OPS document was 50 pages it didn't mean it was flawless. Was Sully protecting the team's mental state? Not wanting them to dwell on WHITEOUT's capabilities and past and be paranoid that the hunters could end up the hunted?

As Sean flicked the kettle on he noticed an Iridium satellite phone on top of some paperwork on the side. It didn't belong to Icarus. It was Conrad's. Thinking quickly he grabbed the phone assuming that it was sure to have a pin but luckily the dopey Geordie had no pin code. Sean immediately hit the contacts list trying to find 'Harry Decker', 'Harry' or 'Decker'.

Nothing. Fuck he thought as he heard a car pull in. With twenty seconds to spare he quickly thought of Conrad mentioning a call from him the other day so he immediately looked at call history and received calls. There was one number it received on the call log not attributed to a name and it was definitely a satellite phone. He furiously began to memorise it. No time to write it down Conrad was opening the door. Only having enough time to run it through his head twice Sean had hopefully logged it. This would make things so much easier for the technical team with both sat phone numbers now if this one was different from the one they reckoned they had traced.

Quickly placing the phone back Conrad walked in. 'Hey up Sean how are we diddling?'

'Great Conrad, you?' The light on the display screen was still green, it hadn't gone into standby mode yet, as Conrad walked closer to Sean he prayed that he wouldn't spot it behind him. However, Conrad was more concerned with the kettle he could hear boiling in the background and simply asked Sean if he was getting a brew on. Sean sped into action. 'Well Conrad it would be rude not to after the two days together, it might not be spot on like yours but I will do my best. Why don't you rest your bones and I'll make you a cuppa?' gesturing for him to sit down on the chair which had no line of sight to the phone.

'That's all you can do kid, your best but sometimes that just isn't good enough to cut it.'

'Ha you bloody Brits and your tea.'

'I was talking about life our Sean, but then again making tea too I suppose,' Conrad corrected himself as Sean busied himself making the tea repeating the number he had begun to memorise over and over in his mind. Casting a quick glance back to the phone he breathed a sigh of relief that the green light had finally begun to dim then fade away completely.

It then hit Sean what a foolhardy move that had been and for no gain. Sully had already intercepted WHITEOUT's calls, the number was already in the system. Cursing himself, he knew those foolish moves would be punished later on.

With the kit all packed, secured and loaded they were ready to go for the next phase of the intense preparation period involving Sean working on camera equipment knowledge and studying the history of Tom Crean, whilst Mick and Robby got their hands on the parachuting equipment. Sean had checked in with Sully and he was pleased with the progress all round.

Walking out of the lodge all three assassins politely thanked Conrad and wished him all the best before jumping into their wagon.

Without warning Conrad quickly sprinted down the driveway. Sean's ears pricked up, what the hell was happening? Had they been busted, he grabbed Mick's knee to steady him as he could tell he was also thinking the same thing and was about to give chase.

'Fuck, move,' Sean whispered. Realising just how wired they all actually were, heading towards the gate, they realised Conrad was simply going to open it up for the guys driving out. Sean sensed Mick's apprehension as his arm was clenched still ready to strike if needed. Quietly gesturing under the windscreen level for him to take it easy Mick relaxed.

Winding his window down, Sean drove up to Conrad who was now holding the gate open personally for them. Sean hit the brakes and reached inside his jacket whilst keeping eye contact with Conrad. The team remained silent, only the sound of the engine could be heard over their breathing.

Conrad's look instantly went from a mellow relaxed look, knowing he had a chilled weekend ahead to one of instant surprise and shock as Sean brought his hand to bear. Conrad's face still had the rabbit-caught-in-headlights look as Sean's hand came through the passenger side window and was a foot away from his chest.

A darting look at the object in Sean's hand before he regained full eye contact, Conrad waited for Sean to say something, if he was going to say something.

'Thanks for your services Conrad. You're one hell of a character mate.'

He handed over a thick brown envelope that Conrad had to take with both hands. Before Conrad could put up a feeble argument to decline the huge bonus Mick tore the Land Rover away, this time with the correct ratio of gravel, ice to wheel-spin gusto that one would expect from a group of city boys training and goading each other before an iconic stag-do at the South Pole.

CHAPTER 20

Roman was wearing a grey polo-neck top with a lightweight blue paisley scarf wrapped around his neck. More of a fashion accessory than an item of clothing to prevent heat escaping up through his jumper when he was walking the streets later, eccentric in nature, he dressed like this as a natural occurrence rather than a statement of mental instability. His bright red cheeks were covered with burst capillaries lending to more evidence of his fondness for late night drinking, his overhanging gut indicating his passion for food. The down draft of the fan caught his grey hair that he quickly moved to correct, covering his receding hairline. He enjoyed striding around on his days off from landing a 210-tonne flying projectile on to Blue Ice runways carved out of the snow. Whether it was Union Glacier in Antarctica, a frozen Lake Baikal in Siberia or a dirt strip in deepest darkest Africa, the precision required was not generated and executed by an autopilot function. This precision was the pure function of his mind guided with experienced intuition on occasions.

When he decided to commit a projectile to land there would never be any final abort lines or turning back when the landing gear was down and locked in place. His final call would be made and it was going to hit the Blue Ice or dirt tracks at 160 mph without any doubts.

A Blue Ice runway qualification course for pilots wasn't another additional certification such as a short runway licence. It was just a thing he did; he had flown the first Ilyushin prototype in the 1970s and had never ceased control since.

Roman had a natural ability and nerve to make last-second judgment calls, whether the vodka running through his veins helped him to harness this judgment and nerve, was debatable. Probably always over the limit, but then, destinations of his chosen runways lacked a police reception party.

Besides, the Ilyushin was a legendary airframe that could land anywhere. Roman and his rogue crew were known as being the Rolling Stones of the skies and Roman encouraged this persona.

The man sat opposite listened to Roman and watched as he gestured his arms whilst recanting another dodgy landing story. Looking like a classic tourist, he was sporting a new signature North Face fleece zip top fresh out the packet, cargo-style bottoms with gloves and hat on the chair next to him. The waiter had him down for another climber, or another mid-life-crisis guy who thought skiing to the South Pole for a trophy photograph will get his broken life back on track.

Fresh-faced it was obvious he was on his way out and not back from an expedition. Clearly he must know Roman the waiter thought, by the way Roman was freely expressing his flying antics with such enthusiasm, or maybe Roman was just relaxed and pissed, again.

As the waiter approached the table with a bottle of red wine, Roman paused his stage show. The man sporting the North Face top halted the waiter to inspect the bottle of red.

'Cabernet Sauvignon, Carmenere, hey, this new grape is gaining a big reputation in the winemaking world, 1997/8 I believe.' Pausing he quickly tasted the drop of red that had been poured into his glass. The man looked like he was a seasoned sommelier, swirling the glass, checking the body then gargling a mouthful before swallowing.

The nod of the head indicated the bottle would stay for a while.

'The thing you will like about this red Roman is that it is best to be drunk fast once opened, right Sir?' Directing the question at the waiter.

'That is correct sir, always best drunk fast once opened never let it sit with Carmenere.'

Either a smart paraphrase or clear knowledge of the wines he was serving, the tourist nodded in agreement.

★★★★★

'Zero. Darios check.'

'Darios,' came the reply from the Team Leader. Indicating he was ready to receive the next transmission.

'That's B2 no change about to have some wine. No food ordered yet.'

'Zero roger that Darios, no change.' The surveillance team was

142

back in action. November was on the far table with her back to Roman, clocking all of Roman's actions in the display mirror to his front. A good 10 metres away it was easy to covertly transmit into the microphone whilst pretending to blow on her spoon full of soup.

Due to Roman's loud gregarious personality and the fact that only those two, plus another couple were in the restaurant, she could actually pick up some of the conversation.

★★★★★

Roman raised his glass that was now full to the brim as a toast before taking a good glug.

Gerry remained silent, waiting for him to calm down and lose the theatricals. Roman spoke: 'So Gerry, your free-fall attempt you crazy man, tell me more...' nodding appreciatively as he sipped his wine then chugged back a good mouthful.

Gerry loving every second of this encounter nodded. He was back on the grid lying as naturally as breathing. 'So Roman,' he leaned in, 'will you let us jump out of the back of Ilyushin? I heard there is an increased chance of survival that way, rather than us landing with you on the ice,' Gerry smiled.

Roman got the remark and laughed, 'Ilyushin does anything. Well I mean she will try anything once! We have launched food containers off the tailgate in Uganda, dropped off weapons in Sierra Leone and would even drop bombs off if the price was right.' Nodding his head at Gerry and grinning away he followed up by saying: 'We're Russian for Christ's sake, course we will drop a free-fall team on to the South Pole. We will even pick up your coffins at the Scott-Amundsen South Pole station.' Both laughing it was nice to know that the sick humour they shared was building the rapport that Gerry was playing for.

'I see you have been flying Ilyushin for 40 years, how many more years Roman do you think you will get out of her? Or even yourself?'

'I think I have another good five years. I think Ilyushin may have less time left but we will find out if she starts free falling herself.' Full of quick witty remarks he was a likeable character. Gerry was feeling good about this so far. The question circling in his head was whether he should just cut to the chase or keep putting the feelers out. Roman was a menace,

143

slightly mental but that was a precondition for his occupation backed up by being Russian. He decided to continue and use his instinct to know when to launch into it properly.

'After five years what will you do then? I take it you'll miss these crazy seasons down here hitting the Blue Ice every few days?'

'Yes it's exciting, but it's only challenging when the weather is really bad. I have over 500 ice touchdowns. Last year we miscalculated the fuel. We were only 100 kilometres from the landing strip and the weather was way too bad. Normally we always have enough fuel to make it back to Punta Arenas if we abort. This time we didn't. Sometimes I do misread the dials, as it's such an old aircraft and it's not all computerised.'

'You what?' Gerry interrupted feigning shock but with an appalled grin on his face at the same time.

'Yes, but it happens. I'm sure you have free-fallen a little drunk and forgotten something, but not your parachute I can tell that looking at you.'

Again the hard and fast funnies kept coming.

'So what happened Roman?' Gerry asked like an excited schoolboy desperately wanting the outrageous answer.

'Well, we told the passengers we were heading back due to bad weather and they could see and feel that anyway. After a few minutes I realised we did not have enough fuel in the tanks, well, in fact it was Andrei my co-pilot who noticed it. Lucky because he's normally asleep. So I calmly told the passengers that a window had opened up and we were going for it. They were happy with that. Not knowing we were sweating and panicking in the cockpit I told Union Glacier we had to land as we had a technical fault. It would have been commercial suicide if I told them we had forgotten to fill the fuel tanks up properly. We would have been jailed and our licences taken away. It was a white-out so I ordered them to set the runway flares off. As long as I caught sight of one of the front markers I was confident I would pull it off. We caught the marker. It wasn't the front one, but not the last one so we had a chance. I put her down and prayed we had enough ice left. Like a movie we did it, I had to reverse her, as there was not enough ice left to turn. No one knew anything was wrong, just the ground crew, but I blamed the surface for not allowing heavy braking due to the snow condition. It was almost a disaster, but we did it.'

Gerry was convinced now that Roman was the man for this back

144

channel insertion. He knew he could fast-forward his retirement plans. But before he got in to the figures he needed to covertly establish the check-in procedures the crew went through.

'Roman you're an iconic character in this part of the world, scary but impressive. It seems like it's cowboy country out here. I mean you like your drink and like you said, I have done lots of free falls pissed with people attached to me, but doesn't anyone check you before you get on the plane?'

Roman threw his head back and roared. 'This is Chile, Punta Arenas. I have worked 20 seasons here. We drive past in our van in the cargo entry point, give them a wave and drive on to the Iluyshin, we are like family here.'

This was great news for Gerry. This meant Mick and Robby could be in the back of the van without being checked. It really was cowboy country. In the ass end of the world why would you bother checking the crew flying to Antarctica? And it was Latin America, a culture that considered itself too 'cool' for doing anything properly. Gerry quickly added, ' I take it they don't stop you on the way back either then when you're really pissed.'

'No, no, we go as we please. I mean what can you smuggle out of Antarctica apart from ice creams.' Laughing yet again at another one of his own quirks Roman raised his glass.

Touching glasses, Gerry smiled genuinely with Roman, liking the cut of his jib. He sighed inwardly hoping that he would not have to resort to blackmail, it was always a last resort. Years of recruiting agents or handling sources had taught him a few things; for longevity of any professional relationship, how you get the initial buy-in is critical. He had found that most people normally want to offer their services for the traditional exchange of money, obviously through the medium of working for the greater good. Wanting to 'make a difference' was the sort of bullshit most agents added to give them credibility and distance them from simply being a grass or blatant deserter. This type of false play just flew over Gerry's head. Unless they really put their bollocks on the chopping block to gain hardcore information, or contact with really bad people, it was for the green, the US dollar. Money talks all the time. However this was different. It was a one-off job. Benign country. No hostilities that Roman knew about. How would he react to a favour for a few million odd bucks? Without having to apply the pressure with the honeytrap ace card. Gerry just knew he had to act as professionally and seriously as he could and to demonstrate that he was not winding him up. He would give him half of the plan, and half of the money.

'Roman that last story about the fuel shortage and your amazing landing in complete white-out was outrageous. Have you ever committed an act of lunacy or covered up a mistake that no one will ever get to hear about?'

'Ha Gerry, a question like that means you must have, right?'

'We all have our secrets Roman, for the greater good, and to save marriages of course.' Laughing and raising his glass again they both have another toast recognising their deceitful similarities once again.

'In England we say, "What goes on tour stays on tour" so what happens in Punta Arenas, stays in Punta Arenas hey?'

'Exactly, "what goes on tour stays on tour" I like that one. But Gerry I have a few things I will never tell anyone. In fact sometimes I hate reminding myself I actually have done some of these silly things. But there is always a good reason at the time I think, you agree?'

'Totally. There is a reason for everything we do in life. Sometimes we don't know why we do these things but it's for the right reasons I believe.'

'Yes. We do Gerry, we do. I'm not a bad man just a little crazy.' Gerry paused while Roman seemed to analyse himself and be content with the results.

'It's a good crazy though from what I have witnessed and read about you,' Gerry placed his elbows on the table both hands clamped together and briefly stroked his lightly stubbled chin, signalling to the team surrounding them that he was about to break his proposition to Roman. Smiling at Roman, nothing was out of place. They were both having fun, and Roman had turned out to be a right character.

'Roman,' Gerry said with a crisper and more authoritative tone. Roman simply nodded and instinctively took the glass away from his lips, before placing it back on the table.

'I don't want to be the first team to free fall in to the South Pole. Therefore I don't want to carry out any reconnaissance or dry runs in the Ilyushin. I am here for another reason. This reason will change your life forever if you want to be a part of something I consider extremely special.' Roman's face lit up with this, and a certain degree of soberness gave clarity to his eyes. He was focusing intently on Gerry's words now. The jokes were gone, the games were over.

'In two days' time on your planned logistical flight to Union Glacier I want you to fly two men into Antarctica. Undetected.' Roman lent back a little, raising his eyebrows, about to talk, Gerry placed his palm up to indicate him to listen, before continuing.

'I want you to take my two friends in your van and get them onto Ilyushin with no one else knowing. They will have all their own gear. All you have to do is open the tailgate of Ilyushin at the release point, they jump out, parachuting of course and you continue as normal. That's it.'

Roman looked completely confused. Squinting his eyes and just looking at Gerry in amazement. He thought it was definitely a joke. Gerry interjected again as Roman was about to ask for an explanation.

'This is just another one of "those secrets". This secret will earn you and your crew two million dollars. You will never see me again or the men you meet briefly. I have half a million dollars for you tonight and you will receive the rest when we are all gone. And believe me, this conversation is taking place Roman, and I am deadly serious. Any questions?'

'Are you fucking crazy? Is this for real?' Roman was starting to get a little agitated glancing around the restaurant and bar before looking back at Gerry.

'I am a highly professional man within a highly professional group of people. We are good people but doing a sensitive type of job, that everyone will benefit from in the future. We need your help Roman, and we will pay you substantially. I am British, but working for a lot of people and countries. Maybe in the future you may realise you helped more people than you can imagine.'

'But, what is happening in Antarctica. Why a secret Gerry?'

'We both agreed earlier some things never need to be disclosed, but that doesn't mean it's about a bad thing. This is just a sensitive secret. I want literally six hours of your time. Six hours means you and your crew could quit after this season is out,' Gerry purposely tried to make light work of the situation.

The waiter came to the table and asked whether they would like to order. This gave another opportunity for Gerry to show his expertise. In fluent Latin American Spanish, he effortlessly told the waiter that they were fine for the moment, and the wine was extremely well balanced and light on his palette.

Roman immediately tuned in to what Gerry was attempting to exemplify; his knowledge, expertise and highly intellectual capacity. Almost reassuring Roman he was a consummate professional and English gentleman.

Gerry handed over his iPhone to Roman. 'Scroll through these photographs.' As Roman did Gerry kept talking. 'We are a top-end asset as you can see. We're not here to intimidate you. Those pictures are not there to threaten you. I am just reassuring you we are at the top end of our business working for powerful organisations. We don't muck about. There are other ways that I could ask for your help, but that would not be asking then, that would be telling you and we don't want to do business that way do we?'

Roman was looking at images of him and Andrei from the previous three days. Leaving their hotel, eating in cafes, drinking in bars. Even visiting the penguin farm on a one-day boat trip to an island off Punta whilst Gerry's smoothly articulated tones ran over him.

The honeytrap images and film were not there. Gerry was playing clean, at this moment. He was hedging his bets on the fact that Roman would be impressed by the clinical approach to his request, without applying undue pressure.

'Roman let's drink up, pay up and go for a quick drive.'

'A drive where?' Roman inquires, still a little unsettled but no doubt running a few figures through his head.

'Around town then I will drop you back. I have something to show you and we can talk properly.'

'I don't know Gerry. Things have changed a lot in the last five minutes.'

'Yes they have, you can plan your retirement and I can plan the next two days for my two men.' Nodding his head at Roman to indicate agreement, this subliminal gesture was a classic technique to get the other person nodding too.

'Come on Roman, there is nothing to be afraid of. Let's talk more.' Gerry reached inside his jacket and pulled out a handful of notes and placed them on the table to cover the bill. Standing up he gestured for Roman to walk before him, as any polite friend would do. Obliging, the men headed for the entrance.

'Zero. November that's B2 and Gerry walking towards exit.'

'Roger November, standby Yankee for pick-up.' This instructed the driver that it was time to pull up and pick up Gerry and Roman.

'Yankee, that's me approaching the pick-up point,' Gerry was walking Roman outside to where Yankee had just pulled up in a Black BMW 6 Series. Opening the rear left door, Gerry gestured Roman inside.

Within seconds of the car pulling away Gerry continued his pitch. A brown leather bag was in between them, the size of a weekend bag. This was the type of bag that Gerry had lived his whole life out of.

'Open the bag Roman,' Gerry asked. Roman paused. 'Go on open it,' Roman still a little shaky located the zip and pulled it open to look inside. 'There is five hundred thousand in there as a deposit. That's yours now to keep. Count it back at the hotel but I assure you it's five hundred. I have a few bags like that. If you prefer I can wire transfer to an offshore entity, but I thought you would prefer this type of transaction for returning to Russia, right?' Gerry confirms.

'Do I have a choice Gerry about this whole thing?'

'Make the choice that is best for you and your family's future. This car is obviously not a taxi Roman. You are a pilot of a very unique taxi. We want to use that taxi for a drop-off. Think of that money as a tip. The only risk you run is getting caught with the two men in the back of the van entering the runway. If you do get caught they will tell the authorities you knew nothing about it. This I can assure you.'

'What are you people? Spies, an assassination team or CIA? I don't believe this is happening. It's a lot to take in right now,' Roman said still shocked by the disclosure and proposition.

'I know that, but it's so simple. In two days' time you will open the tailgate and your passengers will jump out. Done.'

'If I say no, though, I'm getting the feeling that "no" is not a possible answer.' Gerry remained deadpan and stared straight ahead.

'What will happen to me?'

'We have been following you everywhere Roman. I think you know that the images I have shown you are very tame in comparison to the other stuff we may have possession of. The other stuff can go viral instantly, globally. The email addresses we have for you, you would find interesting. As I said, let's do this the right way and everyone wins. The cleaner the better for us both, no friction equals no problems. I won't lie. Whatever you do, say or send we will know about. That's our insurance policy for the next few days, your insurance policy is in that bag.'

Gerry knew he was on the tip of turning Roman. Though it was coercion, no direct threats were issued. 'We are going to drop you off now at your hotel. I will phone you in two hours to get your answer.'

Roman let out an uncomfortable sigh to suggest he was only ever given one choice. And he was right.

He held the bag firmly in his right hand, and walked thought the revolving doors of his hotel. With his back to Gerry it was difficult to imagine whether Roman had a huge smile on his face, or whether he was going to do something stupid.

Either option the surveillance teams had him covered physically and their technical infrastructure had all of his communications monitored. Roman had an interesting two hours ahead of him whether sweating it out or jumping around on a bed full of dollars.

CHAPTER 21

These two hours were crucial for Gerry who had to co-ordinate the next item on his to-do list, acquiring the weapons to kill WHITEOUT. Arms dealers could be very touchy characters to new clients especially foreigners. However this Santiago dealer was another favour from his Venezuelan friend so Gerry hoped suspicion would be avoided.

So far all his requests had been honoured perfectly. No doubt this would be the same. Whoever was dropping the weapons would just want the money then to be as far away from the weapons as possible.

Pablo's Bar had all the markings of a seedy little side-alley establishment that offered refreshment both in the form of liquid and in women. For a small town, the micro-economies of drinking and prostitution seemed to be flourishing.

Parking one block away to the west Gerry and a surveillance team operator started walking to the bar. The rest of the team carried out the standard drill of providing 360-degree coverage of the area so that in the event that things got heated they could be in close support of Gerry and also catch the arms dealer if he tried to make a quick break. Gerry was seasoned and never really fazed by these encounters. It was what it was, and he had a reliable source saying this dealer was okay. In his eyes the meet would involve the introduction, the inspection of the goods, then the fee exchange, probably in a backroom that the whores used. Arms dealers usually had a sidekick for safety. He might be with him or over watching inside the bar, or even parked up somewhere just like Gerry's surveillance team. The team would pick this up for sure. This was a classic scenario called 'watching the watchers'. It was this aspect, when one inexperienced asset's cover gets paranoid and jumps the gun, instantly turning an innocent handover of weapons or drugs, into a horrific bloodbath. The authorities loved these types of exchanges. Self-policing and culling by gangs themselves was something happily reported on numerous occasions in South American enclaves. Gerry pushed these thoughts out of his mind knowing that the team could handle themselves. This was Latin America, one layer of protection in a ruleless world, not Eastern Europe where they would do dead letter box exchanges or brush contacting information to the drop point knowing the layers would be deeper.

Rapid tones came across the network, Gerry blanked them out knowing that his team were merely reporting back that he and Marco were entering the bar. Anymore rapid tones would indicate that the meeting had not gone as planned and everyone would pile in to resolve the situation.

Gerry looked around, it was more of a shack than a bar. The smoke-filled room that housed around five people was no bigger than your average-sized front room in a council house. Maybe it was someone's front room Gerry mused for a moment.

The six-foot-long bar was being attended by a greasy little local who was currently serving two males, both wearing hats and not acknowledging the two new arrivals.

Gerry ordered two Coronas in Spanish. This made the little grease ball wise up. The two locals cast a quick glance at Gerry and tipped their hats as they recognised a fluent accent with a respectable amount of slang to it.

As Gerry turned to sit down at a table another individual they saw on the way in now had a bag on the table. Simply tilting his head towards the bag with a slight point of the finger, this was clearly their man.

Gerry nodded back wincing inwardly at the really bad tradecraft from the dealer's man, but then this was bandit country in Punta and not cosmopolitan Europe.

The man stood up, short with a dark tan and a trademark jet-black bushy moustache, he walked through a door to his left. Gerry and Marco a surveillance team member, both followed. Immediately through the door, they entered a small hallway with a number of closed rooms either side. One was open, they entered the room to see the man waiting there and Gerry greeted him in Spanish. The man nodded then placed three black small boxes on the table. These were clearly holding three pistols. Gerry already knew they were Glocks by the design of the box. Without talking and with the door closed behind them.

Gerry walked over to a transistor radio, clicked it on and turned the volume up. Latin American music bellowed out as he started to open the first box. Nullifying his weapon checks wasn't needed but it was habit.

Picking up the Glock 17 Gerry felt a little rush within himself. This was a weapon he was familiar with. Holding the pistol grip in his right hand, he just looked at it, canting it to the left.

He wrapped his fingers around it remembering … After a brief search at a checkpoint his pistol was missed as he always shoved it down his front. The rebels knew that he was an agent and subsequently frogmarched him to his intended final resting place in a small wooded area down an embankment under the threat of three AK-47s.

Deciding it was now or never he carried out a drill designed for the situation unfolding. A quick rehearsal in his head before time ran out, he went for it. Pretending to trip over a root on the forest bedding he fell forward, looking like he was about to hit the forest floor.

Fear had activated his reflexes to lightning speed and by the time he turned to face the three rebels whilst falling backwards, he had shot and killed the first rebel with shots to the body and head. The two behind him had not really established what was happening. Chaos had erupted in their minds but he was in control of it, firing a further eight bullets into their bodies. They dropped to the floor immediately. Before they hit the deck, he was all over them. As they screamed in pain, he remained silent as he emptied a further two bullets into their foreheads. That was the last time he'd used a Glock pistol. Those three rebels were the only three people he'd ever had to kill.

Breaking the silence, he now depressed the magazine release catch and slid the empty magazine out of the magazine housing. In systematically smooth and fast movements he pulled the upper receiver to the rear then completely stripped the weapon down in seconds. He was inspecting the firing pin along with other essential parts of the Glock.

No facility to test fire, he began to physically and visually check the critical parts that allowed it to fire. The Glock had a smaller number of component parts than most pistols. This increased reliability, reducing the potential for technical problems. Easy to operate and fire under stress, it had a natural grip that increased instinctive pointing and faster acquisition of the sight picture, while the hammerless design prevented snagging of clothing when carried in a concealed fashion.

Gerry knew this all too well. No external holsters around the waist or ankle in his previous job, a pat-down or cursory search would find the pistol immediately and could get you executed. Feeling the Glock in his sweating palm whilst recalling that past event again, he recalled another essential Glock characteristic; it was polymer material and resistant to all climate conditions, corrosion free, resistant to lubrication. The functions had been tested to -40 degrees. Perfect for this job he thought.

Reassembling it he looked at the man and asked 'What about the longs? The M4? Where are the rifles we requested?'

'I only bring this stuff, it is all they gave me,' he replied.

'Yes but we need at least one M4, we need a rifle.'

'If you need an M4 that will take 24 hours, maybe longer,' he replied in good English.

Gerry refrained from arguing or demanding the M4s; he knew it had to go back up the chain. A few phone calls, more bartering then another location and pick-up time.

Opening the envelope full of money he started deducting the money he would have paid for the M4 rifles.

Handing it over the man quickly counted it up. 'Three thousand, yes?' Gerry looked pointedly at him, 'All there.'

The man nodded, 'Good' as they put the boxes back into the bag they said a few pleasantries before walking out.

Gerry was annoyed. This was the first thing to not go as planned. They needed at least one rifle in 36 hours to give the team an option just in case WHITEOUT got away somehow and they needed to shoot from 300-500 metres away.

With his cell phone to his ear Gerry waited for someone to answer. After about eight rings that someone answered.

'Hello?'

'Sully. No longs at the pick-up. I am flying to Union Glacier tomorrow so this needs to be sorted for the guys sharp,' Gerry contained his frustration.

'Okay Gerry, leave it with me, it's only a small glitch.'

'Fine. No change from what I sent you four hours ago, everything is on course.'

'Thanks Gerry, check in with us before you fly out tomorrow,' Sully added.

'Sure, bye.'

On the other end of the line, Sully knew Gerry was pissed off, but then he had also expected that call. He'd only ever asked for three pistols to be delivered this evening in the first place, zero longs.

CHAPTER 22

C ruising at an altitude of 36000 feet the Boeing 777 banked left altering its course for the final leg of its flight path. Below, a white wilderness, another void on planet Earth. It was hard to imagine how anyone could actually be down there at ground zero surviving in the Andes mountains, Mick thought. No civilisation for hundreds, if not thousands of miles.

Mick began running the script through his mind once again. Comprehending what the change would be like if he were to immediately eject from this beautiful aerial view, only to find himself fighting for his life down there.

Identifying a small black dot, he couldn't help but think of WHITEOUT in Antarctica. Knowing WHITEOUT was now battle-hardened on the ice, even enjoying the physical and emotional trauma, he wondered what WHITEOUT would think in this role reversal. If he saw a Boeing 777 vapour trail parting the clouds above, would he transport himself into Mick's seat wishing he could fly the hell out?

Or was he institutionalised? Content grinding away in his living hell. Mick was thinking hard before Robby woke up and broke his train of thought. That little black dot he could see from the comfort of his seat triggered his attention implicitly. Two days' time, there would be three little black dots. Three black dots no one could give a shit about or knew about. Playing out a vicious game of cat and mouse. Two contract killers trying to kill a former SAS sergeant.

Having a smile to himself he wondered if the man in front of him was playing out these type of crazy thoughts, as he looks down at the Andes also.

In fact Mick knew all too well that only a handful of people in the world play out these sorts of movies in their wildly outrageous, but very real minds.

'Anything interesting Mick?' Robby had woken up and immediately erased the image of WHITEOUT's face exploding from Mick's thoughts.

'The Andes mate, looks just like that place we're off to. I was just imagining what that cunt would be thinking of down there as he sees aircraft miles above him. That's if he even notices,' Mick mentioned, taking his eyes from the window and facing Robby.

'The blogs I read pretty much told us what he thinks. The weirdo explains how he enters an almost trance state sometimes, waking up whilst skiing due to exhaustion and hallucination. He mentioned how his ski mask was always iced up, literally only being able to see through a scratch mark. Wearing this massive hood with a wolf tail as fur, wrapped around the hem, he said it was like surviving in a little microclimate of his own. Only looking out through a small aperture directly at his chest-mounted compass, to navigate. Some days in white-out he recites only just being able to see past the tips of his skis.' Robby paused. It was quite a tale. 'I mean he is on day 36 now for fuck's sake. Probably delusional, exhausted and even if he saw us, I think he would welcome us with open arms completely confused about the whole scenario.'

This was twice Mick had picked up the undertones of Robby's admiration of WHITEOUT and put this down to him being younger and not having the same exposure that he and Sean had had over the years to hard-line characters.

'As if, you dopey bastard. Don't feel sorry for this guy he would kill us in a heartbeat if he could.'

Robby nodded and was quiet for a second, 'I'm feeling sorry for you Mick.'

'Oh yeah, why is that?'

'Well you'll have to try and keep up with the Jedi Knight of skiing on the ice shortly mate, I noticed you blowing hard in Norway, may have to leave you behind, you old bastard if you start dropping back…' Robby maintained his grin whilst Mick shot him an unconvinced look.

'Fuck off you twat, now get some coffee in, I'm falling asleep listening to you recite that bloke's diary and bullshit about your delusional skiing talents.'

Robby remained silent, still smirking as Mick hit the attendant's call button about five times.

'You're such a knob,' Mick muttered.

Four Chilean porters jumped all over them in the baggage collection hall. The mere sight of six 100-litre North Face bags was a combat indicator they were here for an expedition.

The yellow, blue and red coloured bags had everything from parachutes, warm clothing, hydrated rations, tents, cookers and anything else besides their skis and pulk. Those two items were to be picked up at the oversized baggage counter.

'Hey tough guy keep all this together,' Mick shouted at a little Chilean guy who just smiled back having no idea who or what 'tough guy' was.

'Okay Mick there's the last one…'

'I've got it mate.' That was a good sign. After transferring from Santiago all the bags were here. Another good sign after clearing immigration minutes earlier. The only thing that the immigration officers were suspicious of at Punta was the mental health of the tourists flocking in, to go skiing in minus forty degrees.

No sensitive items of particular interest to the Chilean government were packed in hold baggage. All the IT equipment was with them in their hand luggage, always within arm's reach. Santiago was renowned for being the Bermuda triangle of equipment disappearance. It was the last major transfer for all Antarctic expeditions. That meant shiny items like satellite phones, palm tops, camera equipment, and expensive clothing got lost in transit somewhere.

Next was the oversized baggage counter. The familiar shapes of ski grips and a pulk were clear to see from 50 metres away. As the four porters dodged their way through the small but manic arrivals hall, Mick kept his eyes on them making sure that one of them didn't go rogue and fleece their kit.

Pushing a trolley each themselves and still herding the porters they saw a guy holding up a white A4 folder with 'CREAN' on it.

This was actually a member of the surveillance team. The other members of the team as per protocol, were either in over-watch, or standing by in the car park area holding the parking position for the quick pick-up position.

'Hi there, I guess you're taking us from here my friend?' Mick asked. The man nodded and said: 'Yes come, come please.'

Mick knew he and Robby were a pair of worked up professionals but he quickly realised too that they had made a novice mistake. It wasn't going to get them killed, but could easily cause offence. Neither of them had any local currency on them to sort the porter guys out. As they both confirmed this fact, a van pulled up straight in to a free parking space, that another member of the team had just vacated in order for this to happen smoothly.

Throwing all the kit in before making the embarrassing admission to the porters they had no currency, the guy who met them fortunately squared it all away.

Everything loaded on, Mick and Robby jumped into the back seats of the twin-cab. Sean had flown in six hours earlier and they were keen to meet up with him and Gerry.

The driver passed a package back. Mick grabbed it, knowing full well it was two locally sourced phones with relevant contact numbers loaded in them and some credit he thought.

They simply sat back knowing this was the final leg of the 18-hour journey they had undertaken today. Not being bothered to admire the coastal scenery to their left that witnessed waves brutally crashing into the shale beaches. Windy as promised this time of the year, it was running riot along the coastal reaches without a soul in sight to challenge its advances. Mick and Robby both sat back. They knew the driver was a part of the surveillance operation, and that they were currently being followed or protected. There was no point in small talk. Everyone knew the drill. Each element had their remit within the grand scheme of things, and wondering or pondering who was doing what, where and when was a waste of energy.

The handbrake was wrenched upwards clicking on a 35-degree-plus gradient hill. The driver gently removed the pressure off the brake until he knew the handbrake would hold.

'This is your hotel,' the driver turned around and said to them.

'Great, thanks,' Mick replied whilst letting out a huge yawn. They both took their small overnight bags with them. The brief was to leave the rest in the van. The van would take everything else to a lock-up, serving as a final bolt-hole to carry out their final preparation, and to confirm any last-minute changes with Gerry and Sean.

CHAPTER 23

The strip light hung gingerly on a set of rusty chains from the ceiling of the lock-up. Dark, dingy, damp and full of useless shit previous transit users had left behind, this was a perfect bolt-hole. It reminded Gerry of the Balkans. Over a three-year period he had orchestrated some of the highest profile arrests of war lords accused of mass killings. As the spook heading up a multi-national intelligence unit in the Balkans, his team ran a network that eventually led them to dozens of detainments and a few unplanned deaths. Working intimately with the SAS, this partnership embarrassed other NATO allies with the sheer intensity of covert operations mounted, but more importantly it was the audacity and daring they executed them with.

Hardened Bosnian-Serb warlords or former commanders who committed genocide were scared shitless of the SAS, they'd all known their days were numbered back then. Especially when a few of their former high-ranking commanders were killed in cold blood along with their protection teams in their own backyard.

The SAS were scared of nobody, and would go anywhere to capture these animals. As Gerry stopped and sat on a wobbly dust-covered table he grinned. Even though his teams had executed the most fierce and sophisticated programs in the region, it was always launched from little shit holes like this one, he thought.

The direct link back to COBR or more importantly to the Prime Minister for the final sign-off came from these small bolt-holes. No plasma screens, live downlinks or predator drone feeds circling above like the movies portrayed.

It was just a load of professional hard asses wearing jeans, jumpers, Barbour jackets and sometimes wellies, coming together at the last safe moment, for the final brief on what was exactly going to happen.

In Bosnia some of the deep cover guys would turn up stinking of alcohol, completely pissed having followed people around bars and whorehouses all day and night. Working with them had been the happiest and most exhilarating time in his life.

Gerry took another sip of his Starbucks that he and Sean had just picked up, surprised to see one in this neck of the woods, it tasted alright. He focused his mind to the current mission. 'Crean Team' as they now called themselves, was all packed and ready to go. Gerry had spent two years working under the cover of a news crew team so had plenty of on the job experience, the camera kit hadn't changed that much so he volunteered himself as the cameraman. After spending a few hours going over all the kit, especially the video camera they would be filming with, he'd initiated a number of quick role-plays ensuring their knowledge of Tom Crean was sufficient to fool any nosey annoying spotter that you meet everywhere you go.

Hearing the sound of a vehicle outside he put his coffee cup down and squinted out of a slight break in the wall. Driving through the double gates that were both barely hanging on though completely open. The car lurched slightly as it made its way over the broken tarmac which local weeds had served to destroy before they pulled up outside their set of steel doors, two warehouses back from the sea and two fast-rotting jetties.

Gerry and Sean popped out through the small five-foot door within the huge steel chain-pully doors, squinting their eyes a little, as they adjusted to the natural light levels.

As both rear doors opened, the frames of Mick and Robby appeared.

Sean waved his right hand that caught Robby's eye. Waving back they both headed over to the reception party.

A few quick handshakes and pleasantries, and they all moved inside. The driver drove off to join his team in an over-watch position.

'Okay guys this is what's going to happen,' Gerry got everyone's attention. 'In the next four hours or so we have a lot to cover with updates and final briefs. This is how it's going to work. First things first, I want Mick and Robby to sort all your equipment out for the jump in and subsequent shake out on the ice. I mean everything. Get the pulk all packed, individual kit all fitted, test cookers, and put the tent up. The full nine yards please. Sean and I will sort all your communications kit out.

Set your GPSs up with the right settings, test all your satellite phones and Sims. Test your beacons and video cameras, along with the handheld radios in case you use them. I know it's quick-fire stuff, are we all on board?'

Mick, Robby and Sean nodded rapidly.

Gerry stepped outside and began the process of activating the two phones. Iridium had a global footprint and were generally foolproof. In Antarctica it was only the odd polar storm or sunspot that denied connection to the orbiting satellites.

Communications was essential to mission success and Gerry wasn't going to take any shortcuts testing kit. Most operations that went tits up in a bad way was either due to miscommunication, or just no communication at all due to technical faults or user error. User error normally meant not updating security crypto or failing to follow proper security protocols. This was another thing he would address later, correct protocols.

Sean was entering all the GPS settings for this part of the world. Once he configured the GPS he entered a number of waypoints. These were vital co-ordinates in case things went wrong. It gave a number of Extraction Points (EP) sites. This would all become apparent in Gerry's final brief.

Gerry double-checked all the co-ordinates that Sean had plugged in. They were fine. Last few things were the video camera, dictaphone and point-and-shoot handheld camera. In fact the most important pieces of kit were the lighters and matches. Without a stove to melt snow into water to cook food, and also warm them both up they would be useless.

'Where are we at lads?' Gerry requested wanting to start moving.

He rose and moved over to the table which had a few maps laid out on it. Gesturing for the guys to come and join him they looked in curiously. From a distance the paper looked to be blank, on closer inspection it was indeed a map of Antarctica.

Everyone sat down at the table, it had an annoying wobble on the far right leg that Mick and Sean immediately counteracted with their elbows. Gerry clocked it.

'This place is a far cry from the futuristic operations centre at Langley I know, but it's growing on me. It will be sad to say goodbye shortly, but it's served its purpose so let's give you the latest before it collapses.'

Gerry's dry humour had begun to grow on the guys. He always maintained one level to work at, never raising his voice, getting worked up or losing his temper. Gerry just stayed in neutral to an outsider. Though his neutral was the equivalent of most operators going flat out in 5th gear, he simply went about business in cruise control.

Gerry placed two pieces of A4 paper on the table, then spun them round to face Mick and Robby. They were sketch maps with sequenced timelines, names and scenarios.

'There have been a few changes lads and this will mean a number of things' Gerry said, knowing this next ten minutes might raise huge debate.

'Really Gerry, at this stage'? Mick said, looking at Sean who was stood next to Gerry. Sean nodded slightly, confirming it wasn't a wind up.

'Look at this sketch map' Gerry tapping his finger on the map he had drawn.

'A picture paints a 1000 words and all that shit. ALE have confirmed a few things. One, Trans-Ant team will pick Sean and myself up if we can join them at the South Pole. They seem to have bought into our documentary story.'

Mick looked at the sketch, waiting for the big 'but', as he noted a timeline change. There was also an additional heading of 'WHITEOUT and TRANS-ANT RV'.

Gerry continued: 'Trans-Ant are going to try and meet WHITEOUT in three or four days at approximately this point', Gerry placed his fingers on the spot. 'They have predicted if he skies for four days at 18-20NM per day on a 127 degree bearing, it will place him around this area'. Gerry repositioned his finger to the RV position.

'Don't get flustered.' Gerry saw Mick twitch. 'Nothing changes, it just means you take him down 24hrs earlier than planned. If you don't, then he will make it to the RV with Trans-Ant. If that happens, that's where we take over'. Gerry gestured at Sean who gave a confident nod before Mick started talking.

'Okay.' Mick slid the sketch map closer. Looking at the sketch it was numbered chronologically. Without Gerry needing to prompt Mick, he took control of the operation 'Point 1. 0700 tomorrow you two go to Union Glacier and set up. 2. We jump the night after tomorrow, landing at approx 0230 hrs. 3. You give us his latest position, the bearing and distance we need to ski on to intercept his tracks.'

163

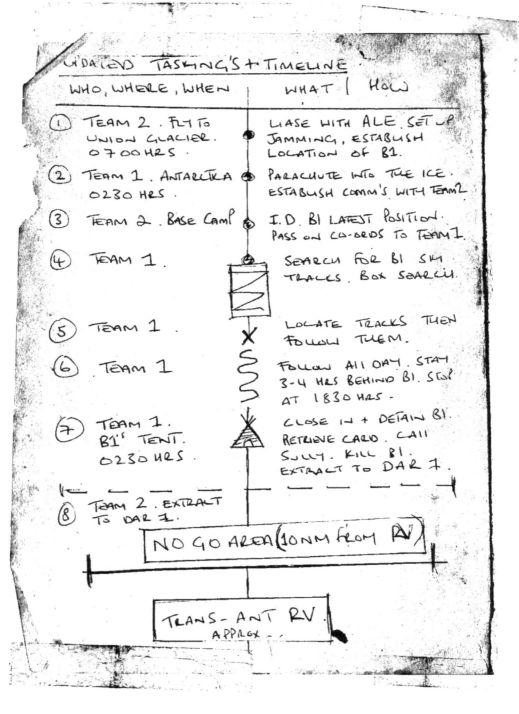

UPDATED TASKING'S + TIMELINE

WHO, WHERE, WHEN	WHAT / HOW
① TEAM 2. FLY TO UNION GLACIER. 0700 HRS.	LIASE WITH ALE. SET UP JAMMING, ESTABLISH LOCATION OF B1.
② TEAM 1. ANTARCTICA 0230 HRS.	PARACHUTE INTO THE ICE. ESTABLISH COMM'S WITH TEAM 2
③ TEAM 2. BASE CAMP	I.D. B1 LATEST POSITION. PASS ON CO-ORDS TO TEAM 1.
④ TEAM 1.	SEARCH FOR B1 SKI TRACKS. BOX SEARCH.
⑤ TEAM 1.	LOCATE TRACKS THEN FOLLOW THEM.
⑥ TEAM 1	FOLLOW ALL DAY. STAY 3-4 HRS BEHIND B1. STOP AT 1830 HRS.
⑦ TEAM 1. B1'S TENT. 0230 HRS.	CLOSE IN + DETAIN B1. RETRIEVE CARD. CALL SULY. KILL B1. EXTRACT TO DAR 1.
⑧ TEAM 2. EXTRACT TO DAR 1.	

NO GO AREA (10 NM FROM RV)

TRANS-ANT RV.
APPROX.

'Correct' Gerry said.

'Okay, 4. After you give us this, we will still need to locate his tracks by doing a box search' A box search was a simple technique of starting from a known point and working outwards in larger size boxes to locate whatever you're looking for, in this case WHITEOUT's ski tracks.

'5. Then we follow them, before stopping short out of distance so he can't detect us'

'Okay I've got that' Robby spoke up, acknowledging the plan.

Mick continued to trace his finger along the timeline of the sketch.

'6. We follow him that day staying a few hours behind him. Wait for him to set up tent, then 7. We close in around 0230 for the retrieval of the Memory Card and then do what we have to do?' He stopped knowing Gerry would have something to say.

'Correct again' Gerry happy with Mick's initiative. 'Now Sully has informed me his preference is to detain him first, then dispose of him as planned after he has spoken to him' Mick rubbed his head with both his hands, before scratching his stumbled chin.

'Right, so if we can we will detain him, retrieve the Memory Card, place our new battery in the camera and delete anything incrimination on it. Once Sully has spoken too him, we dispatch him with the injection and make it look natural, then ski to Point 8, EP 1 for extraction?'

Mick wasn't looking for Gerry's approval, he knew he was spot on, as he followed up with another question.

'So what happens if we don't close in on time? Say we can't find him by the WHITEOUT-TRANS-ANT RV day?'

'Then you pull off. No questions, no pushing it. Sean and I will intercept him at the WHITEOUT-TRANS-ANT RV. You guys will make your way to EP 1 as planned. Once Sean and I have sorted it all out we will pick you up. I don't want questions about Trans-Ant and how we cover it all up, Sully and I have it covered. You two either make your timeline or you don't. This is the NO-GO line for you.' Pointing at the words on the sketch. 'If you have not found him or taking him down by here, you pull off to EP 1. Understand?

Mick surveyed the sketch.

'Right so our NO GO is about 10NM short of the estimated WHITEOUT-TRANS-ANT RV?'

'Correct, and remember guys either way you will get picked up. Clear?'

The scenario's simple and even if they lost communication, they would know WHITEOUT's rough position, be able to hunt him down or not, then get to the EP 1 or pick up site.

Gerry's little scrap of paper made these major changes look simple, though Gerry knew the pressure was on and no mistakes could be made from now onwards.

Robby started talking, which even surprised Mick. 'To keep it really simple, it's the exact same plan, except the take down time has been brought forward 24 hrs?'

Sean and Mick grinning at the honest statement.

'Yes Robby, when you put it like that.'

'So we will leave tomorrow at 0700hrs, set up HQ at Union Glacier, speak to you tomorrow night before you leave here at 2200hrs' Gerry surmised.

Mick acknowledged him, looking settled before asking his final question. 'M4's? Our main weapon system?'

'The M4 Carbines will be dropped off tomorrow by the surveillance team here'

'Sound. What happens if they don't turn up?'

'They will.' Gerry answered.

'Let's fucking hope he's in a coma when you get to him and collapse that tent on him.' Sean added.

'Our ride to the airport with Roman?' Mick enquired.

'As planned you will jump in the back of Romans vehicle and head to the airport. If there is any trouble at the entrance with the guards, the Surveillance team will back you up and rip you out to the safe house.'

'Cool, can they watch the place a few hours before to see if anything out of the norm is occurring?'

'Good point Mick, of course they can. They will also sanitise this place after your pick up tomorrow.' Waiting for someone to say something, no one did.

'Well it's down to business. Let's get in, and get the hell out so you guys can take an extended leave to top up your already tanned bodies, and thaw your frost bitten flesh.' Gerry mimicked lost fingers.

All the guys let a minor smile break their rigid jaw lines. Gerry was actually surprised by the little drama from Mick. No toys out of the pram, just an attitude of hurry up and end this chapter before something else changes.

'Tomorrow this whole building will be sanitised. Not a trace left here. This leads me on to you guys,' Gerry started again. 'It is vital that you leave on Ilyushin tomorrow completely clean. If you are caught, die on the drop zone, or end up getting killed. It is inconceivable you have any information on you of operational, or personal value. The information we have given you is obviously limited for everyone's protection. Let's not make any novice mistakes with regards to personal phones, any notepads or IDs of any sort. Place anything of this nature in the grab bag next to the chair over there. I will take it with me and secure it.

You should have read your cover stories and be able to live them now without thinking. I am not going to test you, just make sure you are all over them. It's the difference between 5 years and 5 days in prison. I have done a lot of talking this afternoon but we are at a place where we all want to be now. Are we all set for the main meat of this operation guys?'

Gerry felt the surge of adrenalin flow through his veins again. The Clinic back in the UK had successfully hacked into ALE' servers and were ready to monitor any beacon updates if they came through. Gerry and Sean would be setting up in Union Glacier, with the ability to also jam any attempted communications at Union Glacier when Gerry and Sean set up, the plan was robust. They would have complete control of the airwaves when they wanted.

The passiveness of OP IGNITION was about to enter the active phase. Seeing that there were no more words between his crew and that they all looked as though they needed a caffeine injection the four men left the lock-up and headed to the wagon that had just pulled up outside.

★★★★★

Sully watched through the covert cameras placed around the lock-up as each member sat around the table and had their last opportunity to air any concerns or last-minute questions. By now they all knew the plan intricately including the contingencies and the possibility of them not returning. This was the eleventh hour of OP IGNITION. Icarus along with Gerry were probably about to execute the most unique assassination ever undertaken. Each of them could argue that there were simpler ways to end WHITEOUT's threat to The Clinic, but Sully needed him dead on the ice to limit any potential risk of him letting his Clinic theories go viral. He had already tried it once via the video diary, and after his historic journey his exposure would be massive. Sully was ecstatic that The Clinic was launching its first live target set and so far the huge barriers had been defeated. The people he had to answer to weren't interfering or monitoring his actions, majorly encouraging. This was also about global reach. The Clinic's capability to be dynamic and reactive to mission requests and rely on widely spread underground networks around the world.

Watching all four men clamber into the large Nissan patrol pick-up, Sully placed his iPad down happy in the knowledge that things were all good after the recent changes. Not one phone call from Gerry or Sean complaining about the goalposts changing rapidly.

Gerry was Sully's perfect right-hand man. His only concern was that Gerry hadn't killed for a long time, and was probably banking on never doing so again in this capacity. The Clinic didn't quite work like that unfortunately and he knew Gerry's days of killing were far from over.

Sully smiled. Whether Gerry was still smart enough to realise this was another question, but the new peli case that Sully had planned for delivery later by the surveillance team to complement their jamming equipment, may ruffle Gerry slightly he thought.

CHAPTER 24

An unexpected double bang sent shivers straight down the spines of Mick and Robby. Even though they were fully alert, desperately trying to listen and gauge what was happening a moment before, it caught them off guard.

In a position of zero control, the situation was painful for them to endure. Remaining motionless in the pitch-black of the van, they could just hear each other consciously trying to regulate their breathing to a shallow depth, and steady their heart rates.

Mick recognised the uncontrollable surge of adrenalin that counteracted these futile attempts and instantly poised them for the fight or flight response, automatically generated by the nervous system.

Tonight was starting to turn in to the worst possible start to this operation. Hours earlier the surveillance team had carried out a serial to collect the M4s from the same bar. This time the man with the bag was not present, the three drunks at the bar were. After waiting nearly an hour the situation remained unchanged. The trail had gone cold.

Obviously Sully was informed within ten minutes that there was a no-show upon entering the bar.

It was made clear that rifles were gold standard, to mean it was the ideal option. This operation would continue with the Glock pistols as the primary weapon system if needs be.

Catching a few snippets of local dialect that were drowned out by Roman's gregarious laugh, Mick's fears were abandoned as the gear stick was clumsily rammed into first and they moved forward through the checkpoint. Feathering the clutch and accelerator heavily, Roman jolted the van forward with the engine revving as violently as the men cursing beneath their breaths in the back.

'Christ I hope he flies an airplane better than he drives this piece of shit,' Mick whispered into Robby's ear.

The erratic noises of the careless gearshifts began to drown out the pounding of their hearts. Robby wiped his brow clean of sweat.

'We are through. No more checks. Told you. Very simple,' Roman shouted back informing the two guys huddled up in the silver aluminium transit box normally used for luggage, not human trafficking.

'Thanks Roman,' Mick shouted forward awkwardly canting his head that was jammed in the metal box's top right corner.

Twelve hours previously Gerry and Sean had been driven to the Ilyushin on a coach with another twenty or so other tourists, climbers and South Pole enthusiasts. Not bent over, cuddling each other in a tin can worrying about being compromised by the security gate guards, immediately followed by an escape and evasion effort with the surveillance team to a safe house.

Though the issue was never raised Mick knew he and Robby had the rough end of the deal, especially now that they had no M4 capability, and just had the living shit scared out of them at the freight entry gate.

The van stopped abruptly. The side door quickly slid open with Andrei motioning them to get out fast. Mick cringed at Andrei's antics that were straight from a 1970s spy spoof. Exiting the van door and immediately walking straight up the retractable stairs still cringing, they were out of sight inside the airframe. This was briefed beforehand so it went as slickly as planned. Even though it was dark and all the freight for the logistics drop at the South Pole station had been crammed in tight, Roman had still been paranoid that anyone could come by unexpectedly for an innocent chat or quick shot of vodka, only to notice Mick or Robby.

This flight was a routine logistics drop that meant the Russian crew and no one else would be present for the flight. The rescheduled logistics drop had worked in Icarus's favour; due to the expected 48hr bad weather window, Ilyushin had been tasked with two extra flights before the bad weather arrived.

'I wish they would hurry the fuck up,' Robby whispered within the sparse shell interior of Ilyushin.

'Ah we're looking at a good 30 minutes mate. You seen how slow Sergei is checking everything, he's not exactly your stereotypical Russian ballet dancer, more a shot-putter I reckon in his heyday.'

Robby smirked at the accurate comparison as Sergei struggled around the interior of the airframe, flicking his torch at various instruments in between losing his footing then finally handing them a bag full of yellow foam ear protectors.

With this done, Roman had started the pre-flight procedure and various pieces of equipment started to power up. Followed minutes later by the four deafening turbine jet engines. Talking was no longer an option. Any communication was left to shouting at each other and pointing.

The tailgate ramp gradually began to close, the lights of Punta Arenas in the distance were disappearing with each second. The long line of lamp posts could be seen hugging the road that ran parallel to the airport fence occupied by a few cars heading back into town along the coastal road.

It was to be their last sight of urban civilisation for a few days. Mick for some reason always thought about what the people he saw last before an operation would be doing that particular night. This time he observed a car driving along the fence-lined road and thought the car may be full of a family heading home from the airport, tired from a long flight and holiday in Brazil. Yeah, Rio de Janeiro he speculated as the iconic Christ the Redeemer monument with arms outstretched overlooking the city passed through his mind. Not religious by any stretch, a certain thought and image crossed his mind.

It was WHITEOUT.

In his blogs before he left for his flight after a three-week delay, he is pictured kissing the toe of Ferdinand Magellan. '*Legend has it,*' WHITEOUT writes '*that those who kiss the toe of the statue of this god will return safely from Antarctica.*' Thinking back Conrad had mentioned this also Mick concluded.

Mick or Robby had not visited the statue, let alone kissed the toe for a souvenir shot. Mick almost laughed at how he had conjured this quick story up from a set of rear car lights, brushing it off with a closing thought of 'what a load of old bollocks'.

Talking of bollocks, Andrei tapped Mick's shoulder and signalled for the guys to fasten their seat belts. An ironic gesture to two men that would be jumping off the tailgate from 10000 feet in approximately four hours and thirty minutes.

Belts fastened, lights off, Ilyushin's 4 roaring jet engines catapulted the silver bird in to the skies high above Punta Arenas. Wrapped up warm and wearing all the kit that they would hit the ice with, Mick took advantage of the next few hours of solace and knew Robby would be doing the same.

A flash flood of thoughts entered and quickly exited his mind. Professionally executing a flawless murder is an art. Like any professional sportsperson or world-class violinist performing on the world stage, perfection was the only outcome that was acceptable.

Mick was a seasoned killer.

He had his pre-match routine or rituals all honed and mastered. Simplicity was again at the heart of him containing any anxiety caused by undue stress or mission arousal.

His self-belief was paramount followed by true belief in the strategy or plan that will get you to the point of execution. He always accepted the plan may not be perfect but knew his A-game would always make up for any shortfalls or gaps in it.

This was his biggest challenge to date, though reading the Sun Tzu Art of War he remembered a certain quote that always made him rise to the challenge. He couldn't recite it perfectly but in short it acknowledged that in order for a warrior to continue to improve and hone his skill towards complete mastery, each subsequent fight he undertook must stretch him far beyond the previous one he had fought the day, week or month before.

This philosophy gave Mick the resolve and confidence to overcome what he possibly deemed as being out of his depth.

This philosophy was at the forefront of his mind as he again began rehearsing the final closure of WHITEOUT. Four deafening jet engines was light background interference to Mick, as he focused exclusively on killing WHITEOUT.

Robby dealt with the pre-takedown nerves in a different fashion. He was happy-go-lucky. Thinking more about his family than WHITEOUT or the operation. For him the planning, preparation and final tuning in had been done. The machine was well oiled and thinking about it anymore just led to indecision, questioning the strategy and causing undue complacency. He knew he wasn't as strategically mature as Mick or Sean in this team when it came to planning or reacting to events. But, he was sharp on the ground, could operate under pressure and got the job done. His lack of strategic intellect didn't bother him, he knew his place in the team.

If he were allowed an iPod he would have been wearing one right now and no doubt listening to some underground grunge, hip-hop shit that would have driven Mick to despair. Robby was happy enough running the images of his wife and two children through his head on a continuous loop. Getting back to them was his priority, above and beyond anything else in this world.

Mick's continuous death loop was broken when the lights came on that signalled the 30-minute call to jumping in to the white abyss.

Not awaiting the signal from Roman, the guys were up and about. A few things needed to be checked over before they threw their jumping rigs on. First was their personal locating beacon. Set up for sending a pulse every two minutes, this was essential. If they had a fatal jump, got separated in the air or could not establish satellite communications at least Gerry and HQ would know where they landed and could monitor initial movements.

'Okay mate, they're both set to two minutes and I've just done a check-in with both of them,' Mick informed Robby as he stuffed the beacon into Robby's jacket pocket whilst tying it on with a clove hitch so it wouldn't separate. As per standard Mick had also put some masking tape across the red emergency distress lever. This made sure any snagging did not accidentally set it off. 'Cheers mate,' Robby responded as he fidgeted with his altimeter.

'GPSs are both on and here's your sat phone ready to go.' Mick naturally took the lead with all procedures. The last technical piece of gadgetry was the two-way radios. If they were separated at the drop zone they could establish communication regardless of bad weather, to within 4-5 kilometres. These would work even if the satellite phones didn't.

All these critical pieces of equipment were placed in the interior pockets of their Mountain Equipment Gortex jackets and secured the same way Mick secured Robby's beacon.

'The only left thing left to do is calibrate our altitude metres mate. I'm going to brief Roman on the run-in procedure to the release point. I will determine the altitude on his dials too.'

'Okay Mick, I will just give the tube a once-over and check all the straps and hooks,' Robby shouted back.

Making his way to the cockpit past all the other logistical supplies he tapped Roman on the shoulder.

Andrei handed him a set of headphones and indicated to flick the pressel switch to talk.

'Roman how long till Release Point?'

'20 minutes,' he replied whilst flicking his right fingers out to indicate physically.

'Wind speed?'

'Only 5 knots south-westerly good conditions,' Roman looked up at Mick with his thumbs up. Mick was trying not to laugh at Roman's goggles. They were a classic set of Biggles World War Two numbers that a spitfire pilot would wear. Like a crazy professor of the skies, there was a surrealism that gave Mick comfort. Having this mad, crazy bastard in the jump seat seemed to cap off this whole fucked-up assignment he thought.

'We need to have a headwind run-in remember Roman.'

'I know you stupid man, I have dropped jumpers off before and it's how we always land you know,' Roman annoyed and sarcastically answered Mick's novice request.

Without trying to patronise Roman again, he asked to view the Release Point co-ordinates on the internal navigating system.

Comparing them to that of his GPS, they were spot on. Mick put his thumbs up then asked for the altitude reading.

Pointing at a dial they were currently at 28400 feet.

Mick calibrated both of their altimeters.

This would start to decrease shortly as Roman began to descend to the correct drop height of 10000 feet, at the exact release-point location. Even the Ilyushin had the technology to automatically calculate and execute this.

Roman would only really manually take control on the final 30 KM run-in. Everything was set.

Robby gave Mick two slaps on his left shoulder followed up with the thumbs up. Having thoroughly checked off every essential harness clip and tightened each strap into a comfortable position, Mick's free-fall rig was fitted correctly and ready for the jump.

Mick had done the same for Robby. The only difference was checking the 50kg transit tube, made from lightweight reinforced cardboard. Inside the tube was all the mission essential equipment ready to go, once they hit the Drop Zone. Mick had attached the tube to his quick-release harness, via a slightly stretchable umbilical cord measuring 12 feet. If the tube was causing Mick major problems for some reason, and he couldn't get stable in the air, he could jettison the tube by simply pulling the quick-release strap. Independent of his parachute set-up Mick would then descend without it, as the tube would free fall to destruction below him.

174

If this scenario happened it was mission failure. The kit would be destroyed depending on what height it jettisoned from, plus the visibility. They would probably never locate it as it had no locating beacon inside.

Robby had a bivvy bag stuffed down his jacket. This provided a simple shelter and a good windbreak to limit wind chill, if they entered pure survival mode. They had enough kit to survive a few days if the tube got trashed to pieces and never retrieved.

Before they put on their Pro-Tec helmets and goggles they both checked their altimeters.

12000 feet.

In about 5 minutes they would be at the drop altitude of 10000 feet.

This was the vector Roman was flying to, for a direct fly-past 7 nautical miles North of WHITEOUT's tent. Roman had WHITEOUT's location loaded into the internal navigation system. Mick had passed this on from Gerry's update hours before they took off. The perfect approach to the release point put them directly to the rear of WHITEOUT. This meant if the drop were spot on, they would end up about 5 nautical miles from WHITEOUT on landing. If there was a delayed exit it could mean 10 nautical miles. Distance equalled time so any mistakes put the team behind schedule.

The GPS mounts on their forearms had the intended landing point. Opening their chutes at about 6000 feet gave them roughly 4-5 minutes of playtime or transit time. Depending on wind they could cover well over a kilometre in the air before touching down. This should be plenty, enough for them to hit their landing co-ordinates if Roman nailed it straight off.

0237 hours.

10000 feet.

Andrei comes walking over with his hands pushing against his headset earpieces. 'He has obviously just heard what I have,' Mick thought.

Mick throughout had been listening to what was going on in the headset he kept on. Most of the communication was in Russian between Roman and his co-pilot Sergei. Every 10 minutes from the 30-minute call Roman spoke to Mick. His latest transmission was 5 minutes till Release Point.

Pointing to his headphones Mick gave the thumbs up. Andrei nodded his head and squeezed past them. Attaching a harness around his waist, Andrei buckled it up as tightly as possible. Momentarily breathing in before his huge gut embarrassingly flopped over the harness. Sweating profusely he was obviously absolutely shitting himself. In a moment he would initiate the hydraulics system that lowered the tailgate.

'Okay mate, once we're at one minute we'll get a few feet from the edge with the tube laid flat.'

'Roger that,' Robby responded

'Once I am set I will give you the thumbs up. All I need from you is two slaps on my shoulder. I will nod a few times. You then start pushing the tube out and I will follow. Obviously you jump a few seconds behind me.' Mick was literally face-to-face with Robby as he shouted commands in his ear. Both were sweating, but had an alertness and intensity in their eyes that reassured each other. Holding the gaze Mick said: 'This is it Robby boy, if you lose me, follow your own GPS as planned and we'll talk on the ground. Keep an eye on the Altimeter near landing, these flat light levels are a fucker to judge. Keep everything tight prior to impact. We both know this shit inside out so let's have a good one brother.'

'No worries Mick see you on the ice-'

'Mick this is Roman.'

'Go ahead Roman,' Mick replied.

'Two minutes wind speed three knots on our correct heading, 10000 feet. Cloud base clear at 6000 feet.'

'Thanks Roman, have a vodka for us when you get back. Good job,' Mick replied.

CHAPTER 25

Mick removed his headset and throws it to the side. Placing his Pro-Tec helmet on over his heavy-duty Gortex hood with only his eyes visible through his balaclava, he gave Robby the nod before placing his Oakley ski goggles on. Hood drawcord pulled completely tight so only his goggles were on view in the middle of a mass of fur. Gortex jacket and bottoms protected every inch of his body. Underneath that were layers of insulting down jackets and bottoms with inner and outer gloves to protect their hands.

They would be in the air for at least eight minutes at high altitude. Luckily the wind was relatively calm which reduced wind chill and made hitting the Drop Zone easier.

Andrei and Robby started helping Mick move the tube to the edge of the tailgate. They were finally set as the one-minute call was given by Andrei.

A last visual check of each other, they indicated their pull handles and reserve handles to each other. A quick thumbs up by Mick. Both the men were two feet away from disappearing into the white nothingness of Antarctica.

Looking out the tailgate there was a cloud base present that was not penetrable. It was a blank screen. Roman had said the cloud base clears at 6 grand so this was not a problem. In all honesty this was a preferred view when leaving the tailgate with a 50kg tube attached to you Mick thought.

Two slaps on Mick's back.

A couple of nods to confirm he felt them.

The tube was edged over the tailgate. It got to the halfway point and started to leave the plane by its own momentum. This was Mick's cue to step over the edge in order to avoid a shock loading effect of the tube, once the umbilical was at full stretch.

Mick stepped into thin air, hitting the 120 mph jet stream and was thrown aggressively into the clouds.

Robby was just looking at Mick's back almost touching him. Leaving a gap of two seconds he was also at the pure mercy of gravity as he entered the clouds.

Hidden in complete white-out, almost suspended in time, the only indicator of them plummeting to the ice was the rushing noise of air as it was displaced beneath them. An initial rush of adrenaline and the violent exit caused by the slipstream delayed any immediate thoughts. After a few seconds Mick took stock, flashing the internal checklist up in his mind and started to perform life-saving procedures.

Mick was talking himself through it ' *Okay, okay Mick, happy days relax, let's gets stable, that's it. Okay check tube below, that's good, all round me, check altimeter, 8000 feet.*'

Robby was no different. It was common practice and a universal teaching to throw the inner monologue away, and just shout out the checks through it all. Once they got to the point where they knew everything was okay with respect to being stable, things calmed. Even falling at a terminal velocity of 120 miles per hour they did actually relax.

Being stuck in the clouds was akin to being stuck in the pitch-black boot of a car driven at 120 miles per hour, having no control over anything.

Suddenly without warning the cloud base was clear. The first look at Antarctica was below them and closing in fast.

'*Check altitude,*' Mick told himself.

5800 feet.

'*Okay Mick, stand by for opening. Look and locate pull handle. Done. Pull.*' Mick ripped the handle aggressively like ripping a rag doll from a Rottweiler's jaws. He then anticipated the canopy opening that would feel like he was being ripped back up towards the clouds. Though really it was just rapid deceleration from the canopy drag.

A violent tug on both his shoulders ensued and he rode out the ferocious whiplash that was deceleration. His head being thrown forward he watched the tube swing out of control beneath his legs.

As soon as he had control of his body again he immediately checked the canopy. '*Good canopy, all cells inflated. Locate steering toggles.*' These were Velcro-strapped to the canopy risers that were the main four straps that connected the canopy to his body harness.

178

'All good, full pull down on left riser, full pull down on right riser, happy days steering is okay. Check Altitude check GPS.' He could now concentrate on tracking toward the LZ. First he looked for Robby. Nothing to his front and above, he pulled down on his right riser handle. This slowly turned him ninety degrees to the right. As he started to face rearwards he caught sight of him.

'Happy fucking days,' Mick grinned.

It was clear Robby had located him as he was starting to spiral. This was a move that allowed Robby to rapidly lose height. What he was doing was dropping close to Mick so he could track him closely so they landed together.

Mick recognising what he was doing automatically checked the GPS direction arrow and set himself up to follow it. He knew Robby would stay behind him now.

Bearing 058 degrees. Distance 1.8 kilometers. Altitude 4 grand.

'Thank fuck this is all going as planned,' he thought. Two other setbacks in the previous 12 hours had rocked them a little. This was great news, actually easier than he thought it would be.

It was only now that he could take in exactly what they had just done. The first ever free fall into Antarctica out the back of an Ilyushin at 10 grand, and living to tell the tale.

With that thought he quickly remembered why they were doing it. Straight away he started looking to locate WHITEOUT's tent. A small red dot was all he was looking for. There were pockets of cloud and mist so it was difficult, but curiosity kept him observing.

Robby was doing the same whilst tracking Mick all the way in. As promised the flat light was about to make the landing tricky. For Mick it was not too bad as the tube hit the ice first 12 feet below him, this let him know to brace for landing.

Robby had no such luxury. Ground-rush was starting to kick in as he saw Mick land safely. Trying to approach virtually on top of him, so he could gauge the height to the ground from an object as a reference as opposed to white ice.

Literally ten feet away Robby flared his canopy that almost suspended him in air 3 feet off the ground. From there he calmly touched down whilst still remaining standing.

'You flash cunt,' Mick shouted over as he was still brushing the snow off his jacket. His landing had been more sporting and certainly didn't involve standing.

'Whoa. That was something Mick, aye?' Robby shouted back as he pulled his riser straps in to stop the chute catching any wind. This could drag him dangerously out of control across the jagged ice field.

'We did it Robby. Good work. Let's get our shit sorted.'

Without any instructions Robby got his chute together and then collected in Mick's.

Mick was on one knee looking at the GPS while pulling the antenna out on the satellite phone. While the phone was initiating Mick took in his surroundings.

His eyes were met with absolutely nothing. He took in a 360 view. It was all the same to each horizon. No beautiful backdrop of the Ellsworth Mountain ranges, as they were too far south now, just nothing. 'So that's why WHITEOUT calls it the white nothing,' Mick mused. WHITEOUT was right, there wasn't even snow on the ground, it was rock solid ice features called sastrugi. The light wind caused spindrift but this was just a powder getting blown across the white wastelands.

The sun was high in the polar skies. As he noticed his shadow slightly behind him again he thought about WHITEOUT. He could navigate by his shadow alone during the long days using a clock ray method. The angle of his shadow would let him know what direction he was travelling in.

'Fuck WHITEOUT,' he thought as the phone lit up with five bars and an Iridium logo on the screen. Hitting contacts, he located Gerry's number and pressed the dial key. Already he started to realise how bitterly cold it was as he exposed his bare flesh momentarily to use the phone.

'Fuck me it's cold,' he muttered curling his fingers up and blowing on them. Then he realised he was facing into the wind and has been for nearly ten minutes. 'Novice mistake you idiot,' turning and putting his back against it bowing into a crouched position.

The phone began to ring then was picked up after one bell.

'Gerry?' he said down the phone as it is answered.

'Mick it's great to hear from you, you both okay?'

'Everything is good no problems. Stand by for our grid.'

'Send mate.'

Mick sent the co-ordinates and Gerry repeated the grid back exactly.

'Give me two minutes Mick, I will work out your approach vector to intercept ski tracks.'

'Okay but make it snappy it's getting cold being static here,' Mick added with urgency in his voice.

Robby had rammed the two chutes in the tube and rolled it into a natural hollow in the ice created by the large sastrugi formations. The pulk was fine with the equipment inside looking almost undisturbed by the transit and landing. Skis were not damaged along with their poles. Arranging the trace and harness Robby started to put on the shoulder straps then tightened the waist harness securely. Like Mick he had forgotten how fidgety it was wearing thick gloves. In frustration he, too, ripped his gloves off and made the final harness adjustment. Immediately the cold had a vicious bite that warned Robby not to do this too often, or for too long.

Due to being completely insulated head to toe with a small aperture through their goggles, visually locating pockets or straps was impossible. It was a case of feeling for everything. Just checking the time Robby realized his watch needed to be on the outside of his jacket as pulling back four layers of clothing to see his watch face was proving a logistical nightmare with his mittens on.

Doing the simplest of tasks in extreme cold weather was a pain in the ass.

He'd read that most of the time Decker couldn't see past his goggles as the condensation from body heat that escaped into his goggles turned to ice, blocking his view.

As Robby finally adjusted his waist straps and relocated his watch he thought: 'Norway was way too warm, I never even realised these little things could cause so much frustration.'

'Mick,' Gerry said down the phone.

'Send Gerry.'

'Good news, you are North of him, so no doglegs required to hide your ski tracks. Simply punch in waypoint one. That is the 5 nautical hold off location behind him where you should intercept his ski tacks. Copy?'

'Got that waypoint one as planned,' Mick had already anticipated this and was already on the 'Go To' option on his GPS. This had a direction arrow pointing to exactly this location. Below it were numerous data fields. The one he was interested in was the distance.

'Gerry we're 3 Nautical miles away from the ski track intercept. That's not too bad. Roman did a good job.'

'Good that's about two hours skiing and we have just received a beacon update from you,' Gerry quoted.

'I bloody hope so. That's about the ski time not the beacon update,' Mick slatted back.

'WHITEOUT's blog from last night.'

'Yep fire away Gerry.'

'Like we knew, his phone is dead. However we got a beacon reading and it gave us his latest position, and base camp don't have this. As per the plan, he will still try and meet Trans-Ant at 1800hrs tomorrow. So that was good to hear. We can now predict the location more accurately as we've got the beacon data. I suggest you write this down now in case we lose communications.'

'Yeah okay, give us a second,' Mick scrabbled for his waterproof notepad and thick chinagraph pencil. Pulling it out of his chest pocket attached by a piece of cord he was ready to receive the RV co-ordinates.

'Okay.'

Gerry read the co-ordinates out slowly, repeating so Mick could scribble them down before repeating them back then plugging them in to his GPS.

'Bang on Mick,' Gerry confirmed them right back. 'Everything is okay here at base camp too. We may have an RV ourselves with Trans-Ant team. Our intentions may be a flight in literally five hours' time to meet them at the Pole for midday. Spend a night with them and head out for the RV the following night. They only have a few more nights here. The good thing is Steve Jones has told us that if Decker does not RV with them, it's not a major thing, they will wait from 1800-2200hrs before they head off to Ilyushin for extraction. This brings me on to weather. You have a shit storm heading your way I'm afraid. Hence if Decker does not make the RV this will be the reason. It's a good contingency for us like we spoke about.'

'Weather Gerry, what we expecting?' Mick asked.

'A low-pressure system is about 8-12 hours out and will be moving through your area. They reckon it will last around 36-48 hours. Mainly the wind will pick up and a low-pressure system will bring increased fog. So expect it to be white-out conditions. This can work for us in all honesty. Be diligent tomorrow when following WHITEOUT if it does close in rapidly. He could stop for any reason and we don't want you being right up his ass.'

'Copy everything Gerry. Right we need to get moving it's fucking freezing mate and as you can tell I'm starting to shiver and shake like a shitting dog.'

'Great work lads. Check in when you get his tracks or actually see his tent. You have about five hours before he moves. Don't push it too early. Get in his tracks and be diligent. Tomorrow is the big push remember. We may fly at 0800hrs and be airborne till 1400hrs, so we will not be contactable until we reach the Pole. Anything else from you two?' Gerry enquired.

'No. Right we're off. Catch you later.' Mick closed the conversation and cut Gerry off as he was about to say something else. Collapsing the antennae and turning the phone off he put it away in the chest pocket of his fleece before quickly zipping up his outer Gortex jacket.

Robby was next to him for the last few minutes and had heard everything.

'There's your skis and poles mate,' Robby said handing them to Mick. A distinct crackling in his voice complemented by the visible sight of his breath in form of a vapour cloud confirmed it was cold and they needed to start skiing.

'Okay mate, we're on. Got the bearing all plugged in. We're three nautical miles away so a few hours will warm our bones. Once we're near the predicted ski track location I will let you know. You tuck in behind me and let's get going.'

'Roger that,' Robby responded waiting for Mick to clip into his skis.

The guys had been on the ice now for about twenty minutes and both were feeling the effects of the biting cold. WHITEOUT had called Antarctica Goliath and him David in his blogs, he had mentioned that this was a place that any blatant show of disrespect would be met with punishment that would be life-changing. Whether that was a few missing fingers to frostbite, blindness neglecting the use of goggles when the weather was nice, or skiing over cracks that could swallow you up in to the depths of the unknown if they shattered. Twenty minutes had confirmed Antarctica was the gatekeeper and the boss here.

It was real now.

The real game was about to commence. Almost like the main event at a boxing night. All warm-up acts had finished and everyone was eagerly awaiting the main card.

★★★★★

There was a frenzy of activity behind the hi-tech screens that were in front of the two operators monitoring the tracking screens. Similar to an advanced radar detection system you would expect to find on a submarine, the detection probes ran a continuous 360-degree loop identifying any new movements or objects.

The activity of all other incursions in Antarctica was also being monitored. On a featureless plateau it wasn't difficult to locate every person, vehicle or movement across the continent.

A combination of expeditions, climbers, researchers or tourists produced various dots on the flat-screen displays to the operator's front.

This wasteland had nothing of any interest really to an unsuspecting eye watching the updated activity unfolding in front of their eyes. The reassuring fact was the technology was all working properly. Multi-million pound investment into sensitive programs that had this global reach capacity, with an almost instant tracking and monitoring system had to deliver results.

When the two new blips or signatures appeared on the screen it was reassuring the technology was working seamlessly. From out of nowhere Mick and Robby had made an entrance and were placed about 5 nautical miles behind WHITEOUT.

WHITEOUT had been monitored now for almost 40 days and the operators watched his slow progress to the South Pole.

The emergence of Mick and Robby so close behind him and to have come from nowhere was easily explained to the operators at The Clinic's HQ.

The operators taking an incredible interest in the newcomers were not at The Clinic's HQ. They didn't even speak English. They couldn't be any further away from The Clinic's HQ. For 15 minutes the operators were rerunning the radar tracking systems acquisition software to try and work out when and where these two infiltrators came on the grid.

They all knew who Harry Decker was. He was the soloist trying to create history. They had all been following him on this radar screen and on his blogs. They knew he was a former SAS agent as this open-source information had gained intrigue from supporters of his epic journey.

The operators were his biggest followers as his daily statistics and blogs broke up the monotony and gave this green blip on their screens a personality.

The problem they faced was this.

Why have two people just turned up from nowhere in the middle of the most extreme continent on planet earth, 7 nautical miles behind a former SAS agent.

The operators after futile deliberations decided to inform their supervisor who would be more adept at filling in the blanks but who was currently asleep.

The senior operator turned to his colleague and announced, 'This situation is a little strange I don't understand it. Go and wake the commander.'

'Yes Sir,' was the quick response followed by his swift departure.

The fact these commands were given in Russian added another dynamic to Op IGNITION. Something wasn't right and the Russians were about to take a vetted interest in every single activity and piece of information that they could intercept and collect.

Vostok the Russian weather station like the British and American ones was always a subject for speculation and suspicion. Each side played their cards close to their chests and had always mutually left each other alone.

In the grand scheme of things what did Antarctica actually have to offer strategically to any of these great nations?

For the first time it wasn't the continent itself that was a strategic asset, the strategic asset that was unknowingly skiing for his life was no longer mutually exclusive to himself.

WHITEOUT was 24 hours from death.

The Russians were a 4-hour helicopter hop from WHITEOUT.

CHAPTER 26

Decker took in the mantras clearly spelt in capitals to inspire him when times were bad. Listed next to them, in red marker were all of his daily distances and position co-ordinates. Like a schoolboy's essay, the first lines were neat and tidy, the last few barely legible on the tent inner.

'Maybe it's all washing away for a reason,' he smirked to himself as he read out 'WHO DARES WINS'. The SAS's motto he noted, was his philosophy for guiding him through life, and yet now another chapter seemed to be opening to erase the previous one.

He jumped up throwing his sleeping bag off exposing his skintight undergarments. Quickly putting his duvet-style snow boots on, he grabbed an item from a stuff sack, then gripped the shovel from the tent outer and was out of the door in a shot.

Rushing a few metres to the side of the tent he drove the blade of the shovel into the ice. Quickly whipping his bottoms down, squatting whilst resting his right hand on the shovel, he paused. Expelling a deep breath before allowing nature to take its course, officially marking the start of another day.

As he admired the crisp morning ice particles flickering to infinity, and relaxed with the relief of the obvious, he noticed something else.

'Today is the first time I have not unzipped the tent slowly, looking to the front and rear before moving out.' Relieved to be noticing this change, he cleaned up. Normally this scheduled morning activity would allow him to try and locate smells of a human nature, including cooked food, or litter flying in the wind. Always looking for early-warning signs that there may be a killing squad nearby, who had dropped the ball.

Looking at his shit, it was solid as normal. Dehydrated rations did that to the digestive system. 7000 calories a day produced a pile of shit the size of a molehill back home. Thinking whilst still looking, he chuckled as he thought out loud, 'Fuck me I have to pick up all my shit from 120NM out from the Pole.'

Antarctica had a strict green policy. Not only would he have to do a huge box movement taking him miles off direct course, to avoid scientific areas, he had to pull his own shit too.

One hour of rustling inside the tent saw him emerge fully kitted with only the tent to pack up. Quickly rolling it up then lying it flat on top of his sled, he pulled the heavy duty zips to close it all up.

Without even consciously thinking, he looked at the shadow the sun cast off his body. Shuffling on his skis he turned until the shadow was lying directly to his 9 o'clock position. At 8am every morning he knew this would be his line of travel for the next two hours.

He always used nature as opposed to technology if he could. These little observations when stacked up made life easier all round and came naturally to him. Many a time he had grabbed an ashtray to ram into an attacker's face in a pub, or used his car as a deadly weapon instead of his gun. Life to him didn't need to be complex, he started to ski.

He knew that two had passed when his shadow was now at his 11 o'clock. Looking through his Oakley shades instead of his mask surrounded by a thick balaclava, and Gortex jacket hood, he felt amazing. This was now like a ski holiday he thought. Admiring the view.

'Polar expedition tours,' he said to himself. 'That's an idea, I could be a polar guide, take people to the North and South Pole.' That idea alone made him drive his poles in harder, really pushing down on his skis to get a bigger kick to slide forward. Somehow the idea was fuelling his energy and enthusiasm. Why wouldn't it? He loved the solitude of the outdoors, relished the extreme challenge and was a great leader.

'Yeah I can do that, yeah fuck it,' knowing that the going price for leading an expedition of 3-4 people down here would be at least 50-70K a season. His mind was starting to race away. '3 months work down here, a few training camps in Greenland for 7-10 days, online support, training programs…' He then thought of Conrad. 'Maybe we could team up together for the first season to show me how it's—

WHOOMP!

'Fucking hell!' he screamed out, trying to spin his body around. In a state of full panic with no ice beneath his skis. Quickly registering this was a full-blown crevasse, and no underlying patch of ground to break his fall, he was free falling with nothing beneath him.

In the spilt second, he acknowledged he was in the shit, and recalled this area was riddled with crevasses. A novice mistake. So high on life and riding the FEAR from his mind, he had forgotten to check his maps for these danger areas.

Managing to twist his falling body 90 degrees in the air, he could see the sled a few metres from the crevasse edge. With no tension on the trace line yet, it was static, but that could change quickly if his body kept heading south. Nothing would stop it falling in after him, when the strain of his body started to pull the sled. Ironically, not one boulder or piece of jagged sastrugi was present to wedge it and stop it tumbling in on top of him, then past him, dragging him to his death. His right ski was kicked and scratched the ice wall in blind panic. With his body at a ninety-degree angle to the crevasse ice wall, the right side of his body slid down it. Reaching out with his right hand to grip whatever he could, he was powerless, even the right side of his face was trying to halt the fall, tearing his flesh instantly.

'Fuck, fuck, no, no, please,' he screamed.

Terrified it was all over and this whole epic was supposed to send him to his resting place.

Before his last scream echoed his right ski hit a firm edge that turned out to be some kind of ledge, breaking his fall, smashing his body into the ice wall and painfully jolting his knee socket. He pulled his left leg in immediately to join the right.

The noise of his ski edges gripping a second ago were akin to a set of jumbo jet wheels screeching to an emergency halt. Then it was silent. The only sound were the pieces of ice bouncing off the crevasse edge past him into the abyss.

Too scared to even breathe, his face was squashed against the ice wall with his upper body twisted inwards, arms spreadeagled touching the ice wall. Trying to stabilise himself as a temporary lifesaving balancing act, miraculously his feet seemed to be dug in to the side wall of a jagged ledge of ice.

Feeling around with his skis on a firm footing next to each other, he gingerly pushed the left ski out to feel how much spare room he had to manoeuvre with.

'Fuck, fuck,' he whispered, as his leg shot off the ledge, making his whole body judder. Whipping the ski back onto the ledge, he remained dead still once again.

'What if the ledge breaks away under my weight?' he whispered. 'Shit.' Tilting his head upwards he could see the edge 5 feet above him. Then looking timidly to his back left, he could see the gap width of the crevasse. It was a three-metre diameter. 'Options aren't looking great,' he noted.

Keeping his breathing as shallow as possible, trying not to disturb the ice shelf beneath his skis again, he looked down the edge of the ice wall. Making out the ledge he was standing on to be about a foot wide, he only had about two inches spare to work with.

'Fuck's sake,' he cursed with his lips touching the ice wall, blood now seeping into his mouth from his friction wound to his right cheek. Not really wanting to look down again he couldn't help it. With minimal movement he captured a quick glimpse. Ironic that he had now caught a glimpse of the black nothing.

'Yep, definitely prefer the white nothing.' His left leg started to shake uncontrollably. Known as disco leg, this reassured his mind that he was shitting himself in fear of imminent death. Years ago this hadn't been a problem, as he was normally clinging to a cliff, firmly attached to rope, anchored to a strongpoint. And, with another person.

The rope attaching him to his pulk still had some slack in it due to the ledge breaking his fall and saving his life. One problem was the trace line was attached to his daysack on his back. If the ledge gave way, his body would fall then the sled would follow. Even if he hit another ledge to break his fall, it wouldn't be enough. Over a 100kg sled acting as an anchor on his body, would rip him off and down into the abyss.

A Catch 22-scenario was now being played out in his mind.

'Will the sled grip the ice with my weight on the rope pulling on it? I can then climb out…Or if it doesn't? In my attempt to climb out it hurtles past me with all my gear and hits me too?'

He made his decision, knowing he had to take his rucksack off, and try and free-climb out by removing his skis, using his ski pole tips as ice axes to climb out and maybe kicking his feet into the snow and ice wall.

'Okay no time to mess about,' he said to himself, his breathing under control again after the initial shock. He eased his left arm back through the rucksack strap. With his ski pole wrist loop still attached to his wrist this was tricky. Halfway through, he flicked his loop off his wrist, risking the pole slipping off and becoming lost forever. A few seconds later he mastered it and got one arm free. Using the slack on the rope he simply dropped his right shoulder and allowed the rucksack's weight to cause it to slide. Whipping his arm and ski pole up through it, the rucksack dropped and hung near his feet.

'Good stuff, nice and easy Decker, skis next…'

Forcing his body into the ice wall harder, his face crushed painfully once more. Lifting his shaking left leg up to get his foot up higher, without looking down he felt for the ski binding release catch. His ski pole was getting in the way and making it fidgety, but he managed to flip it open, releasing the rear wire binding so the ski was free. Only the toe of his boot was holding it in place. Flicking his left foot up to bring the tip of the ski near his face he slowly wrapped his hand around the ski, took a look up, then launched the free ski back over the edge with the most overarm throwing strength he could muster. It sailed over.

'One down. Come on we can do this,' he said calming himself down knowing he was halfway.

Placing his left foot back on the ice he couldn't help but see the disturbed ice drop away in to darkness. With his right ski jammed in against the ice wall he braced himself for the next move. Moving his right hand down to meet the binding, desperately trying not to rush, he blindly fumbled around trying to locate the binding release catch.

'Got it,' feeling the sweat roll down his cheeks.

He replaced his right arm back on the ice wall for stability. His left arm grabbed the ski tip, the sweat was now in his eyes, he squinted and threw it over the edge with the same aggression and precision to follow the former one.

Looking at the trace rope hanging attached to his rucksack he gave it a little tug, it moved the sled slightly. Climbing using the rope was a no-go.

As he pulled the rope he looked at the daysack and realised his Leatherman multi tool was in the top flap and had been since the start. Always at hand to adjust his ski binding settings, or cooker valves when his fingers were too cold. Unzipping the flap, he grabbed it and clumsily unfolded it by using his hand and the ice wall for purchase. What was now in his hands was a mini saw. Only four inches long but built for purpose.

Minutes before he had weighed up the options of ramming his ski pole tips into the snow, then hauling his way up with brute arm strength. Left arm, right arm, legs kicking to scrabble out. He knew deep down it was too risky.

This option was now going to have to work or it was the end.

Moving fast he held the trace rope with his right hand, whilst leaning down and starting to initially chip away at the ice, before sawing it to create a foot hold around knee height. Working furiously his hands were still starting to go numb. This black hole was like a freezer.

Minutes later the first hold was cut. Looking at his right shoulder he decided to cut the next hole just below. Years of climbing in Mountain Troop with SAS had taught him that climbing was all in the legs, arms were simply the support levers of balance. He could climb out using his sharp ski pole tips for balance and the foot hold for support.

Chipping away with his right arm this time he cut the second hole.

Looking up left he started cutting another higher than the right side. A simple set of shallow steps. Luckily he was wearing old-school Alpha boots. Though people had ridiculed him for wearing a 1950s leather boot, this decision would potentially save his life today. At the toe end of the boot was a rubber wedge that slots into the ski binding. Like a small square bolted on the end perfect for him to cut slots for them to fit into to allow him to climb out.

All done, he looked at the hole. Ramming the saw into the ice, he gripped it tight for balance. Placing his left boot into the first hole, applying a downward pressure, he tested it.

'That's good to go mate,' reassuring himself.

Placing the Leatherman back in the daysack, he grabbed the ski poles close to the tips, holding them both behind the baskets. These baskets were plastic and leather webs, set back two inches from the ski tips to stop the skis protruding further into the snow. His fists were clenched tightly behind them. They would aid his dagger-like thrusts into the ice.

Eyeing up a spot to thrust both poles into his ice-climbing skills kicked in. Avoiding a massive power thrust that would smash the ice, he gently tapped away, then drove the tip in about head-height. Normally using ice axes, the principles were the same, never put your hand above your head as it strained the arms.

Both tips dug in, he pulled down slightly. The ski pole tips held but the ledge beneath his feet began to have other ideas. Feeling the ledge fracture slightly, he bent his knees to test it again. At this point instinct fuelled by adrenalin kicked in. He failed to control his nerves, as the panic set in, seeing him pull his body up slightly on the poles. Holding his body weight, with his left foot quickly kicking at the ice to locate the hole cut. Hearing the ice shelf start to slide away, there was only one option on the table.

Locate the hole or die.

More random kicks flew onto the ice wall. Composure was a luxury at this moment as the left pole started to break the ice and loosen. Another few kicks then he felt it hit the hole. Pushing his toes down hard inside his boot, it felt as though his toenails were clutching the ice. Finally getting purchase with his feet, his left pole ripped away swinging his upper body off the wall. Counter balancing, he managed to throw his body back into the ice, desperately trying to dig the pole tip in again. No petite swings this time to hook the ice, just pure power driven by a will to survive.

Bang.

It stayed in.

'Calm down, calm down, control, come on,' he whispered to himself. Resting his head on the ice wall for a second. 'Composure, composure.' He looked up, no need to look down, there was nothing there.

Fully stretched on his left leg, he brought his right one up to find the hole he'd cut out minutes earlier.

'That's it, here we go,' egging himself on. 'Two more to do.' Now straddled unevenly he took a breath before throwing his left pole back up near his head. Taking a few swings it finally caught. Without pausing he pushed up on his right leg, fully extending it to hurl his body upwards. Left leg now hanging, it was one move away from safety. Scarpering around trying to locate the hole, his forearms were burning with lactic acid whilst his left foot was scraping down the ice wall, until he could feel the recess he had cut.

Wedging it in, he felt himself losing his calm composure as the crevasse ledge was almost at his eye level. 'Calm don't lose it now and fall…' Knowing he was one move away from safety he pushed down on his left leg, not even checking that it would hold. Jumping up, trying to reach over the ledge in a scrappy move, he made it. As the Antarctic plateau reappeared to his eyes once again, his elbows dug in on top of the ice ledge. Both legs now loose beneath him still hung in the crevasse. Scrabbling forward like a madman he moved forward until his thighs crossed the ledge. Crawling an extra few metres to be safe he threw himself over on his back.

Breathing uncontrollably, he knew that that was one of his closest calls to date. Panting on his back, arms and legs spreadeagled he was motionless. Feeling the burn on his left cheek come back, as the adrenalin drained away, he tossed his body over.

Lying face down he felt his cheek. The blood stuck to his gloves as he inspected the damage. Knowing it was just a friction burn, he scratched some snow up then forced it into his cheek. Hand placed against his face pressuring the wound, he looked back across the Antarctic plateau.

He'd known this area was dangerous country but had missed the signs. A sigh of relief now washed over him, he lay on his back exhausted. 'I need to get the fuck out of here fast before this place kills me.'

CHAPTER 27

Mick looked down at the arrow on the GPS screen before following it off the screen as far as his eyes could see to the blank horizon. The weather was still clear though a little overcast taking the edge off the sparkling ice surface.

Mick took stock of the expansive landscape and immediately registered what WHITEOUT meant when he talked about depth perception in his blogs. He'd shared how it could be deceiving out here and Mick knew it was almost like a virtual enemy that they had to get a grip of fast. What he perceived to be a wide expanse stretching for miles to his front could in fact actually only be a few hundred metres or so. Making a wrong judgment would be critical, once they got within 5 nautical miles of WHITEOUT Mick understood that failure to judge depth perception could mean compromise, resulting in a premature pursuit across the Antarctic plateau to take down their prey.

As Mick inspected the snow and surface conditions with his ski pole he couldn't help but be mesmerised by the erratic sastrugi formations carved out of the ice. It looked like art to him, a true exhibition showpiece, Mick crossed his fingers in his mittens that the 100 mph winds that Gerry had mentioned would hold off a few more days, these looked tricky to navigate as they were.

As Mick forced his eyes to visualise any cracks in the ice, he could make out a dip in the ground, only partially visible. 'Dead ground, shit.'

Dead ground was a problem; the area of surface you could not see between two points could be where WHITEOUT was skiing or tented up. Further away squinting his eyes he could that the ground regained height and became level again. In between these points was always going to cause major deliberations at this early stage on the ice. Mick knew WHITEOUT could identify easily now the perceptions of depth between two points of high ground. Mick didn't have this luxury and would have to always play it safe, which meant going slower than he'd like.

'Does the ground disappear for 200 metres or two miles?' Mick pondered.

WHITEOUT had described in his blog how he would sometimes look to his front and see a steep drop that entered a huge patch of dead ground. This dead ground WHITEOUT estimated to measure around 4 miles in distance before it rose up, to gain its lost height once more. It shattered him as he knew he would have to descend into the lower reaches only to climb back four miles out of it. He had described the surreal experience of stepping off to take on the challenge and after only 20 metres had passed, he had skied both down and back out of the dead ground. Even being the most experienced navigator that he was, he still couldn't get his head around it but also noted this had happened to him around the North Pole as well. Mick understood it perfectly now, he was now thinking that he was staring out at a huge valley that stretched on for miles to be proven wrong in only twenty steps.

Unfortunately the opposite was true also. This was the dangerous part for Icarus. Mick knew when he skied into a perceived area of dead ground to only be 500 metres and it actually opened up into a three mile valley, they would have just committed to skiing on a downward slope for miles which equalled a long time. If WHITEOUT were only a few miles in front, he would be able to see them on the downward slope higher up behind him if he stopped and looked back.

Did WHITEOUT ever look back? Mick mused, and how far back could he actually penetrate with his mark one eyeball? Does he only look back when he stopped with his back to the wind? And how much attention did this man actually give to a backdrop he was desperately trying to escape? 'Too many questions.' Mick muttered.

Mick knew it would be WHITEOUT's instinct to scan the path he had skied when he rested every two hours. Surely he must look back to give himself the satisfaction of viewing exactly what he had just accomplished? Mick was sure he would, otherwise it was all for nothing.

It was when WHITEOUT took in these moments to appreciate his progress that the pursuers would be at greater risk of compromise.

Thinking quickly Mick decided upon a solution, from 0800 hours he knew exactly what times WHITEOUT would stop, this was when he would look back and admire the real estate he had just covered.

Before Mick committed to any vast area of dead ground he would check his watch. If it were before WHITEOUT's break time, say 20 minutes, he would hold off, not commit. Once it was past his stop time, they would then proceed. To add to that Mick decided they would always stop 10 minutes before his breaks and lay low, until 10 minutes after his break time.

They had speed and time on their hands. Both fresh they only needed to locate his tracks then trace his movements so after 1800 hours when WHITEOUT would stop for the day, they could really put a surge on to get within visual distance of the tent at their stop-short position.

As he looked in the distance on the bearing he saw a jagged piece of ice maybe two miles away. This was his marker to ski to. Once they reached it he would check the GPS again then pick another point. This was classic point-to-point navigation that was fast, accurate and saved GPS battery life.

Turning to Robby he whacked his ski poles together in the air indicating they were off.

Robby waved his right ski pole up in the air to let Mick know he was ready. There wouldn't be much talking now apart from the two hour stops, or when they reached one of these features Mick was navigating to.

'The Death March' had just taken its inaugural steps Mick thought. They had officially entered the world WHITEOUT was thriving in.

The chase was on. You couldn't make this sort of shit up Mick thought as he drove his right ski pole spike into the hard pack ice.

Picking up a rhythm and making sure he was not leaving Robby behind with the extra burden of pulling the pulk, they began to cut their own virgin tracks across the ice.

To gain traction from the snow and sheer ice beneath their skis, each ski had skins screwed into the soles. A suede type of material, it allowed them to power the skis downwards without slipping or sliding. There wasn't really any black art to skiing with skins on, you simply walked but actually slid your toes forward close to the ice as opposed to lifting your foot.

Both now encapsulated within their individual microclimates they moved. Robby was admiring the surroundings that were flowing past him nicely after 30 minutes of skiing before stopping abruptly when Mick slowed around to speak to him.

'Shit mate, schoolboy error, I'm sweating,' Mick yelled against the balaclava and the wind. He was sweating. Sweating profusely was not acceptable Conrad warned them. Regulating your body temperature was essential. Sweat equals overheating, damp clothes, misted up goggles. All their equipment and clothing will freeze instantly whenever they stopped.

Mick looked at Robby through his misted and frozen goggles, it was like looking into the mirror, he too was the victim of a schoolboy error.

Without a word they both started stripping off their sweaty excess layers of undergarments and throwing them in the pulk.

Their goggles were another story.

'These are frozen solid mate. We'll have to warm them up next to our bodies later or something.' Robby was finding it impossible to clear them, wipe them clean and throw them back on his face without a pocket of air getting inside ready to refreeze again.

'Hence two sets of goggles each. When one set are fucked just get the others out until you can clear them both later in the tent,' Conrad advised.

'God bless Conrad mate.'

'Yep definitely,' Mick agreed as he pulled the fresh pair on.

They had only experienced skiing with misted and frozen goggles for 20 minutes. This period alone had already caused Mick extreme frustration, as it was hard to see the ice pack beneath your skis. Mick just wanted to rip them off as he kept losing his navigation point in the distance.

Another strange uncomfortable feeling was hacking away at Robby. Your face fully covered with only a few small breathing holes gave you the overriding feeling of being suffocated. He had borderline hyperventilated a couple of times, just stopping to pull the layers off his face created an air gap allowing him to take in a couple of massive breaths, alleviating his distress.

In a panic for breath Robby was lifting both layers off his face to create an air pocket. Once he collapsed the air pocket releasing the garments again the situation would repeat.

As Mick looked back at Robby to check he was still there he caught a glimpse of Robby again ripping his balaclava clear of his face to breathe. Taking in a few breaths before placing the balaclava back over his face

Mick saw the painstaking process he went through to ensure all his face was fully covered again. The thought of frostbite had put Robby in a paranoid state and Mick was witnessing him taking no chances out here with his constant readjusting. Luckily there were two of them and they could visually check each other's faces for any pieces of flesh that became exposed.

This shouldn't have surprised him. They had read all of WHITEOUT's blogs – he described them as the minor things that caused you a colossal amount of mental and respiratory trauma. The goggles were beyond a joke Mick pondered. He was losing his temper and wondering how the fuck he was going to put up for another 20 hours with this shit.

Two of them were airing their frustrations in the comfort of their own minds, and also giving themselves stick for it. They knew they couldn't keep comparing themselves to the maniac they were hunting. Robby refocused. 'I'm not competing with Decker, I am here to capture and kill him. These fucking goggles are just the small price to pay for a day. Stop whining. Tomorrow night it will all be done.'

Both readjusted, the signature double pole tap from Conrad had been adopted by Mick as he used it to signal round two. They were off again hoping this was their last episode of novice mistakes.

Mick was approaching the sharp ice feature and was pleased to confirm that two miles had been clocked up. One more mile and they should be at the predicted interception point of WHITEOUT's tracks. So far the terrain was user-friendly, the weather still overcast with a murky grey backdrop ahead of them that was becoming darker by the minute. It was still around 30 miles away, Mick figured that it was clearly the low-pressure front heading their way.

'Two clicks mate. How's everything?' he asked lifting his goggles to see Robby's reaction.

'Yeah that was better, I was sweating my tits off earlier and I can actually see now.'

'It's an impressive place isn't it, never imagined it to be so bad but beautiful,' Mick adds describing what he was looking at pointing his ski pole at the limitless horizon.

'Once we get his tracks I will be happy, you noticed the weather front moving in?'

'How can you miss it, it looks pretty angry doesn't it?'

'Let's just find his tracks and hopefully that weather won't hit us until just before we find him tonight,' Robby indirectly hinting to get a move on.

'That's here in three or four hours mate. We'll batten down the hatches for that fucker. Okay let's keep going,' placing his goggles back on and no sooner realising they are frozen up after lifting them off his head. 'For fuck's sake,' he muttered under his breath.

0530 hours gave them another two hours before WHITEOUT was up and about to start his daily routine of melting snow to cook food and boil up flasks for his day's skiing. Finding his tracks was priority especially before the weather front descended upon them.

Both now squared away with small clothing adjustments it became apparent how man-hour intensive it was, constantly adjusting items for comfort. The head was a critical area as you had three or so pieces of clothing stacked around each other. The white balaclava protected the face but was difficult at times to breathe through as it iced up fast.

Digging their heels in, an hour flew by and the GPS indicated a few hundred metres till the expected interception of WHITEOUT's tracks.

Flat light levels and frozen-up goggles meant locating a single set of tracks was no easy feat, the heavy weight of the pulk didn't even make an imprint on some of the hard pack ice.

Mick stopped.

Robby came up alongside.

'We're almost at the intercept point, that means WHITEOUT is around 5 miles away,' they were both looking to their front as Mick was talking. 'Obviously the ground to our front is rolling at the moment so we're safe from compromise. I think we need to spend the next 20 minutes trying to locate his tracks. There is no point heading towards his location until we do, in fact two seconds…'

Mick flicked through the data fields on the GPS. Clumsily pushing a few more buttons with his thick gloves he found what he wanted. 'Right he is 4.7 miles away mate and in that direction,' pointing to the 2 o'clock position in front. 'He is over there somewhere.' Scanning the general area, the ground rose up gradually for a few miles but on an oblique angle sloping left. This was good news at this stage of the pursuit, they were out of sight for sure so once WHITEOUT's tracks were identified they could be bolder and close in a few more miles without compromising themselves.

'Who was it that said "There are no straight lines in nature and this is the fundamental reason for detecting something out of place in the wild" mate?' Robby asked Mick. Antarctica was certainly different. Surrounded by razor-edged ice formations, some perfectly linear fracture lines crossed the different layers of snow pack. 'We've got a ten-metre radius maximum to catch a glimpse of a sharp set of manmade lines.' Robby nodded. A tricky find with frosted goggles but a find they needed fast.

'I reckon we just do a quick jack box search,' Robby suggested. Mountain rescue talk for avalanche areas. Starting at the centre point and taking one step forwards, turning 90 degrees and taking 2 steps, turning 90 degrees and taking 3 steps, this process continues for as long as the area allowed.

Mick agreed as it effectively covered a box area ensuring that all of it was searched within a metre. 'OK I will start from 100 metres over there on this bearing. If you do the opposite and head out across that way, it will give us a fighting chance with two boxes. Okay let's turn our radios on, as we will be 3-4 hundred metres apart when we reach our outer limits. Just smash your ski poles in the air if you discover them Robby, if the radios don't work.'

'Okay I will keep the pulk on, let's do it.' Robby was keen to get this bit nailed as the idea of just tracking WHITEOUT purely on a bearing without his tracks worried him a little.

Walking off in opposite directions all eyes bored in to the ice and snow to discover the tracks. Their alertness naturally heightened one more time, their competitive natures overriding anything else as each one of them wanted to be the one to discover the tracks first.

To think they were a few metres from WHITEOUT's tracks was madness. It was only seven days ago that they had had a briefing in the back of the VW camper in London Mick recalled. He remembered looking through WHITEOUT's file and hiding his shock the moment Gerry told them it was on this continent.

They were only a few hours behind him now, freezing cold, without M4 rifles but with an optimism that boded well. Mick was in his element.

As he skied along looking for ground signs a momentary glance up sent a chill down his spine. His heart raced uncontrollably as he dived to the floor for cover. He started fumbling around frantically for his Glock pistol inside his jacket pocket.

Only when the Glock was tight in his right hand did he try and compose himself to take another look at WHITEOUT. It felt too close to speak to Robby via the handheld radio. He was on his own for this encounter. The adrenalin was flowing and the fact his bare hands were grasping the Glock, resting on the ice had no bearing. Minus 20 degrees did not imminently factor into this equation. With his knuckles white as the ice beneath him, Mick quickly and silently slipped out of his ski bindings trying not to raise his profile above the ice formations. Running a quick script through his head, he braced himself for what he was about to do next. WHITEOUT was sat down on his pulk with his head slumped in his hands. The only thing that divided them was 30 metres of sastrugi and ice rubble. Mick knew as soon as he got up he had to run at him, the risk of crawling up without being able to see him would be dangerous. Mick ran a quick combat appreciation. 'WHITEOUT still has skis on and is sat down, if I run for it I will make it, no problem. Once he sees me coming with a pistol he should freeze. If not I will shout and fire a warning shot off to get his attention.' Mick could feel the familiar effects of adrenalin around his body as he was shaking internally. Flight response had elapsed this time around as it wasn't an option. Fight response, or total all-out aggression was about to kick into action when he got himself together. Taking a few deep breaths to regulate and gather his thoughts for the next ten seconds of his life, Mick was primed.

'Okay Mickey boy, here we go, over the top straight at him. Don't shout until he sees you. When he looks up just shout STOP. Then move in with the pistol trained on him. He won't try and escape as he is attached to the pulk. Okay we're good'. He ran a three count through his head, on one Mick exploded up on to his feet and made a beeline for WHITEOUT. He felt slightly disorientated upon standing, and he didn't pick him off straight away, after fives metres he stopped, pistol extended in front of him. Breathing heavily, he scanned the area. 'Where the fuck is he?' Quickly looking behind him. His heart pounding in his panicked state. There was no way he was falling for that trick, but there was nothing to his rear. Dammit WHITEOUT was too seasoned for mistakes. 'Where the fuck is he?' he said again. Looking back to his front he finally makes out the pulk with a body slumped over. Remaining completely still and undisturbed by Mick's antics, WHITEOUT remained motionless.

Mick squinted and then relaxed. 'Fuck. What's happening to me?'

Heightened paranoia in imminent anticipation of WHITEOUT had allowed these ice formations to play funny tricks on his mind Mick thought to himself, relieved. Like the clouds above you can interpret all sorts of shapes, objects and figures. Mick had a quick dig at himself knowing he had just fallen foul to the beauty of naturally formed light and curvatures reflecting off the ice. 'Shit my heart is still pounding.'

Trying to smile at his buffoonery, he breathed out fully then turned around to go and put his skis back on.

No sooner had he turned his heart was sent racing again, Robby was waving his poles frantically. Evidence of WHITEOUT had just been located in a physical form, not the imaginary mirage version Mick had just tried killing.

Mick skied over to Robby hoping that he hadn't caught a glimpse of him hunting a holographic enemy in his mind. Mick berated himself inwardly. 'I am losing it, why would I possibly think an ice formation was WHITEOUT? I must be on edge? Come on sort it out, you're well up for this.' Robby was proudly pointing to the tracks, visibly chuffed he had found them. It was a relief. 'Well done mate, that makes the job ten times easier now.' The wind was beginning to pick up, so with their backs bolstered against it, Mick got his phone out and looked at his GPS data whilst dialling.

'Gerry?' Mick asked.

'Mick what we got, everything okay?'

'We have his tracks and these are the coordinates, stand by.'

'Send,' Mick relayed slowly and concisely the track coordinates and listened as Gerry repeated them back correctly.

Mick had already loaded the new coordinates and the data field told him they were precisely 4.5 miles away from WHITEOUT's position. The time was 0621 hours, nine minutes before WHITEOUT awoke.

'I expect you have done it Mick, but he's just over 4.5 from your position. What's does the terrain look like on his bearing?' Gerry was debating how much further they could push forward without any possibility of compromise

'It's good Gerry, a gradual incline for about 2 or 3 in his direction on an oblique angle. I am happy to push forward and go firm before the brow.'

'Your decision Mick, just don't get greedy too early. In two hours he will be on the move again. You have got his tracks to play it safe for a few hours, what do you reckon?'

'We'll push forward to the brow and see how the terrain turns out Gerry, but yeah you're right we have time. No need for any compass rush antics,' Mick responds cupping his hand around the Iridium voice mic and his mouth to shield his transmissions from the wind that was picking up.

'Gerry, we'll play this out with caution for a few hours. When the weather starts to pick up even more we can get slightly more ambitious if the visibility closes in. We're all sorted and good to go from here on in. I will check in again in two hours,' Mick confirmed eager to get on with skiing again, the wind was freezing them both.

'Negative Mick, we're flying out of here in under two hours at 0800. Unless there is something urgent don't call us till 1400hrs. We should be at the South Pole by then to meet Trans-Ant team. Once we know exactly what we're doing with them we can give you a clearer update reference the RV. As it is at the moment there is no change, WHITEOUT will meet them in 36 hours, again that is 1830 tomorrow.'

'Got it mate. Right it's fucking freezing again so we need to get moving Gerry, speak in eight hours. Out.' Mick looked at Robby to make sure he understood the conversation that just took place.

'Robby as you have gathered we'll head off on his tracks to the brow ahead then cool it for a bit. We need to stay calm and not get too tunnel-visioned. The plan is going to script so let's not take any shortcuts. You happy?' Mick enquired.

'Fine mate, fine I will keep the pulk.'

Mick nodded whilst checking his bearing that was now pointing directly at WHITEOUT's tent position before heading off once more. In front the low-pressure system was starting to show its hand. Lower cloud base and visibility was down to about three miles.

Both men were draped in white overalls, white balaclavas and white sprayed skis, poles and pulk and Robby felt as though they looked like a pair of Arctic-trained commandos. In a white-out the only visible signs of their presence were the black lenses of their goggles that lit up against the white backdrop. Moving in unison they closed in on WHITEOUT.

★★★★★

Smoke clouds filled the dark room that was now occupied by more people than it ever had seen before and certainly the conversation was more stimulating than anything witnessed in the past. A six-month posting to a small station in Antarctica was a time to embrace solitude, read, research and save every penny you were paid.

Despite the crowded arena, the mini operations room was silent with only the tracking systems bleeping every second in the background as they scanned radar screens. Everyone was a little confused as to how this scenario was developing. Vostok was a Russian outstation that only those listening directly to the Commanding Officer's orders knew of its real purpose, and potentially not even then. However, this situation had aroused huge suspicion and the CO was not going to let it go undetected.

'Interesting. This is very interesting. What the hell is going on out there?' the base commander mused openly before giving his appreciation to the team thus far.

'We have Harry Decker, former SAS Agent, now a Polar explorer attempting to create history.' This he read from a printout of WHITEOUT's expedition website profile page.

'Today, four hours ago two other men appear from nowhere. We can only assume it was from a US aircraft heading to the South Pole station maybe? Correct?' he asked the men listening. They simply nodded. Knowing better than to interrupt him.

'Look here,' directing the men to stare at the flat-screen computer generating the positions of the three men in real time.

'Decker started at Hercules Inlet and has continued on this bearing for the last 38 days covering over 600 miles,' tracing the route with a pencil the Russian commander then pointed to where Decker was now.

'Decker is currently here. Now the two men, well one called Mick whose accent sounds weird appeared here.' Again the man pointed with his pencil.

Intercepting conversations out here was standard and 'Mick' and 'Gerry' were the only two names associated with this strange development.

'They have moved about three miles to here then made that call we have just had replayed. They are tracking this man Decker obviously. But why? They have not mentioned why. We need to find out if this is some sort of military exercise maybe, is Decker still working for one of the cells wings we know about at Hereford? We know the British do some crazy exercises and maybe this is another?'

No one responded, whether this was because that's the way the Russian command structure worked or the others in the room had no idea what the commander was talking about.

'Okay, let's keep monitoring this situation. But I want a team on stand-by. Work out the helicopter flight plan to their locations. What fuel caches do we have out there that will get us there and back if we need it? Re-calculate the no-fly zone in case we need to carry out a legitimate exercise of our own. We don't want to upset the Americans at the South Pole station, and cause an international incident by flying in their protected areas of scientific interest. Get to it men, I want an operations order for a team to locate those men if they need to. I want it in the next hour and I want more information on Harry Decker, who the hell is this man because something tells me he isn't just an explorer.'

CHAPTER 28

Mick knew exactly what he was looking for at the two-hour stop point, especially as the weather had become inclement. WHITEOUT's blogs always included a photo of him flaked out next to the pulk, exhausted. He always placed the pulk across the line of the prevailing wind and dug a quick hole to sit in. With the raised height of the pulk and a foot-deep trench, he was completely sheltered from the wind.

This way he could eat and drink in slight comfort for seven minutes whilst donning his huge down expedition jacket, looking back on his line of travel if the visibility was clear, no doubt admiring his daily stint.

Five metres visibility and a frosted ski mask, Mick squinted his eyes to try and pierce through the wall of whiteness. It was then that he fell. Slamming into the ice beneath his feet. 'Fucking weather,' he shouted in frustration. He felt as though he'd been poleaxed by a few mugs from behind.

Robby observed Mick crawling around on the ground trying to get back on his feet, it was a classic Bambi on ice moment, as he tried to get up as fast as possible to limit his embarrassment, which resulted in hitting the deck again even harder.

Taking a moment to cool his head Mick got it together and realised something. He had fallen because of a dip in the ground. This dip actually calmed him instantly as the sideswipe from nowhere was due to WHITEOUT's little pit he had dug to protect himself, exactly as he had described it.

The hollow was clearly man-made.

On closer inspection Mick noticed the telltale signs of broken crumbs resting on the snow and ice.

Fuzion flapjack bars, 780 calories to be exact Mick thought.

'That fucker,' Mick bellowed out.

This was a surreal feeling for Mick. The man he wanted to kill badly was sat here a few hours ago chewing away on his flapjack bar. Mick was face down in the exact place WHITEOUT's ass cheeks would have occupied.

Thinking that Mick catapulted to his feet with the aid of his two ski poles in a nanosecond. Brushing himself down he once again contained his anger, bitter frustration and eagerness to end this ordeal.

'This is the spot Robby,' he shouted over choosing not to use his radio and instead competed directly with the wind. Shouting felt great to vent some tension as his voice caught Robby's attention.

Robby closed in tight with his face inches from Mick.

'This is where his first 2-hour stop was. Look...' Mick pointed at the small trench peppered with the remainder of WHITEOUT's flapjacks that fuelled his day's exertions.

'Right I am going to work out the time-distance equation, give us a few minutes.' Robby gave Mick the thumbs up before turning his back to the wind.

Frantically fumbling with GPS rubber-covered buttons Mick was collecting relevant data from various data fields. Looking at the distance they had covered from the tent pitch and their start point to this first stop point.

The distance covered was 2.4 miles.

It had taken Mick and Robby 2 hours and 4 minutes to cover this distance as they had backed off to be cautious. Mick could only assume this was exactly WHITEOUT's two-hour stop point due to his mechanical nature and extreme discipline. Using the calculator function he started to work out the distance covered divided by time to equal WHITEOUT's speed. Then he stopped, thinking, *'What a twat.'*

2.4 divided by 2 hours wasn't exactly brain science.

WHITEOUT was travelling at 1.2 miles per hour.

This was slow but he had 120Kg to pull behind him. Mick could easily do 3 miles an hour but this wasn't a cut-and-chase pursuit, it was a covert stalk, letting WHITEOUT have the distance advantage until he stopped for the day.

'Robby,' Mick yelled out. Only a few metres away Robby shuffled backwards. Face to face once more.

'He is travelling at 1.2. I estimate he is 3 hours ahead as we started to move at 0830, it's took us ninety minutes to get to his tent position and just over ninety to get here. That equals about 3.6 miles ahead. That's a good buffer I think, even if these brief weather windows open up a huge expanse, 3.6 miles is a massive distance to see us even if we're caught in the open.'

'This weather is doing my nut in with these bizarre white-outs. Sometimes I think I am moving but have come to a complete halt, it's ball-breaking annoying,' Robby said.

'Ha, it's not just me then mate, I keep doing the same. What a weird feeling when it happens hey?'

'Fucking roll on tonight is all I can say.'

'Not wrong. It's killing me knowing we're within touching distance but knowing we still have to wait.' Taking a quick glimpse at the GPS to check the time, Mick confirmed, 'About 15 hours and we'll be done, finished tonight.'

Mick and Robby throughout the day had confirmed that WHITEOUT was indeed a mechanical mechanism. Almost to the minute and distance his two-hour stops were spot on. Discipline was critical in every aspect of this endeavour. WHITEOUT carried every element out to the letter, whether that was time travelled, the way he looked after his body, to the exact bite-size of flapjack he would tear off to eat at each stop.

From what they could gather from his blog he never thought about family or finishing this ordeal as Robby was, WHITEOUT was always living in the moment on the move.

After the third stop position they both knew this is what he called his lunch break, having 20 minutes to give himself a hot meal from a small Stanley flask. On days like this one with crap weather he'd commented on what a real morale booster it was to eat hot meat, peas and mash.

Both guys were now living and breathing WHITEOUT's daily existence. Each clue to his presence was treated like a scientific area of interest. The physical evidence of his activities was immediately rolled into their own imaginary screenplays. It was like a superimposed character was walking around them, an almost ghostlike figure they could watch in complete silence going about his business.

Lunch break signified another key moment in WHITEOUT's day as he then broke his legs down in to three ninety-minute stints on his skis as opposed to two hours.

Mick knew he would have to factor this in again to make sure he was still locating WHITEOUT's stopping positions. Each stop position was in effect a countdown marker, a tick-off feature and unknown to WHITEOUT, the diminishing existence of his life.

WHITEOUT in his blogs described how he only played upbeat dance music during this period to drive him forward. Listening to the exact same music each time he knew how much time he had left and adjusted his almost sprint-like finish to perfection. Each day was a race to WHITEOUT and he never stopped early, never reduced his level of intensity and never looked back during this last push.

WHITEOUT had made Mick's job easy from a tracker's point of view. It even made Mick shake his head at WHITEOUT's rigid regime and strict routine. As Mick smirked to himself, 'You might have been unpredictable at home WHITEOUT but you should know that predictable patterns are what kills and you sure as hell are predictable out here,' he noted with a sly smile. Mick again signalled for Robby to close in.

'This is our three-hour point. WHITEOUT will travel another three hours from here that works out at roughly 3.5 miles. We move any closer and this weather lifts, we may be too close and exposed. Let's play it safe, use this natural trench over there and hold tight.' Mick had seen a natural trench that afforded them protection from the elements, and most importantly cover from the view of WHITEOUT if the visibility became wide open.

'Roger that mate,' Robby as usual agreed with Mick which was no surprise as Mick generally did make good decisions.

'I will phone in and give an update of our position and also see if WHITEOUT has checked in yet, if his phone is not completely dead again. Hopefully he will have checked in for the last time to give an indication of distance, before we ski in later to take him down.'

'Okay Mick I will get start getting the tent up.'

'Wait one mate. I will make the call and if he has checked in we will know his position. If he has got a major spurt on then we can move closer first.'

'Okay.'

Both jumping in the natural ice trench Mick got the Sat phone out and hit a few buttons. Shielded from the wind he awaited a response.

'Gerry,' Mick shouted in to the phone, awaiting his response.

'Mick,' Gerry replied. 'Send mate.'

'All good here, we have located all his stops and are currently at his second from last stop, approximately 3 hours from him. Has he sent an update?'

'No news and we probably won't know now either. We have just landed at the South Pole station. We will pitch a tent here tonight and, depending on your success later, cancel our meeting with Trans-Ant team tomorrow. We told them it might not happen so they won't be spooked.

'If for any reason there is a delay taking down WHITEOUT then we will go with Trans-Ant and RV with WHITEOUT. Again this is the contingency plan in the instance that any unforeseen scenarios get played out. This is the final cut-off position effectively. Don't worry if this is the case, Sully is working up the projected extraction for this alternative play. If you guys are stranded due to weather or just can't locate WHITEOUT by tomorrow night head to EP 1. Do you copy this Mick?'

'Yeah got it, so if we don't close the deal at 0200hrs and can't locate him by tomorrow's RV then head to EP 1. What's the met report for next 24 hours?' Mick asked.

'Straight up it's getting slightly worst hence my last comments, it's only the weather that will fuck this first attempt up so stay tight guys,' Gerry said.

'We are going to throw the tent up and wait till 2200 before moving. I reckon by 0100 we will be in the Final RV position ready to launch the takedown,' Mick added.

'All copied mate. Give us a comms check at the Final Rendezvous – FRV, so I know you're about to launch so I can carry out a time appreciation if it all goes tits up due to weather or unknowns.'

'Will do Gerry.'

'Anything else to report?'

'Found a lot of blood at one point, next to a crevasse hole, but no more since, probably fell and smashed his face or something. Everything is going as planned. Weather is fucking hideous at times but we are both in good shape, no cold weather injuries.'

'Great stuff guys, glad it's all panning out. Another 12 hours we're out of here on the Ilyushin, homebound. They have a flight in later tonight and overnighting. The skidoos are on board for the EP 1 pick-up.'

'We're all good Gerry. We will check in at the FRV,' Mick said.

'Okay speak later.'

Robby had got the gist of the conversation and had started getting the tent ready to pitch. Knowing the powerful gusts of wind could rip the tent out of his cold hands and across the plateau he stopped short of erecting it himself. If the tent went flying it would be a cold twelve hours huddled up to a very pissed-off Mick counting down the clock.

Mick unclipped his skis and moved over to start bellowing in Robby's ear as his gripped the tent that was now acting like a windsock.

'No change mate, as you heard he is over three miles away. We will stay here. Let's get this tent up then we can chat once we're out of this wind tunnel.'

Both began to pin the tent down in order to erect it. The force of the wind threw the tent all over the place. Like a spinnaker on a sailing boat, once it caught a gust it exploded into a red sail requiring both men to rein it back in.

After ten frustrating minutes the tent was up as they both shook their arms violently to get the blood flowing again before finally taking refuge inside to regroup.

With minimal cooking equipment and dried frozen food rations they melted snow in the pan, boiled the water and served up a quick meal. Due to the wind blowing downwind from WHITEOUT's anticipated position, Mick was happy for them to eat hot rations. He deemed the threat of the Thai green curry scent piercing through the upwind and alerting WHITEOUT as impossible.

Looking at Robby's tired face as he hungrily devoured the food, Mick spoke: 'Mate now it's time to relax if that's at all possible. All the drills are in our minds, discussing any further now is going to develop more unlikely scenarios and effectively skull-fuck us both.'

Robby thinking more of his family nodded.

For now they had the luxury of letting the stove burn away on a low-level flame and enjoying the heat engulfing the tent. Both men lay silently addressing the thoughts that flooded their minds.

★★★★★

2304 hours.

Judging by the battering the tent walls were receiving they knew a full-blown Antarctic hurricane was in session, terrorising the landscape around them. A sudden huge blow to the tent wall was akin to a bomb exploding beside them and lucky too as Mick jumped up in shock and habitually took a glance at his watch. 'Shit, Robby wake the fuck up. We've overslept,' shaking him in a moment of panic. With the weather drowning out his alarm on his watch, Mick quickly checked the phone paranoid Gerry may have called. Viewing the standard screensaver without a 'missed call' notice he sighed, knowing the wrath of Gerry on his back now would put the weather into mere insignificance.

'All right Robby, it's obviously the perfect storm by the sound of it, so let's make sure we are all sorted before we leave the tent.'

'Yeah, it doesn't seem too friendly out there, let's hope the visibility is okay.'

'We will know soon enough aye, fucking Antarctica, come on!' Mick shouted to spur himself on.

Five minutes later and they were both fully wrapped up and ready to face the elements. Only their ski masks left resting on their heads.

'Robby, we will collapse the tent, stow it, then head off following the tracks again. It should take about two hours to get a visual on his tent I hope. Once we have a visual I will decide how close to get before we stop, but around 500 metres I reckon, ground dependent. I will make the call then that's us ready to rock and get this fucker out of the way. Okay?' Mick asks.

'All good let's do it mate.'

Unzipping the tent Mick eagerly anticipated what the visibility would hold for them on this critical leg. From inside the weather sounded atrocious but this was magnified due to the tent bashing.

As he peered out he was surprised. Visibility was still around 500 metres as the spindrift was being thrown about violently. Mick shook his head. 'Fucking weird continent.'

Quickly disassembling the tent and throwing it in the pulk for Robby to pull, Mick started skiing off after checking his watch.

2328 hours.

The terrain was still a boulder field that made the going slightly slower, but this also made them more vigilant as it acted as a natural braking system. Complacency due to anticipation of locating the tent had to be avoided at all costs and Mick was being vigilant as he scanned the horizon ahead as they skied solidly for an hour.

'Fucking hell,' Mick shouted, almost shitting his pants on the spot, he threw his left arm out to signal to Robby whilst kneeling down. Heart almost jumping out of his jacket he almost made a conscious effort to catch it.

About a hundred metres away Mick caught a glimpse of red underneath a thin layer of accumulated snow spray. It was clearly the red fabric of WHITEOUT's tent. As suspected, WHITEOUT had put it smack bang behind a huge ice bolder to act as a windbreak. Mick closed his eyes and opened them again to ensure it was real this time.

It was only when Mick went to ground and looked closely the whole picture unfolded. He could now make out the pulk in front of the tent almost completely covered by snow. This would have WHITEOUT's skis and poles inside plus all the other stores as he'd explained in his blogs.

Behind the snow-covered pulk was the front end of the tent known as the bell end. Facing away from the wind, snow walls about a foot high surrounded the tent, pinning down the valet sheet, acting like a small fortress wall. It was only the entrance that didn't have any walls. This was so WHITEOUT could get in and out of the doorway easily if nature called.

Behind him Robby had already guessed something was wrong watching Mick kneel down, Robby could see for himself exactly what had startled him nearly into cardiac arrest.

Thinking WHITEOUT was at least 3 miles away they were completely wrong, he was in fact half that distance and had caught them out completely. Focusing on the good news that they had located the tent, Robby closed in without Mick having to signal. This part they both knew like the back of their hands. They had rehearsed, talked through, and rehearsed it again many times over.

Both lay down facing each other.

'That shat me up, I just caught a speck of red. Do you see it mate?' Mick asked.

'I got it.'

Heart still pumping hard Mick took a moment to compose and gather his thoughts.

'We're about an hour ahead of time, let's drop our kit down behind that ice boulder and get ready.'

Without saying anything Robby pulled the pulk into the ditch, Mick slid in behind.

The preparation was simple.

Weapons needed to be ready. Plasticuffs accessible for the quick detention of WHITEOUT. Next the camera and satellite phone.

Minutes later they were both ready.

Mick made the call burrowed in tightly to Robby's back.

'Hello Mick,' Gerry answered.

'Gerry we're at the FRV. The tent is about 100 metres away as we were taken by surprise but it's all quiet. Here's our grid.' Mick spoke as quietly as he could despite the roaring wind drowning out his voice.

Repeating back the grid Gerry continued, 'Mick you all set?'

'Once we get him under control we will call Sully for the interrogation. I will call Sully now to prove communications after we have finished,' Mick confirmed.

'Good stuff guys. You have time so be cautious out there. Keep it simple mate and take no risks, if he fucks about shoot him cold dead.'

'I hear you Gerry.'

'That's all from me Mick; this is what we came to do. Well done for getting there. Have a good one,' Gerry finished up.

'Okay Gerry, out.'

Ending the call to Gerry, Mick quickly scrolled for Sully's number.

'Got it all Mick,' was the short response from Sully before Mick could say a word.

'Okay Sully we will call you when we have him pinned down and ready for you to question him.'

'Well done Mick, speak soon.' Mick rolled his eyes, he was as clipped as ever.

Collapsing the antennae again Mick turned to Robby.

'This is it mate, let's just take a look at the ground in front.'

As both men looked from behind the ice boulder to survey the ground, Mick was trying to access the best approach route in. Terrain-wise he knew it was perfect. Loads of boulders as opposed to it being a billiard board. Robby was thinking the same. It was a no-brainer. There's always going to be that paranoia associated with moving across open ground with WHITEOUT watching them approach, but this had been played out in Norway. Even though he should be asleep, Mick wasn't taking any chances. Aiming for worst-case scenario was always a good safety mechanism.

'You see the last bolder near his pulk?' Mick asked.

'Yeah.'

'I will hold at that position and cover you from the spiked ice formation a few metres to the right, once we are both at these two positions, we can close in completely. Before that we can both walk up together to the halfway point then split off. I will let you fan out right first then we move to our final assault positions.'

'Halfway together then break off?' Robby asked.

'Yeah. Let's check comms in case we need them in a second along with the weapons.'

Looking at each other they both checked their pistols giving them a quick confidence check which simply involved racking the top slide of the receiver a slight way back to ensure a 9mm round was chambered.

Mick was surprised at how easy it was to pull the top slide back; he had expected a little more resistance. Good sign that the weapon would fire without malfunction.

Robby had the same result. Both Glocks were ready to go.

'Plasticuffs' Mick said tapping them with his left hand. Both sets were attached by a karabiner on a short piece of cord.

'Phone, video camera,' talking to himself Mick tapped his pockets then quickly pulled out the camera and checked it functioned. Within seconds the screen powered up showing 3 battery bars, but a blank screen due to the lens cap still covering the aperture.

Still transfixed on Robby who was waiting Mick cracked on.

'Okay we're good. On my command we will move forward fifty-fifty until we hit the halfway point. I will hold out my left arm at that point. You then split off right and loop around to the spike. I will move to the boulder. I will do a quick comms check before we commit to the takedown. Once I give the signal, you dive on the tent whilst I shout the commands to calm him down. We don't know if this lunatic has a weapon so no warning just collapse the tent on him. Once he stops fucking about we will cut him out of the tent then cuff him, happy so far Robby?'

'Fine.'

'I will then phone up Sully, you hold the camera ready. I will hold the phone next to WHITEOUT's ear. Any fucking about from WHITEOUT take a shot, no risks Robby.'

'Understood,' Robby replied without hesitation.

'Right let's just take a moment mate the talking is over,' Mick relaxing leaning against Robby. 'Fuck me this task seemed like a wind-up, even impossible sat back in the VW. What we thought was a barking mad option is about to become a reality mucker.'

'I'm with you mate, let's just get this done and get home,' Robby said whilst giving Mick a reassuring clench around the shoulder knowing they were less than 100 metres from WHITEOUT, or Harry Decker to his loyal followers, whose life was about to be brought to an abrupt and possibly violent end. Sleeping after another 14 miles of skiing he would shortly be awakened with the same shock of capture violence he had inflicted on terrorists with ruthless conviction. A short violent interrogation would lead the way to a shock execution, though Mick vowed to honour Sully's wishes and send him off unsuspecting, and not facing a barrel.

'Ready?' Mick nodded at Robby. Robby nodded.

Leading the way Mick moved over the brow of the trench. Creating an inch indent with each step and cringing at the crimping sound which sounded magnified through his senses.

Moving about 30 metres with his Glock aimed at the tent, he stopped and gave Robby the signal to start moving, flagging his left hand in the air whilst remaining still.

Robby slowly bounded forward and moved up near Mick. Both of them were feeling the physiological effects of this ordeal. Minus 30 with a 20mph wind, anxiety was creating sweat this time, not the wind. Noticing his mask was steamed up fully by his sweat Mick removed it, and placed it on his head so he could see properly. A wise move, any moment now he may have to make a snap judgment shot that involved complete accuracy.

Robby closing into Mick realised that he had to do the same now with his.

Mick took a few quick blinks before focusing directly on the tent entrance, almost expecting a random WHITEOUT to pop out for a piss. Taking no chances he kept his weapon trained directly at the tent door. The clamminess on his hands was now evident to him. Trying to counteract the nervous shaking of his hands he gripped the pistol tighter even though his training told him that it would amplify the feeling.

'In control, you're in control, nice and easy, that's just the adrenaline pumping you up,' he whispered to himself.

Knowing that this was the natural activation of all his impulses with his pupils dilating for heightened awareness to channel his vision, he remained transfixed on the perceived threat.

Taking comfort from his body's flight-or-fight mechanism charging the blood to the muscle groups that could be needed to stand and fight, or react in an explosive and dynamic manner if called upon, it was as though his central nervous system had just become his best ally.

Mick saw the boulder clearly a few feet away and knelt beside it waving Robby forwards. Picking up the pace slightly Robby quickly moved in.

A quick nod at each other signalled the initiation of the final approach. Both men registered each other's eyes almost popping out with excitement, terror and anticipation. Both were relieved that they looked and felt the same.

Moving off to the right-hand side, Robby moved in closer. Mick aware of Robby in his peripheries stood his ground training the Glock directly on the tent's entrance again.

Taking time to cautiously move and swing around in a semicircle to take up a ninety-degree angle to the spike. Robby was almost holding his breath to be quiet, even though the wind was ripping through and slapping the tent fabric without remorse. Robby still thought he was making too much noise as he moved up behind the spike, cursing himself frantically.

They both paused at their final assault positions, well beyond the point of no return.

Mick looked at Robby 30 or so metres away and gave him the signal via hand. Zero radio.

Robby felt the final supercharged rush of adrenalin hit his limbs that automatically drove him in to action. He moved forward, exploding into action grabbing the end tent hoop and diving in towards the tent knowing this would be where WHITEOUT's upper torso would be. The poles snapped out of their rubber housing beds and extended allowing the rear end of the tent to collapse.

'Stay the fuck where you are Harry, just stop, no moving, we are armed,' Mick screamed firing a few shots in the air to prove it.

'Stay fucking still Harry I mean it you're outnumbered and we're armed,' Mick repeated.

Robby had tensed his muscles up, bracing himself in anticipation to feel the battered and tired torso of WHITEOUT laying inside his sleeping bag. Driving his knees down hard first for shock effect to at least bruise a few ribs.

'Stay still you cunt, stay fucking still,' Robby was pumped shouting away.

Mick covering and still shouting as Robby's knees ploughed into WHITEOUT's sleeping bag. Something wasn't right.

Wearing salopettes and two other layers Robby tried to make sense of what his knees had hit.

It definitely wasn't a body.

Like a madman Robby started to feel around, his arms crawling over the tent, then started beating the ground hard to locate WHITEOUT.

Mick was observing what looked like a blind tramp desperately trying to locate a passer-by's coins thrown on the deck. 'Shit the bed, the tent's empty,' Mick realised. Robby also stopped and jumped up both quickly turning around in opposite directions, weapons ready.

'Where the fuck is he?' Robby yelled over. Mick shook his head negatively recollecting his premature smirking remark about WHITEOUT setting patterns, being disciplined so it would be an easy takedown. This assumption was now biting him sorely in his ass.

'Cover me Robby, I am going to check his pulk.'

'Roger,' Robby replied.

As Mick closed in he reached down, his left arm fully extended to locate the zip. One jagged rip back, pistol at the ready, he turned to Robby who was panning the horizon.

'He's fucking gone, the skis and poles are gone, he's done one.'

Still remaining alert, as WHITEOUT could be anywhere watching from close proximity. Mick ran through a quick battle appreciation.

'Has he gone for a piss, shit? No. Has he just gone for a quick ski to exercise his legs? Don't be so fucking stupid idiot.'

Robby started checking the tent's contents. Ripping the tent doors open instead of cutting the fabric Robby got inside the collapsed tent.

Creating a dome with his arms he could see everything due to the tent being so small. He panned around clocking the items that confirmed WHITEOUT had not merely gone for a shit.

Neat and tidy were his two satellite phones and one beacon, his entire communications lifeline.

'Over here,' Robby shouted.

Poking his head into the dome created by Robby, Mick was silent, staring at the comms equipment. This moment lasted a few seconds, before they both panicked back to their feet.

Robby whispered: 'Is this guy fucking with us?'

CHAPTER 29

EARLIER THAT DAY

Rolling back onto his front, he had shaken off his near-death experience. Looking up Decker paused. Squinting his eyes to refocus before looking down to the snow he shook his head, then slowly looked up again. Balling his eyes into the distance, there it was again, the clag cleared for a few seconds, and then again.

As he looked up a brief uninterrupted glimpse through clag gave him two miles of visibility. Looking into the lower ground he could make out two dark figures skiing. Cam whites might be okay at shorter distance, but anything over 300 metres offered no concealment. You might just as well be wearing fluorescent orange bibs. And there they were, two figures skiing straight on his bearing, one pulling a small pulk following him in his freshly cut ski tracks.

Catapulting himself into action in a state of sheer panic he put his skis back on, grabbed his poles and started to ski around the huge crevasse hole to hide. Naturally hunching over to lower his profile he started to ski as fast as physically possible.

'*They have finally turned up,*' he thought as his heart started racing as he drove his arms back and legs forward like titanium pistons.

'*I knew it all along, I am not mad, I'm a genius after all, I knew I was, I knew it,*' he continued to mutter to himself. Any self-doubt that saturated Decker's mind throughout this journey was ripped clean out of his body. Thinking a near breakdown fuelled on self-pity and blame to cover his weaknesses was gone, forever. He started talking to himself but the script was fresh, this was real, this was happening, NOW.

'*Not a chance Decker,*' he bellowed out as he just discounted the last 5 minute conclusion of his life.

'This is fucking happening and you never let anything but instinct rule your mind till you drop dead. You hear me boy?' Ordering himself along.

After a few minutes Decker was sweating due to the explosive pace driven by the adrenalin flooding his body. Instantly remembering his training he slowed down and retained his normal pace knowing full well that it was considered rapid to many other people.

In those brief few minutes Decker had just run through an advanced set of operational estimation processes that would take the smartest group of military officers hours. Based on the evidence he had just seen, The FEAR was in fact real. He had some serious life-changing, if not life-saving, decisions to make instantly.

It didn't matter now about the what, who, where or when. He wanted to know the 'how'. How the hell were these guys planning on capturing him, or killing him if he believed his gut instinct.

There was still need for extensive cross-examination about his theories of how The FEAR had maybe mistakenly given him accidental insight to their existence, but that could wait, they were here and coming to collect. Survival was priority not getting back to the enigma of this whole fucked-up situation.

It was about dealing with the facts now, and this was no mean task as his thoughts started to implode openly.

'Fact: this is them coming to capture or kill me. They could have just waited for me when I returned home but they are here, that means I'm high priority, right up there on the kill list. I can see two operators but there may be more. How long have they been behind me? It must only be a day or so maximum as I would have pinged them earlier. How exactly did they get here? The last three days has been boulder fields so impossible for a Twin Otter light aircraft insertion. That is the smallest airframe that could reach with fuel cache stops on route. It would have had to have landed at least 50 miles away, or three days ago to make that possible.

Helicopter? Nah nearest fuel dump is the Thiele Mountains and a return trip couldn't cover that, it's over 500KM.

Mobility? Not a chance unless they have come for the South Pole station and looped in behind me, but why would they get on skis and stalk me? No one else is in this quadrant so they could just as well have driven up to me when I start crossing flatter ground.

It's got to be a Parachute insertion from a Twin Otter or maybe even bigger if they have government assets. C130 I reckon and it must have been a high-altitude *free fall, or I would have probably heard a 5 grand static line come in, but then again the noise of the wind, I probably wouldn't have.*

His mind was on overdrive, reeling insertion possibilities off his head. He knew you didn't just rock up at the South Pole station, thumb down a skidoo snow taxi to ride out and kill someone, or borrow an airframe such as a Twin Otter to throw someone out, free fall to his rear, then creep up and slit his throat.

Covert insertion, it has to be.

This will be their signature so however they got in was either without the person dropping them off actually realising their true intentions, or they have bribed them if it's a commercial plane.

Maybe they have used the cover of a United States C130 aircraft if the US government is helping?

Decker was not convinced the US Government were involved and his gut instinct was they hitched a ride without the facilitator knowing their mission set.

My last tent location must have been known or worked out. ALE base camp is compromised and Steve Jones has no idea, or my beacon may be working after all and they have been tracking it?

They must have a tracking platform but how do I know its depth and sophistication? I will have to completely ditch all communications equipment, it's almost dead anyway. Even when the phone or beacon is off, or in sleep mode it can still be monitored if the right asset is covering it from above. Christ when I was serving we could turn phones on to listen to people, or maybe they're just tracking my body via Satellite downlink?

Nah, no chance this is not Central Baghdad or the Hindu Kush mountains in Afghanistan. Sourcing those assets is a ball-ache for tier one Special Forces Units taking down top AQ leaders. Committing satellite coverage for me is ridiculous.

Decker's estimation process continued as he had to think about what assets or technical capabilities they had to continue hunting him down.

Why the hell do they want to kill me here? Why not wait till Punta or back in UK? Decker was convinced this was a hit not a detention operation and nothing was going to change his mind. Thinking hard he rattled on.

This is obviously time-sensitive, what is it that I can compromise so badly if I get communications again, or reach the mainland. My video? They must have intercepted it and erased it.' He then saw things slot into place and was pissed at himself.

This scenario now centred on the release of information and damage-limitation. Decker knew the exact drills to be carried out when they knew they were going to be captured, then ultimately killed.

'It was the same drill his old drug dealer mates from school would carry out: get rid of the job lot fast, anything that could compromise what you were doing and where, now or in the future.'

The safest way to protect sensitive information was not to let people possess it in the first place. He had been involved in covert operations ten fold. He was never given the full picture or certainly never told the truth on certain target sets. He would be updated with intricate details as the operation went from phase to phase.

Each phase was normally 24 hours or so. This format was an insurance policy and controlled damage-limitation. If he was caught and immediately tortured, it was accepted each operator would tell all that they knew.

There were parameters in place to control the release of information but Decker and his colleagues were playing the big boys' game with big boys' rules. That's why they were in the business.

Decker was having trouble really nailing the exact reason why they would come all the way down here to get him.

How did they know he had cracked their existence for sure? Wouldn't they just think that this was just his imagination sticking to what he knew best, embellishing an idea into a clandestine operation or did he genuinely believe they were an active, deniable asset. There was still no proof, only two shadows behind him.

Right two men, maybe four.

Weapons? Longs or shorts, I couldn't see…

Mode of transport? On skis.

How do they want to kill me?

They would know my sleep routine, I would have done it that way.

So they kill me then what?

Extraction plan?

Who is going to meet them, where and when? They have to be sneaky as fuck down here. The South Pole station is paranoid as it is, let alone a load of blokes turning up mob-handed then disappearing soon after. Activity is monitored down here I think pretty tightly, but I may be wrong.

Unless this is fully backed by the US and they're using assets at the station in partnership, this is a deniable operation. Everyone involved will have a cover story to protect random activity or out-of-place requests to move around the ice.

At this moment gut instinct tells me two men are following me to kill me. Like the hackles on a dog's back rising when danger was all around, he was feeling the tension.

Do they know that Trans-Ant are trying to meet me tomorrow night? We arranged this days ago as I planned to cover 20 miles a day and they were heading 50 miles north of the Pole.

Another paranoid but sanely possible thought passed through him.

Trans-Ant? Are these guys involved in all this?

What Si? Mike, John and especially Dave? He was an ex-Marine, surely not. They would never have got so friendly with me back in Punta Arenas during the three weeks we were delayed together. They flew in one day after me and their expedition has been planned for two years. They were also here three years ago.

Nah not possible. They're not involved in this and they could be my only lifeline out of here. Who knows about the RV? Steve Jones and Trans-Ant team. Have they posted that I am meeting them bearing in mind people don't know where I am and this RV would put everyone at ease, as they will probably give me another solar panel to continue the expedition?

Because I have no communications, will this exposure be highlighted in their blogs and the explorer's website?

Fucking hell, I hope the guys on my tail have overlooked this.

Trans-Ant are good guys, seasoned adventurers and they could have killed me out at the hotel on many a pissed-up night out, when they carried me back to my room if they were involved.

My only concern is, no it's not a concern really, they are in the middle of nowhere right now, they can't have an insider or can't pick anyone up to meet me?

Go with your instinct remember Harry.

Right that's it Trans-Ant are clean, that's where I am going but I have to burn off time to not get there early as I have nowhere to run once I'm at the RV.

The Pole is another 50 miles plus, after the RV. That's too long for me to make that so I have to make it to the RV even if it kills me.'

There were no two ways about it, he was in for some extreme suffering physically. The RV was still 36 miles away but it was too risky being there before 1830 tomorrow night.

It was his next move that would require extreme balls of steel.

Knowing they would wait till he was asleep later, would give him a good head start with what he was starting to concoct in his mind.

A dummy tent pitch is my first plan of action. I can stop as normal, pitch my tent and behave as I would do normally. They would surely hold back to anticipate my clockwork 1830 finish then move in about midnight to kill me.

So if I pitch my tent as normal but ditch all my equipment apart from the skis and poles plus my large backpack... Decker gritted his teeth, he would take what he called mission essential kit to survive for two days or so in this shitty weather to make the RV with Trans-Ant.

As he skied back along to his pulk he played out the scenario.

'Pitch the tent; keep an eye out in case they make a move. In this weather they might, but why take the risk? They know I will stop and pitch.

Next what do I need to be as lightweight as possible as I have to try and out-ski these guys and I have 600 miles under my belt and being ski-fit doesn't matter, they are fresh.

I will have to get the cookers on and melt snow for water before I leave, this will be a vulnerable point but I will keep my guard up, this is unavoidable.

Water in all three bottles, four or five flapjacks, that's nutrition sorted.

Bothy bag and roll-mat for survival shelter and shovel to dig a snow trench. That's my lifeline in case the mother of all storms comes in. In fact I will take the tent inner and spare poles...

GPS, compass and a few batteries to get me to the RV.

Warm North Face jacket for insulation.

What do I have to kill these people with?

I need to kill these fuckers badly if I can't out-run them.

A slow torturous death wouldn't be enough to compensate the years of trauma they have inflicted.

All I have is my Leatherman knife blade, wire from my repair kit, tent pegs? Tent cord? Not much really if I have to defend against an M4 rifle or pistol, I can only assume they're carrying weapons.

Ah, actually I have my hunting knife, well all six inches of it. Thank god I didn't leave it at cache one like I was planning. This may be all I have.

Inside he knew he wouldn't have the steam to outrun them if they were fresh and competent skiers. Again he thought of another team being in front of him. Suddenly Decker realised how they'd tracked him down. He caught his breath for a second before instantly figuring out how to entrap them right back, if he had the balls to execute it, as it was a one shot, one deal affair.

'They must have seen my 127 degree bearing comments. All they will have to do is take the back-bearing from the Pole and it will lead them to me. This must be how these guys found me, unless they have come straight from the Pole and overshot my position, turned around to come back and look for me?

This scenario made Decker rethink his initial plan of action.

Right, after I pitch the tent I will ski off then take a dogleg bearing to avoid a contact to my immediate front, in case a second team is tracking my back-bearing to box me in from both sides. A dog-leg meant leaving his intended ski bearing, heading off 90 degrees right before turning left and skiing roughly along the same bearing.

This still means I have to burn off the time and make my approach to the Trans-Ant RV from another direction, not the one they're expecting.

Decker was sold on the fact this was a four- or six-man team and another two were in front of him. He had to assume the RV was known. It meant lots of extra miles but desperate times meant tactical measures.

Is the RV the right choice Decker?

Yes, stop questioning it.

They would definitely have some sort of cut-off plan in place for me if I headed straight to the Pole without any support, and I would be exhausted by then so the Trans-Ant RV it has to be.

Another paranoid thought entered the equation.

Trans-Ant? Could they have been infiltrated unknowingly?

If my killers have managed to get in with them it will still be covert. How would they plan to capture or kill me? Surely they wouldn't kill Andrew and his team just to get my scalp cleanly? Would they just have a quiet word with me so I wouldn't shout my head off and compromise them? Do they have a ransom or bargaining chip with me? Nah, nothing.

In fact I am not convinced Trans-Ant have been compromised. They are clean and it is my best option to get out of this mess. Put this to bed full stop, Trans-Ant is my safety net, not another problem. Sold.

Contingencies?

What contingencies do my pursuers have in place?

Weather for starters can easily delay my interception, or they could simply lose me out here.

They have already fucked up getting too close which confirms they definitely don't have the capability to monitor my current position real time, without attacking my satellite phone or beacon.

The team must be small to limit exposure. Only a few people come here each year to the point everyone knows each other's business, or story as to why they're down here. Union Glacier base camp is a classic 'everybody knows everybody's business'.

How do they actually want to kill me, and how do they cover it up if that's what they plan?

Shoot me, poison or even drug me, that's a classic these days. Maybe that's it, capture me to get all the information I have then inject me?

That way it looks like hypothermia, I said on my blog it's a fine line here between pushing a little too hard to the point I may not notice exposure setting in. At this point all logical thought processes are lost, along with feeling. Next thing is hypothermia, then death.

I only have a 6-hour window to meet Trans-Ant and if I don't turn up it doesn't matter, that's what we agreed due to weather and possibility of no communication. This would increase their window again by a few more days.

What is their last safe moment to take me down?

They must have some sort of transport in place. After they kill me they would need to get picked up fast and get the hell out of here without suspicion. The support elements will not come looking for me till at least another six days due to the plan I agreed with Steve Jones at ALE. Do they know this plan? Probably, so they have time on their hands.

Something doesn't add up.

I mean two, possibly four guys requesting that they do some scientific research or documentary-style affair around this area, it's too random, too short notice, things like this take months to put in place.

If I was Steve Jones I would be suspicious.

But they might not be using ALE?

They could again be under the cover of the US banner?

I just have a feeling that no one knows they're here. They must have come in under the radar either by the US cover, or by buying someone, even Ken Borak airlines to drop them off somewhere. I know Ken Borak is struggling financially too. Is he going to pick them up too if this is the case? It's flat enough about 50 miles from the Pole to touch down, not like this shit I've been skiing through for the last 100 miles or so.

Decker was trying to understand his pursuers' modus operandi to enable him to make the best judgment calls early. All this raw data was ricocheting around his head endlessly. Getting a grip of what was the most realistic scenario was painful.

Skiing onwards he knew for certain he would do the dummy tent stop, ditch all his technical kit and start skiing for his life with the bare minimum kit on him.

Knowing it was fast approaching 1830 hours, his daily stop to pitch the tent, he finalised his intentions. Running a quick checklist through his head of what kit he would take. Feeling a touch nervous about stopping for 30 minutes to melt snow for water, this was a risky but critical move. Crux of the bluff he thought, but that's why they are called 'cruxes' he grinned. Vulnerability came to mind, whilst he would frantically pack and melt snow they could stalk up and pounce unannounced if they skied like maniacs once they saw the red flysheet erected. Decker like the professional operator ran his latest plan through his already saturated head. In fact, he quickly ripped his notepad out of his top pocket and started scribbling frantically. As he ran the plan through, the dots all started to join.

Stop. Wait five minutes for a soak period; observe my rear with this weather bouncing in and out.

Prep all my kit for the move off before I erect the tent and melt snow. Leave the technical kit behind as planned.

All set, erect the tent as I would normally so they don't get suspicious if they come in for a recce first before the strike. Get 3 litres of water boiled and hydrate one meal and stow it for reserves along with a load of flapjack bars.

Head off on 127 degrees then switch to a dogleg after a mile to avoid any possible ambush by a team in front, coming at me on a back-bearing from the Pole direction. From then it's ski like fuck aiming to hit the RV in 36 hours coming in at the last safe moment. Also observe the RV first to see any suspicious activity.

However I know I will have to stop at some point and take these men on. Hopefully the weather will get worse allowing me to put an ambush in.

You are going to survive.

Decker once again felt the surge of blood and survival running through his veins that he had been deprived of for years. This was what he was born to do, kill against insurmountable odds. No one else could tell him that or take it away. These bastards were not as good as him. A feeling of indestructibility mobilised every single muscle to twitch with nervous anticipation.

Nervous anticipation was the sign he grew to respect.

It let him know he was alive and primed for action.

This was the trigger that he needed to stimulate his own self-worth back into a game he had to win no matter what.

'I will have to hit and run,' he whispered. 'One member at a time in this visibility is possible. Take one out and get any weapons they have on them if they are carrying. They will always be chasing me down, all I have to do is get the first one then I am truly back in the game. If I get a weapon they are fucked. I will murder these callous bastards in a heartbeat. The weather and environment is my equaliser at the moment, add a weapon and that's me, game over. In fact a weapon puts the end result beyond all reasonable doubt, my only problem then is getting out safely if they have cut offs. If Trans-Ant are clean and I RV, I think that's it, until I reach the mainland. That can wait. I have 36 miles to ski, at least two men to kill and Christ knows how many to evade after that. He paused for a sombre moment.

'I must make the RV with or without blood on my hands. Final.'

He stopped and took a brief moment to suck in the cold air, close his eyes and breathe out slowly. He did this three or four times leaving his eyes closed throughout. A process during his old days he'd called 'recalibration', during which everything that had happened in his life previously was of no consequence. The only script that needed to be running through his head was the one about to unfold before him.

All his thinking now was geared toward the immediate future. His brain would continually start updating the current scenario and how he could best adapt it.

The film frames were now running smoothly through his head.

He felt composed now and at peace with what he had to do. Search for solitude was a figment of the past; he had unwanted company with an unwanted agenda. He opened his eyes.

'You are going to survive.'

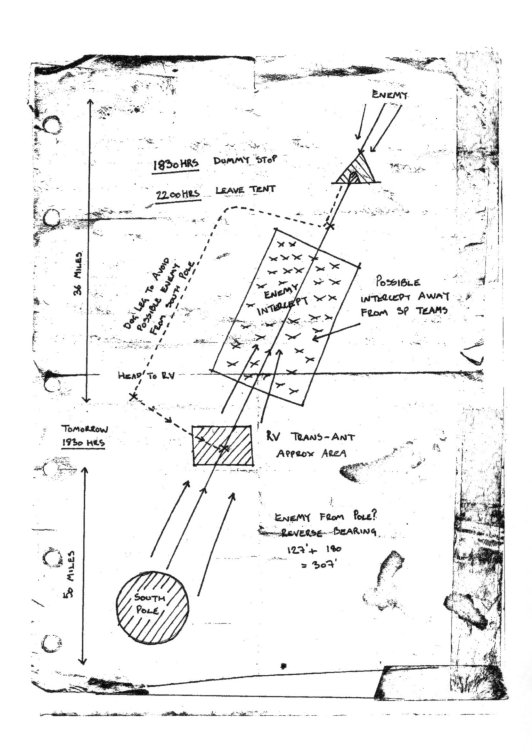

CHAPTER 30

'He's gone, fucking off-ski, literally Gerry,' Mick vented his anger down the sat phone.

'Run me through it Mick you're speaking in riddles, what's happened, where is WHITEOUT?' Gerry stuck to his usual monotone in an attempt to calm the situation from his tent at the South Pole, clearly Mick was in a flat spin about things.

'You say he is gone?' Gerry asked again. 'Give me a rundown of what's gone on between the FRV and the tent?'

'Tent. WHITEOUT's tent is empty and he knows we're on him, big style.'

'Explain Mick,' Gerry repeated.

'We both came in for the hit, everything was normal like he had stopped; pulk was there, tent surrounded with snow walls. We ambushed him, but when Robby jumped on the tent it was empty, not a trace. I just opened up the pulk to find that his skis and poles are gone. We can see his new ski tracks heading away from the tent too,' Mick ran out of breath.

'Okay does it look like he stopped for long or just set the tent up?'

'I don't know.'

'Cookers? Are the cookers there? If they are, are they still warm?' Gerry started firing on all cylinders. 'Diaries? If they are in the tent has he made an entry for tonight? Phones? Check the last call if he had any battery life left? Get on this now Mick,' Gerry impatiently requested.

Mick shouted at Robby barking the requests for immediate information for Gerry, cursing himself that in his heightened state of panic he hadn't thought to check those things beforehand.

'Robby is just checking Gerry.'

'Okay we need to know if he has seen you prior to stopping, or whether you spooked him when moving in close to the FRV. We can gauge how far he is ahead by what I have just requested.'

'Got you Gerry, nice one,' Mick saw the logic in the questions and felt his heart rate begin to decelerate.

Gerry's experience was showing. A man used to controlling high-level operations and human assets on the ground in real-time scenarios knew one thing. The operator in the heat of any high-pressure serial doesn't think as calmly or logically as the person controlling the operation, from the comforts of an operation centre, albeit this mini ops room was a four-man tent in the South Pole, the rules were the same.

'Anything Robby?' Mick shouted.

'Cookers are cold and connected to the fuel bottle so they have been used.'

'They have been used but cold Gerry,' Mick passed on.

'Phones?' Pointing to the phone he's holding he signalled to Robby.

'Got them but no life.'

'They're both dead Gerry.'

'Okay quickly put your spare battery in one and see what comes up. Also, make sure you locate his beacon and check whether the distress has been switched on if it's in the tent,' Gerry added.

Mick and Robby moved quickly knowing that time was passing by and this was now a pursuit that needed to be underway immediately.

Gerry remained on the end of the phone waiting for answers. He already knew them if WHITEOUT still had the edge about him. He would have ditched everything immediately and fled. But that would also compromise his position.

He also knew he wouldn't have hit his distress or contacted Trans-Ant or ALE either, but Gerry didn't know how exhausted he was, after everything he'd been put through he might have panicked and dropped his guard.

It was appearing not to be the case.

If he hadn't and he'd somehow pre-empted the strike, WHITEOUT would initially have limitless questions. How did they track him down out here, how they got inserted? Who they are using for logistics in the air or on the ground, how they are going to kill or capture him. Whether Trans-Ant have been infiltrated unknowingly before the RV tomorrow.

Gerry knew WHITEOUT was thinking all of this and more, he also knew that Sully would be thinking the same and extra.

The picture Gerry had in his head was WHITEOUT now on the run heading toward the RV with Trans-Ant, or straight to the Pole on a death march.

'Gerry,' Mick called out.

'Shoot mate,'

'Fuck all, phone batteries aren't compatible nor is our charger. Beacon here but no distress signal activated.'

'Diary? He has a Moleskine for his diary, and the two others we need, any sign?'

A few more moments passed.

Robby walked over to Mick as quickly as he could with a notebook. The current page was open, held back by the black elastic page divider strip.

'We have it Gerry, the diary.'

Mick paused.

Silence.

'He knows we're on him for sure,' Mick muttered.

'What Mick, any entry?'

Looking at the clean page of WHITEOUT's diary Mick read the passage from Dec 20th. Today.

All silent in anticipation, Gerry with Sean on his shoulder listening in.

An SAS soldier will fight where he is told to fight, but an SAS soldier will always win wherever he fights. Good luck.'

Silence ensued as Mick watched Robby's face drain a little more of colour, and gritted his teeth to will his not to do the same.

Gerry broke the silence down the phone: 'Let's not get bogged down in his psychological warfare. Let's keep thinking about the facts that we know to be true. You have weapons, his set of ski tracks and a shit load more energy than him. He is only four hours ahead Mick so get on his tail and take him down. Caution as always, but let's fucking end this operation within the next 12 hours.' Gerry barked his orders before Mick had time to think of any more questions that might cause delay.

'We've got it.' Mick out of his blind panic checked in. 'We'll ditch the pulk and go light with our daysacks. We have enough gear to keep us alive out here, and we won't be stopping for any rest periods until I have his fucking head on my ski-pole spike.' Mick was enraged, far from calling in any excuses to avoid closing in on Decker. His blood was boiling. Decker was a dead man walking in Mick's eyes. The rivalry between South African

Special Forces and the British SAS was about to enter a whole new meaning.

Mick looked at Robby who was listening in and nodded.

'Right we're off Gerry. Will call when we have him. I will keep one phone on in case HQ track his position somehow and you contact us immediately.'

'Okay Mick, speak soon.'

Mick turned to Robby, 'Ditch that pulk, we're just taking daysacks otherwise we won't catch him. Take the survival gear out with a few days' worth of rations, the cooker and a pot to melt snow.'

'Got it.' Robby knew time was of the essence and knew exactly what to pack as they had discussed such a scenario happening.

All packed Mick gave Robbie the nod and they were off. There was no need for a quick brief, they had covered it all and Mick was fuming. He didn't want any questions off Robby now. All he wanted to do was ski as fast as humanly possible to make up the deficit with WHITEOUT.

After 30 minutes the terrain was becoming chaotic posing difficult drops of 10-20 feet. This slowed them slightly but they rested in the knowledge that it would also substantially stall WHITEOUT's progress as he also negotiated the safest route.

Mick remembered Conrad mentioning that the terrain between the 87-degree line and the Pole was notorious for these brutal knife-edge drops, and towering ice formations rising out of the ground. This was all becoming another grim reality when it was the last thing they needed.

WHITEOUT's tracks seemed to blur in and out as he obviously chose his best line of advance.

Mick was a slave-driver at the moment running on pure hatred and desire to kill WHITEOUT. He felt insulted that WHITEOUT had discovered their presence and the note just added fuel to the fire burning deep inside Mick's ego.

If he was honest the blistering pace was more to do with righting a wrong as fast as possible, than executing a personal vendetta. He had let Sully down and was paranoid Gerry was fuming about this lack of caution, not to mention what Sully's reaction would be. Correcting this mistake in super-quick time was critical to regaining credibility.

Mick drew to a halt at the edge of a huge drop.

Robby closed in behind him.

'WHITEOUT has skied down this without any problems by the look of his ski tracks. Cleanly exiting the run out without evidence of him falling.' Mick turned around. 'You okay with this Robby?'

'Yeah, I think so,' Robby cocked his head sideways to judge the steepness.

'Let me ride it out first. Once I am at the bottom follow me down,' Mick instructed.

The drop fell away steeply into the low-lying fog, gradually flattening out straight back into a load of sastrugi obscuring exactly where WHITEOUT's tracks headed off. Only following the steep drop down would give them the clues to his next ski-leg direction.

Mick was deliberating hard, once he entered the fog WHITEOUT could be there waiting; tapping his Glock on in his drop harness, should he hold it as he skied down to preempt WHITEOUT having a go?

Still motionless, Mick paused before taking on the steep descent, the pace they had maintained was so fast both he and Robby had undone their jackets exposing their base-layer t-shirts, both of them covered with a film of sweat beads that were radiating steam. They were poised like two ski jumpers psyching themselves up for the 60kph ice track that lay beneath their skis.

Without warning Mick went for it with his Glock still holstered. Adopting the classic telemark offset stance he rapidly gained traction and hurtled down the slope, arms spread wide to aid balance. Looking like he was going to pile in with a nervous trip, he managed to stay upright and glided to a halt. 'Phew,' he muttered under his breath. Those 20 seconds of concentrating to stay upright had to be the only 20 seconds he had forgotten about WHITEOUT. As he entered the run-out area he was quick to grab his Glock and cover the area to his front. Everything was clear. Looking over his shoulder he raised his poles in the air letting Robby know to crack on.

Acknowledging the signal Robby adjusted his goggles and started to slide forward to the edge.

Bracing himself, he bounced a few times to relax his tensed-up legs, shook his shoulders out and took a deep breath. Correcting his posture he took one quick last glance behind him, through his steamed-up goggles he caught a glimpse of a blurred figure three feet away.

One millisecond later his thoughts disappeared as he felt the freezing cold serrated blade of a knife being rammed into his face with 80kg of kinetic force behind it. Piercing through his goggles effortlessly the blade punctured into his right eyeball, then further into his socket. Before he could even register the excruciating pain of his eyeball being torn to shreds by the serrated blade and shearing into the eye socket bone, the knife was withdrawn.

Robby screamed out in complete shock. Trying to see what was happening from his one remaining eye whilst stumbling on his skis the blade was now being driven home into the left side of his windpipe. He naturally lifted his hands up to grab the implement. Before his hands even left his ski pole loops the blade was dragged forcefully across his windpipe in a saw-like action, his cartilage causing resistance and agonising pain initially as he remained still partially conscious, feeling his hands flake back to his sides.

Seconds later the towering strength of WHITEOUT's right arm behind the knife severed his windpipe with an almost blunt cutting motion. Standing behind Robby now, holding his head with his left arm to steady him, the knife ripped out cleanly throwing small pieces of human flesh and blood through the air.

Robby dropped to the ground, completely dead. His right ski unclipped and slid away over the edge of the drop.

Decker crouched over him, saw the ski disappear over the edge. Witnessing the bloodbath implode across the icy surface. He was slightly shocked by the brutality of the murder he had just committed. He remained still, it had been a long time since he'd acted in this manner and now he realised what he'd always known, the skills and killer instinct were never lost. Though the emotional vacancy he'd acquired as a seasoned killer years ago was not quite tuned in yet, this slight delay registering this immediate return to the dirty game of war, took a few seconds to digest.

'Robby!' His comrade screamed out grabbing Decker's attention.

He remained silent, looking at the edge. Aware that the other remaining guy could probably see the steam rising up from the dead man's arterial blood as it met with the freezing air. The stench was vile.

A cracking sound of a bullet passing his right ear instantly awakened him from his moment of thought, followed quickly by another. He physically felt it fly past him due to the air dispersion created by the huge velocity the projectile created.

Decker's proactive instincts kicked in. 'Fuck,' he yelled as he instantly hit the deck and started scrambling around on the floor giving himself orders. 'One down Decker you've got the other one to go, what weapon is it?' Judging the weapon could help him judge the distance between him and the other guy on his tail.

Was it a high-calibre rifle or a pistol?

Lying next to this motionless body and looking towards the edge of the bank a load of ice fragments were sprayed up into his face, another bullet that was meant to kill him. Shit. Things were getting desperate, he needed to search this Robby guy for a weapon. Due to the long white overalls the pistols had not been visible to him when they had both passed him earlier.

Frantically searching the body he found what he was looking for, trying to pull the pistol free from the holster he struggled to undo the frozen Velcro. A novice mistake by this guy letting it freeze, it was now stalling his chances of drawing the pistol and fighting back with equal firepower.

He knew the other guy would be closing in, moving back towards the bank, weapon trained on where he last saw him pop his head up. As soon as he had a shot he was dead for sure, as he was only 40 or so feet away.

Finally breaking the frozen Velcro he held the pistol in his right hand, splaying himself out on the ground as flat as he could not daring to lift his head he knew he only had one option left.

If the other guy was over the bank with a rifle or pistol aimed directly at him, even if he crawled away a few metres and popped up at a different position, the man over the bank would get the drop. It was a simple rule of angles; you fire a pistol by aiming it from eye level unless you're a Libyan freedom fighter, firing an AK-47 from above your head or from around a corner. His thought process was entering another rapid decision cycle that would dictate his next move, he needed to decide what to do quickly as to get it wrong could have catastrophic consequences, he knew the other guy would be closing in and fast and would think nothing of seeing him off the second he had a shot, although that was a steep and slippery climb that he'd hoped at least one of them would go down at a time.

Alternatively he could crawl back stand up and approach the edge with the weapon trained, but his head would appear a nanosecond before he had an arc to fire on, without hitting the edge of the bank in front of him.

Again that would be too risky, this man over the bank was obviously a professional and would be predicting this sort of shit.

'Ah fuck it.' With the pistol still in his right hand he crawled like a maniac for 20 metres then got up and started running towards an ice statue without looking back.

As soon as he got close enough he dove the last few metres into the safety of cover. If this guy tracking him had a high-velocity rifle, a burst of ammunition would rip through the ice formation instantly.

Looking around the right-hand side of the ice statue he could still see the motionless body. Weapon poised for the second figure to come over the brow he waited.

A few minutes passed, still nothing.

Hands and fingers now numb and cold he flexed his trigger finger to ensure it was still functioning; he'd taken his gloves off to stab that guy. Wanting to shake his hands out to get the blood circulating he knew he couldn't risk taking his right hand off the pistol grip. So he continued to just keep the trigger finger flexing a little inside the trigger guard without pulling the trigger.

In the opposite direction Mick's weapon was also pointing at the brow of the bank, he waited. He knew Robby was dead and did not bother to call him and compromise his exact position to WHITEOUT.

Known as a Mexican stand-off in the business, he knew that neither of them were going to play their hand first. Mick pushed all thoughts of being cold out of his head.

After three minutes the adrenalin started to drain itself from Decker amplifying the cold.

He'd known after an hour of skiing that he would not out-ski them. Noticing the severity of the terrain and being fruitfully aware he had at least two hours to put in an ambush, he had chosen his ground wisely.

Known as a classic double-back he'd skied down the steep bank and continued for another 100-metres so it looked to his trackers' eyes like he had skied onwards hoping that they would continue to follow.

Yet after 100 metres he'd made a huge loop West and moved back to the top of the bank placing himself behind the huge ice statue. From this position he knew he could see who was actually tracking him close up as they were bound to stop and discuss the drop. He could confirm the numbers, weapons, even accents of people he knew from the past maybe, even a clue as to confirm why he was being targeted. Taking his skis off and priming his knife it would just been a waiting game. Behind the ice statue now he was acutely aware that he was on his back foot at the moment and had to make a decision. Taking a quick bearing on his compass, he decided to move and began to run as fast as he could between all the ice statues in front of him for cover. His first priority was to create a gap between him and the other guy.

If this guy had a rifle he realistically had a good 300-metre kill zone in this weather, anything more and the erratic wind and visibility would start playing havoc with his accuracy. This was the minimum distance of separation deemed safe in his mind. He was erring on the side that the other guy only had a pistol, due to the fact that the snow bank he was nearly shot through earlier was not getting sprayed down with semi-automatic fire, or there was a chance that this guy didn't know his teammate was dead and was being cautious thinking that his colleague was behind the bank too and incapacitated? Either way Decker moved as quickly as he could.

Mick slipped his skis off slowly whilst maintaining his aim on the bank and at last he saw WHITEOUT.

He slowly backed off to another ice statue behind and like WHITEOUT took cover and trained his weapon back on the area of the perceived threat.

He waited.

After ten minutes he made the decision that WHITEOUT must have headed off somewhere, especially if he was starting to shiver uncontrollably like Mick, there was no other option but for him to run and get warm. Mick had the same dilemma with his fight against the cold plus he couldn't let WHITEOUT get away again.

But he also knew WHITEOUT may be waiting for him to come up and inspect Robby's body. Surely a colleague would do this? Check his wingman?

Another ambush in the space of 15 minutes at the exact same point?

No thanks Mick thought, that's an amateur's mistake.

As much as it killed Mick to not see Robby he knew he had to register the co-ordinates of his body, part company, make a call then loop back in and chase WHITEOUT again.

This time they would both be on foot, both with pistols with the identical aim of killing each other or put more elegantly, surviving. Mick couldn't risk staying on skis even though he could potentially catch up with WHITEOUT faster. Skis restricted his mobility at close quarters, especially if he got jumped again or shot at with minimal, if any, warning.

He made the call.

'Gerry it's all gone fucking wrong, Robby is dea,.' Mick quietly told Gerry down the phone.

'What the fuck?' Gerry responded totally caught off guard.

'He came from nowhere; all I saw was him behind Robby at the top of a bank ramming a knife into his neck. I think Robby is dead.'

'Where is Robby now and what about WHITEOUT?' Gerry asked.

'I'm in cover behind an ice formation looking back at where Robby was taken out. I don't know if WHITEOUT is near him or not, but I assume he has Robby's pistol. What the fuck is all this Gerry?'

'You have got to get WHITEOUT Mick, I know it's tough but he needs killing, don't worry about anything else just kill him,' Gerry commanded again, trying to get Mick out of his state of shock and back into business mode.

That inflated ego that most South African Special Forces house, had just had a major puncture. Mick's bottle was in question now and he knew it.

'Not sure I can do this Gerry, I need back-up he's too sharp out here, he could be watching me now.'

'Mick take a few deep breaths, have a moment, come on let's get some composure.'

Mick breathed heavily in and out a few times, the vapour mist rising with each exhalation as he continued to erratically dart his eyes everywhere looking for WHITEOUT.

'Gerry I could be dead in a few minutes or hours, what the fuck are we doing here, give me at least that, you owe it to us. Robby, he's dead for Christ's sake,' Mick began pleading with Gerry.

'Mick, listen, WHITEOUT is theoretically our most wanted at the moment, he is a man we need killing now, today. He's a loose end that is inhibiting the activation of the most covert-psychological mind manipulation programme that will can kill terrorisim from within. It's a game changer. He was an intricate part of the programme. We need him dead mate. I know you're in pain and may be doubting yourself, but you can do it. He got lucky with Robby. Remember he is exhausted. You need to start tracking him again and take him down. CAN YOU DO THIS MICK?'

Mick digested all that Gerry said and took a few more breaths gradually regulating his pattern of breathing.

'Mick, face the facts mate, he is going to hunt you down and want some answers or he may just kill you without question. It's a catch 22 and the only way out is for you to kill him, I can't help you at the moment and he's not going to wait around. You getting all this?'

'I'm good, I'm good,' Mick responded without sounding like he was hyperventilating this time.

'That's it Mick, let's get the game-head on now buddy. He is either going to start moving fast to the Trans-Ant RV in which case we will sort it out then, but between now and then you have to give chase as he might just fuck off on a tangent somewhere else, we can't predict his behaviour so you need to get on it now.' Gerry was trying to get Mick moving.

'Okay Gerry I'm just thinking, give me a second.'

'Mick,' Gerry shouted, 'he's just murdered Robby, your close friend, a friend whose family don't have a husband or father now. Now if you want your family to suffer the same consequences then keep thinking, but thinking won't get you anywhere. Get on the offensive now, take the upper hand again and bury this guy.'

'Fucking too right Gerry,' Mick responded aggressively, snapping into gear. 'Okay but I want in, full-time when this is finished Gerry, this is a massive undertaking now and Robby is dead remember. We can't keep doing this shit without knowing how deep we are.'

'Not a problem, you have my word, you're in. Just get WHITEOUT and then get yourself to the EP site afterwards, you hear me?'

'That's a deal,' Mick confirmed.

'You can do it Mick, you can do it. Now sort yourself out and end this fucking nightmare, you owe it to Robby.'

'That's me I'm out of here. Phone is still on. I'm moving now to pick up his tracks, out.' Mick killed the call and with his eyes barely blinking started moving on the ice to kill WHITEOUT.

CHAPTER 31

Mick had finally got his mettle together and started a right-hand loop to try and pick up WHITEOUT's tracks completely avoiding the scene of Robby's massacred body. Knowing that witnessing first hand Robby's murdered torso across the bloodstained ice, might make him reconsider this pursuit or supercharge his desire for a quick revenge.

He moved at a snail's pace knowing that it was possible for WHITEOUT to be bunkered down waiting for him to walk into his sights, and killing zone. The weather had moved in and now he could only see about five metres to his front.

Stopping immediately he realised he was being too hasty. This wasn't going to be a quick resolution or revenge killing. Patience was now the order of the day unless he wanted to meet the same fate as his fellow South African. A classic case of the hunter becoming the hunted, Mick was in a lonely void where his bravado couldn't hide the fact he was scared shitless. Every soldier needs his wingman to rely on, to turn to in times of desperation but this wasn't an option. For the first time in his life he was on his own and felt alone knowing he had to finish the job to survive, or fail and die.

★★★★★

Decker was finding it tough going underfoot as the ice conditions were fragile. A mixture of soft snow in between hard pack ice meant one second it was solid ice, affording good purchase the next he was up to his knees in snow.

Employing anti-tracking drills he was erratically moving from one ice formation to the other, constantly checking his rear, the same five-metre visibility was starting to take a strain. If he didn't check his compass or GPS direction arrows every 20 metres he would become easily disorientated chancing a head-on with this guy. 'Bring it on,' Decker thought under his breath forcing the words out against the catabolic windstorm that was now murderously in session, gusting winds of 70 mph straight at him, rocking and spinning his body.

Naturally dipping his head to avoid his mask getting ripped up off his face, he stuck to his bearing, moving left and right to confuse his tracker and keep him guessing. From the moment the shot was fired he knew that this person was not going to stop, he had to keep progressing till Trans-Ant saw him tonight.

This weather was the worst he had come up against in a good while and was starting to dictate his tactics. Any sane man knew it was only a matter of time before continuing would be suicidal, and stopping soon was the only option. Wind chill, the combination of the cold temperature and the wind, magnified the temperature drop. 'It must be at least minus 40,' he thought as he was staggering blindly. Visibility was zero, energy levels were running dangerously low and progress was stinted.

It had been nearly 90 minutes since he'd ripped that unsuspecting guy's throat clean out.

Decision point.

'I have to stop, get into some sort of snow trench and get my North Face jacket on or I'm going to die of hypothermia, not a fatal gunshot wound,' Decker mused to himself, finding a natural hollow in the ice pack was now his priority to shield himself from the wind. He faced the direction he had just travelled. He could only work this out by a back-bearing on his compass that just involved looking at the direction of the white end of the needle, as visibility was now at zero. This would be the direction of his pursuers' approach if he were still in pursuit and somehow following his tracks.

Mick would only find him now if he tripped over him such was the storm. His instinct honed by military training had told him to make the wise decision to survive and fight another day instead of continuing with the death march. It was again a waiting game. Only a weather window could set him free again to continue the manhunt.

Finding a hollow he sat crouched up and threw his huge North Face jacket on, knees tucked up inside. Wind still riding across his back, it was still bitterly cold but better than dying on his feet trying to evade

Mick. He took a look at his watch, 0403 hours. Just as he was about to close his eyes the crimping of compact snow underneath heavy-duty boots made him freeze as he peeked out to his front. Unable to react the boots were only metres away, three metres then two. How the hell had this guy managed to find him? How had he actually managed to keep going during this onslaught? Decker was in a complete state of shock, had his arrogance got the better of him? Was it due to the other guy being fresh, unlike him, or was he that pumped up and determined to revenge his mate's death he had adopted a crazed manic type of resolve to close in for the kill? Still motionless he was there finally on top of him. Paralysed he looked up hopelessly to see the legs above him. In a complete catatonic state he prepared himself for it to go dark when a mammoth gust of wind propelled a chunk of ice at his head waking him back to life and setting him free from the nightmare he just had endured.

'Fuck that was a vivid one.' Panicking then double-checking, Mick's imaginary legs in front of his face had gone. Ripping back his jacket sleeve he took a look at his watch.

0456 hours.

'Holy shit,' quickly checking the weather he looked outside of his jacket hood. Sighing with relief it was still a blank canvas, no change.

This whole experience was wreaking havoc with his mind and his impatience was eating away at his consciousness. 'I need to keep moving, I have to, I can't drop off again.'

Logic batted this thought away.

'Don't lose your nerve there is no way that he is moving in this weather. Only a team of at least three or four men would dare move in this, and normally that is only to rescue the stricken mountaineers like him, and only in the most extreme of circumstances. Stay here it will get better.' Reaching for his watch Decker set the alarm for 0600 to give him some much-needed sleep then shut his eyes again.

At 0620 hours he awoke with a shock.

'That's it I'm out of here, nice one with the alarm call dipshit I can't even hear myself think let alone hear the idle beeping of my watch shaking against my jacket.'

He checked the weather again, 5-10 metres visibility wind slightly weaker.

'This is it now, no excuses. That's workable out there, time to get your ass in gear and make this RV.'

With over two hours' rest he jumped up, stretched out and got a spurt on to try and warm up and also increase the distance before he decided what his plan would be to take his tracker down.

He made good progress, the ice pack was once again favourable underfoot and the visibility was opening with small breaks in the weather. He moved his feet faster knowing that the other guy would be feeling the same.

★★★★★

Mick stopped and knelt down. He could see the footprints of WHITEOUT but no sign of any blood, knowing his shots fired earlier were not effective.

Scanning his front the mist was as clagged in as ever. Rising to his feet he gingerly moved forward with his pistol up ready to fire the moment he saw WHITEOUT. Instinct told him he was close by. Moving in, out and around the ice boulders he sensed something was happening. Pausing he took cover behind the ice to centre himself.

Waiting and briefly checking over his shoulder, he looked to his front again and there he was. WHITEOUT was moving across his front slowly only just visible, probably ten metres away. Mick clenched his pistol hard as he saw him stop. Resisting the initial urge to pull the trigger, WHITEOUT then turned right so his back was facing Mick.

Fighting to compose himself Mick moved out of cover and slowly moved towards him not making the mistake of rushing in and firing too early.

'This is it, he's in my sights, stay calm,' Mick whispered to himself.

Five metres away, Mick barely breathing couldn't contain his adrenalin-fuelled instincts. His calm plan went out of the window as he pulled the trigger and shot 7-8 rounds straight into WHITEOUT's back. He watched as he began dropping to the ground falling to his knees first as another few rounds punctured his back. Mick ran forward then fired another barrage of rounds into the body that was now laying lifeless on its front in the snow.

Emptying his magazine, he breathed out hard, relieved, his chest burning.

245

He knew WHITEOUT was dead, as the figure remained splayed across the ice with blood starting to flow freely from it.

He paused then walked to WHITEOUT's legs. He felt a sharp blow to his right side with an immediate burning effect to match the feeling in his chest. The two sharp blows spun him violently making him drop his pistol.

Falling to the deck and trying to take stock of what was happening, he caught a glimpse of two figures clad in white overalls and holding rifles. Awaiting more muzzle flashes to come from the barrels indicating they were firing again to finish him off.

No more flashes came.

Face on the ice, grimacing in pain, Mick knew he was bleeding heavily. Looking up there were two or three figures closing in.

★★★★★

Decker felt as though he was flying as he moved down a gentle slope, so much so his eyes were fixated on the ground to the front of him, even so it was not enough to stop him tripping and catapulting himself through the air. Tumbling a number of times, and being stopped abruptly by another ice statue.

He got to his feet swiftly and started moving again before coming to an immediate halt, motionless. He pinched himself to ensure that this wasn't another hallucination triggered by a hypothermic state.

Nope this was real, this was happening. About 100-metres away he saw two figures standing up with their backs towards him. These guys were there, right to his front completely oblivious to his presence.

Gently dropping to one knee Decker pulled his pistol out whilst the other guys remained static looking at something on the ground. With the clag moving in and out, they were obscured at times, he was trying to piece it together.

One guy moved off ninety degrees to the right, he blinked confused. This was getting more interesting by the second. Squinting his eyes and concentrating once more he saw that two figures were lying on the ice. One had his hands behind his head as another figure knelt down to start searching him. The other guy on the floor was being cradled by another figure. He also noted they had white camo overalls on like the guy he killed earlier.

The figures were holding rifles, M4s possibly and had it trained on the man on the floor. It was now clear this man was a prisoner and maybe was about to be executed?

'Is that the other guy who was trying to kill me on the floor? Who's the other dead guy being cradled? In fact who the fuck are all these people?' He wondered.

These questions could wait. Looking behind him he started to move back slowly to greater cover. If these figures looked back now, he would be compromised in the open with a pistol against a high-calibre weapon that could easily shoot semi-automatically to the 100 metres where he was.

His heart beating rapidly, he kept his eyes transfixed on the two figures as he continued his cautious retreat to an ice block about 20 metres away. His pistol was no match now and didn't offer any danger at all to either of the men in front of him.

Currently this situation was helpless. It was one of those scenarios where the fight-or-flight mechanism chose wisely without hesitation.

'A little bit more Decker, nice and easy.'

Both figures still facing away oblivious to him creeping backwards, this close encounter was almost over.

The ice formation that was to the left of the people standing came to life as another figure in cam whites holding a rifle stepped out.

Decker's heart instantaneously missed a beat.

The actions of the new figure said it all as his weapon was raised and aimed directly in his direction. Wind shielded any communication being made by the figures, but the two figures standing now also turned and faced him.

Without hesitation Decker turned and legged it to the nearest ice formation.

Bracing himself for the impact of 5.56 bullets entering his torso from behind, he tensed up, gritted his teeth and just ran.

Looking at the cover he was heading for, he saw the ice splinters jump up metres to his left and right side. Experience told him to stay on his flight path as he launched himself hard off his right foot into a last life-saving effort, diving three metres directly to his point of potential safety.

Jagged shards of ice merged in with the bullets as they continued to splash up around him. He was expecting the ice statue he was hiding behind to get decimated along with his head within seconds so he crawled away from it.

Miraculously this didn't happen but without delay there were more blisters of ice spraying up five metres away pinning him down.

'They are not trying to kill me, they want me alive, they would have got me by now, 100 metres away is .01 of a second for a bullet travelling at 960 metres per second. Four men on foot with one prisoner and another dead? I have minutes to get the fucking hell out of this entire situation that I have no idea about.'

No bearing, just sheer adrenalin-fuelled energy transported his body across the ice as fast as possible. Heading for more cover to shield him from view, he ran and didn't look back for at least two minutes. Falling down trenches, but picking himself up instantly he literally ran for his life.

A huge ice formation was to his front and he chose it as his next point for a quick rest.

Immediately chunks of it were shot to pieces as he heard the familiar crack of a bullet travelling past his ears.

He turned to look back and saw two figures about 200 metres away, before the mist obscured them, only to be sighted again seconds later.

'This is fucking insane but keep going you're 200 metres ahead. The ground is perfect for evasion and they have a prisoner to deal with.'

He rationalised with himself. 'By the looks of it they aren't trying to kill me and that's a fucking first in my life when an enemy has been shooting towards me.'

Another final charge of 20 metres got him to another trench that ran deep and seemed to continue for around 50 metres to the right. Without hesitation he headed right down into it unsighted to the gunmen, his internal rhetoric keeping him focused.

'Let's get to the end of this trench pop up and head off in a different direction, even back towards where I came from. What is going on? Who are these guys? Who is the one on the floor, it has to be the other killer…'

Decker began praying for another bout of bad weather and no visibility, but that wasn't happening, all he had was 100-300 metres in and out, and it was getting clearer.

★★★★★

The man in pursuit breathed calmly and followed WHITEOUT's tracks right to the point of entry to the trench. It was a 5-metre drop down into the trench system that was narrow and veered off to the right.

The man continued looking down into the trench but did not drop in. Scanning his weapon and walking along the top, he looked for WHITEOUT.

About 6 foot 2, fully clad in arctic warfare equipment consisting of white camouflage clothing wearing a commando cache over it, he was military. Face covered with a white balaclava and goggles he remained static just scanning the area to his front looking for WHITEOUT. 'Brilliant,' the man sighed. He muttered into his radio to his colleague covering from behind before jumping down in to the trench.

'I need a condor moment,' Decker thought, like a time-out in basketball to figure out your next play. He was feeling slightly disorientated and tried to establish his bearings. With no time to boot up his GPS he quickly checked his compass. Looking at due south, the general direction of the RV, he decided to get moving towards it.

The terrain was a mass of trench systems, sharp drops and short areas of flat ground. Despite the moment of complete turmoil he thought, 'It could be worse I could still be pulling that fucking iron bath of a pulk across this shit hole.'

Keeping glued to the compass was essential as the terrain kept throwing his bearings as he ran, climbed and crawled his way amongst the labyrinth. It felt so slow with the sudden bursts of explosive energy creating lactic acid that only served to fatigue his muscles quicker. Rubbing them to keep them warm and the circulation going, he knew he needed them more than ever to haul himself up sides of steep drops. Crawling rapidly over flatter areas to avoid detection was draining him quickly to exhaustion again. Only his mental resolve and focus from his previous life would help him to once again exceed previous thresholds.

'Fuck this crawling. If they see me they see me. Just head on the bearing now and keep looking over your shoulder. No more silly buggers jumping around, I just need to stay a good distance away and out of their sights. Remember, I don't think they want me dead.'

Pep talk over, he adopted a normal walking pace and started to take each obstacle in his stride. He had to play the long game. Becoming delusional due to exhaustion would get him killed within hours, at worst, minutes. It was all about pacing himself now and using his energy conservation to keep his body in check with a fresh and re-focused mind.

CHAPTER 32

Soon after intercepting Mick's report of Decker's empty tent to Gerry, the Russian CO ordered his intercept team to fly to the co-ordinates of the tent. They touched down, cleared up the mess, taking all of the kit.

During the 4-hour flight they also intercepted the call that confirmed Robby had just been killed. Not only did this confirm that this whole situation unfolding was of strategic value, it gave them a closer co-ordinate to aim for to begin their very own intervention operation.

Managing to fly close and avoid a catastrophic air disaster due to the weather, the 5-man team were dropped off within a few hundreds metres of Robby. Forced to take off, fly high and fast out to the area, the helicopter was now stranded until the weather window opened again.

The Russians were on their own for a while, no back-up, no support. Just increased firepower, energy levels and expert knowledge of the Antarctic terrain, although even they were starting to get cold on the trail of Decker and Mick.

Ivan, the Russian Spetsnaz Captain, closed the remaining good eye of the man they knew to be called Robby, he then inspected the gaping knife wound. Judging from the death scene he figured Decker was unarmed at the point of kill. It was clear he was a ruthless operator that looked to be surviving on instinct and improvisation. Ivan squashed the torn eyeball that was hanging on his cheek by the cartilage and tendons back into its rightful resting place, back into its socket using his right thumb.

Ivan clocked the empty holster on Robby's leg, working on the assumption that Decker was now armed with a pistol and spare magazine. As he looked at Robby's face Ivan pictured how the fateful scene had unfolded. Was this man Decker desperate when he did this? Or was he thriving in the moment?

Ivan assumed that the other guy known as 'Mick' who made the satellite phone calls would only be armed with the same type of weapon as his dead partner, as there was no evidence of larger calibre weapons. No 5.56mm or 7.62mm magazine pouches. This was good news as it meant the threat to his team with their superior weapon systems was low. The manhunt could continue safely in the knowledge that they had potentially huge stand-off capability against two men with 9mm pistols and a few hunting knives.

Not hanging around to cordon off the area and create a crime scene, Captain Ivan quickly made the task simple. He and his fellow operator would follow the tracks of both men to capture them. It didn't take them long to see the footprints of two men, heading in the same direction.

Staying on skis and roughing it out in the weather that had grounded the two men, the Russians closed in within an hour.

As the weather cleared they strapped their skis to their backpacks and started tracking on foot again. Once they had either men in their sights, a burst of ammunition around their legs would gain their capitulation pretty quickly.

As Ivan followed his lead scout tracking the prints of Decker or Mick through the thick fog he was shocked to suddenly see him drop to the floor. The sound of the gunshots were muted in the wind, but it was clear by his jerking body that he had been shot multiple times with small flesh segments spitting across the ice.

Ivan brought his rifle up on aim trying to figure out what was happening when he saw a figure come across his front from behind an ice boulder. Holding and shooting a pistol again as he moved at the lead scout Ivan took two shots.

Seeing the body spin then collapse to the floor Ivan closed in fast to dominate. The snow-draped figure lay helpless before him, his pistol on the ice, top slide to the rear after expending all his bullets.

Rippimg his mask and balaclava off, he instantly recognised him not to be Decker from the images of his face from his blogs, Ivan looked down at him whilst another soldier checked the guy who had been killed by Mick.

'Stay still Mick, don't fucking move,' Ivan shouted at him.

Mick returned his gaze, clearly accepting his fate.

'Who the hell is WHITEOUT?' he whispered before the initial butt stroke across his face and numerous kicks in the head attempted to produce any groundbreaking intelligence.

251

Ivan was convinced Mick was who he said he was after spilling the story about working for an unknown agency tasked to hunt down a man known as WHITEOUT. Clearly Harry Decker.

Another 10 minutes of beatings getting the same repeated answers and Ivan had to get moving again.

Instructing one of his soldiers to cuff Mick's hands with zip ties they needed to leave him and pursue the tracks of Harry Decker again.

Quick as a flash, another member of his Russian team stepped out from the ice statue urgently stating that he had seen WHITEOUT in the distance backtracking towards cover, so started firing.

No capitulation.

No hands in the air from Decker.

Just an instantaneous reaction to get out of their killing zone.

Looking down at Mick, Ivan said 'I guess that's the man who killed your second-rate comrade. Yes?'

Mick's face was covered in claret with visible bruising setting in, he looked bemused.

'As they say in the books Mick,' Ivan paused as his colleague emptied another 10-12 rounds in Decker's direction. "You can take the man out of the SAS, but you will never take the SAS out of the man." I think you people forgot that he was a ruthless killer hey?' Reaching for his pack of cigarettes, he pulled one out, tapped the end on the packet. Looking at Mick he continued: 'Is this Decker man crazy? Or is he a fucking genius that you people just can't catch, not even on his own down here?'

He rapped an order out to his colleague in Russian and without hesitation two men ran past him weapons at the ready, clearly in pursuit of Decker.

Turning to see his comrades head off into the abyss to hunt down Decker, Ivan got his zippo lighter out, shielded himself from the wind and cupped the cigarette and lighter to spark one up.

Sucking in his first drag and blowing it out, he sighed then pulled out his small notepad with his left hand and started thumbing through the pages.

'Here it is Mick,' he announced.

Mick managed eye contact, though his right eye was almost closed due to the bruising from the last ten minutes of field interrogation.

The Russian started reading from his notepad.

'Mick, listen: "'He's a loose end that is inhibiting the activation of the most covert mind manipulation programme that will can kill terrorism from within…'It's a world game-changer in so many different ways I can't explain. We need him dead mate."'

Ivan watched as Mick winced, obviously recognising the words to be exactly what Gerry uttered to him over the sat phone earlier.

'Maybe that tells you why we want this man alive, and not so dead like the British government want him, hey Mick?'

CHAPTER 33

Thundering across the Antarctic wastelands, both of the AT44 Toyota Hilux Arctic trucks did a good job of churning up ice and snow, leaving a cloud of white dust in their wake.

Heading directly to the Pole the AT44s aggressively battled one another to gain supremacy as they approached the final straight, in what could have been an epic final to an ice-tracked Grand Prix.

The sheer arrogance, carelessness and competitiveness of the two trucks' movements reflected the men's personalities that drove them. 'Not long now till we see Decker boy.' Andrew grinned as his team whooped and hollered.

Successful businessmen, hard and fast playboys, with a true tenacity for adventure was the absolute core of the Trans-Antarctica Team's philosophy.

Delayed for three weeks with Decker at the Hotel Cabo de Hornos in the town centre of Punta Arenas, the group of them quickly gained a reputation for being seasonal hard chargers. Fine dining in the evening to soak up the beer consumed after lunch, they hijacked Decker into their very own mini rock band road trip across the Punta Arenas district.

Decker had done his preparation by this time in Punta Arenas and was more concerned with increasing his body fat for the expedition ahead whilst he was delayed waiting for his ride in.

Andrew, co-owner of Trans-Ant threw a pint of Heineken in his hand one night, rudely interrupting Harry's daily blog from the hotel table he sat at religiously, he didn't blink.

Simply slapping down the top cover of his laptop Decker had nodded his head, saying, 'Cheers Si,' and with that he'd joined the Trans-Ant road show.

Andrew and the guys grew to like Decker fast. A true modern-day hero in their eyes, he embodied everything they thought an SAS man could and should be. A quiet and private individual who had gravitas whilst maintaining complete modesty about him. The way he'd talked about his ambitious and life-threatening world record attempt with such matter-of-fact conviction gained the respect of all of them. Clearly a fearless individual who was somehow settling a score, or planning his own destiny to move forward in, and that was what Andrew loved about him. A man after his own heart Andrew thought as he charged the vehicle forwards casually over the ice.

An instant synergy formed between them all, whether this was eating over breakfast or propping up the bar at a local dark spot, Harry was one of them.

A few late-night drinking sessions had led him to vent some of his past angers and grievances to a team that sat around him in awe. Never disclosing the where, what or who most of the time, Harry would let the team live out their schoolboy dreams through his intricately crafted stories that would leave them always wanting more.

One moment he was breaching into a stronghold in Central Baghdad coming face to face with AQ suicide networks in order to free hostages, the next fighting his way out of an attempt by AQ to take him hostage during an undercover mission that resulted in it being a failed attempt, and another few less extremists to worry about.

Other stories centred around him narrowly getting out of situations that involved huge volumes of alcohol, fit girls and a few right uppercuts.

Decker had brought a beauty and romance to the war experience. To him it wasn't a diehard job, a war of attrition or simply kill-or-capture missions. It was his life, his journey on the road to mastery. War was the canvas in his life, one where each brushstroke was created by an operation, an experience or thought. On their last night in Punta Andrew had made a pact with Decker that they would meet in Antarctica before Trans-Ant headed home no matter where he was, just to say goodbye. He was going to honour that promise he thought. Catching the truck next to him signalling to slow down, they both drew to a halt.

Andrew in his Trans-Ant expedition clothing stepped out to greet Gerry and Sean. 'Hi guys, I'm Si,' as he outstretched his hand.

The man taking it spoke clearly: 'Hi Si, I'm Gerry, this is Sean, thanks for having us onboard.'

'Our pleasure, we're all one team down here. Let's get your kit on the trucks.' Andrew was keen to get a move on as they still had some scientific testing to do before they met with Decker later this evening. No one had heard from him for a day or so but Andrew was still heading for the RV he had made with him a few days back before his phone cut off at base camp with Steve. It was the last stop on Trans-Ant's expedition that had seen them break land-speed records across the continent, as well as gathering much needed scientific research. Nothing would stop Andrew making that RV. At roughly 1830 hrs they would find him, come hell or high water. In their eyes he was the man, the legend.

★★★★★

Decker stopped, he felt heavy on his feet and needed a moment to take in his new surroundings with the awe that they deserved. He was standing in a labyrinth of tunnels marked out by steep sharp drops into the abyss, it looked like the entrance to an icy maze at a theme park.

'This is exactly what Conrad was talking about, in fact it's the photos he showed me when he said guess where this is?' Decker paused longer, taking it in. They were the opposite of the mazes created by high, immaculately trimmed hedges at country estates that his parents used to take him to on Sundays. 'Dad wasn't chasing me like he used to either, when I craftily evaded his futile attempts to capture me.' The six-foot-two man mountain called Dad was now replaced by trained killers. Quite the change, Decker mused.

Now I am alone.

Now I am outnumbered.

Now I have inferior firepower and reach and I don't know who is who.

He laughed slightly as an image of his dad popped into his mind.

'These things are meant to test you son.' He heard his dad's voice ring out clear in his mind, like he always had done in any conflict zone or whenever he'd hit times of extreme adversity.

'You can only control what's happening now boy, never think of the past, just dream of the future and live in the now, control the now.'

Gosh those words have shaped my life, as the comforting voice interrupted him again.

'I never ever once doubted anything you attempted, I always knew you would do it.'

He was right I have never failed at anything. I have doubted myself but that was all part of the process of being human, that doubt reinforces self-belief and makes us who we are.

'It takes a real man to walk away from a fight than one to stand and fight son.' That last statement snapped him straight back into reality.

'Ha, god I wish you could see me now Dad. This is one fucking fight I can't walk away from. This is the only fight I have to walk straight into, if I ever want to pass on the wise words of wisdom you passed on to me.'

Memory lane over, Decker thought hard as he surveyed the terrain around him trying to establish another plan of action.

A thick ground fog that came up to his waist-height moved eerily through the labyrinth, the wind had died down and without it a deathly silence had crept in.

Moving at the same pace as the slow-flowing blanket of fog he reminded himself that every step he took was now vital, either from slipping off down a crevasse or turning a corner to find his pursuer waiting to meet him. He moved with caution, always training his pistol to his front. With so many sharp corners and changes in trench directions the man could appear at any moment. If he did, he was poised to take him down, the SAS training engrained into his every move. No warning shots or shouts to gain capitulation, just a clinical and highly accurate set of double taps aimed at the head if the guy was within ten metres. Any distance further was two to the body initially or as many as it took to ground him, so he was motionless and no longer a threat.

His direction was dictated by the maze now, not his compass or tactical intuition, Antarctica was again the master in his high-stakes battle.

He moved forward looking over his shoulder every few steps knowing a man with an M4 rifle could appear and start firing in his direction, killing him instantly, he went over his plan in his mind again.

'Right, I reckon they are both still on me but they will be spread out, the two other guys will be guarding the other man or taking care of bodies. They know I have a pistol. That tells them they have superior firepower and reach. They also know they will have to spread out to limit the threat I pose with this pistol. If they are within 5, 10, 20 metres of each other, I will kill them both within a second if I get the drop. They must know

257

this, so I think they have split up unless they're scared. Safety in numbers could be an option especially in this maze with limited visibility.

'I still have no idea who they are. Is it this covert organisation I named The Fear that are real now or was that the guy earlier helpless on his knees being taken hostage or prisoner?'

Decker brushed this debate from his mind, 'It doesn't matter who it is. I have to kill them all.' He bent down low and started to crouch as he walked methodically, poised with only his head clearly visible above the fog.

Luckily for once the environment was on his side. The ground was hard ice pack making it impossible to track his footprints especially with the lingering fog.

With little wind present WHITEOUT removed his goggles and let them hang around his neck, his instincts told him that this situation was going to erupt shortly. Classic indicators were present, his hairs were standing up on the back of his neck to match his sweaty palms, as he held the pistol directly in front of his eye line. Removing his goggles gave him twenty-twenty vision again, primed to lock on to anything that crossed his path.

Stopping sporadically, he could clearly identify the white tip of the foresight blade on the top of the pistol's upper receiver. This white tip would be aimed at the centre of any intruder's face, before two bullets penetrated through it in quick succession. He gritted his teeth as he approached each sharp corner of the steep trench banks where he would expose his body, in doing so he made a dynamic move punching hard and fast around the corner, pistol up on aim waiting to acquisition the target who might be lying in wait.

He kept his SAS training constantly in his mind, it had flooded back to him today like the natural born instincts of a professional killer.

'If he's at 15 metres or more close the left eye, gain a clear sight picture aiming at his body mass and squeeze the trigger gently. Double tap again, but a little slower for accuracy.

'It doesn't matter if he's aiming at you, just keep it slow and keep it smooth. Slow is smooth, smooth is fast. You know this worked the day that attempted kidnapping happened, they shot at you first from only 5 metres away and you still nailed those assholes.'

Sweat was starting to run down his temples, ironically it was the slowest he had moved in nearly a month and the weather was probably the coolest, being trapped down in this labyrinth was creating a pressure-cooker nearing the point of combustion.

As the droplet of sweat ran past his ear and flowed fast down his neck, he knew it was time to listen to his body.

He paused.

50-60 metres to his front he could make out a kind of crossroads. It was four trench systems meeting, with walls 15 feet high all around. Crouched over just above the fog line he was motionless watching the choke point.

This was a great place for an ambush if he was the first to get there, providing of course that they came this way.

Remaining static and running the decision cycle through his head he was sold on it.

'Right let's get to the ambush point, tuck myself in tight on one of the walls so I can see all four routes meet in the centre. That's the killing zone. I can wait there until it gets too cold to wait any longer, but I've got an hour in me I reckon before it gets dire and hypothermia sets in.'

Checking over his shoulder before moving to the identified ambush point he turned to move off again.

'Holy fuck.'

Crouching down beneath the fog line Decker caught sight of a figure crossing his killing zone. 'Damn my ambush plan is two minutes too late.' It was too far to fire he observed. Tucked into the snow bank and hanging low beneath the fog, he predicted that the guy would stop and have a look this way, he waited 20 seconds without looking up, bracing his body once more to receive high velocity gunshot wounds. 18, 19, 20 seconds and cautiously he raised his head.

Just catching the back of the figure passing through the killing zone he knew he should just remain static and observe, knowing full well that he may come back.

'In a minute or so the other figures should pass by behind him, then I can start pursuing them.' Decker felt infuriated.

'Fucking typical, two minutes earlier I could have had them. Right just stay cool, the others will pass by shortly then I can get on their tail and hunt them down.'

After another two minutes he concluded that they weren't together and made the decision to stand up and start walking to the killing zone.

Okay now's the time Decker . Let's get to it and end this nightmare.

He froze along with his inner rhetoric to decipher the new immediate threat.

That's a barrel of an M4 rifle in my back and that voice that just said stay fucking still and don't turn around or I will kill you is the other man, and he's Eastern bloc but must be Russian, they have an outstation here.

He just asked me to drop my pistol. My pistol is in my right hand about shoulder height with my arm bent at about 60 degrees pointing forward.

My left arm is to my side.

Barrel of the M4 firmly in my back still, I don't have much time and it's now or never. I know it's the worst move you can make to put a weapon in someone's back. It means you have closed down the immediate space to maneouver and he is attached to the weapon. I know exactly where he is in simple terms.

I would have stayed a few metres away, shot a few bullets or shouted a warning not to turn around, simply drop your weapon. You need that gap for the variables.

One of those variables I have to do now if I want to take control again.

Fuck it! I have to go for it. I have practised this move but I have never heard of anyone having to use it for real.

Make it clearly visible you're going to drop the pistol by raising your right hand high in the air. He will be watching this like a hawk, tracking my right hand taking his attention away from my left lower arm.

The moment I drop it, I spin anticlockwise smashing his weapon away with my left outer upper arm. It will be an almost reverse elbow strike. He may have fired but in training when the gun fires it's too late and misses the target. I then lock my left arm over the weapon underneath the armpit then I either go for a dynamic chop or blow to the head or neck.

After that it's just sheer physical violence, fighting to the death trying to keep the weapon away or trying to get hold of it. I know it will be on a sling so attached to his body, more bullets may be fired during the struggle my pistol will be on the floor a metre away.

I don't even know how big this fucker is but all-out aggression is my only hope. No hesitation.

Again all he could hear was a Russian accent telling him one more time to drop the weapon.

'Okay, okay. Who the hell are you anyway?'

The Russian began counting to three.

'3,2,1 drop the pistol. Turn, turn'

He dropped the pistol, his instincts were correct and the window of opportunity had arisen. He spun as he'd vividly rehearsed in his head and smashed the M4 violently with his forearm, the M4 fired four rounds into the ice bank. Clearly shocked, the Russian had pulled the trigger as many times as he could before he saw the maniac eyes of a ruthless killer screaming in a voice that can only be described as a sound of a man who thought he was about to die.

A ferocious two punches to the Russian's temple stunned him as his weapon dropped and hung on his sling attached around his neck.

Decker quickly wrapped one of the loose sling straps around his neck creating a noose, immediately followed up with four rapid close-range headbutts to his face. Only his balaclava prevented his face exploding into the air. The sling wrapped tight around his neck prevented the screams ringing out throughout the trench complex. Throwing the guy on his back and tightening the sling around his neck, Decker felt back in the zone.

Ripping his dented and cracked goggles off he saw his assailant's eyes looking at him in complete shock as they rolled to the back of his head.

Shaking his head violently Decker started his shock-of-capture treatment.

'Who the fuck are you? Who are you, who are you?'

Holding him till his eyes began to focus on him Decker started again.

'Who the fuck are you?'

In true Spetnaz fashion the Russian had a large hunting knife attached to his outer left thigh. Decker in full control of an almost unconscious casualty ripped it out of its scabbard.

The Russian's eyes quickly focused on it as Decker held it in his right hand.

Decker now had his left knee rammed in the Russian's throat. His weapon was lying across his chest but it was in no position to be grabbed. Competing with Decker now was impossible; negotiating was now on the agenda.

'You understand English I take it YES?' Decker asked.

The Russian just about managed a slight head movement and blink to signify yes.

'Good because I want answers or this knife will be rammed straight into your right eyeball.'

Blinking again Decker took that as a yes.

'Right, why are you trying to kill me? And again who are you?'

Decker eased the sling that was restricting the Russian's capacity to breathe.

Spitting out blood and breathing heavily the Russian prepared himself to give an answer.

Decker moved the knife in front of his right eye.

'We heard the team following you and trying to kill you communicating with their satellite phones to their HQ,' the guy managed to answer.

'Who exactly? Who is trying to kill me, is it The FEAR? Are they British? Are they called The FEAR?' Decker pushed.

'We just know you're so important to something that they want you dead, some psychological programme, warfare or something you know about. A world-changing thing they say, we don't know what it is, we just had orders to catch you and bring you back before they killed you.'

'Was the FEAR mentioned, The FEAR?'

The Russian grimiced with pain.

'You Spetnaz? Are you Russian Special Forces?' Decker was unrelenting.

The Russian confused asked, 'What do you mean by The FEAR?' Decker tightened the sling again digging his knee further into his chest.

'Who they are? What they are a part of, their organisation's name, do they call themselves The FEAR?' Decker was desperate for the Russian to say yes and put all his assumptions to bed.

'We just know they call themselves The Clinic, whatever they are that is what they are called.'

'The Clinic you say?'

'Yes, yes, The Clinic, they want you dead and it's British voices.'

'How many of you?'

'Just two.'

'Don't fucking lie to me, how many?

'Four asshole,' but this time with a grin as he knew what Decker's intention was. Telling the truth wouldn't save his life but it may save his comrades.

For the second time that day Decker held the knife with a reverse grip and rammed it clean into the Russian's eye, placing his hand over the Russian's mouth.

Twisting anticlockwise then driving the palm of his hand hard onto the knife handle, he felt the knife grating fully into the socket and beyond into the softness of the brain tissue. Already short of breath and exhausted with Decker on top of him, the shock of the knife in his eyeball sent his body into complete shutdown.

Leaving the knife in his eye Decker grabbed the weapon sling with both hands and pulled the tapered sling in opposite directions completing closing off his airway.

As hard as he could pull the sling, the Russian's movements faded away as he watched his left eye roll back and become completely still.

Within a minute all signs of life had disappeared.

Another man killed, another resident in the graveyard.

Decker let go of the sling and pulled the knife out and wiped the blade clean of partial eyeball fragments, frayed ligaments and brain tissue.

Panting with all the exertion that had just taken place he remained on top of the Russian, knees either side of his punctured head.

Looking down at another dead body he was exhausted yet elated to be alive and feeling the effects of yet another adrenalin hit.

In cold blood he had just racked up another number on his reactivated kill list, that he thought had had its last member years ago.

Things were getting hazy, trying to understand this latest killing, he closed he eyes and sucked in a few more breaths.

Opening his eyes and looking for the last time at the Russian, he nodded his head and gestured to himself to crack on with the task at hand.

'This is fucking mental I have some guys called The Clinic who want me dead, a number of Russians want me alive. The Clinic has to be The Fear, it has to be, it must be, I must be right this really is happening.'

It was a moment he was almost relieved to be proving his insanity to be a sane theory. But he still had no conclusive evidence to completely confirm his wild assumption.

He also knew to get to the bottom of this meant getting on his feet again and heading to the RV. With that in mind he assessed his current situation. One M4 weapon and the guy's equipment lay around him leaving him in a much better position to go on the real offensive with true latent force. He felt positive for the first time in a long time. He might even let himself have a smile he thought, before everything went dark. A perfectly pitched hard blow to the back of his head knocked him clean out and he fell forwards over the Russian's head and face-planted into the ice.

Decker was down.

CHAPTER 34

Frozen ice pack had totally numbed Decker's left cheekbone and eye socket, adding to his sense of helplessness and confusion upon awakening.

Remaining immobile, keeping both eyes closed he tried to take stock of his new-found circumstances. It was evident that he had taken a huge blow to the head. Squinting through his one good eye he saw a trail of blood seeping out over the snow, no doubt from his head as it felt as though an axe had been driven straight into his cranium.

The localised pain and swelling that was causing him acute distress was possibly cerebral spinal fluid, pressing against his arachnoid space. His SAS advanced trauma training told him that with no puncture or fracture to release it, the pressure would eventually crush his brain, reduce blood and oxygen supply and kill him. He lay still and tried to calm his breathing, hoping against all hope that it was just mild concussion.

Fuck I got caught out by the other Russian, he must have side-swiped me or butt-stroked me. My arms have been pressed behind my back and my hands are bound. My legs are bound too, I won't move at the moment but it's only a matter of time before he knows I'm conscious.

Coughing Decker moved his head slightly back and forth and licked the thick slush-puppy-like blood he felt around his mouth.

He was greeted instantly with a kick to his ribs. It was not a full-blown kick meant to injure, just one to get his attention.

Rolling over to face another Russian he knew what to expect. He was met by another Spetsnaz figure clad in white camouflage clothing and training a weapon on him. Standard. *Wannabes but they have got me this time so box clever, the last guy was a lying shit. Remember I have something they want and they need me alive so hold a strong position in this imminent negotiation, no matter how brutal. It's time to be the prisoner for the first time in my life. God knows, I've dished out the good news, punishments and ruthless executions in my time. Looks like the bitter karma pill could be finally here for me to start choking on,* Decker thought.

Still tightly bound, he let himself be hauled aggressively into a seated position against the ice walls of the trench. It would only have been a waste of his valuable energy to struggle. This made him consider that this Spetsnaz wannabe may be more swept up and experienced than the last piece of roadkill, especially looking at the barrel of an M4 trained on his every move from a few metres away.

Ivan had witnessed how Decker had just disarmed his fellow comrade from a near-impossible position of power, so he was taking no chances.

He also knew that Decker was of severe importance and had to be captured, not killed, only 'tortured within reason' were his commander's orders.

Whilst he had been unconscious Ivan had confirmed by handheld radio to his other comrades including Mick, who were now moving to his position.

Earlier they had collected all of Decker's kit, they wanted all traces of him gone; if any subsequent rescue party found a tent it gave them a search point to start from.

They were working on their knowledge of Antarctica where the snow never settled that deep, inches if at all, enough to cover all ski tracks and evidence of stopping points, but not deep enough to prevent finding a body.

With one member of the assassination team captured, one dead and now Decker, the man the other two were supposed to be assassinating captured, Ivan knew they had a strong hand.

Speaking to his Russian Commander back at the Vostok Operations room, they intended to make it even stronger after listening to a few other interceptions of The Clinic's communications.

Ivan's satellite phone started ringing, his commander at Vostok was primed to give Ivan an update on current developments.

'Ivan we have intercepted more communications from a man called Gerry, confirm you are copying this?'

Ivan pressed the phone to his ear, 'Yes I copy Sir,' maintaining eye contact with Decker at all times.

'Okay it seems Gerry is a key person in this thing they called The Clinic, copy?'

'Copy Sir.'

'Gerry and another man called Sean are now with a team called Trans-Ant Team. These are the guys we saw Decker drinking with on his website. The Trans-Ant Team have no idea who the two men are for real, copy?'

Purposely keeping the transmissions short knowing the weather conditions were bad and he had Decker in front of him to keep an eye on. Ivan remained brief.

'I understand Sir.'

'They will be heading to meet Decker at an RV position that is not fixed, we do not know where this position is yet but Decker will know roughly for sure, as that's where he was heading whilst evading you, copy?'

'Copy Sir.'

'Okay wait for the others to meet you. By then I will have thought how to resolve this RV location.'

'Okay Sir, out.'

Stakes were getting high if the Russian Commander himself was hatching a plan of his own, Ivan mused. It would mean leaving the helicopter three hours away at the fuel cache. He couldn't afford any large signatures to appear on the radar at this point. The team was only 50NM from the Pole. He felt they had pushed it enough already and reinserting the heli could compromise this operation that was gaining significant traction.

Ivan turned his focus solidly back on to Decker.

'Harry Decker, yes?' Ivan asked him kicking some ice up at his face.

'No shit, Mr Spetnaz what can I do for you?' Decker was obviously still a little concussed as he slurred his words slightly.

Training his weapon on Decker, Ivan simply smiled.

'No need to play the tough guy Harry, I know you're tough, I know you're a professional, just look at the damage you have caused today.' Ivan pointed to the dead body laid next to him. 'It's not just my comrade you have murdered. You have murdered another person's comrade, someone you will meet shortly.'

'I have no idea who they are and why they want me dead or captured.

I know you're Russian, from Vostok no doubt. That little quiet airbase where you Spetnaz monitor the weather? I mean what the fuck are you guys doing in Antarctica? Do you always have a presence in case a random bloke like me shows up with a load of assassins chasing me across the Antarctic plateau?'

Ivan could see the funny side to Decker's last comment though he remained silent waiting for him to finish his rant.

'I'm just trying to get to the South Pole and you fuckers keep delaying me.'

'What do you have that they don't want anyone to know about Harry? What have you decrypted or what do you know that is so revolutionary the British government has sent in a crack team to carry out a deniable operation? Have you deserted your Government? Were you so involved in a project that your departure from the military a few years back has now crept up on you? Are you happy the British government attempted to kill you today?'

Feeling slightly smug at his barrage of hard-hitting questions Ivan casually started to pace up and down. Mindful to keep his distance, he was itching to find out what Decker was hiding.

'I don't know why they want me dead, I came here to create history and find my own piece of solitude that I thought I deserved after years of fighting and suffering. I just protected myself like anyone else would. I'm here to create history not become a part of it. I have nothing that I know of that could be so dangerous to the British government.'

'Well you have my friend and we will find out exactly what it is. We are the same Harry but my government is not trying to kill me, and will not continue to hunt me down till they do. At the moment I am the only chance you have of surviving and I know you don't want to die.' Ivan paused. This whole situation was intriguing. He'd heard obviously of the British SAS for years but never met someone who had served in it. 'It's only when you leave the Special Forces you can begin to live, my former comrades tell me. Is this true?'

'I didn't come here to get killed, I came here to return to the former greatness of my past, and yes that meant living again. Obviously some fucker isn't happy with that scenario and who's to say they are the British government anyway?'

'It is your government, under what guise we don't know, but it is. I am your only chance of survival and that's why we are going to work together and you will do as I say, or more innocent people will die.' His phone rang again. Taking a firm grip of his weapon in his right hand so that Decker knew he had him covered Ivan spoke. 'Hello Sir.'

'Ivan you have his phones and sim cards intact. When the other team members are co-located with you this is what you will make WHITEOUT do, copy?'

'Good copy.'

'Using our batteries, but his phone and sim he will make an emergency call to Trans-Ant explaining he has slight battery life after his solar panel wires managed 10 minutes of connection before failing, copy?'

'Send.' Ivan replied.

'He is to tell them that he is injured and they need to meet at these revised coordinates, soon as they repeat correct coordinates, turn the phone off immediately, you getting this?'

'Copy all Sir can you send the relevant information now?'

'Negative we will work the coordinates out then talk to you shortly, that's all.'

'Copy all Sir, out.' Digesting the information whilst holding eye contact with Decker he continues where he left off before the commander's interruption.

'We know where you are heading but you lost communications a couple of days ago. They don't know if you'll turn up and they won't wait either. Once my friend's arrived with one of the men who tried killing you, you will make a call to them.'

'Fuck me you have their number do you Mr. 118 118?' Decker said half laughing referring to a phone search company that helps you find any number anywhere in the world. Ivan just tutted seeing through Decker's sarcasm. Ivan registered this, his training had taught him that if a prisoner became humorous about his situation of capture he is either destitute, ready for execution or playing a cool game.

'No but we have your two phones with no battery power and Sim cards by the way, and I'm sure we will find them on your contact list. I guess you thought you buried that one deep didn't you Harry but not deep enough this time, but don't worry even professionals make mistakes in the heat of the moment.' Ivan smirked.

'That's mega. So put your batteries in it then make the call right?'

'Simple hey,' Ivan added.

'Genius you really are Einstein aren't you?' Though Decker was furious they had the Sim cards. He had thrown them earlier, knowing how he should have buried them deep.

He was fully aware the man he was talking to was an officer. One his English was perfect and two he had not been brutal or that rough with him. He appeared to know where this game was going and was playing all the right moves, or his commander certainly was. Decker pondered his situation: 'He's working to a bigger picture for sure, directed by higher formation, I imagine there is a very busy operations centre somewhere directing his moves. This is at Kremlin-level for sure now, and they know they have to box clever politically. In the real world people think I am just without communications, everyone thinks I'm fine and expect me to meet Trans-Ant later tonight. The Russians can't maneouver that close to the Pole; in fact I am surprised they got dropped off this close without popping up on a few people's radar. Maybe I am wrong, who gives a shit down here and how well is it monitored? Well apart from by the Russians, I've found that out the hard way—' He was interrupted.

'Your friends from the Trans-Ant team, you look like you had a few good nights out in the photos on their website Harry?'

'It's allowed in the West, having a good time you know?'

'Well you do as I say and they all live, you have my word. One soldier to another right? I will meet you halfway on this Harry.'

'Anyone who asks to meet you halfway is usually someone who is a poor judge of distance I believe. You'll kill them.'

'We won't even meet them face-to-face to do that.'

'Really what's the plan then shit head?'

'You will call them on your own phone, which is plausible to the real world as your solar panel could have worked again to get enough battery life in your phone. You will make out that you are injured and that you need picking up instead of meeting them. You will give them the coordinates I tell you. Simple 'shit head', yes?'

Decker knew not to give anything up as he thought through the scenario posed. He could call Andrew and ask for a pick-up due to injury, that would not be suspicious at all and would lure the team in.

But why on Earth would Ivan want the Trans-Ant team to meet them? They offered no benefit, no information and were not part of this operation.

Shit. There was only one plausible reason as he thought back to the last call with Steve. So initially happy the video hadn't been uploaded back then he totally forgot about the documentary guys. They must be the other members of The Clinic with them and the Russians must have intercepted this knowledge from their phone calls.

Bollocks. He willed Andrew and the crew to be alright. The Clinic may be next to Andrew without him knowing who they were, Decker thought. They would still be listening no doubt to Andrew give an innocent answer by just telling him they did have new people with them. At this point it still wouldn't tell him if he was being held at gun point as they would be working to a foolproof cover story.

When he spoke to Andrew he mustn't ask either, they were smart and if The Clinic heard this sort of question, they would know he suspected them.

So The Clinic is with Trans-Ant. I arrange a pick up and the Russians arrange an ambush. Why would they not be happy with just me, and the guy who has tried to assassinate me? That's enough information without having to risk compromise or an international incident if the Trans-Ant RV goes wrong.

Why risk it? They could cut and run now. Fly a helicopter in and go straight to Vostok. It would be another six days before anyone will be worried about me, plenty of time to have me back at the Kremlin with a set of crocodile clips clenching my bollocks.

But The Clinic... Decker paused trying to see how it all came together in his mind. I reckon the two muppets attempting to kill me wouldn't know fuck all about The Clinic, they would just be a hit team tasked with taking me out.

Whoever is with Trans-Ant is important, well at least important enough to know about The Clinic or high up in it. These guys must be here to clear up any mess, or me, basically.

It must be the only reason for insisting I call Andrew and bring forward the RV time at a place of the Russians' choice. It's classic tactics, the Russians are making the calls, luring them in on their terms.

Shit, The Clinic and Trans-Ant are driving into an ambush, they want me alive but at what cost?

Would they gun down Andrew and the team to clear all this up? How the heck would they pull that off? It's not the fucking Bermuda Triangle down here.

No sooner had he pondered, he had his answer.

This is the Russians for fuck's sake Harry, get a grip, they will clear it all up for sure.

Decker went straight back to his survival instincts, he would never want the guys to die in the crossfire, and did not want to take Ivan's words of trust about not killing Trans-Ant team.

This RV was the only real chance of survival for him the more he thought about it, an RV would now bring total confusion, more chaos and a substantially higher chance of evasion, if The Clinic put up a major battle with the Russians to get to him.

It's the classic rock-and-a-hard-place type scenario but I will have to go with it. I can't let personal relationships get in the way of what makes sense for my survival. Andrew and the lads are great guys, proper gents and seeing them get mowed down unarmed would devastate me as it's my fault.

Before any potential guilt got the better of him he heard his dad's voice again.

'Son never base arguments or decisions on emotions, always base them on facts.' The facts are on the wall, I have to make the call to facilitate the new RV, I won't ask any questions. What Ivan and higher command have planned after that I don't know, but he has slipped up already and he will slip up again for sure. Be patient, be sharp.

Ivan shivered and delved into his backpack and pulled out his big down jacket. It was getting cold remaining static guarding this guy.

In an act of kindness he pulled out a small down sleeping bag that was stuffed away and undid the zip so it was a large blanket to place over Decker knowing that he would be feeling the same way.

Does he genuinely give a shit about me? he wondered, before brushing that thought off. He is not feeling sorry for me I know that. I am an asset they need alive and not hypothermic. Keeping me alive involves these acts of kindness. In all honesty I think this officer is kind-hearted, you don't meet many who are as ruthless as me and my mates back in the day.

He forced himself to go back to rallying all of his thoughts and battle appreciations through his ingrained filtering system. He was trying to work out the RV scenario, his fingers itching for a pen and paper to map the ambush scenarios out from every person's angle to predict the best line of action.

Ivan knew Decker had little to say but noted he was obviously thinking to himself, he reminded himself to stay on guard, this man had proven that he could be lethal. He looked at Decker wondering what the hell it was that this man knew. Not knowing was killing him for sure though he purposely avoided striking up needless conversation, as it would only create hostility. Ivan didn't want Decker worked up and pissed off, that would just alienate him. He had also worked out that Decker was ridiculing him continually but he refused to bite back.

Ivan's phone started ringing.

He moved away from Decker and took the call.

It was his other team member with Mick giving him an update on expected time of arrival.

Collapsing the sat phone antenna he walks back over.

'So Harry this is what will happen. When my man arrives with the man who is trying to kill you, I will instruct you to call Trans-Ant and speak to Andrew, yes? You're a seasoned professional so I expect no covert tactics from you remember. They will die if you try anything foolish. Talk as an expeditionist and not a ruthless killer, you will tell them that you have regained slight battery life so you have to be quick. Then you will tell them you have twisted your knee badly and can hardly walk, possibly a spiral fracture. Due to the time, quickly ask them to record the coordinates I give you. Once they are happy, request they pick you up as soon as possible, and ask what their expected time will be. That's all Harry, that is all. Simple yes?'

'Sounds like a great plan,' Decker responded with sarcasm of the highest order.

'Good, we are clear,' Ivan happily pronounced.

Ivan dialled his phone and moments later he started to wave his hands as he caught sight of them in the trench system ahead.

Decker followed Ivan's line of sight and noticed two figures walking towards them. One huge Russian in front, the other would-be assassin bound dragging behind on a leash.

Decker gritted his teeth hard out of contempt for their prisoner as he eagerly waited to see his face. He was actually anticipating it was someone he knew, but then again everyone he knew in the business were seasoned pros, the best would have got the job done. Not this pair of halfwits who had compounded The Clinic's problems, by failing to do their job and were now handing him over to the Russians. It was highly embarrassing for them and despite his current situation bound helpless, bloodied and bruised he couldn't wait to gloat.

Stopping 30 metres away, the huge Russian moved forward to meet Ivan. Both looking at their GPSs the huge Russian started pointing due South-East.

Ivan must have asked them to try and find an opening outside of the trench systems Decker surmised. Trans-Ant would never be able to negotiate the terrain here. Hence Ivan requested to find a suitable location to set up the ambush.

Speaking in Russian the huge guy was getting louder pointing more strongly in the direction they had come from.

He was clearly confident that he had seen an area suitable whilst moving here that fitted the bill.

Decker listened in to catch the gist of what was going on. The Russian who was talking and pointing was explaining to Ivan that only 1 nautical mile away the labyrinth became clearer, it ended at a rubble field. In Antarctica these rubble fields almost form perfect demarcation lines or boundaries. One second you would be in the worst rubble field ever with these types of trenches, then five metres later you can pass through the rumble field and find that it opens like a gate, and you will enter a completely flat landscape.

The Russian had obviously found this type of break in the terrain and Ivan agreed it was a perfect ambush setting.

Without hesitation Ivan walked over to Decker.

'Right Harry I am going to free up your legs so we can move to the RV location. It is only 30 minutes away. I don't want you shouting at the guy over there looking for answers. If you try and make a run for it I will shoot you in the legs, understand?'

Decker continued his vacant stare before Ivan placed his goggles back on his face, and stowed away the sleeping bag.

'You move I will shoot you, clear?' Ivan's last words before they began to move off, staying about 30 metres behind the others.

Decker's hands were still bound to the rear which was harsh and a little foolhardy. A fall could result in a serious breakage but Ivan was taking no chances. He didn't complain. He was too busy playing out his next couple of moves and secretly wanting to rip Mick's head clean off.

It was ironic that the weather had cleared up completely. The wind had died down, the haze had cleared and the sun was shining high. Visibility was the best it had been for two days. This was good news for Decker maybe, as it would make the ambush more challenging. If the visibility was still low then the Russians could have quickly closed in and taken control, without giving The Clinic any time to react.

The Russians would have to use the terrain or Decker to their advantage when the RV happened.

Decker knew he had no safety networks save for Andrew and the guys, if they had not already been taken captive or executed.

If the Russians offer me up as bait, where do I run when The Clinic see I have company? Will The Clinic kill me without hesitation once they see others involved? Will the Russians protect me at all costs? Options were at the forefront of his mind as they journeyed over the ice, so much so they had reached a large rubble field wall already denoting the ambush site in record time. Decker had crossed similar terrain many times, it was an almost perfect wall of rubble that separated the horrible terrain behind them, and entered an almost billiard table-like terrain ahead.

Ivan and the other Russian were looking out to the flat ice to their front and discussing the ambush options no doubt. They would have time once Decker made the call to finalise their execution of the plan.

Playing around with their GPSs and switching batteries from satellite phones Ivan began to walk over to Decker.

'Okay your phone is powered up. I will explain this clearly, you deviate I will kill you. Phone Trans-Ant and speak to Andrew.'

Ivan pointed to the display screen on his GPS.

'Once they read these co-ordinates back that's it, say you have to go as you are saving all the power you have left. No questions, don't answer any of theirs.'

Ivan flicked through the contacts list and found Andrew on the phone.

'Is this Andrew from Trans-Ant?' Ivan asked.

Decker nodded silently.

Another Russian came over to cover Decker as Ivan dialled, checked it was on loudspeaker then held it next to Decker's head.

Both Russians were silent.

Decker was thinking what to say whilst thinking how stupid Ivan was to keep saying he would kill him. If he was dead the game was over, checkmate.

It was ringing.

'Harry how the hell are you buddy?' Andrew sounded genuinely excited to hear him.

'I only have minimal battery life Andrew so listen and get ready to take my position…'

'Sure, go ahead,' he replied.

Ivan pushed the GPS up in front of Decker's face with his left hand. Nodding to the other Russian who instantly pointed his weapon at his head as Decker read the coordinates out twice.

'You have to come and meet me, my knee is injured badly and I can only move a small distance.'

Andrew read back the coordinates.

'That's correct, how long Andrew?' Decker asked hating this.

'Umm, umm… Fuck me, about four hours mate, hang in there okay?'

'I will, I have to go Andrew.' Ivan pressed the red end-call button.

'Was that okay for you?' Decker said to Ivan.

'Perfect Harry, that was perfect,' Ivan smiled before lashing out at Decker's sarcastic tone and pushing him back, but Decker managed to stay on his feet.

Decker was almost about to leg-swipe Ivan in return but saw sense and took the hit instead. He had to stay friends for now, for at least another four hours.

A linear ambush Decker thought.

Hiding behind the rubble wall looking out to the front, The Trans-Ant team would roll in with their trucks to this location. The Russians could stay behind cover until they were literally metres away, so as long as Decker was visible on his own they would come right up to him and straight into the ambush, or the killing zone.

A liner ambush was the simplest ambush to execute if the enemy did what you expected. And why wouldn't they? Decker thought.

If The Clinic don't know the Russians are here this is exactly what is going happen… The Clinic don't know they're here so this will happen.

How the fuck can I sort this out in this position? I just pray the lads are okay. Hopefully The Clinic have not topped everyone now they know where I am.

He reprimanded himself, Decker you don't know for sure that The Clinic are with Trans-Ant, that's just your prediction based on an assumption that the Russians have intercepted some calls from The Clinic to the assassination team.

Are you racing ahead again? Being too quick and smart for your own good and seeing things that simply aren't there?

Decker took a moment to calm his thoughts and think rationally. Closing his eyes, he took a few long breaths before twitching them open again.

'Maybe I am actually missing the real reason for the Russians wanting to meet Trans-Ant team and have missed it from the start? I have 4 hours to work it out…'

CHAPTER 35

Sitting behind Andrew in the rear twin cab, Gerry quickly sat bolt upright, moments earlier his head had been almost pressing against Andrew's headrest trying to eavesdrop as much as possible to ascertain what WHITEOUT was saying, whilst masquerading as staring out of the window during the long drive.

At this point it would have meant serious decision time if WHITEOUT had mentioned what had happened, although Gerry would have banked on Andrew reacting like a civilian, either thinking WHITEOUT was having an episode of post-traumatic stress disorder making him delusional, or he had just lost the plot completely with his past experiences finally taking control of his mind being in this insane environment on his own for too long.

However, what Gerry was catching snippets of was nothing of the sort.

WHITEOUT sounded injured and was squeezing the last blip of battery life out of his phone to make this desperate call for a pick-up.

He thought it through, the injury to WHITEOUT's leg was plausible.

Mick was not communicating and the last they knew was that he was about to seek revenge for Robby's murder.

Had the two met? Was Mick the latest victim of WHITEOUT's plight for evasion? Had WHITEOUT got injured or shot during the fight?

Gerry thought this was most likely the logical conclusion.

WHITEOUT had killed Mick and had sustained a serious injury. Maybe life-threatening, he would have taken Mick's battery out of his phone due to the severity of his injury, and called Andrew for a pick-up instead of the planned RV at the prearranged spot. WHITEOUT would not have risked making such an emergency call otherwise.

Covering his tracks by saying that he had managed to get some power out of the solar panel was a simple explanation as opposed to telling Andrew it was from the phone of the last guy he had just murdered in self-defence.

Gerry knew he had to make a call to Sully ASAP. His thought process was cut short by Andrew.

'Wow, that was him Gerry if you hadn't guessed. So it looks like we will meet, and earlier than expected. I must admit I didn't think we would see him since his communications went down, but such a shame, he says the exped is over due to his knee being twisted, we really thought he was going to make it.'

'Least he is okay,' Gerry faked back. 'The weather has been horrific these last few days; especially for one man to endure on his own and I know you guys were concerned. Like you say, a shame. Still it will be great to see and speak to the guy, no doubt he will be pretty devastated by the recent turn of events.' Gerry held his own with the seemingly innocent conversation whilst doing the maths inside his head at a rapid rate.

The Trans-Ant team was static as Andrew pulled his teammate John over and told him to go firm as soon as the call was received and they knew it was Decker. Gerry knew he had to act fast now and activate the jamming device. Andrew would call Union Glacier and Steve Jones immediately to update them on WHITEOUT. This could not be allowed to happen, it would equal Mission Failure and the fallout would be unfixable at this point. The Peli-case with the specialist equipment stored in it was in the back of the truck hold.

Without hesitation Gerry made his move.

'Andrew I'm just going to get a spare battery out of the Peli-case for my camera, it's on its last bar.'

'Go ahead Gerry, we're here for a few minutes plotting the route to Harry's location.'

Gerry jumped out and headed to the rear of the wagon.

Whilst this was happening Andrew talked over the two-way vehicle radios and let everyone know the news about Decker.

Sean reacted instantly as he observed Gerry upfront moving to the rear of Andrew's wagon, moving to meet him.

Gerry pulled the handle to bring the tailgate down and saw Sean walking over clearly aware that something was up.

Gerry whispered: 'Right I have to activate the jammer before they make the call to Union Glacier. WHITEOUT has just called in with an injury and Andrew is planning the route to get to him so we have literally minutes. In fact you activate it. It's in the second peli-case underneath the black North Face bag there.'

Sean jumped straight on it and began moving the black bag to access the peli-case.

'I need to quickly phone Sully. I will move to the front so I can see Andrew. If he picks the sat phone up I will switch mine to my other ear. Activate it on Alpha Setting when I do this, we don't have much time mate. Also bring the remote with you,' Gerry confirmed.

Gerry talked to Sean loudly explaining where the spare batteries were so the crew can hear him, Sean continued the role-play to start buying time before Gerry let him know that he's going to make quick call reference work stuff.

Audible enough for all to hear Gerry scrambled for Sully's number, locating it he hit the green dial button.

Anxiously watching Andrew finishing up on the laptop he saw the prominent 'GO TO' button get tapped on the screen.

Mike from the rear vehicle jumped out, immediately reaching for his zip to take a quick piss. Only five metres from Gerry and even closer to Sean, they prayed that a piss was all he needed. Sean paused on extending a small antenna that was integrated into the peli-case, he had to do it for it to start jamming calls. If it was seen by Mike it would be suspicious, especially as he was the tech geek, he was just going to have to employ a bit of stealth and speed.

Gerry was watching Andrew holding his satellite phone in the wagon. Clearly scrolling his way through the contacts list, Gerry knew Andrew was flicking to find Steve Jones at Union Glacier Base Camp. Sean still had his head buried in the Peli-case and Gerry gritted his teeth against shouting 'Get a move on'.

'Gerry how's it going?' Sully's voice bellowed down the phone breaking his concentration.

Gerry answered without sounding rushed. Composing his relaxed posture was complicated as he was worried about Andrew, any second now he was going to make the call...

'Gerry I will call you back, this is a bad connection.'

The intensity of the situation was clear to see on Gerry's face as he held Sean's gaze and moved his eyes towards the cab. This was the signal that Andrew was in action.

Sean was poised knowing as soon as Gerry moves his phone from his ear he has to activate the jammer.

'Okay will get straight on it and talk in a bit,' Sully replied.

'Thanks mate,' Gerry changed the phone from one ear to the other happy in the knowledge that "bad connection" was a codeword that meant sat comms was compromised. Gerry knew he would retrieve an encrypted data message on his beacon soon.

Sean hit the switch activating the Alpha Setting jammer.

Gerry looked at Andrew as he moved the phone to sit against his other ear, his lips mimicking a conversation.

Inside the truck, Andrew held the phone to his ear and Gerry started to hold his breath.

30 seconds passed, Gerry watched Andrew intently, he still held the phone to his ear his lips hadn't moved.

Had the jammer had enough time to power up and actively start jamming the phone signal?

Andrew brought the phone down in front of him.

That was the sign Gerry was waiting for and with it he sighed.

Andrew checked the number and dialled again but Gerry grinned inwardly knowing that this was a no-go.

Walking over to Sean he handed him the spare battery that doubled up as the remote for the jamming device. Pushing the tailgate back up both men rejoined their respective teams.

After a few minutes of everyone loading up, Gerry de-activated the jammer.

Gerry's beacon made a small beep, he only heard it as he was expecting a message to come through within minutes of Sully ending the call.

It wouldn't take the techy too long to suggest to text to Union Glacier if Andrew wanted to get a message back. It wasn't rocket science; even your average person tries to text if the phone was not connecting, sending a text message, you know it will get delivered at some point.

Gerry scrolled down to the received message icon on his beacon, entered the inbox, accessed the message and began to read, fast.

It was clear Sully had pre-written most of this message possibly anticipating he would have to give orders in a secure data format if he suspected the satellite calls were being intercepted.

'Good work Gerry. A few things have been going on here that are unclear, but your last message has locked this all down in my mind. I'm alone with what I am thinking but here it is:

Russians, I think they have WHITEOUT and it means one thing. You and Trans-Ant are driving straight into an ambush. The guys are working on intercepting more transmissions from the Russians but it's not proving too successful.

Mick's phone is an Iridium 9555 model, a different battery pack to WHITEOUT's 9575, not compatible. There is no way WHITEOUT has recharged via his solar panel, all his gear was left at the tent site, even Mick confirmed the solar panel was there.

I think the Russians have WHITEOUT but I am not sure about Mick. His phone is off. His beacon has been static for hours. This either means he's dead or the beacon is fucked.

I reckon the Russians must have been eavesdropping and know what model phone he's using. It's not rocket science it's an older Iridium so they will have them anyway like us.

These are now direct orders and trust me this is how we end all this.

Go to the new RV but put the normal anti-ambush drills in place. You have the weapons to deal with this.

Hence you got the high-calibre rifles and Icarus team just got the pistols so they would have to get up close and personal with Decker and not take the easy option and shoot him from 300 metres away. That was my insurance policy they would do the job properly and not bottle it.

The Russians, if they have been intercepting our conversations will know you're with Trans-Ant and more importantly that you're a big player Gerry. They will want you and WHITEOUT alive. This is the only edge you need to get the drop first and get back to the runway at The South Pole station ASAP. Ilyushin will be waiting and ready to go, Roman is expecting Trans-Ant back at 2000hrs he will be turning and burning with logistics from the station.

This is critical Gerry and I'm sorry I never told you before but I know you'll understand this. Do not disclose this to Sean.

In fact you are the only person apart from me who has this knowledge.

It's getting too close now, and what I am about to tell you next will be hard to swallow but it's the completion of The Clinic's inception and activation...'

'These flipping solar hotspots do my head in we had this the other week. Well least we received his call and know where he is,' Andrew said to John and Gerry, interrupting Gerry's disbelief as he read through Sully's final paragraph of his new orders.

'Probably that weather system that's just blown through,' John concluded. Clearly having no idea what he was talking about being the grease monkey mechanic, and much loved village idiot on this adventure.

'Yeah nice one Batman, well I will send an SMS, it will get through eventually,' Andrew said.

Gerry quickly scrolled though the last paragraph before hitting the remote jammer button. Any messages would never leave Andrew's phone, or any other, blocking them from even entering cyberspace to be retrieved at a later date.

His relief was short-lived as he absorbed Sully's message that he knew he had to delete immediately. Storing it to memory was the only hard copy he possessed now. Conscious the Russians, if Sully was right, would at some point tap into their data transmissions. Gerry started to ponder...

'I hope I have read and interpreted it all correctly as it's going to be a catastrophic fuck-up if I didn't.'

His reason for being in the thick of it even though this outcome was not expected, was actually looking less likely to be a coincidence now. That said, he trusted Sully to the death. Knowing he had to execute a mission-critical order, these were tragic orders as Gerry's guts were churning. Once he briefed up Sean at the next stop, the next move would have to be made and he only hoped Sean would commit without question.

'What's the plan then Andrew?' Gerry asked.

'We're about 60 miles away so roughly three or so hours to Harry's location. We'll head off for an hour or so before we refuel and try and make another call. I'm starving too so we'll quickly boil up some rations, you hungry mate?' Andrew asked Gerry.

'Not just you then, I'm starving Si, sounds great.'

Gerry was relieved. He and Sean needed a stop to action the orders Sully had quickly sent him. The fact he sent them via encrypted data let Gerry know how serious he was about the Russians being involved. They wouldn't know a tracking beacon had this facility, as it was the newest beacon available so they wouldn't have intercepted Sully's last data message, or certainly not decrypted it.

Gerry had always had that gut instinct that Sully was holding back at the beginning of this op. It gave him satisfaction knowing his instincts were right again, but his instincts were not so sure about Sully's orders.

Instead, what he had just learnt about his whole operation just smelt of Sully's ambition and risk-averse attitude that always culminated in a flip of a coin. A smile crossed his face as he thought about Sully back in his command centre watching this all unfold. Such was his faith and trust in his operators on the ground, Sully knew things always tended to work out. Although Gerry would have put money on Sully being gutted to not be with them and closing in hard with the Russians if he was correct.

All the pieces started to fall into place in this most bizarre scenario. He was a little shocked to think how Sully predicted they would end up with the Trans-Ant team at this point in the game.

Genius maybe or just another well-thought-out contingency?

Sully was a maverick. Orders were orders. To him it just reaffirmed his position in their close partnership of the past. If he wanted this partnership to continue, Gerry had to enter the fray again and get his hands dirtier than ever.

Grabbing the phone off the dashboard Andrew tried it again with the same result.

'Fucking shit,' he proclaimed.

'Okay John let's pull up, refuel and get some hot food on.'

'OK mate, I'll set us down over there,' John pointed to a flat area a few hundred metres away.

Reaching for his two-way radio to inform the other team to stop he can hear the radio's ominous static tone as he lifts the handset to his lips already telling him that it won't work.

'Polar, solar bloody hot spots,' throwing the handset on the dashboard instead of replacing it on its bracket.

The truck came to a halt. The other truck pulled up alongside.

Each team knew what was happening so immediately got out of their wagons and began fixing up the hydraulic fuel pump to the barrel full of fuel.

The rear wagon with the logistics trailer had a mini kitchen that comprised of a two-point stove and Burco boiler with a few electrical items running off the small generator.

Mike got straight on it and placed a load of meals in the Burco and lined up six thermal mugs for a much-treasured brew, once the guys had finished the refuel and maintenance checks.

Weather was clear and the temperature was actually mild. Mild enough for John to place a load of fold-up chairs out to sit on whilst they had their evening meal and a hot coffee.

Sean showed willing and was helping the guys with the refuelling. Meanwhile Gerry paced around thinking about how the next hand was best played.

Making out he was going for a piss he walked 30 metres away for his final deliberation.

Confirming in his mind he had interpreted the data correctly his decision was clear-cut. Turning to walk back he saw John holding up a mug and orange ration bag, indicating to Gerry that his food and hot brew was ready.

Everyone was sitting down as Gerry walked over to join them.

As he approached John who was still standing, John held both his hands out offering the food and coffee.

Gerry pulled his right hand out and before John could articulate what Gerry was holding, he had two bullets in his head.

Dropping without a sound Gerry turned his immediate attention to Mike who was just about to climb out of his chair. Before his ass cheeks left the seat he sat back down. Dead.

Two bullets to his forehead in quick succession just like John.

A quick spray of red mist puffed into the air followed by the solid liquid blood with bone fragments and torn flesh exiting and staining the ice.

This signature technique known as a double tap in the business was pure instinctive shooting. Professionals never fired a single shot, by the end of their training it would be the most unnatural action they could contemplate and it served its purpose.

Two shots equalled maximum trauma to the victim with no time-lapse to evaluate if the shot has been fatal. Victims can be lucky with one headshot as weird flukes can occasionally happen. Two shots eradicates this variable.

Gerry looked at Andrew's face, it was obvious his fear was paralysed by the shock, time for him was standing still in a freeze-frame that gave him a perfect picture of his lifelong friends motionless splayed awkwardly on the floor and slumped in a chair.

He shook uncontrollably and certainly hadn't registered the urine free-flowing down the insides of his thighs.

Dave and Sean remained seated in the same state of shock as Andrew facing Gerry. It was no good, they knew it was over, why run?

Sean who was also paralysed with horror knowing that this wasn't in the script and he wouldn't be able to get his pistol out fast enough to retaliate. If he did he would be dead for sure as Gerry would see the threat and terminate it straight away.

He knew his only option was to sit it out and hope he was still part of this operation that was evidently taking a new turn for the worst.

Concluding quickly that Gerry would have killed him first if that was his fate made the decision to remain still and continue to shit himself like Dave next to him.

Gerry turned to look at Dave wondering if his fight-or-flight mechanism would take over.

Flight would mean staying the fuck still and hedging his bets.

Fight... Slumped down in the foldable chair his ass almost touching the ice Dave obviously decided to get up. Pushing down hard with his arms to generate enough force to push himself up and out the chair he started the movement, Gerry registered it and finished him off in an instant with the exact same treatment as the previous two with a double tap just above the bridge of Dave's nose, almost through the same hole.

Gerry didn't even watch to confirm his shots had been fatal, and instead the pistol was trained on Sean, knowing Andrew was zero threat being in a catatonic state with steam rising though his dampened trousers.

Gerry knew Andrew would have physically shit himself too; one rarely comes without the other on these occasions.

The orders Sully had given him in his last paragraph had just been carried out in the professional manner Gerry always subscribed to.

Calm, calculated and causing as little distress to the victims as possible. It wasn't personal. It was the last thing Gerry wanted to do, ever.

This is why people like Gerry were and still are at the cutting edge of this ruthless business.

'Don't fucking move,' Gerry says in a controlled voice, breaking Andrew out of his current state.

'Sean the plan has changed. Sorry I couldn't warn you, it was an ideal situation so I took the initiative. Get your weapon out and keep an eye on Andrew. We need him, and need him alive,' Gerry casually dropped his weapon down to his side now the formalities were over.

'No problem, thanks for that one,' Sean replied with a lump in his throat and still a bit sheepishly shocked by Gerry's behaviour.

In the still of Antarctica three bodies were splayed out with blood running from the exit wounds at the rear of their heads.

Andrew was clenching the foldable chair's arms like he was on a white-knuckle ride. Relieved he wasn't dead, Sean got busy telling him to remain seated but twist his chair around so he wasn't facing them.

Dignity was needed Sean thought, as he knew Gerry must have received a fast set of orders from Sully in order for this massacre to happen at such lightning speed, and in such a heartless fashion.

Gerry stood next to the front wagon looking to the horizon, pistol still in his right hand hanging at his side, he could feel the minor tremors rushing through his hands shaking the pistol slightly. Not tempted to tense his hands to counteract the sensation, he knew all too well that to counter tension, you didn't resist it, instead you embraced it with total relaxation.

He looked at his watch. In three hours they were entering an ambush situation to meet WHITEOUT.

The Russians knew they were coming.

The Russians couldn't know that he knew about them.

The question running over and over in Gerry's mind was how the hell is WHITEOUT playing this? He must know that he holds the strongest possible position for all of them even if he is captured, he mused.

If The Clinic is to get out of the killing zone alive, with the Russians all dead WHITEOUT must surely know how to orchestrate this Gerry thought. WHITEOUT will set something up whether it's stalling tactics, a diversion or maybe he has pretended to turn if somehow he now knows he has been the target of a failed assassination.

Gerry actually contemplates this.

Thinking that if he was WHITEOUT and had just evaded death from the British government would the Russians then become his safest option?

No, Gerry knew that WHITEOUT would never trust the Russians even if he didn't trust us anymore, but deep down Gerry knew it was a weak conclusion, only based on what he wanted to think WHITEOUT was thinking.

In three hours Gerry knew that he would only have one chance to read the scenario perfectly without any of them showing their hand too early. Deciding what side WHITEOUT had chosen would dictate the outcome of OP IGNITION.

Three hours…

CHAPTER 36

All three bodies were placed in Bivvy bags, normally they were only used as body bags in times of war when the proper body bags ran out. It wasn't a logistical predicament expected on the Antarctic plateau.

Andrew wept as he was ordered to help Sean throw the lifeless bodies of his best friends into the back of the rear truck trailer. Visibly shaking and no doubt wondering if he would be next to go on the pile no dignity, no story to tell or questions answered.

'Get your hands on the steering wheel Andrew,' Gerry commanded.

Throughout this episode there was one thing that managed to penetrate deep down inside Andrew, cutting through the layers of raw emotion and stabilising his current shock state.

Who is Harry Decker really?

Has he played us? What the fuck is actually happening here?

Another guy they trusted looked after and adopted as one of their own in Punta. He knew in some way this was his fault, or certainly the result of something he was caught up in somehow, it had to be.

Using 4 doubled-up zip ties to attach his hands to the steering wheel of the first wagon, Andrew was now officially a prisoner.

Following Sully's hunch, Gerry and Sean now had to plan a counter-ambush. Limited equipment and possibly outnumbered, it was another scenario where the odds were stacked against The Clinic.

They had enough weaponry to give the Russians a really bad day; it was just how they employed them initially without giving the game away, they needed to get the upper hand. Surprise was needed, but all the surprises had come from them at the moment, the balance needed addressing.

Walking to the back of the truck Gerry turned to Sean to get him up to speed. 'This isn't ideal mate but we're about to enter an ambush.

Sully is certain WHITEOUT has been captured due to him calling in unexpectedly with his random excuse for us to pick him up.'

'What the fuck, when did this happen?' Sean replied, clearly still a little shaken after Gerry's murder rampage 30 minutes previously and probably feeling completely out of the loop.

'What about Mick? Is he dead, with the Russians or still out there?'

'There is no beacon activity so we must assume he is dead, still out there or captured with them,' Gerry replied. 'Let's just look at what we have got to go with on this Sean, I'm under the pump too here just following Sully's orders.' Gerry calmly started talking already forgetting about the whys, the whats, the what ifs, even momentarily forgetting about the three calculated head shots he'd just dished out.

'Well the Russians are expecting us to roll up in two trucks with six people if they have done their research. And for us to turn up in three hours or so. They know we want WHITEOUT, and if Sully is right about the Russians, they won't be handing the fucker over for the spare cash we've got left with us.' Looking at Sean and sighing he lightly scratched his chin his go-to movement when the odds were complex.

'How do we know the Russians know we are with the Trans-Ant Team?' Sean asked. 'I mean does Sully know this for sure or is it just another wild swing of the bat Gerry?'

'Could be an assumption but his assumptions normally have some beef to them. We have to plan as if they know we are here to collect, but also play it out as if they don't.'

'Meaning?'

'I reckon the Russians have intercepted our transmissions. Vostok is only 400-500 miles away, they must have launched from there if Sully is right. When we start to plan this next part we do it so it looks like Trans-Ant do not have us with them. It's a little more risky and will mean getting up close without weapons on show. Maybe you holding back and hitting them from a longer range may be possible, but again even more risky,' Gerry stated.

'Yeah it's another shit deal. The Russians will also be wondering whether we have Trans-Ant under duress, or if we have remained covert to the last safe moment without them knowing that WHITEOUT is our target. Would the Russians know we're playing the part of our documentary makers?' Sean suggested.

'Your guess is as good as mine Sean. In fact it doesn't really change the price of fish mate what we're pretending we are now.'

'Yep so we will have to plan it from both perspectives. They'll be looking for the initial telltale signs of Trans-Ant being under duress. Anything suspicious will spook them.'

'Like three dead members of the team in the back of that trailer for example and Andrew strapped to the steering wheel?' Causing Gerry to smile, it wasn't often that Sean showed his dry sense of humour.

'Yeah there is that I suppose,' Gerry chuckled, 'we hide that small point, we have a fighting chance. Like I said a minute ago, if we get close enough without them knowing for sure what's happening, we might just get our window of opportunity.'

'How do you see the Russians posturing themselves for our arrival? Full-scale ambush or more of a blaze reception party, safety in numbers and all that?'

'I reckon a tent inner will be set up with WHITEOUT in it. They will be hidden close by with clear arcs of observation and fire, or he will be in the open. They will watch it all unfold to the part where we approach the tent or him. This is their only opportunity to gauge what the facts are. They will be trying to identify us for sure, and it will be hard for them if we're not showing weapons.'

'I agree mate. What are you thinking?'

'They may have photos of Trans-Ant off the website but those will be of no use as we'll be wearing goggles and jackets etc. They will have to make a decision to close us all down, and I reckon they will make it before any verbal contact is made with WHITEOUT—'

'Otherwise WHITEOUT will blow it for them by shouting his head off.'

'Exactly.'

Gerry felt good inwardly, his instincts giving him faith that he was thinking along the right lines. They would turn up as the Trans-Ant team and once they saw WHITEOUT on his own waving at the wagons they would approach him. Hiding behind cover the Russians would wait till they were close enough before initiating the ambush, but the Russians had some problems too.

Killing Trans-Ant team was a must but they needed Gerry intact, even Sean too and they didn't know what he looked like. How they differentiated this in a matter of seconds was their problem. They couldn't shoot the wrong people – Gerry had all the answers and WHITEOUT was useless without him.

It was obvious Gerry and Sean would be the ones that had pistols or high-calibre weapons, they needed to choose their time carefully to disclose these items to identify themselves clearly to the Russians watching.

As Gerry weighed it up he aired his fears to Sean.

'Let's focus on what we do know to be fact and that starts with us two. Weapons? We have two Glocks plus the M4 rifle, a H&K G28 that will give us a stand-off of 500 metres plus and these two Arctic Trucks, that's the tangibles covered. Importantly we have Andrew as the point of contact to meet WHITEOUT. We have communications but we can safely assume the Russians are intercepting the satellite phone but probably not the handheld radios as we close in, unless they have a frequency scanner with them.'

Sean nodded not wanting to interrupt Gerry's flow.

'Now I think they must have been intercepting the sat phone calls. If I was the Russians, the only time I would have realised WHITEOUT was vitally important was when I gave Mick the pep talk after Robby was killed. I mentioned WHITEOUT was a lynchpin in the next phase of this revolutionary psychological warfare that we're going to launch soon. My fuck-up, but if I was a Russian and heard that amidst WHITEOUT killing the men after him, I would want a part of the action, agree?'

Sean nodded his head in silence again.

'So, I think the beacon data to communicate is secure for now but I don't really want to send another message unless it's critical. We can choose to break radio silence to use it deceptively to our advantage, as another weapon of manipulation to feed the Russians a false game plan? But again it's a balancing act, I think it's better to not give them any clues we're here.' Gerry paused.

Sean jumped in, 'How do you think the Russians will play it, any idea of numbers, are they on foot, in trucks, any heavy weapons? We could be walking into a fucking shit storm Gerry. I mean who knows what those fuckers have stored at Vostok?' Sean looked pissed off that he was now in this mess with no warning, not to mention whatever the hell was happening to Mick.

He continued, 'WHITEOUT has probably killed Robby and possibly

Mick, the Russians have WHITEOUT we think, and it's only a possible mate. He may be on his own for Christ's sake. Even Sully could have played this one out wrong?' Sean had a valid point, Sully could be wrong and all this planning may be for nothing.

Gerry paused, he knew Sean was getting a bit twitchy and he had every right to be, but in his mind they had to trust Sully's instinct and intel, they were definitely walking into a shit storm and he needed Sean's A-game. Going home was a long way off, it was time to dig their heels in.

'Yeah you're right and I hope it is the latter and we take him straight out of the game and go home but we have to plan for the worst-case scenario. This means we will be postured for the shit storm you mentioned with the Russians. Now, I reckon they're light in numbers to lower the footprint for sure, they must be on foot and have been dropped off by helicopter or light plane, logistically this is the only way as their base is hundreds of miles away.' Gerry had seen Vostok on the map when he was researching Antarctica and read it was the Russian scientific base. Shrouded in the same secrecy the South Pole station was by the Americans and Brits it had all seemed a bit far-fetched from his laptop in London. Out here however...

He carried on: 'Right let's work on a four-man team, so a maximum of four shooters. One or two with WHITEOUT, the other two in left and right cut-off positions in a linear ambush. What's their mission and main aim?' Gerry asked his questions out loud to aid his thinking and also prompt Sean for his input. As per usual Sean was too slow to react and Gerry was off again.

'They need WHITEOUT alive as well as us two. The intercepts would tell them we're higher up in the food chain with all the information. This gives us our critical window to take them down, once we have them located. The hesitation period they need to identify us is the edge we need.'

'Yeah for sure,' Sean agreed his curiosity starting to get the better of him.

'Andrew has to meet WHITEOUT to give us that initial stand-off distance to locate the Russians. They won't know if Andrew is one of us or one of the Team.'

'Yes that's a good point, I see where you're going with this one.'

'Tactically I'm thinking one wagon stays in depth initially. That will be you with the Sniper rifle. Initially we will stop and look like we're setting something up, even a weather balloon just to take their attention away to get you in position from 500 metres or so away—'

'I can get under the truck and start observing and dialling in.' Gerry knew that by 'dialling in' Sean meant he could locate targets and estimate distance and wind to deliver killer shots with his sniper rifle when required.

'Andrew and I will go forward but not all the way to WHITEOUT. We'll park the truck 50 metres away. Andrew can walk out to meet him. The Russians now have three things to watch, your truck, my truck and WHITEOUT meeting Si. This is our window. Hopefully you can locate a few of them from 500 metres away through your telescopic sight, cross hairs on their bodies preferably.'

'Carry on,' Sean nodded.

'You're in position 500 metres away and we move forward and stop 50 metres short from WHITEOUT. Andrew jumps out waving and ranting at WHITEOUT and starts to walk forward. Surely the Russians will now be suspicious and maybe know something is up, but they can't commit to shooting Andrew, as it could be one of us and they want us alive remember.'

Sean tracked every word.

'I am even thinking we could give Andrew a pistol to give to WHITEOUT so he can fight at close quarters. It's a dangerous option but WHITEOUT will know it's part of a bigger thing. If you and I have taken the others out by then, we just put some bullets around his head or feet from our positions, WHITEOUT will drop the pistol and be at our mercy.'

'Hold on mate,' Sean put his right palm up at Gerry. 'Bearing in mind he's killed Robby and possibly Mick, do you think he will just drop his weapon? I mean this guy is a fucking maniac and will be massively pissed off by now.'

'I don't know Sean, I really don't know. If he decides to fight we take him out. But if he complies I will interrogate him, we will kill him them put him in the back with the others, and head to the Ilyushin. Sully will have our extraction at the South Pole all sorted by then.'

Sean breathed out slowly, clearly not convinced, 'Fucking hell Gerry, this is borderline insanity, but I have nothing better at the moment. You're right about the time of WHITEOUT meeting Andrew being the only window we have to take them down.'

'It's not great, but it's possible,' Gerry confirmed.

Sean nodded in agreement knowing full well that his brain couldn't match Gerry's when it was going at full pace. The weather was closing in, they were getting cold and time was running out.

Gerry knew it as he pulled the think velcro flap back on his top right pocket and pulled his notepad out. Leaning against the truck he started drawing, with Sean peering over his shoulder. 'A quick sketch mate to show Andrew our masterplan.'

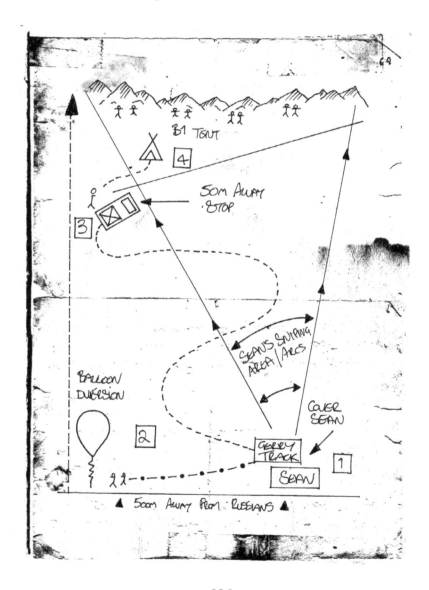

Both managed a small chuckle, then the sober light of day hit Sean. Both of his mates could be dead, Robby already was. The smile left his face.

Within a minute Gerry ripped the leaf of paper out of his pad and presented it to Sean.

Quickly taking a look it was simple to follow. He had a quick laugh at Gerry's signature signed Gerry aged 5 years.

'Yeah, old British joke' Gerry watching Sean tap it with his finger before handing it back.

'Okay let's get on with it, I will explain it all to Andrew.'

'Good luck with that one buddy.'

'This ride isn't going to be the most topical I've experienced,' Gerry said as he walked to the front of the truck.

'Do you think it might be a good idea to give WHITEOUT the weapon handover with Andrew telling him we're here to "capture, not kill him" or something?' Sean suggested to Gerry, 'builds some trust up doesn't it, and keeps him thinking.'

'Good point and I think I have a piece of information that will do this. It can only increase our chances Sean, yes let's do that.'

'Yeah okay, I am sure he would want to kill a few Russians if he hasn't already, it may even help us out a little.'

Looking hard at each other they knew this was the best they had. It had finally sunk in to both of them that they would potentially be fighting for their own lives shortly, that hadn't been in the script.

'Right let's brief up Andrew,' Gerry said tapping Sean on the shoulder. 'It's important we let him know he will not get killed by us and in all honesty I will push Sully for this, poor fucker. No one was supposed to die. Look now, five possibly dead with us now facing our own fights for survival.'

Collateral damage was expected during war but completely frowned upon by Gerry in this commercial setting. It was effectively mission failure when innocents got killed in the contracting world.

With less than three hours to fine-tune the plan a few things had to be squared away, they both knew what was coming next.

'Sean, you need to battle zero the G28 rifle for complete confidence as he would need to put people down from over 500 metres away.' A quick zero at 100 metres would suffice but 300 metres was more realistic for complete confidence especially as he would be the first to shoot if it went to plan. Confirmatory zero ensured that Sean could adjust his sights for distance and wind to distances beyond 300 and still know his shots would hit, theoretically back to 1000 metres and more. Sean nodded in agreement and moved to carry out Gerry's orders.

Without delay, Gerry, with Andrew still loosely zip-tied to the steering wheel, drove off to 300 metres using the GPS trip metre to judge the distance exactly.

Gerry grabbed the foldable table and erected it, turning it lengthways and standing it up. Finding some duct tape and piece of an A4 document he turned it blank side and taped it to the table. Using another small piece of duct tape, he ripped off a small square and stuck it to the middle of the A4 paper as an aiming marker.

Happy no-one had sent a message on the sat-phone, Gerry switched the jammer off. Using the two-way radio he gave Sean the go-ahead to fire when he was ready. He could visualise Sean's preparation, which would be nothing short of gold-standard marksmanship principles, building a strong firing position around the weapon so he would be naturally aligned to the target, so that he wouldn't have to muscle in to force the scope sights onto the duct tape aiming mark. He would also start his breathing cycle noting his mil-dot sight moves perfectly up and down on the duct tape centre point with no diagonal movement left or right.

Closing his eyes he would continue the cycle three more times before opening them after exhaling for a few seconds. If the millimetre dot sight is still perfectly centred on the duct tape, he had confirmation that his position was rock-solid and perfectly balanced without having to force the shot.

Big-timers at local gun clubs tended to hold their breath then pull the trigger, either snatching it in anticipation or flinching as the shot release surprises them causing the shot to go high right. Pros however knew that you had to breathe out slowly, almost emptying your lungs of oxygen causing no internal diaphragm movement, then after three or four seconds the slow trigger pull suddenly releases the shot without warning to the firer.

Sean had obviously just executed this cycle perfectly as the first bullet smashed through the plastic table.

A single round that he knew would hit low from a cold barrel was initially ignored as he primed himself for the second. Hearing the second bullet penetrate the plastic Gerry walked over and checked the fall of shot. He shivered, actually feeling quite exposed, Sean could just kill him now if he wanted. He wondered if Sean was thinking the same?

Inspecting the table and A4 paper the bullet hole was just inside the left hand edge of the A4 paper by about 2 inches and slightly low of centre.

Feeding that back to Sean, he informed him that he needed to adjust four clicks right for deflection and one up for elevation.

Sean fired his second round.

On quick inspection it was on the outer left edge of the duct tape but smack on centre. Gerry transmitted 'one right elevation good,' before moving out of the way again.

As Sean split the duct tape perfectly in the centre Gerry nodded. The battle zero was complete.

Sean rejoined Gerry and they quickly switched over positions for Gerry to zero his M4 rifle from only a hundred metres. After two rounds Gerry was dead-centre and happy.

'I will lead off with Andrew driving,' he instructed. 'Keep up with us and we will stop about thirty minutes out. We will quickly go over the plan and add anything new we come up with on the way. Andrew will not be briefed until this point.'

'Understood, let's go then. It's high time we finally meet WHITEOUT and more importantly have the satisfaction of letting Robby's family know that man who killed him is now in the dirt too,' Sean said.

CHAPTER 37

For the first time on this expedition Decker was not alone inside the comforts of his Hilliberg two-man extreme-weather tent.

It wasn't an extreme-weather tent anymore as it was only the inner of the tent. The outer flysheet had been left standing when he made a run for it to look like the tent was normal. He had thrown the inner into his rucksack with the spare poles though he never expected to be sharing it with a Russian.

Either way it did keep some of the wind out and offered a limited form of protection. Decker was amazed that the Russians hadn't brought their own tents, but then again they'd had no idea what they were getting themselves into and probably thought it was going to be a simple few hours out.

Bound with zip ties around his hands and ankles, he was out of the elements but by no means out of danger. Held captive in what could only be called an ad hoc detainment facility in Antarctica, his destiny and future were in the hands of the Russians.

Fortunately so far, the Russians had cottoned on that beating and attempting to torture him for information would be futile.

Ivan had a dilemma to thrash out in his head.

Had the Clinic members disclosed their real identities as calculated cold-blooded killers? Or were they still playing the grey incognito bullshit?

This mattered, it was essential and he knew he would have to work it out fast; he wanted this ambush to be executed with minimal fuss with maximum casualties minus Gerry, Sean and WHITEOUT.

The Commander at Vostok had already told him that a clean-up operation would happen once they had secured The Clinic members. How this would happen he didn't know, that wasn't his problem.

The big two were all he needed and he already had one, the rest were simply collateral damage.

Decker was lying on his side in the foetal position with his back towards him.

No doubt reading all the writing on the tent walls. It seemed to be a combination of mantras that Decker could look at, every waking second on his back in his sleeping bag.

Next to the mantras was the daily statistics of each day's work. Miles covered, hours spent walking and finally his final position for that day.

Written with a thick black permanent marker some of the early statistics had faded a touch but were still readable to Ivan.

On the other hand the mantras and mission statements were bold, black and readable from 10 metres away. Decker had obviously meticulously kept retracing over the original statements to ensure they kept the crisp, sharp and penetrating thoughts clear in his head.

Like the ice he skied on every day they were crystal-clear and clean. No room for pink fluff or outdated clichés that normal folk spewed up everyday, in a vain attempt to be inspiring or turn that negative situation into a thriving positive.

It was a pure language he believed in.

'In order to win, you must suffer,' Ivan said as he read one out. Decker rolled his eyes back awaiting the cocky, patronising follow-on comment.

'Ha, "Who Dares Wins" now I like that one. It is the greatest Special Forces motto in the world I have to admit Harry, and B Squadron hey?' Ivan commented seeing it written underneath the quote 'Who Dares Wins'.

'Bravo Two Zero I recall, they were B Squadron. It is a great book, it would have been even more enthralling if my English was better when I read it over ten years ago.'

Decker had seen little of Ivan's features apart from his face and that was through the large eyeholes of his poorly fitting balaclava.

He placed him at around 28-30 years of age, judging by his lack of laughter lines, or maybe that was because the Russians weren't renowned for their sense of humour. He wasn't a seasoned hard man or killer looking squarely at him in the eyes, but what officer is? Decker concluded. They simply unleashed the dogs of war; and he had been one of those dogs for years.

Decker knew he had the psychological edge over Ivan. He sensed an almost childlike nature about him, a kid that read action-hero books especially the American and British Special Forces' books, hence his knowledge of Bravo Two Zero. Now he had his little prize, a burnt-out, exhausted former SAS Sergeant as his prisoner. Though he tried to be cocky reading off the mantras it was all a show, a dick-measuring contest to let Decker know that he was not intimidated.

Decker knew he could rip this guy's throat out in a heartbeat. Simply grabbing his throat and staring into his greyish eyes that had faded from a piercing blue over the years, would make Ivan piss and shit himself.

Ivan was smart though.

Not engaging Decker for information but merely repeating the fact that he was being hunted down by his own people almost kept him neutral.

'How do you think this is going to end Harry? You are lucky, I have saved your life today. Christ knows how many else are out there after you.'

Decker pondered this in relation to the RV.

If I asked him why we are meeting Trans-Ant what would he say? There is no tactical reason for meeting them. Why possibly compromise this mission when he could cut and run back to Vostok.

Now I know he knows there are other members of The Clinic with Trans-Ant, this is why we're meeting them.

He has no idea I have figured this out.

Does he want to detain them, kill Trans-Ant I assume then take us all to Vostok, then Russia. Or maybe everyone, it would be a Bermuda Triangle moment for a lot of people to try and work out, but that could be his plan.

Fuck it I will ask him.

Rolling onto his back in order to look Ivan in the eye when he asked the question, Decker grunted as the pain of rolling on top of his zip-tied arms shot through him, before rolling fully on to his left side.

'What is the point in meeting Trans-Ant team? Why get them involved they are good people?'

'To buy time,' Ivan replied immediately.

'How exactly?'

'They meet us, they can make a call back to Union Glacier telling them you're okay, that way no one is worrying, no one is looking for you.'

'Andrew would have already done that straight after I called to report that I was injured and the expedition is over…'

WHITEOUT purposely started putting Ivan in a corner.

'That's not true. They might not have done so I need to make sure this is done to keep the heat off,' Ivan began to take the bait and defended himself instantly.

Smirking inwardly enjoying the beginning of the mental mind game he knew he could unfurl on the Russian, Decker continued. 'Are you for fucking real buddy? You have just added another moving part to this whole fucked-up situation. They would have just waited a few hours then left, they have a flight later tonight hence it was a leaving visit. Now you're going to have to kill or detain them. No wonder you lot are stuck in Vostok asshole.'

Decker knew the reason but couldn't show that, and was happy just to get a quick dig into him and hoped that he would bite. He was starting to work on his mind, placing a bit of doubt in his mind to shake him up a bit.

'There is a reason for everything Harry, not even you have all the answers. In fact at least I know the answers, it appears you don't even know what answers you're being hunted for, but that will come with time for sure.'

'So how are you going to play this RV out?' Decker cannoned forwards, choosing to ignore Ivan's attempt at one-upmanship.

'Seeing as you ask so nicely, I will tell you now instead of later. You will remain in this tent, bound as you are the bait. The team and I will be in an ambush position behind the rubble. Trans-Ant team will pull up in their vehicles, no doubt they will think you're resting or asleep and approach the tent. At this point they will all be static, probably a few members out of the vehicles to see their little hero. Then we will ambush you all at close quarters. Anyone messes around they will die.'

'Then?' Decker asked seemingly nonplussed.

'That's umm, how do you say it? "On a need to know basis" I think. You like this Mr SAS man?'

'As we say, it sounds like a plan,' Decker sarcastically replied.

He knew there was no point in idle banter so did not labour the conversation. He had got the plan out of him though. Ivan thought of him as a prisoner at his mercy. What did it matter if he disclosed the plan, he was bound hand and legs? He supposedly could not affect it in any way. Trans-Ant and the Clinic would turn up, come and check the tent with him bound inside it.

Then the ambush went in, simple but effective. Three Russians with automatic weapons could deliver this blow easily. Any fast moves by the Clinic or Trans-Ant would result in their deaths.

As Ivan finished reading the daily stats off the inner tent he too started to think more. A few scenarios crossed his mind.

Would The Clinic let members of Trans-Ant greet WHITEOUT then only disclose themselves as The Clinic once back in the wagons with WHITEOUT, he thought.

This would be a major problem for us. Or will they just hold WHITEOUT at gunpoint immediately after they are introduced as the documentary team taking Trans-Ant team by surprise, and then getting them all to obey their commands at gunpoint?

Had they already got Trans-Ant team under duress? All held captured, tied up? This was another consideration for the Russians.

No matter what the situation was, WHITEOUT had to be seen initially on his own and meet them on his own to have the element of surprise intact for the Russians. This had to happen Ivan realised and this part was the weakest link in the chain of events but was the strongest link for The Clinic to get the upper hand in what could be a raging gun battle.

Ivan knew he had some serious thinking to do but at this point he knew leaving Decker on his own while all the guys were in the ambush ready was risky.

He was even considering staying in the tent with Decker himself but this had potential to go wrong and deep down knew he didn't have the balls to be alone with him when someone entered the tent.

His last excuse was he had to be in a position to command and control so had to observe from outside. He could risk putting another Russian in there but then he would lose one vital source of firepower.

His mind kept thinking. All alone in the inner tent he'd gone full circle. Only days ago he was relaxing after an exhausting day on the ice, flaked out on his sleeping bag knowing another hard day had been cracked.

Now he was bound, laid on his side waiting for 'The Clinic' that he'd always profoundly known to be The FEAR who were on their way there. Time for thinking had ceased. He knew a member of The Clinic or Trans-Ant would be entering his tent soon, whether they would leave together, or at all, wasn't even worth contemplating he thought.

It was all back to being reactive. It was instinctive; when it happened he knew he would react and go for it. 'My survival is their deaths,' he reminded himself.

Another thought entered his head, a thought that always comforted him before he slept at night, beautiful Larnaka. He imagined running his fingers through her hair, smelling her warm skin on his. Pure beauty in its true essence. Then quick as a flash she was gone.

Some Russian whistling through their fingers to another member of their team broke his reverie. He caught a quick exchange of Russian dialect followed by footsteps crunching through the snow, then silence.

He pushed all other thoughts from his mind. Forcing himself to focus with one solid fact, one single thought over and over in his mind: 'The Clinic are finally coming to collect.' His blood warmed with rage at the thought of it, it had been a long time coming.

CHAPTER 38

Andrew looked somewhat blankly at the sketch map that Gerry and Sean had decided was the master plan to take the Russian's down and rescue Decker. For the last 30 minutes Gerry had been talking him through it.

Two trucks, one sniper weapon, an M4 carbine, air marker balloon and Andrew, an unwilling volunteer who now had a critical part to play.

Andrew reluctantly spoke, like a school boy in a strop. 'Okay so we stop 500 metres away from where we see the tent or RV? Both trucks close together so I can set up an air weather ballon and Sean can establish a sniping position from underneath his truck?'

'Yes you got it' Gerry answered, a little taken back by a sudden injection of interest.

'Hopefully he will locate their positions, then we will proceed forward to within 50 metres of the tent or end location.'

'Carry on Andrew.' Gerry ignored his shaking voice.

'When we stop I get out, I shout for Decker, you take some photos to buy time and locate the Russians. Then I enter his tent with the pistol and say 'Old Harry Rocks, they need you alive.' Then I cut him loose if he's alone or shoot anyone else in the tent? Then just lay low until you collect me?'

Gerry paused for a second looking at Andrew. He did feel guilty though emotions weren't a problem to him, he just knew how to override them.

'I'm truly sorry Andrew. I wish I could explain but it's not that simple. Harry Decker is a wanted man, and wanted long ago. In fact he is called WHITEOUT, Andrew. We set out to kill him but now we may need him alive, and that includes you. I was ordered to kill your friends because my boss knows we are going to meet the Russians when we meet

WHITEOUT, if your team knew about all of this we could not risk the secrecy. This won't help, but it's bigger picture bollocks and you've just been caught in the crossfire.'

As Gerry waited for a response, even some sort of ridiculous understanding or empathy from Andrew he saw it.

Like a red beacon glowing in the dark to warn aircraft of an imminent high-rise building, the bright red doors of the inner tent lit up the horizon. Purposely designed in this bright colour to enable easy recognition for Mountain rescue teams it had done the job. From over a kilometre away it was visible and Gerry maintained his breathing at a calm pace, eyes barely blinking taking in the rest of the surroundings.

Driving into harm's way without any real actionable intelligence was the hallmark of the SAS's motto 'Who Dares Wins' but even then you had numbers and equipment, a robust team of operators with a true desire to kill the enemy and high-tech infrastructure to back things up if it all went to rat shit.

Gerry knew this plan was lacking all of those constituents, they were literally winging it, back of a fag packet stuff. He was no stranger to letting this type of operation be sanctioned with even less intelligence in the past, but he was normally sitting next to someone akin to Sully watching it all erupt. Now he was in it himself.

This thought hit him hard, if he had been briefing Whitehall he would have had to have maintained a straight face as he uttered the words: 'A dynamic risk assessment has been conducted and we will be executing an Emergency Response directive.' People in Whitehall actually got paid to make this sort of jargon up, but that's the way the government liked things; professionally distorted terminology that conjured up images of fast-thinking individuals, surrounded by high-tech equipment, executing strategic-level ops to save the day. This always got a 'yes' vote. Would this ambush plan get a yes? No time to wonder he cracked on.

'Sean you got this?' Gerry transmitted over the two-way radios referring to them having a visual marker on the red tent doors that was now the RV position.

'Roger mate, seen,' Sean acknowledged.

'I make it 1100 metres North-West to the RV,' Gerry said reading the GPS data. 'It looks about bang on, let's just slow it down a touch, come to my right mate so your view is not obscured,' Gerry requested knowing that they now had to start looking for the Russian ambush party without letting them know that this was what they were up to.

'Will do, are we still looking at a 500-metre stop-short?' Sean transmitted manoeuvring to Gerry's right.

'Yeah, do you see the massive rubble field with a few pressure ridges behind the tent stretching East to West? I reckon that's the classic linear ambush site Sean if I was a betting man.'

'Yeah got it, on the money. It looks like a good position if you ask me, unlike ours at the moment,' Sean replied, knowing that they were wide open now on the wrong side of the rubble field, in the open or killing zone with no protection if the bullets started flying.

'That's what I expected, they chose well but the tent is up mate. That's a good sign. That puts us back in the game, we still have one card left if WHITEOUT is inside it.' Gerry quickly switched his thinking to the plan he had envisaged for the tent option. He glanced at Andrew who was obviously nervously listening and driving them carefully forward under his directions towards the ambush site.

'Sean when we are 700 metres away I will count us down to our first stop position for the weather balloon serial. As we planned, stay on my right side, close and tight. I will traverse East to West parallel to the tent and look for a clear line of sight position. We don't want any sastrugi or ice formations blocking your view of the tent and ambush site.'

This part was essential. Sean had to be able to see the ambush area with no obstacles to his front. Gerry knew that with a 'line of sight' he could acquire a target through his scope with no terrain getting in the way of the bullet as it hurtled faster than the speed of sound to the recipient's instant death. A 7.62-calibre bullet was designed to stop people, not hurt or injure them. A sniper rifle had one purpose and one purpose only. Kill with every single round, one round, one kill.

From 500 metres out this job was a walk in the park for Sean. A conventional sniper on a battlefield would look to stand off between 600-1500 metres picking off strategic targets, their fellow soldiers would be engaging at closer ranges with smaller arms.

'200 metres to stop-short,' Gerry transmitted.

'200,' Sean repeated scanning the terrain towards the tent; things looked promising so far as the Russians were clearly being slack.

'Gerry look at the ice formation jutting out North of the tent or behind it.'

'Got it mate.'

'It's like a dog shit on a snooker table,' Sean joked.

'That's got to be the ambush site for sure,' Gerry said looking around and taking in the surroundings.

700 metres out and scanning the area closest to the tent there was a linear formation East to West about 50 to 60 metres long that had three large lumps of ice and rubble occupying it, almost like three perfectly formed ice pyramids rising from the ground. Equally spread apart it formed three dream positions for the Russians to hide behind and launch an ambush.

Directly North, behind the tent was the smaller of the three pyramids only two metres rising out of the ice rubble.

Gerry quickly muttered under his breath, 'You fucking twat,' before transmitting to Sean.

'The sun,' Gerry spat down the radio.

'What Gerry?' Sean transmitted back a little confused.

'The sun is high right to them if they're behind those three larger ice formations North of the tent, do you see?'

'Yeah, do you reckon that's where they are?'

'Yes I do so we are going to have to loop around to the West then come back in on a North-East bearing so that the sun is behind us and in their eyes as we approach the tent. If we stay like this the sun will be to their South and it won't bother them. Do you copy?' Gerry again playing his 'A-game' waited for Sean to understand what he was thinking.

'You're right Gerry, I will just keep following and wait for the countdown.'

Repositioning as Gerry was suggesting would make a huge difference. The sun in the Russians' eyes would buy them a fraction of a second each time they fired as they would be squinting and adjusting to filter out the brighter light. Those fractions meant the world in close-quarter battle, it would be the difference between living or dying out here.

'Roger that.'

Gerry redirected Andrew to carry out exactly what he just described to Sean.

After moving West for a few minutes Gerry called it in. '50 metres to stop point.'

'50,' Sean replied.

The trucks now had the sun directly on their backs, this would definitely cause problems for the Russians Gerry thought as he looked to his rear. A novice mistake by whoever was organising this ambush.

'Sean when I stop, pull up on my right, there is a piece of sastrugi there, pull your truck up over it, it will give you a great cover position under the truck.'

'That's a stop, stop, stop Sean,' Gerry ordered.

Andrew brought the truck to a smooth halt.

Sean got a visual of the sastrugi and went static on top of it alongside the other truck.

Looking at his GPS Gerry read 512 metres North-East to the RV position.

WHITEOUT's tent was clear to see, alone with no activity present as of yet, Gerry summised before winding down his window to speak to Sean.

'Right, I have just noticed something else mate and it's definitely a sign the Russians or whoever are with him. His tent has been set up with the wind hitting it broadside, WHITEOUT would always set his tent up with the prevailing wind hitting the bell end. I know he is only using the inner tent skin but the principle is the same. The wind hasn't changed direction today or the last few days for that matter. Maybe he's letting us know he is under duress.'

A big assumption from Gerry, though Sean wouldn't be convinced totally until he pinged a Russian through his sights. In some respects Sean thought Gerry was searching for a signal from WHITEOUT that just wasn't there.

'Well spotted mate,' Sean was impressed by Gerry's attention to extreme detail but still sounded a little dubious.

'Okay you sort out your sniper position under the truck while we set up the weather balloon. Start scanning hard as we will take about twenty minutes. Designate prefix positions of objects too and obviously locate any Russians mate or activity of interest.'

'Roger that,' Sean confirmed, his adrenalin kicking in to both be on the hunt and eager to confirm this was all for real and not just in Sully's imagination.

Gerry now switched his attention to Andrew. Though Gerry was sorry for murdering his mates and was going easy on him it was business mode again and this was serious, the nice guy part had worn thin. Gerry now needed to instil a sense of fear into him again. He slammed his hand down on the dashboard loudly. Andrew jumped out of his skin as he was focusing on the tent in the distance.

'Andrew.'

'Yes, yes sorry I was thinking.'

'Andrew I am going to cut you loose. Do not fuck around with me, there are Russians behind that rubble field 500 metres away. We're the only fucking way you're walking out of here so we are a team now right? They catch you they will torture you to death, literally cut your bollocks off and throw them in your mouth. They learnt that off the Mujahedeen in Afghanistan in the eighties. Trust me, do as we planned and we might all get out of here.'

'I have no intentions of pulling any stunts Gerry, I'm shaking all over look at me,' Andrew stammered holding out his hands that were shaking uncontrollably.

'Don't worry that's natural. Once we get into this you won't be thinking about your hands shaking, you'll be too concerned being face down in the snow crawling for your life. But you will make it, we will all make it out,' Gerry looked at him to give reassurance and he meant it. He wasn't going to die on this job today, today wasn't his day to join the fast exit club.

'Let's do it, you get the balloon off the back seat and let's just act normally, they will be watching us through binoculars,' Gerry added just to put Andrew on edge even more.

Walking 20 metres to the West of the truck Andrew started to erect the weather balloon. Gerry surveyed the area naturally to try and pick up any novice mistakes the Russians had made. The tent was the first schoolboy error, there were bound to be others he thought.

'That's me set up, scanning for targets,' Sean confirmed.

'Roger, keep giving commentary,' Gerry acknowledged.

'All static at tent, I have clear arcs of fire East to West. Let's prefix the pyramids with cardinal positions as this works easy Gerry.'

'Sounds good Sean, crack on.'

'Okay, left pyramid is West, centre pyramid behind the tent is North and the pyramid to the right is East,' Sean transmitted as he made himself comfortable underneath the truck and tucked himself into the right edge of the sastrugi.

'That works for me Sean.'

Continuing Sean used his binoculars as it gave him a wider field of view of the target area without moving so much, as opposed to using the scope on his sniper rifle. Normally a sniper would have a number two who did this job but double-hatting was their only option today. Sean sensed things could start to unfold rapidly as a quick rush of adrenaline flushed through his body. As he was panning East with his binoculars something caught his eye. Panning back West it wasn't imaginary. Sure enough the huge white hood with a furry wolf ruff around the rim, had caught his eye. It was to the East of the tent, right behind East pyramid.

'Fuck me this is happening, Sully was on the money,' Sean muttered under his breath.

'Stand by, stand by that's one Russian behind East Pyramid with an assault weapon, wait.' Wait means do not interrupt.

Gerry turned without showing any signs of surprise or anticipation as he knew he was being watched closely. Novice mistakes like touching his earpiece or talking down into his radio were mistakes he had ironed out over 20 years of operating under this sort of scrutiny.

Tradecraft wasn't tradecraft to the likes of him, it was simply daily life in a world of double-cross, double-bluff.

A burst of compressed air screeched out breaking the silence, catching Gerry and Sean off guard. Gerry did his best to not flinch at the sound as Andrew immediately knelt down to peg the balloon cord in to the ice.

'Fucking hell Andrew, cheers for the warning,' grasping his heart Gerry tried to joke in shock.

As the balloon filled with helium a bright orange ball grew to the size of three beach balls. Gerry thought that it was the size of his heart ten seconds previously.

Attached to the guideline Gerry held it while Andrew continued to peg it to the floor with a large titanium ice screw.

'No change, one Russian East Pyramid,' Sean updated him.

'That's it Gerry,' Andrew informed him standing up.

Mimicking a few final checks with a notepad for the Russian audience, they started to make their way back to the trucks.

Both jumping back in the truck Sean came online with a little more urgency.

'Stand by, stand by I've got another Ruskie almost directly behind the tent, next to North Pyramid. Just caught him with binoculars so be aware they're on us.'

'Sean do you have clean shots? How exposed are they?' Gerry asked wanting a definitive answer.

'We're talking chest and above when they pop up for a look.'

'Well let's hope they keep popping up like meerkats for a look then, we'll go forward and stop. Last time guys listen in. Here's the final brief. We stop, get out, do the mock photo-shoot to look random. Andrew then walks forward with the weapon and knife concealed calling to WHITEOUT like you would do naturally Andrew.'

'Yes, yes,' Andrew stuttered. Gerry knew he was getting uptight again now but he couldn't do anything for him now.

'If at any time those two Russians make a move then don't hesitate to drop them Sean. I will be behind the bonnet with the M4 on the seat at this point faking the battery change on the camera.'

'Got it,' Sean confirmed.

'If I see a few and think I am in a good position to start killing them I will initiate with rapid tones on the radio, step out from the truck and start shooting. You start shooting too Sean. If I don't have time to let you know I'm about to shoot you will see, and hear it hopefully. In fact you better see it or else we're fucked, if they're that close I will need some serious support if there's two or more,' Gerry added.

'So gold-standard is Andrew making it into the tent. When that happens you should have eyes on a few Russians too and hopefully I will have clocked the rest of their team.' Sean paused before finalising, 'Main thing is anything that looks life-threatening to you I will start dropping them, no hesitation.'

'Yep we're all clear on that now,' Gerry now happy it was clear-cut. 'Right Andrew let's get moving,' Gerry said as he pointed to the tent.

Ivan patiently watched the men go about their business. Exposed to the elements having left Decker protected in the tent, he had anticipated that the Trans-Ant team would turn up a lot earlier. He and the others were now paying the price frantically flapping their arms behind their cover to avoid them seizing up against the cold, especially their hands.

As they saw the truck pulling off, Ivan signalled down the line for everyone to stay completely still, any stupid moves now would risk compromising the ambush position entirely.

He had hidden Mick with a colleague East of the tent and he was occupying the ground directly north behind Decker's tent, heading up the killer group.

With just the West pyramid still out of view, Sean had two out of the three in his sights intermittently. Poor discipline had seen them pop their heads up and down like a group of meerkats just as Gerry had said.

Gerry was conscious a Russian must be behind the West Pyramid area as this was the missing position in a classic ambush formation at the moment. The centre men forming what was known as the 'killer group', whilst the left and right side were called the cut-offs, being the East and West pyramids on this occasion.

The idea was simple. The left or right cut-offs would inform the killer group when the enemy were entering the ambush area, they would not fire but just watch them walk or drive past. Once the enemy was in front of the killer group they would step up and engage and start shooting to destroy said enemy. Any escapees running for their lives would be shot by the cut-offs as they try to escape and evade left or right.

For centuries this tactic had been used and for centuries it had always worked. As long as the enemy didn't know they're walking into it of course.

Gerry knew he was driving into it.

Insanely he knew he would then be walking into it.

He also knew he had to walk out of it with WHITEOUT.

Directing Andrew to drive towards the tent he got him to stop 40 metres short of it, checking the right wing mirror he knew he had to keep Sean's arcs as wide and clear for a possible shot to the West of the tent.

'Here is golden,' he transmitted.

Sean had a clear vector for all possibilities, enabling a shot for anyone popping up West of the tent behind the rubble.

Sean started to tighten up his position so the sniper rifle was now in a comfortable position to be fired in rapid succession. Once they came to a halt he would have to be on his game big style.

Observing his front he still had the Russian at East Pyramid but the guy at the North Pyramid had battened down the hatches and was out of sight behind the rubble.

Observing past the tent to the West, Sean still had no Russian in his sights. There were a few large obvious pieces of ice rubble but no evidence of another Russian at the West pyramid. It was the one you didn't see that always got you, but he knew they couldn't see him facing the sun 500 metres away. For Gerry's sake though he had to identity a shooter from that position. 'Haha there you are you fucker, right on time,' Sean snarled under his breath.

'Just saw a reflection off a scope or binoculars Gerry left edge of West Pyramid, can't identify a person just saw the glint off an optical sight of some sort,' Sean quickly updating Gerry of the latest find.

Gerry hit the transmission button twice to confirm he had received the information. About to come to a halt 40 metres away he didn't speak into his mic as he knew the Russians were watching him through telescopic sights or binoculars and he didn't want to trigger their paranoia kicking everything off, prematurely squandering the planned encounter.

Sean automatically started reporting.

'Green on East, Red North, Red West,' as they all knew this referred to the pyramids Sean just transmitted West, North or East now to save time. Green meant he had a clear shot, red meant no shot.

Bending down in the truck Gerry started talking into his radio, 'Okay Sean we're about 40 metres away from the tent, when Andrew gets out I will take photos from behind the bonnet, rifle on the seat ready to go.'

'Okay, still only green on East, standing by,' Sean replied still anxious to get at least two targets in his sights. Due to the 500-metre stand-off, the North and the East positions could be engaged rapidly, as it would only take Sean a slight shoulder movement to realign his sights without taking his eye away from the scope. This process was literally a few seconds from adjustment to letting a second shot deliver a fatal blow.

With the engine turned off to avoid arousing suspicion Gerry turned to Andrew, 'You know the drill Andrew. You have the pistol in your inside left jacket pocket and the knife in your right one. When you get out act normally, give him a call, walk to the tent then turn around after 10 metres and shout at me. Simply say, "John take a few snap shots" then point to the tent etcetera. Just play about for a bit. When I say, "the battery is dead" and head back to the truck you proceed forward, just shout to me "He must be asleep lets get this prick up or something" then just get in the tent. You must get in that tent and hand over the weapons. Understand?' Gerry demanded.

'Yeah photos, dead battery so I walk towards him saying let's wake him up, then no stopping till I'm in the tent quickly say about Old Harry.' Andrew was trying desperately hard not to go into shock and garbled his words like a drunk person. Gerry looked at him in concern. 'Decker needs you Andrew. You have to get in that tent.'

'Ok let's do it,' Andrew gritted his teeth together and clenched his jaw tight trying to psych himself up.

'Good, then just stay with him, listen to me shouting, then keep low and get back to this truck, we're all going to make it out, that's a promise, trust me Andrew.'

Andrew hesitantly nodded his head. This assurance from a man who had just brought hell and unimaginable pain on three widows, and now fatherless children was a hard one to believe.

He took one last look at Gerry and one last deep breath.

'Okay this is it, and I will do my best.'

'Great, okay, let's up the fucking antie,' Gerry said before immediately transmitting to Sean: 'Stand by, stand by that's us foxtrot out of the truck,' Gerry informed Sean.

'Copy, green East,' Sean replied.

Things had to be kept even shorter and sharper now. Transmissions to the minimum, Gerry knew that Sean would now only report green for Russians in his sights, and not bother with any red Russians that he couldn't see, it just wasted time.

Both guys got out of the truck and Andrew true to form had shredded his shock-like state and started shouting: 'Decker! Wake up, city boys to the rescue.'

This was what Decker had referred to them as. Rich city boys gallivanting around the globe, just spanking money like it was going out of fashion, and drinking like it was their last day on the planet.

'Harry!' Andrew yelled out again.

There was no reply.

'He must be asleep Andrew, stop there mate and let me get a few photos,' Gerry commanded so it could be heard by all. Cringing inwardly slightly at his role-play, Gerry knew it was buying them time they needed.

Andrew turned around following the internal script listening to Gerry's commands.

'Move left mate so I can get the tent in the photo,' Gerry ordered him like a seasoned pro bossing a slutty page-three model about.

'Keep moving, that's it,' Gerry began his covert pan starting out on full zoom, wide angle looking West of Andrew trying to locate the West Pyramid Russian. Snapping away he brought the camera down to his front inspecting the imaginary shots.

'Stay there mate the sun is killing it a bit from behind, let's try again.'

Bringing the camera to his eye Gerry desperately searched again for the Russian knowing that this was his last chance before it became ridiculously suspicious.

Holding the camera still looking straight at Andrew, Gerry scanned out to the West through the lens again and his patience reaped dividends. Peeping around the ice formation, unable to control his curiosity, the Russian had dropped his guard, Gerry knew exactly where he was. This didn't mean too much at the moment, Gerry was two metres from his rifle and all hell could break loose any second if any of the Russian's lost their nerve.

As Gerry lowered the camera to check his photos he shook the camera, pressed a few buttons before declaring.

'Fucking batteries, this place does my head in. I will get the spare.' Then started to walk back.

Andrew knew this was his cue for the long walk, the walk of death maybe. Fighting for the survival of himself and Harry. Shaking, the thick outer clothing disguising it, he continued his walk like a bomb disposal expert approaching a device.

He couldn't help but look for the Russians before he remembered his job and how vital it was.

'Decker you knobber you awake old chap?' Andrew called out before turning to Gerry for reassurance as he continued shouting, 'I think he's getting his head down Jim.'

Good work Andrew, Gerry thought, as he mimicked playing with the camera below the dashboard, instead priming himself with the rifle. His right hand was wrapped around the trigger handle, finger on the outside of the trigger guard. Picking the weapon up with one hand and turning to initiate a contact would be easy. It was just a matter of timing; he was still convinced the best time would be when Andrew was in the tent. No way would the Russians shoot at the tent. They would be too busy trying to identify The Clinic members from the innocent Trans-Ant team.

His thoughts were interrupted.

'Green East,' Sean confirmed. Not responding Sean was just updating. Gerry held his breath.

Andrew was at the tent door fidgeting with the door zip, looking back timidly as he started to pull it down.

Casually looking up Gerry took a casual glimpse West to locate his target. Nothing.

'Fucking arsehole where are you?' he said to himself.

Andrew naturally moved down on his knees as the zip approached the floor. He felt like he was a prisoner of war, kneeling down to receive the bullet to the back of his head.

Briefly closing his eyes he said a final few words not knowing what would occur when he unzipped the tent doors fully.

CHAPTER 39

Mick couldn't take any more, he had bled out to the point where he was feeling his consciousness slipping away. It was now or never, the freezing cold had numbed the pain of the gunshot wounds, he knew this was it.

With his hands bound at the front he'd been dragged along like a slave for the past eight hours, and now they'd finally stopped, his feet were bound too. Despite the tape tightly clamping his mouth shut, his teeth still clattered uncontrollably as the cold cut into his bones. Enough was enough, the Russian who was guarding him was doing a good job, although this latest hype of activity had caught his attention, the voices 40 metres away had lured him in, Mick watched him try and get a slight glimpse around the ice boulder. Mick had identified the voice shouting as Gerry, good to know he was no longer without allies out here, but he had to act. Staring at the knife strapped to the Russian's leg all day Mick kept running through his own plan, that knife was his sole mission right now.

With the Russian's attention still hooked on whatever was unfolding on the ice, Mick dug his feet in and used the ice wall next to him for leverage. Barely blinking to maintain his watch over the Russian, he managed to shimmy up the ice wall and stand, still restricted by his bound hands.

Knowing he had to make two big hops with his bound feet to cover the three-metre distance to the Russian, he bent his legs, primed for two explosive moves. The zip-ties was keeping his arms locked straight meaning that strangling this guy wasn't an option, but causing a loud reaction and letting The Clinic know something was wrong, was.

Sucking in some air and knowing it was now or never, he launched himself on the Russian's back, trying to clamp his arms around his neck.

The Russian gasped, obviously stunned as Mick's arms moved over his head and around his upper arms making him lose complete grip of his weapon, which hung on the sling attached to his body.

The two men engaged in a full-on bear-hug as Mick requested every last ounce of power he still possessed in his body to come forward and help him fight and create some noise for attention. So far his attempts to scream and shout were nothing but futile murmurs as he was being driven back to the ice wall that he had used to gain purchase to stand.

As his back was slammed into the wall his face met with the Russian's head in an ear-splitting headbutt that immediately broke his nose. Not even having time to readjust and power out of the situation the Russian released four or five consecutive reverse headbutts, he was obviously no mug. Mick in his dazed state saw the guy quickly spin around so he was facing the ice wall, he felt his legs go numb beneath him as he was administered a classic judo-style kick and he hit the deck back first as the Russian jumped to his feet leaving Mick a moment to try and work out what had gone wrong through his blurred vision.

His eyes watering from his broken nose, he was conscious enough to make out the object that was fast approaching his face as he gritted his teeth.

As the butt of the Russian's rifle struck him in the face, he vaguely heard the blunt thud and sound of broken teeth echo across the ambush area.

He stared up at the Russian, waiting for the second butt stroke to hit that would surely knock him out completely, but the man was staring in the direction of the tent. Mick licked his blood as it ran from his nose into his mouth and tried to focus his eyes. He blinked and saw the man staring right through him convulsing as though a freight train had hit him in the back.

The Russian spun around in an almost perfect pirouette, dropping to his knees. Mick gasped, what the hell was going on? As blood began to pour out of the frayed exit wound in the man's chest Mick breathed out a sigh of relief, the fucker had been shot. Mick watched silently as the shockwave travelled across his captor's body.

'Come on die you fucker,' he whispered through his broken teeth. The man was clearly shocked that he'd been shot, he remained staring at his hands now covered in his own blood. His eyes started to roll to the back of his head and he spat out some of the blood clogging up his mouth onto the ice before his face hit the deck followed quickly by his body. Dead.

Ivan behind pyramid North had been literally an inch away from getting his head blown off. The burst had miraculously missed him as he was raising his head. He dropped back to the floor and waited for the ice splinters to stop, he knew he was under severe fire.

'Fuck.' He knew he had to find out what was happening, all he'd heard was the man he believed to be Gerry yelling 'Get in the tent, Si.' The loud clatter created by the bullet smashing his colleague's slung weapon as it exited his body chilled him to his core and he'd looked East to see his fellow Russian spinning to the ground. Crawling away a few metres so he wouldn't pop up in the same place he crawled frantically for another 5 metres, still noticing bullets smashing into the ice behind him by the continued onslaught.

Hyperventilating he rose from around the side of an ice ridge, located a man behind the bonnet of the truck and started to fire in sheer panic before composing himself and taking proper aim through his sights.

His bullets struck the bonnet, shattering the windscreen. Obviously startling the man from The Clinic who hit the deck. He squinted, the guy's head was tucked in behind the thick rubber front tyre.

Ivan continued to harass him with more fire.

With no fire coming back from the man, Ivan briefly took his finger off the trigger watching the undercarriage of the truck. He then quickly looked at the tent. Without warning a zipping sound of a bullet passed the truck and hit his weapon. The sheer velocity and force catapulted his unslung weapon out of his hands.

Sean from over 500 metres away had the satisfaction of seeing the impact of the weapon flying to the ground as the Russian's body was tumbling straight on top of it. As he witnessed the man hit the deck he quickly transmitted: 'North is down, East is down.' Without one command from anyone the fierce firefight had begun.

There was movement near the tent and Decker remained alert. He'd heard the gunshot and was hoping against all hope that it was one of the Russians that had gone down first. As the zip pulled up he threw himself, fully bound onto his knees, ready to headbutt his way out of the tent if needed.

As the gunshots increased in volume, Andrew scrabbled his way inside the tent.

They were immediately face-to-face with each other, Andrew grabbed hold of his shoulders clearly trying to blurt out something but he was obviously in a complete state of panic, knowing bullets were flying around him he couldn't get the words out. Stuttering then gasping for breath, Decker couldn't make sense of what he was saying.

'Andrew, Andrew what the fuck is happening?' Decker shouted out, trying to snap him into gear as the gunfire continued to erupt outside the tent.

'Andrew get a grip, get these zip-ties off me now,' fuck being patient Decker thought, no time for that, he was getting irate as he heard the firefight intensifying outside.

Suspended in shock Andrew managed to open his jacket that was already unzipped and pulled out a pistol. Decker dove straight at him side swiping him with his bound hands, knocking the pistol away then driving his forehead straight into Andrew's face. 'Fucker. No chance you're killing me today.'

As Andrew rolled back clutching his face he started screaming, 'They know why you didn't jump off Old Harry that day, we're here to get you out.'

'You fucking what?' delivering a double-handed blow to Andrew's face.

Momentarily Decker was stunned. Andrew was a civilian who had just pulled a pistol out on him moments ago. How the hell did he know about that day at Old Harry? What the fuck was happening?

Andrew was on his back with his palms facing up in submission, pulled his jacket wide open showing him the hunting knife.

The dots joined instantaneously. Decker didn't delay by asking questions.

'Cut me loose, cut me loose Andrew,' Decker shouted cancelling his second double-handed strike that would have knocked Andrew out cold.

He offered his wrists to Andrew, both lying on the floor to lower their profile and chances of getting caught in the crossfire. Andrew clenched the knife and started hacking and sawing his way through the zip-ties, trying to stabilise his shaking hands.

As the zip-ties broke the momentum of the cutting motion threw the blade deeply into Decker's hand.

'Fuck!'

'Sorry, so sorry…' Andrew naturally apologising, shook some more.

'Cut my legs free you idiot,' Decker winced slightly resisting the urge to swing for Andrew's jawline as penance. Instead he started shaking his hands out to improve his circulation before pulling back the top slide of the Glock to check if a round was already seated. He knew the magazine was loaded, but he always did a quick confidence check to see that a round was ready to be fired when the trigger was squeezed.

Pulling the top slide back a few millimetres he observed the chamber, glancing momentarily at his hand that was pissing out blood from the cut. That could wait. The pistol was loaded and ready to kill.

'Come on Andrew, hurry up we need to get away from this tent before it becomes a bullet magnet for the Russians,' Decker shouted.

With both hands on the knife now, Andrew focused and cut away like a man possessed.

'Okay you're free,' Andrew said, panting away like he had just sprinted 400 metres.

'Right give me the knife and stay down, we're going to crawl out of the side of the tent. Who is out there?' Decker demanded.

'They know why you didn't jump off—'

'You just said that,' Decker interrupted, he was not interested in remembering that right now.

'How many with you Andrew?'

'Only me and two assassins, they killed the rest.'

As WHITEOUT was manically cutting his way through the lining of the tent hopefully out of sight of the Russians, he couldn't even process that last comment. As he cut through, the sun's powerful rays shone into the tent temporarily blinding him. He could see the truck in the distance. He looked at Andrew who nodded back, 'Yes that's Gerry's truck.' No doubt Gerry was somewhere behind it using it as cover. Decker looked at Andrew, 'That's where we've got to get to.'

Gerry sensed a lull in the firefight, no bullets were flying so he turned to his left instinctively knowing the Russian just west of him must have got the courage to start shooting by now.

Things went into slow-motion for him as he saw a Russian Spetnaz Commando dressed in white camouflage drapes with his weapon up on aim, pointed straight at him.

There was no way that Gerry could get a shot off before him, milliseconds of the difference between life and death.

Gerry braced himself for impact of a high-velocity round tearing through his body. Knowing how the effects of a gunshot wound would work, his immediate image was the secondary trauma of the bullet tumbling uncontrollably through his organs creating a vacuum before exiting.

However the Russian hesitated as a flicker of movement occurred in the direction of WHITEOUT's tent. Not waiting to work out why, Gerry got his weapon up pointing roughly at him and let another burst go from the ground. Two or three bullets spat ice up in front of the Russian before another few bullets clipped his legs.

Tripping backwards the Russian let a burst of fire off into the air as he screamed and fell back behind cover.

Gerry jumped straight to his knees closing in tight to the wheel-arch again watching where the Russian had fallen.

Suddenly a huge block of ice was tossed up in the air from where the Russian fell. Sean was on him. Gerry breathed out. Another chunk flew into the air.

Gerry then looked to locate the Russian that was beyond the tent but again saw nothing. Even though Sean's comment 'North down' repeated in his head, his instinct told him that he wasn't necessarily finished. Out of his periphery he saw WHITEOUT exiting the tent crawling out through the side with Andrew crawling behind him.

'Move, fucking move Harry!' Gerry screamed as he got to his feet and began to give covering fire into Ivan's position just in case his instincts proved to be correct.

Watching him intently, WHITEOUT continued crawling forward with Andrew right behind him, his head almost up WHITEOUT's arse.

Still looking towards Ivan's position Gerry knew he was near the end of his first magazine, he had to make a decision to either change it now, which would take 3-4 seconds, or hold on aim until Ivan popped up again.

'Keep crawling, keep crawling,' Gerry shouted to the lads as a burst of fire came from behind the tent leaving a trail of spat-up ice only feet away from the two men crawling and in line with Gerry.

Knowing that the guy must be low and behind the tent somewhere Gerry stood up and let rip with a first burst of three to five rounds from his M4.

His second burst was followed by the worst sound and feeling he knew you could have on a two-way range.

Silence. 'Shit.' Gerry cursed.

The bolt carrier of his rifle locked to the rear instead of releasing forward and picking up another round to continue firing another shot.

Diagnosis simple.

Empty magazine, no bullets left.

Out of pure habit and to let WHITEOUT know that he needed to change a magazine he yelled: 'Stoppage, stoppage,' as he pressed the magazine release catch to eject the empty magazine off the weapon.

Out of his periphery he saw WHITEOUT register his call by immediately spinning onto his back, firing back through his legs with five shots intending to pin down whoever was firing from behind the tent. His shots had zero significance as another hail of bullets struck the ground around him and Andrew. As Gerry expertly switched the magazine the seconds seemed like hours as he watched WHITEOUT spin back onto his belly again and continue his crawl to the truck.

Magazine reloaded, Gerry instantly got trigger happy shouting, 'Move, move Harry, I'm covering.' Firing to suppress the Russian's position.

Completely catching Gerry off guard he saw Andrew scramble to his feet, unbeknownst to WHITEOUT, obviously in a stricken panic and started to run towards the truck completely cutting his arc of fire.

'Get down, get down!' Gerry screamed desperate for Andrew to move so that he could give cover against the Russian again.

As he watched Andrew look at him with the fear of death in his eyes his arms flayed up and his right leg stumbled as he spun around.

A millisecond later a bullet missed Gerry's head, clipping the windscreen frame. 'Andrew, no,' he looked out to see WHITEOUT shouting at him as Andrew's body tumbled to the ground.

With his arc free once more, Gerry re-engaged again giving more covering fire as WHITEOUT crawled as fast as he could to Andrew who was groaning on his back. Lying beside him he grabbed Andrew's right hand and rolled onto his back. With all of his strength WHITEOUT rose to his feet holding Andrew's arms around his neck so that he could drag him the remaining few metres.

Without looking back he started running to the truck.

Only 5 metres away Gerry remembered the Russian whose legs had been shot up West of him. Panicking and pissed off he had forgotten this in the chaos. Turning just as WHITEOUT dragged Andrew past him obscuring his view he realised that Sean would have stopped firing as all the commotion of Andrew and WHITEOUT moving would have blocked his view. It would have been too risky to keep suppressing the Russian's position West in case he hit one of the guys.

As they both passed him, the Russian crawled back up over the bank, weapon almost ready to fire.

Gerry instantaneously brought his weapon to bear knowing it was too late and that he wouldn't make the shot in time.

'Fuck!' he screamed in terror watching as the Russian's head got split in two, replaced with a giant chunk of flesh and bone. A 7.62 bullet from Sean's sniper rifle had terminated his threat.

'Get behind the truck into cover,' Gerry shouted at WHITEOUT.

WHITEOUT obeyed, carrying Andrew to the rear of the truck, dropping him down behind the tailgate.

Gerry quickly moved back to join them when one more shot was fired and he felt his right shoulder explode. He felt the bone shattering into his flesh as he let out a scream, dropping his weapon. Dropping to his knees he huddled in next to WHITEOUT and Andrew.

WHITEOUT looked at Gerry who was in agony clenching his right shoulder.

Decker, who had never forgotten a face, thought to himself: *'Metal factory, Bosnia, Sept 2000.'*

'Pass me that weapon and have you got any magazines,' Decker demanded not really bothered about Gerry's shoulder wound, that could wait he thought.

'Left pocket,' Gerry replied.

Quickly digging around in his pockets he found the two magazines. 'Best you fucking keep him alive,' WHITEOUT said pointing to Andrew who was now barely conscious. 'And get that other prick of yours out there in here now to back us up,' referring to Sean.

With that Decker did a quick confidence check again with the M4 then placed the pistol in his pocket.

Pausing momentarily and looking back at Gerry again, he pulled the pistol back out and handed it over to him knowing that Gerry may need to protect to himself if any Russians on the other side of the rubble were still alive.

His gaze switched to Andrew as his friend's head moved and he stared at him, the look was short-lived as bullets started to strike the side of the truck again, ricocheting away breaking their gaze.

'Stay with him,' he said to Gerry, gesturing at Andrew. 'This needs fucking ending now. I'm fed up of watching amateurs piss about.' He said it with such venom and disgust that he could tell Gerry was insulted. Decker didn't care, he was a big boy he'd get over it.

'I think two are dead Harry. How many are there?' Gerry asked.

'Three, I'm going to sprint out to the West near that Russian over there and work through clockwise to the East side to finish all these wankers off.'

Without waiting for a reply he started shooting multiple bursts North behind the tent before sprinting West over to the position to where the Russian just had his head split in half.

As he moved he kept the weapon upright in the air, his left arm pumping he canted the M4 to check that the bolt was fully forward ready to engage again. These advanced skills were designed to never catch a professional out, it told him instantly his weapon would fire again and not jam.

Approaching the Russian's last known position he was up on aim, creeping forward ready to finish him if needed however the sight that he was met with caused him to lower his weapon.

He looked at the body slumped over an ice formation, the head completely deformed by an angry 7.62 strike, the surrounding ground was covered in claret with fragments of flesh and brain.

Not hanging around to admire the shooter's handiwork he quickly started searching the Russian for any other munitions. He found nothing. He looked at the Russian's radio, to take it could be double-edged, as he didn't have an earpiece so any static noise could give his position away.

Leaving it where it was he rolled the man over on to his back, the bullet's small entry hole was just below his right eye, almost invisible, as the skin had closed up again. A total contrast to the exit wound that you could put your fist into and then some.

Decker looked towards where he thought Ivan was and heard in the distance the sound of the second truck closing in and fast with his extra cover, could this other guy be trusted Decker wondered? Better safe to assume the negative and carry on with the utmost of care.

The second truck's entrance was met with hostility as accurate fire from what could only be Ivan ensued without stopping. Sparks were flying off the engine block of the truck as it was hammered with bullets, Decker saw the driver's natural survival instinct kick in making him dive below the steering wheel, helpless as another burst of bullets struck the windscreen. Making a sharp left turn the truck headed towards the other guys almost losing control on the ice.

That's when he clocked something else. To his East, a perfect silhouette of a gun barrel was protruding past a bit of snow cover. Each shot released a puff of cordite fumes exiting the muzzle and heading towards the truck.

Without hesitation Decker took aim at the snow mound two feet back from the muzzle and pulled the trigger of the M4, letting out a barrage of fire that smashed the snow mound to pieces.

The muzzle disappeared instantly.

He unleashed another volley slightly more to the left and at ground level. Decker paused and dropped down to collect his thoughts.

'Have I hit him? I didn't hear anything so no I didn't. Right let's stalk this piece of shit in to submission. He's an officer for fuck's sake Decker , lets close him down.

Decker knew not to push it too fast, too soon. He was sure it was Ivan. It was a stalking situation in an Antarctic rubble field that meant Ivan could easily hide and ruthlessly pop up and kill him in the blink of an eye. He took a breath, the feeling of having an M4 assault rifle in his hands again was breathtakingly natural. He had never, ever forgotten how it felt in his hands, how much it weighed or the feeling of the light but comfortable kick you felt in the shoulder from the recoil. He trusted himself, and he trusted his rifle, that was enough. Before he moved off he quickly went to ground and changed the magazine. Knowing he had about 13-15 bullets left he slickly removed the magazine, throwing the half magazine in his pocket and seating the new one into the magazine housing, checking it was fully home and locked in place.

Through his whole career he'd always put a fresh magazine on in situations like this; a slight lull in the battle gave him the moment to ensure he had 30 bullets for the next contact instead of guessing what he had left. He almost smiled as he recognised that pure blood instinct and training was taking over his mind again, flooding into him. It gave him renewed strength.

To come to face to face with Ivan would require a couple of bursts to shatter the ice formation, before the bullets could cut through and take him out.

He began to move out further North with the aim of cutting back East in a box-like movement, then South to where he thought Ivan was hiding. This would confuse Ivan as Decker suspected he would be watching the tracks behind him only, and not expect anyone to pop up from another direction.

Crouched over and taking small paces with his weapon up on aim he started his box move heading off North.

It all seemed a little surreal again as he fanned his way around corners of huge ice formations, many ten foot high and then some. Years of close-quarter battle had taught him to never telegraph or highlight his position by clumsy barrel discipline so he never walked past an ice feature with the barrel leading. This had almost cost Ivan his life moments earlier. Each turn he made around the ice was instantaneous, the moment his barrel protruded so did he, in a position to engage anything that moved behind it.

Now turning East, Decker made his way another 30 metres before stopping again to get his bearings before starting to head South to surprise Ivan. He could see both trucks 100 metres in front now but could not see any activity. Maybe they were all in cover trying to revive Andrew, he figured.

'*God I hope he makes it, Trans-Ant had nothing to do with this,*' he thought before quickly quashing any kind of thought that threatened his concentration.

'*Switch on Decker, this guy is close, his death is my survival.*'

As the wind picked up a little more it sprayed the spindrift into the air again, with this he noticed his own shadow to his left, which spooked him a little as he had missed this initially, his impeccable high standards were still in check, just a little rusty.

Ivan may have called forward the helicopter that must have dropped them off. Ivan wasn't just going to make a run for it, he would stand and fight till his fellow Russians came to back him up with force.

Then again maybe he was heading back towards the trucks, he couldn't let The Clinic escape surely Decker thought.

Or was he actually dead?

Not a chance.

White static from a handheld radio grabbed his attention. This was the exact reason he didn't take the Russian's radio.

Decker froze as he tuned in to the peripherals and listened acutely over the light breeze that seemed deafening.

He knew it was the noise of a handheld radio. It was the noise it makes when another radio is transmitting with no one speaking into it.

Was it a trap to lure him in? Maybe there's a radio on its own I may hear upfront with Ivan pressing his own radio to create the transmission sound? An ambush within an ambush? Is he waiting behind me ready to pounce?

Immediately throwing his head around to check his prediction he sighed, nothing. This was pissing him off. Unless the wind was deceiving him, the static was about 30 metres away to his front amongst some large rubble.

He started to creep backwards a few metres until he got behind a huge ice block and went to ground. This terrain was perfect for concealment to track someone as he was doing, but equally perfect to lie in wait and kill someone like he assumed Ivan was. Seeing the tent he knew he was now directly behind the original ambush position where Ivan was shot.

Five minutes passed seeming like an eternity especially as patience was not naturally in his make-up. All the guesswork had taken its toll and it was time to close the deal he thought.

Fuck it Decker, no more fucking about let's end this shit and stop dancing around. Right straight up the middle let's confront this bastard, he's in this vicinity somewhere.

He was initially going to do another deception leg to cut back in from the East but he had just convinced himself to go straight South to the radio noise.

Stalking slowly on his final attack heading he was close to Ivan, he sensed it.

That intuitive feeling was flooding his body, it was a great feeling that brought immediate awareness, that sixth sense kind of thing. With that came the anxiety, as he knew he was about to brace for a collision course. Either a head-on with Ivan, or the hope that he would surprise him from behind as planned.

20 metres away he spotted a brown mountaineering boot with a pool of blood around it.

Instantly seeing that a leg was attached to it he went to ground and paused. As much as this was an imminently life endangering moment he couldn't help but think, I'm not falling for the empty boot trick to find a gun in my head.

It was not the case as he saw it move slightly in the pool of blood.

Cautiously moving sideways to come slightly behind left of Ivan, Decker got into a position just over 10 metres away, tucked up against an ice pillar, he observed what was in front of him.

Ivan had his weapon held up to his eye obviously observing the kill zone to his front. Five metres away was the other radio on its own in the snow.

In his left hand was his own radio. Watching, WHITEOUT could see him intermittently pressing the pressal switch.

Bingo.

Decker had known that this was a trap and this had just confirmed it.

Moving in silently he had him.

Closing with his weapon trained directly on his back, if Ivan moved an inch he would get a quick burst in his torso.

Decker had the M4 butt in his shoulder, now pulling it in tightly anticipating the recoil when he pulled the trigger, with his index finger pressed against the trigger mechanism.

Wrapping his left hand around the front hand guard he was now poised for action. There was no need to look through the sights he was too close.

What was about to happen next was clear-cut. He'd just rehearsed it in his mind, played it out and was about to rewind and press play for real.

Squeezing the trigger four times in quick succession Decker double tapped Ivan's lower limbs adding to the trauma of the bullet that had already struck his leg.

Letting out a scream and immediately dropping his weapon Ivan naturally spun over. He obviously knew enough to know that there was no point in spinning round with a weapon still in his possession, that would be instant execution.

Still grimacing and naturally trying to grab his lower legs he faced up to Decker towering over him.

Snarling and spitting whilst gritting his teeth he looked up.

'Just do it Harry, I'm not a terrorist. One soldier to another just end this fast,' Ivan asked trying not to wince or show any pain, though it was obvious four gunshot wounds to the lower legs was unbearable.

Looking down at Ivan's shredded legs covered in blood he shook his head.

'I knew they were coming and I knew it would end like this Ivan, you should have got a pick-up. Why didn't you?' Ivan groaned in pain. 'What were your orders, how far away is the quick reaction force from us now? Decker continued asking.

Ivan had respect for Decker and in a bizarre way actually felt embarrassed that he had taunted him earlier. He actually admired the British SAS.

'Yes they are coming, I sent the code word for contact and they will be here in 60 minutes, you don't have long,' Ivan warned.

'What else, who the fuck exactly are these people? Are there more of them to come for me? Decker asked impatiently.

'We don't know but please end this when I tell you that my last intelligence update was that they were now here to take you alive, that's why we needed all of you so badly. I was told to capture Gerry too as the intercepts established he is high up in The Clinic. "Just kill the rest" were our orders.'

Decker looked hard at Ivan to try and gauge the sincerity and truth in his last comment. He made the snap decision it was genuine, well he hoped it was but would still tread carefully.

'Gerry?' Decker said, quickly thinking back to the guy at the truck who had been shot in the shoulder.

Ivan broke his train of thought 'Do you really not know what it is you know?

'I'm not a defector, but I know the guys trying to kill me know that I've uncovered their existence.'

'So you trust they want you alive,' Ivan struggled to get the words out, grimacing in pain, spitting blood across the ice.

'You said that's what your guys intercepted? So yes, fuck it, I will roll the dice Ivan.'

'Don't trust these people Harry. Now please end this humiliation,' Ivan was begging him to execute him.

'This wasn't your problem and you don't deserve to die, so hang on and one day tell your kids you met the explorer Harry Decker.'

'A pleasure asshole,' Ivan managed a small laugh.

Decker picked up Ivan's weapon. 'Stay here and don't be a hero, you will make it.'

Ivan didn't reply, he was concentrating too much on breathing as Decker started walking away.

Hearing a man's voice shouting, 'Harry are you okay, Harry it's Gerry show yourself.' Convinced Gerry and Sean were not going to kill him he jumped up on an ice mantle to see the men both standing 60 or so metres away next to the trucks.

Decker shouted whilst waving his weapon.

'I'm fine they're all dead, just checking.'

'Okay let's get out of here,' Gerry yelled back.

Simply waving his left hand notified Gerry that he understood.

Looking back down at Ivan before heading back something caught his eye about 40 metres to the East.

It was a movement but all he could see was the other dead Russian, the one Sean had killed with the sniper rifle.

Maybe it was his imagination and slight paranoia at this stage of the game. Brushing it aside he started to move off then as he passed a snow mound he spotted Mick.

'That fucking piece of shit that started it all,' Decker said, his blood instantly boiling. He had forgotten about him in the hail of bullets.

Darting over to take a quick look to see if Gerry and Sean were looking. They weren't.

Twenty seconds later Mick received a kick straight into the face. So hard it actually hurt Decker's foot. Still bound tightly and mouth taped, Mick had no retort or verbal scream to alert the others.

Dazed with blood pissing from his nose Decker was straight on to his torso with his hands around his neck. Leaving his mouth taped he started demanding answers.

'Who are you lot? Why are you trying to kill me, who do you work for? Motioning silence with his finger to his lips Decker continued, 'You raise your voice I will execute you'. Ripping back the bloodstained tape slightly, Decker lowered his head to listen.

'Start speaking fast, I want the whole story, do you work for the government? If not, who, and what was your mission?'

Almost unconscious, Mick spat out a load of thick blood with chips of his teeth mixed in from his beatings. Forcing his eyes to focus in on Decker he gasped a few times then started to whisper.

'Fuck you.'

'Really, are we really playing tough guy today?' Decker gripped both of his hands around Mick's jacket collar and pulled him in closer and almost spitting blood on his face Mick continued to whisper.

'You're fucked like me, these Russians will get you soon.' Mick like Decker seemed to be predicting they were closing in soon. Noting this Decker changed his tack trying a more empathetic angle.

'Look buddy, you know I'm the innocent party here, you all know it.

I think you have been crossed on this job, whoever's contract this is they have fucked you too. You sound South African, yes?'

'Yeah.'

'South African contractors on a British Government contract? Really? I think that this was always a one-way ticket for you lot mate.'

Mick was silent. Obviously processing his words, Decker continued.

'So come on asshole, you know the rules of this game what's the score? You've failed, you've been deceived and it's not looking good for you when I leave you here for the Russians to clear up.'

Mick obviously knew he was in a desperate position and was trying to contemplate whether or not they'd been crossed by Sully.

'You killed my best friend.'

'The British government killed your best friend, not me. I'm like you remember, but just a tad smarter it seems looking at this current dilemma.'

Mick closed his eyes, Decker knew that one had hit home. No one likes to come off worst when you're attempting to assassinate someone.

'We're on a contract,' Mick spat out more blood.

'What contract?'

'To capture you, get answers off you then kill you.'

'Who for?'

'I don't know their names.'

Decker knew he was lying but carried on. 'What questions did you need to ask me?'

'We were never told. When we caught you we were to phone in, the Boss would ask you the questions. When you were finished we would kill you. That's all we were told, you know how it works.' Mick managed a slight grin.

Decker took a quick look back towards the trucks and could see someone walking in this direction. Still not knowing what to do with Mick he started to rush.

'What's this outfit called, who are they?' Hoping he would get The Clinic as a response to confirm Ivan's story.

'He never said, none of them did, but it's something new, it's big I know that as my team leader was excited to be working with them.'

'What did they say about me?'

'You could compromise the latest covert psychological manipulation programme or something, I was only told this after you killed Robby, we never asked questions before this.'

Decker knew his self-appreciation society moment could wait as this confirmed his theory.

'Why did he give you this information after I killed your mate?'

'It was only me left close to you and I was going to sack this job off and walk out of here. He said I was in for sure if I pulled it off.'

'The Russians, when did they get here?'

'No idea. I was looking for you, I thought I shot you about 10 times, but turns out it was them out of the fog, then minutes later they started shooting at you.'

'What have you heard them talk about?'

'Nothing, they thought I was you and it's all been in Russian dialect.'

'Did you know who I am?'

'What?' Mick says.

'Did you know I was a former SAS Sergeant, a soldier just trying to make a life for myself again after this lot destroyed it?'

'Yes, we knew you were a retired professional but didn't know the background to this.'

'Retired?' Decker was enraged, 'You can take the man out the SAS but you'll never take the SAS out of the man. Was this what you fucking amateurs expected hey? A quick jaunt to Antarctica, capture me, ask some questions then fuck off home with my dead body frozen here?'

Mick never answered as he sensed the situation was changing rapidly.

'Well this contract killing world is simple when you pick the right targets, this time they got it wrong mate. Wife? Kids?'

'Yes both.'

'You can tell that to the Russians if they pick you up before you freeze to death.'

With that Decker stood up, turned his rifle around and butt stroked Mick as hard as he could. Mick looked unconscious, maybe even dead, Decker couldn't care less.

Knowing he has already been searched he left him and moved over to the dead Russian to search him. He was interrupted by one of the guys screaming at him from the trucks, he quickly checked over the Russian's military rucksack.

'Harry, we have got to go it's the chopper, it's the Russians coming for pick-up, move it.'

This wasn't ideal.

Damn I need my Moleskines. He rapidly shook the contents out, knowing that they were in there somewhere with the kit but there just wasn't enough time to go through everything.

Cutting his losses he started to head back to the trucks with his weapon trained in his shoulder but stopped after a few metres, turned and walked back.

It wasn't just for the Moleskine diaries.

It was unfinished business.

A professional knew that loose ends always bit you in the ass, he looked down at Mick's body. Not sure whether he was dead and not bothering to check, he drove the butt of his M4 rifle hard into Mick's temple three or four times confirming he was dead.

Not a whimper came from Mick as the right side of his head was caved in with visible brain matter and skull fragments on show confirming the job was done.

A few moments to compose the few seconds of rage was shaken off with ease as Decker turned once more and headed to the trucks.

As he approached Andrew was being placed into the back of the truck, in fact on closer inspection Decker realised it was the trailer, shit he must be dead.

The rush of anger he'd just shaken off engulfed him again as he started to run over.

Dropping Andrew's legs, the man he recognised from before quickly pulled his pistol out at exactly the same time Decker raised his M4 in his face. Arms almost crossed, each of them had a weapon a foot away from each other's faces. Both men's fingers had already taken up the first trigger pressure.

'Gerry?' Decker stated. Finally remembering his name.

'Listen Harry listen. We don't have any time left. This is happening. This is real. I will explain when we get on the plane.'

He was clearly out of breath trying to get it all out in one blurb, obviously aware that Decker could pull the trigger at any time.

Breathing heavily and not taking his eyes off Gerry, Decker again recalled Gerry's face and knew somehow he had to trust him.

'Bosnia, 2000, Ustinov was our target,' he thought again.

'Harry we have to go, if I have to put this down I will,' Gerry indicating with his eyes that he meant the pistol.

Decker nodded and watched as Gerry lowered his pistol.

Decker remained on aim.

Throughout this exchange he clocked Sean motionless in the trailer.

'Out the fucking truck you and get your hands up,' Decker ordered Sean who obliged instantly but slowly.

Rotor blades were getting louder, probably 15km or so away now, the reaction force were closing in fast.

As Sean moved out of the van Gerry without moving his feet quickly swung his pistol up on aim to his right and without hesitation delivered a swift double tap to Sean's head, then dropped the pistol again immediately.

Even Gerry was shocked by his accuracy with his left hand, knowing a miss could've got himself killed.

Decker raised his eyebrow. Mildly surprised. 'That little move could have cost you your life.'

'That's the last one, the last member of your assassination team code name Icarus. Get in the truck and follow me to the airstrip. Once we drive straight onto the aircraft Ilyushin I will brief you up fully. Ilyushin crews that you met before have all been bribed so there is nothing to worry about.

'Our evasion corridor back to the UK starts now. We have about five minutes to clear the area. By the time the Russians land and figure things out we will be too close to the South Pole station and US/UK territory for them to enter the air space. For them it's a clean-up operation to deny anything happened back there, you know how this works,' Gerry finished.

Decker had many questions but again focused on the rotor blades was reminded that now was not the time to be asking them.

Looking down at Sean's dead body Gerry looked at him again.

'Come on, it's time we got the fuck out of here. Even I'm starting to get confused about this whole thing.'

Instinct. Always rely on instinct Decker thought again as he held his weapon ready to execute Gerry.

Looking at Gerry's eyes he noticed a genuine look of confusion but not panic. It was a face that could be trusted and a face that had just driven into a suicidal ambush to get him.

Decker stared hard at him wondering what he saw back, before nodding, 'Let's go.'

CHAPTER 40

Decker clasped his hands around Sean's dead body, placing his arms underneath his armpits, linking his fingers together behind his back made him wince, the first time the pain from the cut that Andrew had unwillingly inflicted on him suddenly registered. Exploding from the kneeling position he managed to throw the body halfway into the trailer, Gerry wincing at his injured shoulder made a token effort to push Sean's legs in the trailer. Decker jumped into the back dragging Sean back over the growing mountain of dead bodies. Luckily they had not started to stink of death yet, though they felt stiff and deformed as he laid Sean to rest on top.

He hoped this was the last body to join the trailer of death and it wouldn't be his to top it off.

Surely this can't be another double cross? Decker thought, *I know this guy's face, MI6 Bosnia, 2000. My ordeal is over, isn't it, surely? I've learnt to trust people on instinct and raw gut feelings, can I really trust again after all this?*

Gerry broke through his silence. 'Harry we have to move, their waiting for us to execute extraction. They will be on us soon. I'll take the front truck, you follow we will stop once we see the South Pole station so we can quickly talk. I don't want to use the radios or phone because of Russian intrusion. I am sure you have questions but let's get the fuck out of here now, the flight home is the time for that.'

Decker could tell that Gerry didn't want to appear too forceful, he'd now proved on many occasions that he wasn't a man who needed prompting, antagonising or certainly manipulating.

'Yeah sure, I was having a moment trying to figure this whole fucked-up situation out and you're right, we will talk before and whilst on the plane Gerry, is that clear?' Decker changed his tone so Gerry would take that as an order almost, backed up by the fact he still had the M4 in his right hand as he jumped out of the trailer, Gerry knew the trailer had enough room for his dead corpse if he pissed him off.

'What's the plan if a Russian attack helicopter starts shooting the shit out of us?' Decker enquired knowing full well what the actions on would be.

'There's only one answer to that Harry,' Gerry held his gaze back. Decker nodded his head once, 'Yeah I thought so.'

Leaving it at that Gerry then walked to the front truck and jumped in, clearly and quickly started scrolling through the GPS menu until it displayed the data field for waypoints.

Decker having located the automatic option on the Arctic truck gear selector followed Gerry already thinking about whether the next curve ball on this journey would be a Hip attack Russian helicopter on their bumpers. He actually imagined it firing a Hellfire missile, locking on to his truck as he observed the vapour trail dancing about in the side mirror before obliterating them. He prayed this would just stay a disturbing thought and not be reality in the next five minutes.

They were speeding over the ice now, looking at the backdrop he had called home over the last month he started to worry, *How the hell are we going to get these bodies out? I mean if they have bribed the Ilyushin crew that's fine, but Punta Arenas? What after that?* 'STOP IT, FUCKING STOP IT MAN!' Decker shouted at himself, focusing back on the ice field ahead before another rant at himself.

'It's done just believe this guy. No more questions, what else could test me today? Nothing. Just follow Gerry and keep your eyes peeled to the rear.'

Though Decker desperately wanted all the answers now he knew he wouldn't get them until he was probably in a sanitised debriefing area. Locked in a room, video cameras rolling, tape recorders turning in front of a large mirror on the wall that hid the main man, who would be directing the line of questioning. No doubt they would produce evidence of him murdering an innocent expeditionist in cold blood, with a load of other prefabricated bullshit to hang him on, if he got anti and didn't want to play the game The Clinic were proposing.

That wouldn't happen.

Absolutely impossible, he thought, he was a killer, a calculated tactician. If The Clinic was aligned to what he had imagined, or been mistakenly made privy to, it was a win-win.

Even in such a short space of time Decker was already debriefing his own performance during these last few days.

Beyond this he started to actually make an objective assessment as to whether the pain of the last few years caused by The Clinic was justified. This ridiculous thinking snapped him back into the present. He thought about how they had destroyed his life, his career and almost made him kill himself once more.

Decker knew he was starting to weigh up the suffering with a reward that he still didn't truly understand and wasn't comprehensible at the moment.

Only the future would justify forgiveness he thought.

He was yet to forgive anyone.

Bitterness and anger were his primary driving forces, forgiveness was the sort of thinking that dampened and numbed the intensity of these feelings he thrived on.

No forgiveness.

Ever.

Checking his mirror again all Decker could see was the grey contrast of the skies meeting the white sastrugi surface of the ice, as the truck bounced across the Antarctic wastelands.

'That mirror is the past, the truck in front of me is the present, what happens when we get on that plane is the future' Decker murmured to himself, checking the sky for the Russians again.

In the distance there were some weird shapes silhouetting the horizon.

The South Pole station was in their midst finally.

It was the polar opposite of how he'd imagined his approach to the Pole to be but his relief and curiosity were the same.

Andrew had told him that the South Pole station looked like a number of alien spacecraft from a distance, especially later on in the day when the terrain took on a tint of yellow that actually resembled the moon's surface.

He'd had always thought his last hour of skiing each day was like being on the moon, alone with the combination of his goggles and the sun's glare at that time of the day... even those memories seemed a lifetime ago now.

Everything seemed to be clicking now.

He breathed out a small sigh of relief knowing that the Russians wouldn't come near this place, they were scared shitless of the Americans.

Plus the Americans, being American, would interpret it as an act of war and all chaos would break loose.

Only ten miles away he thought. Andrew had also said that it always seemed to take forever to close in as the buildings were huge and depth perception could drive you crazy. Shit Andrew, he thought sadly. All of that life and optimism now lying defunct in the back of his truck. He'd been caught in the crossfire and Decker wouldn't forgive anyone for that. He gritted his teeth again. Clutched the steering wheel harder and focused on the drive.

They were closing fast at 40 miles per hour across a relatively flat plateau.

Gerry knew they were on the clock and the Ilyushin crew would be on edge. Even though they dropped off some logistics and were scheduled publicly to pick the Trans-Ant Team up they would be nervous.

If all went as Gerry imagined they would simply drive up the tailgate of the huge Ilyushin and stop, the loadmaster would ratchet the wheels and chassis of the trucks to the deck, secure them, then get ready to taxi off down the runway.

Sully had come into the equation with the Ilyushin crew. He would have coordinated the extraction for the team. Gerry was just assuming that Sully would have informed the crew to leave the trucks alone, do their job and just shut the fuck up.

What Sully had planned for all the bodies and trucks in Punta Arenas was another story. Gerry knew it wasn't worth pondering on this part of the plan. That was Sully's bag and no doubt Roman would tell Gerry what was happening when he spoke to him shortly. Gerry hit the brakes and went static and waited for Decker to pull up alongside him which he duly did.

Winding his window down Gerry started to explain to him what he thought they were about to drive into.

Having already been dropped off here Gerry knew the layout of the station and knew that Ilyushin would be held as far away from the complex as possible.

This wasn't an international airport with high fences, CCTV cameras, wandering guards with attack dogs, but even so, given the cargo heaped in the back of the truck they were driving, Decker could potentially cause a massive stink and blow Sully's whole operation wide open. Unable to gauge anything from Decker's trained noncommittal expression, he carried on in the vain hope that Decker was smart enough for them all.

'Harry, we're nearly there as you can see,' Gerry pointed to the weird structures on the horizon.

'From here it's the far right corner; I reckon the Ilyushin will be parked at the bottom near the refuel bunker. It fills up at literally the last minute as the reserve fuel gets pumped into the wings. They do this last minute to prevent stressing out the wings.'

Gerry had had to filter some incredibly useless information over the years, but had cultivated this bit of trash conversation into an important factor in their extraction from an extraordinarily beautiful worker at Punta Arenas airport.

'They always fuelled last-minute to have a clear weather break of an hour before they ever commit to a take off. That's why we get here only to be turned away when the weather window is predicted to change within an hour, to ninety minutes,' she told him.

Gerry continued: 'I suspect the tailgate will be down as they'll be waiting for us. I imagine it will just be us on the flight. The crews are all on the take so don't worry about them. Stay in the truck when we get on. I will speak to the pilot Roman and get a quick brief, as I still don't know if we're flying to Punta. This strategic airlifter has an in-flight refuel capability and as it only needs 450 metres of runway to land with its thrust reversal system we could be landing anywhere,' Gerry pre-empted Decker's next question as to where they were landing.

'Harry I will tell the Captain, Roman, that the guys are staying in the trucks. He knows we're dodgy so it won't bother him, but I don't want to raise any suspicions about why the guys aren't getting out of the trucks.'

'Okay I will stay put, but what if something isn't right?'

'If there is no clear signal as to what's happening I will call Sully. Even though we risk interception I am sure he will somehow encode to me what's happening.'

'Simplicity is the ultimate sophistication hey Gerry?' Decker's face smirked at him.

Gerry shrugged his shoulders instinctively which triggered a shock wave of severe pain through his body. He sucked in his cheeks at the pain.

Decker didn't show any physical compassion as he surveyed Gerry's blood stained jacket and asked: 'Is it okay?'

Unsure of Decker's intentions Gerry grimaced, looked at his bloodied left hand before deciding to return the smirk with a wink.

'Nothing changes Harry.' For the first time Gerry actually laughed out loud recognising the fact that the ordeal was almost over in the field and his desk was beckoning.

'Right keep tight. If I start acting edgy or anyone tries anything with us and it's not in the script, we go hell for leather with what we have and if that means Roman flying that fucking freedom bird with a gun barrel in his mouth on take-off, so be it. Understand?' Gerry waited for a response.

Without a flinch, nod or reply back Decker did up his electric window and stared straight ahead.

'Ok then,' Gerry muttered and clicked the vehicle into drive again.

Pulling away Gerry was relieved the visibility was good. It was time for the extraction, the final phase of OP IGNITION. At least five miles' visibility with a high cloud base boded well for the planned take-off.

Ideally they wanted as little interaction as possible with the Station staff, any delay would put everyone on tenterhooks, especially Roman. Not a seasoned pro or an expert liar, let alone a brutal killer Roman just wanted to get home and finish his part of the bargain and retire.

Ilyushin was on the pan with the external generator keeping all the plane's operating systems on standby. Gerry knew Roman would be eagerly awaiting the sight of two Arctic trucks breaching the runway's perimeter and heading straight to the plane.

From Gerry's relentless research he even knew that as soon as the crew saw them come hurtling through the wire that the fuel truck could start pumping the wings full of reserve jet fuel.

Decker sat behind the wheel of his truck and sighed, listening to Gerry's ramshackle plan was just the usual seat of the pants, back of the fag packet planning he was used to from back in the day. It hadn't fazed him at all, if anything it had humoured him. An hour ago he had just been told he was back in the game unofficially or officially. Now he was getting a really shit brief from Gerry who clearly had no fucking idea what was going on.

'I've missed this shit,' Decker sighed again under his breath.

Looking to the eleven o'clock position Decker could see the main Station building. A three-storey monstrosity that had been a mere speck in the distance some twenty minutes ago suddenly seemed uncomfortably close now. It was casting a huge shadow across the complex. He clenched the steering wheel in annoyance, this should have been his moment, on skis alone powering towards the South Pole, marked by the ceremonial globe surrounded by the Antarctic treaty countries' flags.

He looked for the dome building, intriguing onlookers for years, his mind was littered with all the rumours of secret bunker systems, sensitive military research programmes and NASA projects that had been publicised in the past, adding to the conspiracy theories about this isolated community.

Short tours of the main station building seemed to fill the conspiracy theorists' appetite, many claiming it to be the Antarctic version of AREA 51.

He smiled, screw the conspiracy theories for once, the South Pole station was probably nothing more than the building for where a load of wankers studied ice formations, global warming and other irrelevant shit that cost millions of pounds to fund.

Driving past the complex to a kilometre away he looked for signs of life. It seemed dead, but he assumed they were all inside looking through microscopes.

What he did see was a truck moving between buildings. This sent an initial wave of suspicion across him though he disregarded it when the vehicle went static, just making out a body moving in to a building.

What he saw next was exactly what he had been painstakingly searching for.

Initially he could make out a number of Hercules C130 carriers probably belonging to the US military, as he couldn't make out the markings. Turning his attention to the right of them, trying to work out where the runway was, he clocked a lone aircraft about a kilometre from them.

'Ilyushin you beauty,' he whispered, before concentrating on taking Gerry's lead ahead for signals on how to react.

With no fences or barriers surrounding the airfield Gerry drove directly at the Ilyushin.

Checking that WHITEOUT was behind him he continued towards the airframe. Only 400 metres away, he could already see that the tailgate was down. He could even make out the thick fuel pipe that was now pumping fuel into the wings from the nearby tanker. *This bodes well*, he thought.

Closing in to 50 metres he spotted the loadmaster standing at the tailgate, the man looked directly at him before crossing both his arms aloft his head. This universal hand signal meant stop.

Stopping 20 metres away the loadmaster came over to him, probably wanting to guide him on so the truck wouldn't damage the fragile shell of the aircraft. Gerry wound his window down to receive his instructions checking his wing mirror briefly to see that WHITEOUT was still only a few metres behind him. 'Hi there,' Gerry said breezily to the overweight Russian loadie that had also dropped them off a few days before. After the last few hours the Russians were the last people on the planet that Gerry wanted to converse with but he managed to remain pleasant with a false smile. A little ironic they were here to rescue them from their fellow countrymen he thought, *but what they don't know…*

'Hello,' was the response from the Russian loadmaster who was wearing the same stupid hat with massive furry dog-ears hanging down.

It was obvious to Gerry he was on edge, his eyes told the story. Full of suspicion and an eagerness to get on with the job that was unnatural to a guy who was massively overweight and underworked.

Quickly demonstrating left and right hand signals, Gerry gave him the nod.

'Okay my friend,' Gerry said interrupting him knowing they needed to get a move on. The Russian nodded and turned to slowly make his way back to the ramp. Gerry watched him leave and then scanned the area for other potential threats. He clocked the fuelling truck, it had two men working, one with the hose connector at the starboard wing, the other at the controls just behind the truck's cab. They seemed busy enough.

A third man was at the rear looking right back at him, standing next to a red Toyota pick-up. Wearing a massive red South Pole station jacket and a stupid hat similar to the one the loadmaster was wearing, he maintained his gaze.

What is he looking at? Gerry tried not to make eye contact.

The man then looked at the second truck.

Who the hell is he, logistics? Administration? For the station? His mind started to drive at 100mph.

The man adjusted his hat against the wind and started walking over.

Fuck, he must be looking at the bullet holes or the shattered windscreen of WHITEOUT's truck.

Gerry grabbed and clenched his pistol with his left hand and placed it inside his huge down jacket. Gritting his teeth to suppress the pain of the gunshot wound to his right shoulder, he waited for the adrenalin charging through his body to cancel out some of the pain. He could see WHITEOUT also watching the man making his move towards them and hoped he had his M4 at the ready to blast them out of this situation if necessary.

No one else from the station was close by, just the refuelling guys. If it came to it, all three would be given the good news then put on the plane. What difference would three more stiffs make in this predicament?

As Gerry was looking in the mirror he saw WHITEOUT nodding his head slightly confirming to Gerry that he was ready if needed.

Only a few metres away the man closed in on Gerry's truck. Pretending to be playing about with the Sat-Nav unit Gerry avoided looking at him, as though he hadn't noticed him at all.

Leaning over toward the passenger side, back toward the window Gerry heard two knocks on the window.

Just ignore him, he said to himself.

Another couple but no voice.

Then the knocks turned into a dull sharp stamp of the fist.

'For fuck's sake,' Gerry whispered to himself.

Still feeling the pistol underneath his leg Gerry knew he had to turn and face the music, it could be innocent but it certainly wasn't a 'Can I see your driver's license please Sir?'

Windows slightly misted, Gerry covertly gripped the pistol tighter whilst looking at the figure on the other side of the window. Hood done up and ski goggles on Gerry took a moment. Locating the trigger guard he began to slide the pistol from inside his jacket, looking at the side view mirror he then pressed the electric window button.

As he felt the bitter cold chill sweep into the cabin he turned and faced his next victim. If this guy asked him to get out it would pose problems as the pistol was under his leg, trying to hide it quickly could be tricky, but it wasn't a problem, he would put a hole in his head.

Gerry confidently said, 'Hello mate, how's it going?'

Waiting for the response there was a slight pause.

344

Slightly uncomfortable, Gerry wasn't happy. The figure remained silent and glanced at the second wagon.

Then the figure looked back. About to speak he breathed out producing a cloud of mist as his warm breath hit the -20 air.

'I hope that's WHITEOUT in that truck you fucker.'

Gerry's heart rate went from 200 beats per minute in an instant to 60.

'Sully, what the fuck? I was planning to blow your head off 30 seconds ago you nutter,' Gerry motioning his head downwards, drawing Sully's eyes to the Glock clasped in his hand, ready to rock. He relaxed instantly, wincing from the pain to his shoulder.

'How are we looking Gerry?' Business-like and wanting an update.

Releasing the pistol from his right hand Gerry immediately felt the absent pain return as the adrenalin wore off. He summed up his brief to Sully:

'WHITEOUT is not injured, I am however and lucky to be here. He is obviously confused and pissed off but workable I think. I haven't had anytime to fill him in with details, you can risk that one later. Everyone else is dead in the trailers. I've been shot in the right shoulder so thanks again. How about you Sully? Any injuries, blunt trauma or problems you want to discuss?'

His sarcasm was covering deep-seated anger as he recalled Sully's last request that had led him to four murders; Sean's had been the worst, however quick, it still felt like a complete betrayal.

'I am a little bit cold, but don't worry about me.' Gerry rolled his eyes. 'Right, drive on and meet Roman. Tell him everyone's staying put in the trucks as something critical is going on and they're using the IT systems. Inform him to hurry the fuck right up, with that, add you'll be back in the truck with the guys. He knows where he's going so don't discuss that. Clear?'

'I thought as much Sully. You flying with us?' An obvious question but Gerry thought to ask it.

'Not this time Gerry.'

'What's going on, why not?'

'Right. Once you get back to the trucks after you see Roman, my Toyota will be at the tailgate. I have the manifest for him to sign. They think I am with ALE, not you guys. When I walk past your trucks to go to the cockpit you two need to get out of your trucks and get into the back of mine. I will grab the loadmaster so he will be with me, once Roman signs the manifest I will get in the truck and we will fuck off. Clear?'

'Yes.'

'Make sure the refuelers do not see you get in the Toyota as I have no idea who they are. You speak to WHITEOUT when I'm doing the manifest.'

'Okay.'

'Get the trucks on now.'

Sully walked back to his Toyota.

Gerry checked his mirror instantly for Decker's reaction and saw him visibly relax into his seat as the potential incident obviously passed without any dramas.

Gerry slowly manoeuvred up the tailgate under the instructions of the loadmaster. As he entered the shell of the aircraft he was relieved to see a huge amount of stores piled up in front of him, creating a break between the seating area and more importantly the cockpit, hopefully making their exit to Sully's Toyota easier without prying eyes.

Hitting the brakes on the loadmaster's signal he cut the engine.

From behind the stores another engineer came walking through and immediately started anchoring the truck down with the ratchet straps.

Pretending to play about with the laptop Gerry stayed in the truck waiting for WHITEOUT to drive on. He kept the ignition on so the climate control pumped out hot air to steam the windows up and aid the cover plan.

Noticing his plan take effect he opened the door and climbed out clumsily protecting his left shoulder. Looking over at WHITEOUT who'd had his truck secured, he quickly walked over to his truck and gestured for him to wind his window down.

'Get the heating pumping out Harry to fog your windows up I am off to see Roman up at the cockpit. Stay put I will be back soon enough.' Turning around and walking past the other crew, then through the tight gap on the right starboard side he disappeared.

Decker sat tight, watching, the hairs on his neck started to rise, what the fuck was just about to happen? Instinct told him that there was a crucial part of the plan that he hadn't been informed of. Rage started to boil inside him and his hands clenched onto the steering wheel tightly.

What the fuck had just happened with that guy who spoke to Gerry through the window, the guy I just looked at seconds ago?

Battling his latest bout of anger knowing the web of lies continued, he had to wait for a sign to react.

He knew he had to sit tight and play this out however Gerry wanted it, he was still at his mercy and he fucking hated it. Why had he asked him to keep the climate control heating running on full power?

Four minutes later Decker was beginning to feel as though he was cooking slowly with the heating on at this level. Fortunately he saw Gerry moving quickly towards him.

Winding down his window again he started to give him a quick heads-up.

'Okay we don't have much time. When that guy who spoke to me with the red jacket walks past us we have to get into the red Toyota. He will get the attention of the loadmaster and take him with him, as he has the flight manifest. Our only problem is not being seen getting off the aircraft by the fat guy or the two refuelling men.

'I suggest you go first; I will look out for the fat guy. The refuelling truck should be out of sight so no problems there. No time for questions Harry, you clear?'

Sighing Decker rolled his eyes back and took it as yet another twist to this fucked-up trip.

'Yeah, sure just give me the nod and I'll jump out and jump in.'

'Good, right here he comes,' Gerry seeing Sully walk up the ramp with the loadmaster.

Walking straight past them and moving towards the gap Gerry watched the loadmaster disappear with Sully. Quickly looking over to see that the fat guy didn't start to walk this way Gerry knew it was clear.

Gerry gave WHITEOUT the signal by nodding his head towards the Toyota.

He watched WHITEOUT spring out, careful not to slam the door, and watched him walk down to the Toyota. Checking his right side for the refuellers he could only make out the bottom of the tanker.

So far, so good.

Gerry gave the gap area a final check, happy that it was still clear he made a swift move towards the Toyota and joined WHITEOUT crouched down in the back.

Not daring to take a peep they both lay in silence.

347

A few minutes passed before the driver door opened and Sully joined them. Did WHITEOUT know who he was? Gerry wondered as they hadn't been introduced yet.

Before he could say anything, WHITEOUT quickly started talking.

'The trucks, they're not locked as we left the ignition on for the heaters to mist the windows. We either risk the trucks being unlocked and the windows staying misted to disguise us, or we risk the loadmaster opening the trucks if he wants us for some reason.'

As quickly as he got in, Sully jumped straight out of the Toyota and walked back up the ramp.

Gerry and Decker remained silent. Sully could tell him when he was good and ready Gerry surmised.

Scaling the Ilyushin, Sully quickly opened the door to Decker's truck, ripped the keys out and hit the fob to lock, the lights as expected, flashed twice.

Moving straight to Gerry's truck he did the same then quickly walked off towards the tailgate before stopping again. Swivelling round he walked back to the trailer.

As he did, the loadmaster returned, probably coming to take up the tailgate Sully suspected, shit.

Placing his clipboard up against the trailer door window Sully started to mimic writing something on the manifest, feeling the gaze of the loadmaster still looking at him.

Sully looked up and gave him a nod and a smile.

The loadmaster, still only metres away, started to get the control unit prepared that operated the hydraulic tailgate.

As Sully mimicked fucking about with the clipboard with one hand, he was desperately trying to find the key to physically lock the trailer door, as the fob wasn't doing it.

With one hand he fumbled through the two sets of keys already losing count of which are which.

Each bundle had three keys on them.

Catching a glimpse of the loadmaster walking behind him before moving outside the tailgate for a final clearance check, Sully made a rushed effort to locate the right key.

Second key nothing.

Fuck it, is the door fucked?

348

Grabbing another key and hoping this was the one he forced it into the keyhole.

Come on you little beauty don't fuck this up for us.

Making an effort to turn the key right he felt no resistance, it moved freely.

Get in there.

The door locked.

Turning around he quickly flicked through the papers on his manifest for a few seconds, gave a nod to the loadmaster who was just returning, then walked off the tailgate.

As he walked off he noticed the fuel truck was just pulling away. 'In the nick of time then.'

The hydraulic system kicked in and the audible sound of the tailgate lifting echoed behind him as he reached the truck. He turned to see the loadmaster from the waist up. Giving him a wave Sully got in the Toyota.

As he sat down he let out a massive sigh of relief.

'Fucking hell. Talk about last-minute requests, anything else guys? Anyone left any personal belongings on board?

He put the Toyota in first and drove off.

As he looked in the rear-view mirror the Ilyushin was now starting to taxi, the tailgate almost closed, just the loadmaster's head was now visible with his earphones on.

Turning his focus towards his drive towards the main buildings Sully couldn't help but maintain a grin on his face knowing that The Clinic was now exactly where it needed to be.

Finally he could give the brief he had been waiting to give for nearly fourteen long months now. Unable to see Decker's face hidden behind his seat, he noted a slight tension in his chest of anxiety about the company he was now keeping. He dissolved it from his mind, planted his foot firmly down on the gas and blasted across the ice eager for the next stage to begin.

CHAPTER 41

Driving towards a small hangar on the far side of the airfield Sully noted the Ilyushin taxiing down the runway in his rear-view mirror. Snow starting to fall again he realised that his next planned move needed to be slick. Getting caught in the incoming front that was fast gaining momentum would be costly.

Grinding the handbrake on he got out with the guys still laying flat in the back.

He rolled up a set of metal doors. Jumping back in the truck he drove another ten metres forwards, cut the engine then jumped out. Raising his arms to pull the rollers down, Ilyushin was primed for take-off. No doubt Roman was in a blind panic checking the last few dials on the snow-covered runway. Pausing to acknowledge the one-way destination they were heading to, he gave a saluting gesture, with absolutely no compassion attached to it.

Slamming the roller doors shut he rolled back his heavy-duty hood exposing a fresh face that hid the anxiety that lay beneath it. Pulling the passenger door open he spoke:

'Okay, get out guys we're safe here.'

Decker rose slowly, reaching for the opposite door to Gerry. Not acknowledging Gerry's groans this was all about getting out smoothly and getting the upper hand. Knowing the other guy was front left of the truck gave Decker a blind spot to prime himself.

Standing up on the offside of the truck and blind to the guy who was now bent over helping Gerry, he quickly whipped his pistol out, ready. He quickly and quietly moved around the truck without causing suspicion.

They were both aware of his approach as they both calmly stood up. Decker kept his weapon trained on the nameless guy who still had his back to him. He could see his pistol on his hip. Neither man pulled the spaghetti western stunt of turning and shooting from the hip with his own pistol, instead they both sensed that they needed to face the music from the sheer silence. The unidentified guy turned around slowly first.

Weapon up on aim ready to punch holes into them fast if they started getting twitchy, Decker felt his face turn white with shock, nanoseconds before the gradual build-up of rage sees the red mist heading to explosion point, a point he was happy to be experiencing again.

Sully, his old Commanding Officer was looking straight at him.

He instantly revisited the last two encounters with him. One was giving him the opening brief on the new Cell in Baghdad, the other looking up at him from behind his office desk when he left a broken man.

Pausing everyone was shaken by Ilyushin's jet engines rattling the metal hangar as it got airborne for the last time.

Decker controlled his rage, taking a moment to ponder. Slowly working things out, he clocked a genuine fear in Gerry and a huge front being put on by Sully to hide his uncertainty.

Sully raised his right arm in an attempt to pacify him. No chance.

'Stay where the fuck you are, both of you.' Ready to start his one-way negotiation. Sully remained still, holding his hand gesture.

'Harry, take it easy for a moment. I expected this reaction.'

'You start taking it easy by first dropping whatever tool you have on you. Nice and easy 3, 2...' They both knew that the count of zero meant a bullet in Sully's head. 'Okay, okay.' Sully reached beneath his coat and fished his Glock out, dropped it on the floor before kicking it to his feet without waiting for the request to do so.

Looking around Decker spotted a room to his right. It was a small square office-type room with a window on the right-hand wall of the hangar.

'Both of you in that room,' nodding his head towards it.

'Harry, put the weapon down, don't have to drop it just lower it. We need to talk about this. You need to know what this is all about.'

'*I* need to know? That's the first thing that's made sense to me in the last three years.' He laughed manically, 'I need to know... You're fucking right I need to know, both your lives depend on it.' Both men stared at him. Motionless. 'Now get the fuck in that room, now.'

A desk with a film of dust covering it held the centre ground. Four old metal chairs with wooden seats and backrests surrounded it. A small sink to the side with upturned mugs on the draining board, from a kettle that had three rusty tins next to it, it was obviously a brew room or office for technicians who worked in the hangar previously. Today it had the courtroom feel to it or even an executioner's chamber WHITEOUT thought if he didn't get the answers he came for.

This'll do, he mused, thinking it was both the perfect courtroom and execution room in one.

'Now sit down and shut the fuck up,' he ordered locking the door and pulling the blinds down.

Both Sully and Gerry sat down next to each other, Gerry cradling his shoulder. Decker remained standing, walking left to right.

'Look,' Decker pointed the pistol at them, shaking his head. Placing his finger against his lips notifying Sully to be quiet, he walked behind them. Raising his arm, Decker brought his pistol down, whipping Sully across the side of his face, causing his eyebrow to explode, splattering blood onto the dust-clad table.

'Court is officially in session.' He grinned. He was back.

'Stop it, stop it Harry,' Sully shouted out as he placed his left palm over the first split in his head.

Gerry startled shuffling his chair back to react. Decker kicked him straight in his injured shoulder. Gasping it knocked Gerry off his chair and he slid back to lean against the wall.

Decker watched in satisfaction as Sully's blood spilt onto the table. Sully tried to lift his head back up to get eye contact. Decker walked around the table enjoying toying with his captors for once.

'You move I kill you both. Now let's just talk about how you hijacked my life, in very, very slow time. If I notice something doesn't quite add up, he dies,' Decker pointed the pistol at Gerry.

He was pleased to see that Sully looked awkward. It was obviously not going to his plan.

'Okay, but we don't have time Harry,' Sully continued. 'Look, Gerry only knows so much, this whole thing took a few wrong turns that I had to sort out… Sorry Gerry,' Sully gave Gerry a sympathetic nod. 'I had no choice ordering you to do what you did—'

'Skip over the high drama about choices and start talking to me,' Decker said impatiently.

'Three years ago I was approached and asked to lead a new project that, if successful, would begin a whole new wave of modern warfare. As your Commanding Officer back then I was told to recommend 5 candidates who I thought were the SAS's smartest, and most resilient to undergo a Mind Manipulation Programme called Project 8. Another 100 or so test cases were drawn from the Intelligence Services, other arms of Special Forces.

'When I understood the bigger picture and what this meant for the future I gave them The Cell in Baghdad.'

'I know, I remember your face filled with glee giving us the brief about getting one over the CIA,' Decker said.

'I only gave them you guys because the opportunities it would give the SAS in the future. The controlled setting was perfect and when I let them know we were about to use Larnaka and Mo, it was exactly what the boffins had been looking for. I handed it to them within an environment that was reaping hell as it was. People's changing attitudes and behaviours could go unnoticed and attributed to the intensity of war, if the programme encountered problems.'

Decker wasn't surprised by Sully's smug response and he retorted. 'The Cell, what timing, you must have been licking your lips to know you could hide the real agenda behind this programme, within a new Cell that actually makes sense to prying eyes? A super Cell and we bloody were, putting our balls on the line each day, dodging death, working out our own psychological issues, whilst you lot started cracking on with us too.'

'It was all supposed to be controlled Harry. They were using Ultra-Sound Psychological Burst Penetration though a number of mediums you find in everyday life.'

'Controlled? Andy Rodgers hung himself, Johnny Malbec shot Larnaka and killed her. Mo, had a divine intervention and changed faith. How was that all controlled? I couldn't give a toss about Ultra-Sound-'

'I only had certain knowledge of what they were doing with the new equipment they issued you,' Sully interjected 'I was assured they were looking for systematic evidence that they could break individuals down, then influence new thinking patterns, to create key actions and behaviours across a wide spectrum of areas. These area's would be key to a terrorist's mindset.'

'Didn't you watch my video?' Decker said sarcastically, before continuing. 'I figured all that out by what the guys did, or what you influenced them to do, you say?'

'This program isn't a brainwashing process, it's controlled and subtle, but problems happened.'

'And what's the silver lining?'

'There is none. It's ready, like you predicted, to be used against terrorist cells, people on the watch list and eventually lone wolves if the boffins can work out a few algorithms to locate them.'

'So put me out of my misery. What was it that I was manipulated to think or do?'

'You were just contained to carry on the fight, keep The Cell running effectively until the manipulation program ran it's course.'

Decker paused, looking hard at Sully who had relaxed slightly due to his explanations.

'Larnaka? That was a sick move from the boffins hey?'

'What was sick?'

'Influencing her to fall in love with me, then allow me to drop my guard and tell her things I shouldn't have?'

'Larnaka was never influenced. She was the neutral member of the team. Call her the placebo effect if you will. They wanted an Iraqi or indigenous member to simulate the suspicious character within a terrorist cell. If she had started getting twitchy about members' then this would highlight problems. She never even noticed Mohammed's dilemma.'

This made Decker pause. As he thought of her he quickly snapped out of it. Knowing he couldn't let Sully get the upper hand with his passive aggressive tactics.

'So what else about Project 8?'

Sully remained silent.

Decker crossed his arms, resting his chin on his left fist.

'You watched all this unfold? Stripped me of my life and career I adored. All my mates telling me to get help, stop drinking or simply thinking I had become weak and unsalvageable, "not worth saving so let him run his course, you ruthless maniac"?'

'No it wasn't completely ruthless. Alex the programme's mastermind had his own technology to sift out exactly who was being crippled by the manipulations. When it was clear the softer less resilient cases were heading south they reduced the programme's intensity before leaving them be to—'

'You mean business as usual? Put it down to some mid-life crisis? PTSD for us guys then let them try and figure out what the hell happened to a slightly malfunctioning mind? Nice stuff.' He shook his head in disgust.

'We realised that testing wasn't going as planned when a few of you headed through P3 without showing vital signs of emotional breakdown, so Alex kept turning the screw to see what people were really made of…'

'And me on the cliffs? How did you know I wouldn't do it?'

'I didn't. I didn't even know you were still alive then.'

'What?' Decker barked out.

'When you left my office a broken man I informed Alex you didn't look like a man who had much more to give, but I knew you would get through it and make a life for yourself. That's how Project 8 was running, so the last I saw was you was stinking of booze, three times over the limit heading out the gates of camp that day.'

'That's it? No "stop Harry", no call to Alex telling them to back off. You watched me leave my career a disgrace?'

'I didn't call all the shots back then. In fact, my concern was how I exited the SAS without causing suspicion to take charge of The Clinic. I knew what the Project's Mind Manipulation Programme was trying to achieve, but wasn't given full clearance until you were long gone, and I was away from the SAS.'

'So when did you find out I was alive?'

'I randomly saw that *The Independent* newspaper article about the expedition. As I said, when you left my office you were a broken man, I didn't know what you would do, but I knew it wasn't the end of you.'

'Nor did Alex did he, he kept pushing me didn't he, what a devious psychopath.'

Sully hung his head. 'Yes, Alex, our very own mad scientist. He made all the big calls back then, it was a scientific experiment run by boffins remember. He thought you were different so wanted to keep you rolling longer. I didn't know about this, until we intercepted a call to Steve Jones about the solar panel cable being broken. He had been monitoring you closely without my knowledge.'

Decker started tapping his pistol against his forehead digesting the data dump he had just heard. Sniggering he nodded, he still wasn't satisfied. Remembering the day he stepped away from the cliff and saw a man in the distance looking at him.

As he thought deeper he knew he'd seen this guy before wearing black-rimmed glasses a schoolboy would wear. Once on the water kayaking and again in the café next to the beach. Fighting hard to recall, it all made sense. 'This Alex? Wears glasses with an acne-clad face?'

'Yes that's him, our boffin.'

'The article? What did you do then when you knew I was alive and not in a ditch?' He retrained his weapon back on Sully.

'When I saw you were in Antarctica attempting to create history, I knew you had come back to us, you had gone full circle. My mind was made up then, hence I rummaged around your flat and found all your conspiracy theory stuff on your whiteboard, and then I found this…'

Sully reached slowly into his pocket.

Decker brought his pistol up on aim at Sully's chest.

'Easy, you know what it is.'

Decker sighed to himself, 'Dictaphone I expect, but I wasn't sure then that was still a hunch. I didn't know The FEAR would actually be this fucked-up Project 8 at the time. I even discounted it after I sent the video diary. I had a few days of bliss thinking I could start living again without this paranoia killing me.'

'Yes, that video diary you sent. That's when it all changed. I had no choice then but to launch a rescue mission.

'When the phone call was intercepted, Alex started to panic and brought it to my attention. We knew you were going to send a last diary call but didn't know what. In fact, I had a hunch before you sent the diary that it might be damaging.'

'So Alex didn't know what was on that dictaphone?'

'Correct he didn't know that I had noticed you pop again on the grid when I read the article and saw you were still alive. He doesn't even know what's on this dictaphone. I was about to play it to Gerry and Alex at our initial meeting. Thinking I had uncovered your genius thinking or conspiracy back then as you weren't fully convinced yourself were you?'

'No but I knew Antarctica would be the perfect place to figure it all out, or discount it as I did. So if I hadn't sent the diary then what Sully?'

'I would have continued the brief to the new members of The Clinic about you. They would have heard your dictaphone recording,' Sully shook the object on the table, 'that tells us what you went through, and how you defeated the so-called undetectable. It made perfect sense to me. You had cracked it almost, so you are the one ideally suited to take control of it or certainly take it to the next level. I owed you that at least.'

Gerry's eyes were squinting. Trying to take it all in. Decker noticed his confused expression. He was no doubt asking the question Decker was about to ask.

'Rescue mission?'

'Yes, before you tried something stupid again and exposed this project, or at least got everyone paranoid within government circles that would go looking for dirt.'

Decker looked at Gerry. 'Gerry what exactly were your orders?'

Gerry glanced at Sully.

'Tell him the truth,' Sully said.

'Yes Gerry from the fucking start please.'

Gerry nodded his head.

'Myself and another were called to meet Sully and Alex over a week ago. We were briefed that a new Mind Manipulation Programme was ready to launch and we were called The Clinic. During the brief we were interrupted by Beast, the Intelligence Officer who had intercepted your call about losing the solar panel. Twenty minutes later they watched your video call, that changed everything.'

Standing back up he was piecing it together, looking for irregularities so he could pull the trigger.

'So you heard me talk about the FEAR, this fucked-up programme?'

'No we didn't see the video call.' Gerry looked at Sully again.

'It's true,' Sully cut in. 'I didn't let them know exactly what you were all about.'

'What were you told about me Gerry?'

'You were a part of this Project in some capacity and you had lost the plot, effectively you were a dangerous loose end. So much so, you could compromise the existence to the public and you needed...' Gerry paused.

'Executing? Killing? Taking out?' Decker shouted. Looking squarely back at Sully with a look that said it all.

'You didn't even have the balls to tell them how you had broken me. That dictaphone tells a story about a man's journey to hell and back, not a story about a loose end.'

Sully remained silent.

'So I get it. If you had played that dictaphone, Gerry here wouldn't have signed up to it. Killing a loyal member of his own, sick right Gerry? Especially after hearing how Project 8 hijacked my life, sanity and almost my will to carry on fighting the good fight.'

Silence continued.

'So I ended up back on your radar again after you read the article in the *Independent* newspaper about this record attempt. The title "Man's search for solitude, and quest to win the war within," must have caught your attention hey? Shit I dropped the ball there didn't I Sully? The war within actually created by you lot.'

Sully shrugged his shoulders and motioned toward his watch.

'Sorry we running out of time guys? So this Alex? Where is he?'

'UK in our Operations Centre.'

'In a classified location I bet,' Decker waved his hands. 'Get your phone out Sully and get his number up.'

'That's not—'

Decker took up the first trigger pressure, '20 seconds or I kill you.'

Sully pulled out an iPhone that had an Iridium satellite adapter fitted. Scrolling down he found Alex. Decker nodded. 'Hit call, place it on loudspeaker and place it next to the dictaphone.'

'But the Russians-' Sully's eyes looking up to the ceiling mimicking they could intercept it.

'Fuck the Russians, press call, now,' Decker waved his pistol. 'No in fact let's talk about the Russians as this is how it all went horribly wrong, and turned this place into a bloodbath that you know won't stop on this continent.'

Sully slammed his fist down with impatience. 'You need to listen to what's going on here, because I don't think you realise what the hell this is yet, and how it was only your last video message that fucked it all up. If you had shut up, no one would be dead.'

Decker walked over enraged, raising his pistol to prime another whip across Sully's head. Sully quickly continued:

'Harry you are a genius, how you worked it all out took us by storm completely. Your conspiracy? Wow, you did it, but letting everyone else know this wild conspiracy? We had no choice!'

'What the fuck happened?' Decker screamed out with rage.

'Look, hands up Harry? Things went wrong, but I think you need to understand what The Clinic is, what exactly we had to do, to launch a hit into Antarctica. I had to throw the dice but I always allowed for two outcomes and I gave you a fighting chance.'

'How?'

'The Clinic had not been operational and Antarctica gave me the perfect operational run out for us. The Clinic has a revolutionary MO and is an asset deniable like no other, I was assured by my two paymasters that they would not interfere. For me I could launch this whole operation without over-watch. We could re-enter all the murky waters and back-channel dealings, bribery, sourcing of weapons, outside surveillance teams, even the assassination teams, the whole lot, with a shit load of money.'

'And? Has there been any interference?'

'No, thus far they don't even know we're here.'

'The plan to rescue me?'

'I made sure the assassination team were second-rate, and the two guys on your tail only had pistols so they would have to get up close to capture you, not take a cheap shot hundreds of metres away. Then they would phone me and I would have the conversation were having now…'

'Yes, but you would be the one giving me the ultimatum, not me giving you one now?'

Sully sighed. 'Exactly. You've done us all Harry.' Sully clapped his hands. 'In all honesty I thought you would kill them both then see how you reacted. I expected a call on their satellite phone, or Gerry would have got one from you asking questions when you scrolled the names in the phone.'

'I would have and…'

'I would have told you what I have told you now, or Gerry and Sean would have closed the back door and taken you out the game. But after killing a few people I thought it would snap you back into it. A little insurance policy for us but essentially the result I wanted – you on board.'

Decker was deliberating knowing full well the deviant master-plays Sully could pull out of his ass.

'Time was my enemy. The risk of you causing rumours that would upset my bosses, causing people at Whitehall and Vauxhall to start digging around. In fact, everyone would ask questions and that meant shutting this all down. We were lucky we intercepted the video diary before it went viral.

'Containing you was my objective and killing you wasn't my first choice but a real possibility after we caught you and I spoke to you. With no power down there it was both a perfect window to get you before you spouted off again and a perfect opportunity to stress-test us all. Ironically it was to rescue our future commander if you take your head out of your ass for a second.'

Decker looked at Sully again wondering whether his psy-ops was still in full flow.

'No video call Harry and we could have had this conversation at Starbucks.'

Smirking Decker felt amused by Sully's attempt to try and regain control.

'Tell me exactly how you fucked it all up, and what about our Russian friends? What's the contingency to stop the Kremlin rattling the cage. Four Russians dead?' Sully didn't respond, Decker carried on: 'The Russians? They intercepted it all didn't they? Missed that Sully, slacking?'

Sully paused before talking, 'When did you know we were here tracking you down? How did you know?'

'South Africans Sully? Probably best trackers in the world, but not on fucking ice. Minus 40, limited visibility 70 mph winds. They got lazy.'

'Oversight on two counts then. I certainly didn't anticipate a Russian outstation clocking us,' Sully said.

'No shit, I saw them execute the other guy. Not the one I had to kill.'

'You killed Robby…'

'You killed Robby, you killed everyone Sully, even yourself maybe. When did you know the Russians had me prisoner?'

'When I couldn't contact Sean and I found out that you had called Andrew. I knew you must have got a battery from somewhere. Our guys have a different model Sat-Phone, not compatible. I saw Vostok on the map and it clicked, Russians must have deployed to try and rescue you.'

'Fuck me, wanted dead and alive. You couldn't make this shit up.'

'So Plan B. Our documentary team to the rescue—'

'And in the process murdering all of Trans-Ant team? You fucking sick bastards.' He looked at Sully and pointed at Gerry.

'I knew that didn't add up when I spoke to Steve about two documentary-makers wanting to meet me. That's when I realised for sure you were killers after me as the Russians made me arrange the RV.'

Sully carried on talking, 'I knew you wouldn't tell the Russians anything initially and thought you were lost to them, flown straight out to the FSB in Moscow.'

'No just a few smashes around the face. I'll live,' Decker pointed to his bruised cheekbone.

'But they got greedy…' Sully added.

'You both got greedy,' Decker snapped back.

'They worked out we're called The Clinic when I told Mick, he's the second guy who you killed.'

Decker stayed quiet not mentioning he was caught by the Russians.

'They knew we had men with Trans-Ant. So I changed my mind, and the mission.'

'Oh yeah I remember. Those were probably Andrew's last words, "they are here to save you, not kill you". Familiar?'

'I realised at that point that the original plan could still work. You alive, and us to move on and forget about this fuck-up. And that's true, no traps. I always wanted you to get through this. You gave me no choice, that video message—'

'Who exactly do you think you are? Choice over life and death? We have four innocent guys dead, three South African mercenaries and four fucking Russians? I would be worried about that one. This isn't a fucking game you psychopathic egocentric maniac.'

Slamming both his fists down this time Sully was enraged.

'That's where you're wrong Harry. This is a game. It's no different to the game we all played in the SAS. It's a game that you were born for. I'm blown away that you have won this one. You have to see the potential of where we're going with all this.'

'So what's the plan then Sully? How do you get me to say I'm in and not blow your fucking heads apart? I'm pretty sure after this, I can get my ass off this continent. How are you closing the back door on this?'

Sully looked at his watch.

CHAPTER 42

The loadmaster was doing his usual thirty-minute checks inside the Ilyushin airframe. Squeezing past the first truck he looked into a random control box to double-check everything was alright. Shining his torch deeper into the corners of the box, he confirmed that everything was OK.

Looking at the trucks he wondered what was actually going on but chose not to worry about it as he was under Roman's specific orders to leave them well alone. Switching sides he checked the starboard side control box, again shining his torch to the depths confirming everything was good.

Walking to the tailgate to check that the hydraulics and fluid levels were good something caught his eye like a bolt out of the blue. Walking closer to the trucks again to double-check his vision.

Fluid? he thinks, noticing the rear truck is leaking fuel. A pool of it had run past the rear wheel with the aircraft's movement.

Quickly grabbing a load of paper he scrunched it up, got on his knees and started to soak it up before looking up in confusion; the purple fluid was actually red, disguised by the low-level lighting.

Inspecting it again closely, the consistency of the fluid wasn't that of diesel or brake fluid, it was sticky and definitely red as he shone his torch on it.

Still on his knees he stuck his head underneath the trailer to confirm a leak but saw nothing, moving his head back he felt a drop hit his neck.

Wiping it away he saw it was coming from the bottom of the rear trailer door above him. Freezing for a second he witnessed a large amount of thick red fluid all along the rear bumper. Shitting himself he didn't hang around trying to open doors, he headed straight to the cockpit.

Now sweating and conjuring up horrific thoughts he climbed up to the cockpit entrance and spoke through his headset to Roman.

Roman saw his expression and instantly knew something was up.

'Blood, blood there's loads of blood coming from the rear trailer,' he gasped.

'Where is Gerry?'

'Don't know?'

'Did you knock on the doors?'

'No I just came straight here.'

Roman, the co-pilot and the loadmaster all exchanged looks.

'Okay, take over I'm going to speak to Gerry.' Undoing his three-piece safety harness Roman stood up and moved out of the cockpit.

Following the loadmaster back to the truck he immediately noticed the pool of blood, he moved to the first wagon and started banging on the windows. Confused at the lack of response, he looked at the loadmaster who was turning a whiter shade of pale.

Roman continued banging shouting, 'Gerry, Gerry you in there? You okay?'

The loadmaster started banging on the rear truck's windows.

Nothing.

'Get the fire extinguisher,' Roman shouted to the loadmaster.

Removing the extinguisher from its holder he gave it to Roman who immediately rammed the butt-end into the window. After three strikes the window caved in. Looking inside Roman panicked to find it empty. 'Fuck did we leave without them?' Roman's balls went cold at the thought, Gerry would kill him.

He moved straight to the rear truck.

Again nobody.

Panicking and racing to the rear trailer he shattered the glass, smashing through it. All he could see were large bags with a tent sheet over the top.

Ripping the tent sheet away he was met with the dead corpse of the guy he'd shipped out with Gerry, Sean staring back at him. Roman turned pale instantly and wretched, just managing to hold it back.

The loadmaster quickly took a look to see what had startled Roman so much. The lifeless eyes of Sean confirmd to the loadmaster that he had his blood all over his hands. He threw up instantly and looked back up to see Roman heading towards the cockpit. Bending over on his knees to propel another mouthful of puke onto the aircraft floor he realised that he was kneeling in blood which made him wretch even harder.

Back in the cockpit, Roman didn't even bother to replace his headset, shouting at the co-pilot, 'They're gone, they're not here and there are dead bodies in the trailer truck, blood everywhere. What the hell is going on?'

Studying Roman's features the co-pilot was in no doubt he was telling the truth, Roman was literally white with fear.

Ripping his own headphones off he asked, 'Say that again Roman, who is dead?'

Roman,in a muddle, kept his headset off and told his co-pilot to do the same to ensure nothing was recorded via the black box.

'Dead bodies back there, and Gerry has gone, they have disappeared, something's wrong, something's terribly wrong.'

Shouting again into his co-pilot's ear Romans started talking.

'What shall we do? Still fly to Punta or turn back, pretend we have a problem? They were supposed to take care of things at Punta. If they discover these bodies it's going to be a nightmare, especially if they search our rooms and find the money.'

'I don't know Roman,' his co-pilot responded.

'We either turn back or drop the trucks into the sea off the tailgate.'

'We can't they saw the trucks drive on, they have the details of what came on here at the South Pole. We have to land somewhere, I think we should turn back to Antarctica,' his co-pilot suggested.

'Yes, yes same here, let's pretend we have a technical problem with the airspeed measurements suspecting the pitot tubes are obstructed with ice and turn back.'

'Okay good, let's do it, remember don't mention the bodies, all we know is they got on, we took off and this is what happened. The first we know of the bodies is when we land, let's put our headsets back on and continue as normal.' His co-pilot nodded his head.

Getting into character, placing his headset back on trying to stay calm and fly the plane but flustered by the developing events, Roman started to play out the made-up scenarios about the speed sensor failure.

'Punta Air Traffic control, this is Ilyushin 2031 check.'

'Ilyushin 2031. Go ahead.'

'Punta we are at 32000 feet but experiencing a technical problem with the airspeed measurements suspecting the pitot tubes are obstructed with ice and are heading back to South Pole over.'

'Ilyushin copy, you have airspeed measurement problems suspecting the pitot tubes are obstructed with ice and are heading back to South Pole over.'

'Punta correct, we are turning back to South Pole station in case we have difficulties landing, it will be a safer option over.'

'Ilyushin copy, you are heading back to South Pole station.'

'Punta correct. That's us changing course now and returning. Our ETA is approximately 2 hours 45 minutes.'

Ilyushin copy I make that landing time approximately 2330 hours.'

'Punta—' He was cut off by a seemingly distant rumble that turned into an earth-shattering, eardrum-bleeding explosion.

Roman stopped, his entire body felt like it was red-raw with heat, and then everything went red. A huge fireball ripped through the Ilyushin reaching the cockpit within a second instantly incinerating his crew in 3000 degrees heat, created by the 2000 tonnes of onboard fuel.

Like a comet falling from space the Ilyushin nosedived from 32000 feet towards the hungrily waiting Antarctic Ocean.

Ironically the Ilyushin, known as a bombproof carrier proudly serving Antarctica for 27 years as the Trojan of all workhorses now fell towards its gravesite, decimated into millions of fragments by the sheer heat of the fireball, most of the airframe didn't even make the ocean, what did would simply be the Ilyushin's ashes spreading across the water and finally being laid to rest.

'Ilyushin this is Punta over,' the air traffic controller frantically trying to make contact.

Silence.

'Ilyushin 2031 this is Punta over.'

'Ilyushin 2031 this is Punta over.'

'Ilyushin…' Soberly taking his hand off the pressel switch the controller knew.

Ilyushin had a problem.

CHAPTER 43

S ully still glaring at his watch looked up at Decker. 'That flight out of here has everyone on it. Gerry and you, Trans-Ant and most importantly the pilots we've been bribing. That flight will be at the bottom of the ocean soon. All traces gone.'

Decker sighs rolling his eyes back. 'Of course Sully, since everything else has gone to plan so far, why should I doubt it? Decker sarcastically added.

'We have to get moving Harry-

'Press call,' Decker shouted interrupting Sully's sentence.

'Why Harry? Alex can't change things' Sully shouted back.

'I know, but I want to speak to the guy that manipulated my mind and fucked me over. I've had enough of speaking to the one who betrayed me, traitor.'

Sully reluctantly hit the call button. All three of them stared at the phone as the backlight flashed with Alex's name.

'Sully?' Alex voice came down the phone momentarily breaking the tension in the room.

'No it's not' Decker says.

Waiting for Alex to work it out. It didn't take long and his quick response sounded like he wasn't surprised either.

'Ah Harry, how are things down there?' All of them were a little perplexed by the calmness in his voice.

Sully interjected 'Alex we're all here-'

'Shut it Sully' Decker snarled waving his pistol again. 'Yeah Alex It's Harry Decker or WHITEOUT, whatever you prefer. I have a pistol pointing at your Boss and Gerry, understand?'

Another pause. 'Okay I see.'

Decker grabbed the phone and increased the volume to maximum.

'Alex I thought I would take the opportunity for you to talk to the guy that has not only detected the undetectable, but defeated it too. You didn't see that one coming hey? My crazy concept saved me just before I threw myself over the rocks, remember that day? I saw you didn't I'

Everyone looked at the phone.

Silence, just a small hint of static.

'Yes I do remember the sun was out ironically if my memory serves me correct'

'Shame you didn't follow me back and watch me piece together my strategy to kill off Project 8's manipulations.' Decker snarled.

'I see you know now what this is all about?'

'He knows everything Alex, the whole lot' Sully said.

'That's not strictly true is it?' Alex replied allowing Sully and the rest to stir for a second.

'I didn't need to follow you back Harry' Alex said.

Sully faced Decker. 'Alex hasn't heard this Dictaphone recording Harry, he doesn't know of your crazy FEAR concept that saved you, and made you discover our existence.'

'Again, I don't need to Sully,' Alex raised his voice slightly which agitated Decker. God damn him for being so calm. Fucking boffins.

'It all really started the day you left Sully's office a broken man. Remember? Shortly after leaving the gates Sully called me and told me you were finished, 6 months I think was what you said Sully?'

Sully looked at Decker trying to hide his shameful admission.

'So you spun off down the road then back to Corfe Castle, your spiritual home. As I remember, you went straight into the Greyhound Pub and carried on your death march into oblivion'

Decker was recalling this vividly as he remembered almost having a fight that night if it wasn't for the landlord saving his ass.

'You remember Harry?' Alex teased.

'Oh I remember alright you piece of shit so start cutting to the chase'

'So that's when it all really started for me, that's when the project began getting interesting. When I started to push the right buttons and find out if you were the one exceptional case that could beat my manipulation program. It wasn't pretty to watch as you know the details better than anyone.'

Decker was deep in thought as he knew what was coming.

'We had some crazy moments Harry, and I thought I may have pushed you too far on a couple of occasions—'

'You mean those 3 men on the Swanage chain ferry looking for me that day?'

'No that was all in your mind, just like the night you stormed out the pub thinking 2 men were watching you. That drunken car chase to avoid those two renegades nearly ended with you shooting two policemen'

Decker smirked, nodding his head as this ad hoc courtroom now had him on the stand.

'That would have killed this project' Alex continued 'Lucky they hit the blues and twos, that allowed you the time to throw your pistol when they cornered you in that dead end farm complex'

Sully and Gerry were looking at Decker. Momentarily he was lost in thought that confirmed to them both Alex had him on the ropes. Shaking his head and walking closer to the phone Decker responded 'and the doctor? I knew that fucker was a part of this program when he mentioned neuro-hijacking's—'

'No he wasn't. He had nothing to do with this. You went to him after you knew you needed help. Then you flipped out with paranoia, went back to your place then ripped anything technical that could possibly transmit or radiate stuff. When you didn't find anything you drunk a bottle of vodka, picked up another bottle then headed for the rocks,' Alex pausing waiting for a response.

'I was right though?'

'About what?'

'How you manipulated my mind, how you actually did it?'

'Yes you knew a few ways, but not all of them. You could never decide whether you were a paranoid delusional wreck or it was us'

'How did you stop me jumping?' Decker picked up the phone, wanting to reach his hand down it and rip Alex' throat clean out.

'I didn't stop you and thank god you didn't jump, as it would have wasted the last 6 months of work, or should I say Phase 4. I knew you wouldn't take your own life as you knew something was going on, and you proved me right'

Sully remembered Old Harry Rocks too just as Alex cut back in 'See Sully this was the reason we didn't take your option that day. This is why I said I could take care of it and let Harry get back to normality finally, without repercussions.'

Decker sensed straight away Sully had lied to him minutes ago about the last time he saw him was leaving his office. But too much was happening now, he needed to focus.

'Even that night we watched the video at HQ Sully, you wouldn't let me explain, you just palmed me off for two weeks so you could get back into your ego driven world of running front line operations on the ground.'

Sully didn't rise to the jibe, he knew Alex was about to play his own ace card.

'Phase 4? Project 8? Call this what you want, but it's time to end this all. I will blow their brains out shortly mate if you keep speaking to me like I'm a complete retard, some sort of experimental candidate that went sideways.'

'I'm sorry you didn't complete the journey Harry.' Alex said.

'You what? Are you serious?' This comment was random and threw Decker slightly as he scrunched up his eyes.

Sully's blank expression showed he had no idea where Alex was heading with this. He was feeling more nervous than before.

'Yes after 1400 miles and 85 days you had imagined your Union Jack draped over your pulk as you walked the final few metres towards the press reception. First man in history to do it…'

Decker caught Gerry and Sully looking at him. They glanced away.

'Yes, and let's not forget the song you would play over and over again in your head as you walked that final mile?'

Where was Alex going with this was everyone's thinking.

'We all listen to songs in our head Alex.' Decker said.

'Yes, and yours was the soundtrack to the Gladiator film, it's an inspiring soundtrack, good choice.'

Decker was rattled. He could see Sully twitching to know what the fuck was going on. Alex's posh voice and cock-sure attitude made Decker squeeze the phone tight, imagining it was his scrawny neck.

'You can't mess with me Alex, I've beaten it and have your boss at gunpoint so stop talking shit. I chose to stay alive, fight the good fight and here I am, about to create history until you lot ruined my life again'

'It's true though isn't it about the soundtrack, about the flag draped sled? How did you come up with the South Pole idea? That return to former greatness to create a mental masterclass and rid this poison in your head?'

'I created the FEAR and you need to be FEARING me Alex.'

'No I'm the last person who should be fearing you,' Alex said calmly.

'Really?'

'Yes I created the FEAR Harry, I implanted the concept when I knew you had beaten the Phase 4 intrusions. I had taken you to within an inch of your life by breaking you down but you didn't do it.'

Silence.

WHITEOUT started digesting a few things that were appearing hard to swallow, as he walked around the room deliberating before Alex spoke again.

'The next part of this program was then manipulating high value terrorists with the same manipulative intrusions that had almost killed you off. But once we got them to Phase 4 we could then re-pattern them with a number of strategies that ranged from ideological change, extreme paranoia about their own cell members, combined with a physical program run by Sully to confirm their paranoid delusions by orchestrating compromising situations. Ultimately a tit-for-tat killing spree would start infecting cells across different areas as rumors started to spread. No secret MI6 or SAS war on our own turf, just the maniac extremists killing each other over through fear of infiltration or defections—'

'Yeah I get it,' Decker interrupted, 'and I'm the one guy you had to destroy to get it to this point?'

'So my question was this,' Alex was talking again. 'Can I manipulate this man to take himself to within an inch of his life again by walking 1,400 miles on his own in Antarctica? So I sent you the link to the South Pole expedition. Can I make a man put his life on the line by ignoring the signs and signals to stop when death looks the likely answer? This was another project in itself to run strategies on you, that could work on terrorists after they went past Phase 3'

No one said a word.

Decker didn't know whether to semi bathe in glory that he was an exceptional person after all, or loose it completely and kill them all. His decision was cut short.

'You did beat it you know. You did work it out, you alone realised the FEAR was us. I didn't expect that part to happen and was shocked. If I had heard the Dictaphone recording I would have tried counteracting it no doubt, but I haven't so we both win this one. Both of us together'

Decker had made his mind up.

This whole psychological process had exhausted him. Life meant nothing now, all he knew was he hated Sully for his former Commanders betrayal. Gerry? He didn't know but would be tarred with the same brush. Holding the phone to his lips he makes his play.

'Well Alex any last words for Sully and Gerry? Let's see if your manipulations can stretch this far in real time? Can you stop me pulling the trigger?'

'Alex stop it,' Sully shouted. 'He's got a Glock on us. You do realise he will kill us if you don't start making sense and tell him where this is finally going?'

Decker looked damaged, an enigma he had uncovered and defeated wasn't as it appeared. Alex was quiet, they were all quiet or maybe just shell shocked.

'Well call me a bad loser Alex but it ends here for me, you won't see the guys again.'

Pistol back up on aim Decker took a second to align his sights. Sully closed his eyes to accept his fate. Gerry remained still on the floor watching him.

There was complete silence for a second as Decker focused his aim. Hearing static crackle over the phone, he paused knowing that Alex was about to talk.

'You kill them; you will never see Larnaka ever again Harry.'

Decker looked at the phone and paused.

Alex, raising his voice, repeated himself 'You kill them you will never see Larnaka ever again. She is alive, and your time is running out so follow Sully's plan and get the fuck back here so we can start doing what we are supposed to be doing, eradicating terrorists on UK soil'

When they all thought the tension in the room couldn't get any thicker or the room any quieter, they were wrong. This final spanner in the works made Decker turn to Sully, who felt his stare.

Sully opened his eyes.

Decker was looking at him waiting for something to come out.

Blowing out hard Sully started talking 'It's true, I paid her off with 20 thousand dollars. We knew you were planning to get her out of Iraq so both of you could settle somewhere, leaving it all behind.'

'She was shot Sully. I saw her slipping away that day' Decker was welling up slightly.

'She made it. It was a perfect opportunity to get her out of the frame so Alex could maintain you on the program and I could get you home. I agreed with Alex and told her you had been flown back to UK. And... said you had a wife and kids too to make sure she never looked for you. I ordered her to never surface again if she wanted to live a full life.'

Decker threw the phone on the desk and smashed Sully straight in the face. Sully didn't even try to block it.

'You bastard, you destroyed our lives together, you ended my life!' Sully was on the floor again. In the background Alex's voice could be heard but not understood. Decker walked to the wall exhaling hard, trying to compose himself.

'Harry, Harry,' Alex shouted down the phone in his weak high pitched voice.

Walking back over to the phone Decker spoke 'Start telling me how we are going to rectify this whole fucking nightmare.'

Sully slowly started to get back on his chair, nursing his split nose that was pissing blood again.

'Can everyone hear me?' Alex asked.

'We can all hear you so get on with it,' Decker taunted him.

'We all have a chance here to do something incredible, we've got this far and you lot need to take the fight back out there again. We're ready Harry, we are ready for you to lead The Clinic to hell and back.'

'Larnaka?' Decker replied.

'We can do anything you want us to, to try and find her.'

'Really? I'm finding that a big pill to swallow right now,' Decker said.

Gerry and Sully were feeling a slight change of heart now that Larnaka was back in the frame. Decker's broken body language told them he was in a mood for negotiation and this had all crept up on him. Sully started talking.

'Harry this is what you were destined to lead, forget the rest. This is it, our ticket to fight and kill like we've never done before. And we have to go now or it's over.' Decker turned away from Sully, whose voice was no longer shaking.

He felt tears running down his cheeks.

There was silence from Gerry and Alex.

'Gerry, in your experience where do you think she is?' He wiped the tears away.

372

'If she's still on the grid, the CIA will have her snapped up by now. High grade female operatives in that region are gold dust.' Gerry wheezed, his shoulder obviously causing him some pain now.

'Syria?'

'Maybe, but we all know she could be anywhere on this planet'

'Yes she could be, but can we find her anywhere Gerry?' Everything banked on the authenticity of Gerry's response. He glanced at Sully, who was also looking intently at Gerry, obviously in the knowledge that his answer could get him killed or grant him the chance to live.

Gerry looked up, and took a deep breath that made him wince with pain again. Decker walked over to him and squatted down next to him. Pretending not to notice the fact that he was obviously in pain, he leant his face right up to his and held it inches away.

'Answer me.'

Gerry blew out hard.'Of course we can find Larnaka. We're The fucking Clinic gents.'

THE
TRACE

RAY CAROLE

CHAPTER 1

'Conrad?' Lisa Trent's voice spoke excitedly down the phone, not expecting the call to be answered so soon by Decker's former Arctic mentor.

'Conrad, is that Conrad Dickinson?' she asked again. The voice at the end of the line was hesitant, either trying to place her voice to identify her from the unknown call sign that she knew would have flashed up on his screen, or he was pondering the thought, with dread of course, that it was a woman wanting to arrange cold-weather training and cringing at the potential pains of that.

'Yes, Conrad speaking dear, sorry but who is this?' She smiled at the response and also at the warm Geordie accent. It was just such a likeable trait and so far she'd liked everything she'd researched about him. She snapped back to business.

'Hi Conrad, I'm Lisa Trent.' As soon as she knew that Conrad would start processing the name, Trent was straight back at him with a line of questioning which was the only form of communication she lived by.

Direct and intrusive but well disguised by her seductive voice.

So it should be. This was a woman that worked on the Serious Organised Crime Agency for ten years after spending the previous five on Murder Squad and finished up in Special Branch before freelancing herself as an investigative journalist.

Putting people behind bars had become a routine habit to her, she was now busy crafting her art form of turning them into informants to open networks up in order to crush them. Now?

She knew that others saw her as a women with her own agenda, her own curiosities and paranoias. But to her, a case never closed in her mind until the perpetrator confessed, killed himself or was found guilty beyond all reasonable doubt. Sometimes that doubt had a little edge of circumstantial evidence miraculously appearing or disappearing.

She had read the final conclusions drawn from the Ilyushin catastrophe that lost three Russian Crew, four members of the Trans-Antarctic Expeditionary Team, two journalists and Harry Decker.

Most tabloids had followed it closely but the concluding verdict was catastrophic engine failure or a fracture of the exterior skin. Even a bird strike wasn't ruled out, even at thirty odd thousand in minus 60.

'Hi Lisa, you say?' Conrad asked.

'Yes Lisa Trent or Trenty.'

'Okay how can I help Lisa?'

'Harry Decker.'

The line went quiet. Names always conjured up images and she could just imagine what was racing through Decker's former coach's head right now. Damn she needed to get inside it.

'Conrad are you still there?' Lisa swiftly back to her probing ways.

'Yes, yes sorry I'm on the road.'

'I can hear that, Conrad I need to see you, where are you?'

Direct. Being intrusive was a figure of speech not adopted by Trent.

'I don't understand,' he asked. 'Are you another journalist?'

'No, I knew Harry a number of years back as a friend, sort of. I was in Special Branch but I am now a freelance investigative journalist, stroke Private Eye. This whole thing doesn't make sense to me and I want to follow up on a few possible leads or theories I have.' Theories was a polite and professional way of saying, 'I smell a rat.'

'What doesn't make sense? Conrad seemed confused.

'I followed all his blogs, knew the kind of guy he was and I'm suspicious of a few things. I just want to meet you as I know you saw him just before he left, and I wanted to know when you last spoke to him?'

'I haven't spoken to him since day 16 of his expedition.'

'How often did he call you on his satellite phone, I saw he mentioned you in a few blogs?'

'Every 2 degrees or 120 nautical miles, but what are you getting at?'

'I have lots of questions but don't you find it strange that he didn't call his mentor to explain his failure once the Trans-Ant team picked him up? Surely he would want to explain?'

'Look I'm driving at the moment and you've caught me off guard with what you're asking. In all honesty I'm pretty upset about his death and I don't even know who the hell you are woman.'

Trent realised she had hit a nerve but her thick skin continued to probe a little deeper, she softened her tone to soothe his nerves.

'Look me up, Lisa Trent, I'm legitimate and appreciate that this may seem weird Conrad but please let me call you back as soon as possible. In fact I will text you my number and email address, where are you at the moment? Norway still I take it from the ringtone connection?'

'Yes I am driving back from my Norway training camp, I've been here since November, I'll be back late tomorrow.'

'Okay has anyone else tried contacting you about Harry?'

'Just a local paper, I did an article about him before he left.'

'Conrad, can I ask that you please do not speak to anyone until I see you? You have to trust me. If anything happens, or something you remember pops into your mind before we meet, use the phone, text or email. If after we meet you don't understand my possible theory then I will not bother you again, you have my word.' That wasn't strictly true. Trent could be as bent as they came to glean the truth of a situation, she knew she was a solid detective who used her slim frame and well-rounded particulars when necessary to turn many a hardened criminal to inform.

'Okay text me, I will be back tomorrow night so we can speak then.'

'That's great I appreciate it. Remember do not speak to anyone about this conversation and anything you think of that is not adding up, keep to yourself, we will talk tomorrow.'

'Okay,' was the slightly dubious tone he replied with but Conrad felt okay and all of a sudden had his wits about him, the caffeine injection he was craving could wait. He had some thinking to do.

'Great, safe drive home. Bye.' Trent rang off and put her phone down on the front of her own *Times* paper, next to the article entitled 'Complete White-out, No clues as to disappearance of The Ilyushin 76'.

Conrad's mind raced away from Lisa and the road he was driving down and he tried to calm his mind. Shit. It wasn't happening. Blaming the distraction of the rattling chassis of his battered 1978 Series 3 Land Rover that now worryingly resembled the raging state of his own body, he gave up.

What the hell was happening? Only yesterday he was reading an article in *The Times* about the crash and the Civil Aviation Authority's investigative prediction where nothing had been found due to the geographical location of the Antarctic Ocean. Instead his mind couldn't shake his last goodbye to Decker. In a pub near Hadrian's Wall in Carlisle.

He recalled watching Decker drink a half pint of Guinness out of one of Ernest Shackleton's original silver goblets, it was Conrad's tradition to anyone attempting the South Pole solo. A safe return ritual, not that he believed in them anymore. Now a chick called Trenty wants to meet, he mused.

Something inside Conrad was intrigued slightly by this curve ball. Maybe it was his own past military background and the fact Decker was former SAS. Someone poking about couldn't cause any harm he thought. Also Decker was a bit of a maverick he recalled fondly, so it wouldn't surprise him if this Trent bird had uncovered some quality dirt which could be quite interesting. Now the shock had worn off. He was looking forward to her call.

★★★★★

Decker took a look at Bob and gave him the nod.

They were in a dark suburban street of Bradford that you wouldn't want to be walking down without some serious hardware to hand, with a wingman to help dish out the blows if needed. Sat in a dark blue Ford Focus, Decker had both. Bob a serial hard bastard and two Glock 17s. A seriously reliable and deadly pistol in the hands of two seriously hardened killers.

'I'm good my side,' Bob said in a low voice but not a whisper. Bob was always taught it was rude to whisper, even in a street that hadn't been patrolled by regular police for months due to the nature of its inhabitants.

Perfect for this little trip, and even better that every single CCTV camera had been smashed or torched.

'Okay, good here too,' Decker scanned the passenger-side pavement front and rear. It was a Tuesday night, early hours of Wednesday, so no chance of drunken idiots interrupting their business from a good night out and hence why they had chosen this day.

This little visit wasn't part of The Clinic's manipulation programme on AQ234 Cell.

This was personal.

For the last five weeks the whole team had been working hard on the strategy for when The Clinic went fully operational, after the manipulative results starting showing conclusive results on AQ234.

4

For the physical part of future operations, Decker knew he might need a few sources and some of the previous Muslim operatives that had worked with MI6 in Baghdad were the perfect fit. No doubt most of them were back here as part of the package deal they had signed up to, he thought. Wife, kids and family, council house and a shit load of benefits.

To be fair they deserved it, they'd stuck their life on the line for the country. Decker was actually surprised the government made it happen, if they knew of course, not like those bastards to actually honour their promises he thought as he'd worked his way through the files head-hunting potentials. When he was scrolling through the database a face had jumped out at him. His reaction at the time was pure shock and horror, which had been surpassed with an immediate realisation.

How he was in the UK Decker had no idea, but he had his details, his address and now a crystal-clear image of his face exploding from two bullets that he himself would be responsible for delivering at point-blank.

'What did he do?' Bob asked. It was nearly a whisper but not quite.

'I ran a covert program in Iraq, he fucked me over and also tried raping a team member in Baghdad. First time I met him I knew he was a complete cunt.'

'Rape? A bloke I take it, the fucking sick Arab pricks,' Bob replied.

Decker didn't say a word, just took a quick moment of reflection.

'Cheers for helping me put this one to bed mate, I know Sully wouldn't have approved but this fucker has kept me awake since I saw his mugshot on the file.'

'No probs, it's a pleasure I hate these fuckers. Watching you job one on home soil while I do crowd control is something I've dreamed of.'

'Me too'

'Let's do it then Boss,' Bob insisted as he flared his nostrils sucking up a huge space of air to see him through the formalities ahead.

Decker reached for the inner door handle, slowly but quietly pushing it open.

There was no going back now on this little vigilante job to a place in Britain that they were both completely disgusted by.

★★★★★

5

Stopping to open his hefty five-bar front gate marked the start of Conrad's own domain and the end of his worst ski season to date. The listed building that he'd restored to its former glory overlooked Hadrian's Wall and Northumberland National Park.

He looked fondly up to the centrepiece tower that housed his study, library and life's achievements. It would be good to be back here for a few solid weeks.

After Icarus had said their goodbyes with a small token of their appreciation in the form of a fat envelope, he'd spent the next two months further up north in Norway leading multiple expeditions.

He hadn't had the luxury of following Decker on his blog; his only contact was a phone call from his exhausted disciple screaming down his satellite phone from a wind-battered tent. Even after the aftermath of the crash he lost track of the headlines in the middle of the Hardangervidda. A barren land and the biggest mountain-plateau in Europe offering no real connection with the real world. It was the perfect world for Conrad, no smartphones, no city clutter, no traffic and no random humans, only the serious survived up there.

He looked around, it was good to be home. Now to make it shipshape. Plugging his computer back into the mains, followed by the screen and printer his workspace was back in order. Hitting the 'on' switch he heard the usual internal ramblings of the computer hardware booting up, and the printer reel acting erratically before settling in the idle position.

Seated in his leather retractable chair Conrad leant back and pulled his phone out. He looked at the recent calls list first to see Lisa Trent's number before checking the text message that had her new contact details attached. Her email would be a starting point for Conrad to do a little digging on Google, he figured, prior to calling her.

Conrad then thought about her call and her accent. She was a softy Southerner he thought, and was no doubt nearby soon, as she would have surely looked up his address. It wasn't a close-kept secret. He wasn't Decker, he had no secrets, well certainly none that would make him a target of his own government, maybe an ex-wife at most.

Driving back he had been thinking madly about Lisa's words. *Anything suspicious, anything he said, anything before he went. Don't speak to anyone.* As he mulled over the phrase *'didn't you think it suspicious he didn't call you when he failed?'*

In fact Conrad didn't at the time but on reflection? Yes, he thought, why didn't he? Decker wasn't the type to shun failure or be embarrassed about it. A courtesy call maybe? But then after nearly 600 miles, only 100 from the end maybe he was devastated, not wanting to talk to anyone. *'Would I feel the same?'* he asked himself.

Deciding to not make the call to her for now he logged in and started to get his house and business in order from the previous few months' training. He generally sent his invoices six months after training, such was his busy life. Always great short-term for clients, but probably a pain when that unexpected invoice for 2000 quid rocked up on their doorstep months later.

It was their doorstep too. He still hadn't embraced email to its maximum capacity and didn't care too much about saving trees. All his invoices were printed out and hand-posted from the village post box that was nearly as old as his listed home and Land Rover.

'Right let's get these invoices cracked' he muttered to himself entering into his first client of the season that was 6 weeks before Icarus came on the scene.

First writing a quick courtesy letter with the normal pleasantries and 'don't hesitate to call me again for my services'. He then added the part people hated, the invoice. Attaching it to the same file Conrad hit the print button, before relaxing back.

Groans from the printer, followed by the reel setting its position to print the first line was then followed by nothing. Silence, then an audible beeping. Leaning back up to look at the screen he saw the alert telling him that his printer cartridges were out of ink.

Not a problem as logistics was his strong point and his office stationery locker had the remedy. Ripping the cartridges out he started the process of reloading them all.

Pressing the stand-by button to start the pre-ink cartridge inspection procedure he watched its progress. Upon the last click there is a moment of silence, another little purring noise then the printer catapulted into action.

He relaxed back in his chair again.

The printer seemed to be printing page after page, certainly not just the two pages that Conrad was anticipating. Standing up he looked at the printer's collection tray, picking up the vast amount of sheets and flipping them over to see what was coming out.

Casually expecting a file about symptoms of hypothermia or weather systems that he had forgotten to print, he browsed the opening page.

Feeling an immediate head rush triggered by a heart rate explosion he panicked and grabbed the remaining sheets off the tray dropping a few on the floor in the process.

Looking at the title page he froze. It was blank with four lines of print:

OP IGNITION
CONOPS V4.0
TARGET – HARRY Decker (WHITEOUT)
ANTARCTICA

As he tried to process this he frantically pulled his phone out of his pocket and hit the recent call log.

Identifying what could only be Lisa's number he pressed the green dial button.

Conrad hadn't used the printer at all on his trip away only one other person had tried using it.

Robby.

Attempting to print the latest Decker file to make it easier reading he must have been met with the same resistance that Conrad had just overcome.

No ink, cartridges too low.

But the fool obviously hadn't deleted the file from the printer queue.

A novice error.

Conrad could tell he was shaking as he almost strangled his phone that was pushed tightly to his ear. The OPS papers fluttered in his hands as his shaking intensified.

Two ringtones and Trenty answered.

'Conrad how are you doing?' Without a moment to say hello Conrad let rip at an uncontrollable rate.

'Someone's killed him, he's been assassinated, and my printer, it's all here in my hands, get here fast.'

'Slow down Conrad slow down,' Lisa tried to outshout Conrad and get a grip of the situation.'What has happened?'

'My printer has just printed out a load of papers, it's an orders thing.' Conrad's high level of intelligence wasn't reflected by his thick Geordie accent. He had done his appreciation already and knew the lads that had visited for three days, the same guys who gave him a whopping tip, must be the ones responsible.

'Three guys visited me in Norway before they went down to Antarctica in December. They knew I trained Harry. It is them, it must be…'

'Conrad, listen,' Lisa again tried to stabilise a hyperactive Conrad who was attempting to wrap up Lisa's investigation in super-quick time.

'Conrad are you still at home?'

'Yes, yes and there's more printing out.'

'Listen. Stay there I am about four hours away. Don't leave. Send me the files on email now and I will be with you in four hours. I am driving a Black Toyota Corolla but I will call when I'm near. Understand?'

'Okay I won't go anywhere.'

'Great just calm down and don't worry, remember just you and me know about this so let's keep it that way for now. Okay?'

'I'm not talking to anyone.'

'Fine, look it's late so get some sleep if you can I will be there about 3am.'

Conrad looked at the clock and saw it was nearly eleven pm.

'I will try but I don't reckon—'

'Well whatever I will be with you at 3am and email me the file right now.'

'Right I will.'

'See you soon Conrad.'

Conrad had calmed down slightly and he took up position in his leather recliner with an added tumbler of whiskey to mask his fear and stop his trembling.

Picking up the rest of the printed OPS he shuffled them in order, took another sip of whiskey and started reading.

★★★★★

Tuesday night, or the early hours Wednesday to be precise the two guys cut through the shadows. To a trained eye you could make out the pistols in each other's right hands, and you could certainly make out the guy on the right, casually screwing a silencer adaptor onto his pistol.

Some would call that act unprofessional and argue that it should have been screwed on prior to getting out of the car. Others would say that it was a sign of a cool, calculated operator.

The truth was that it was a trigger mechanism, the final twist ensuring that the adaptor was housed correctly was the trigger, the sign that he was ready for action.

Every solid operator has one, the switch that takes them from being a loving husband and father, to a cold-blooded killer.

When the adaptor is unscrewed after the bloodshed, it was back to being the loving husband and father again.

The nod was given as the house front door lock was silently manipulated and without a secondary chain latch, the two guys were already at the bottom of the staircase.

They made slow methodical movements hugging the edge of the staircase to reduce any creaks from the wood alerting the occupant to their presence. From studying the plans beforehand, they knew exactly which room they were heading to.

The door to the room in question was already ajar. Another barrier to compromise removed as they heard the sounds of loud snoring coming from within.

Even better they nodded again.

Opening the door slowly and fully, the moonlight from the opened curtains illuminated them but they weren't concerned as they appreciated the full depth of their target's sleep.

As the second man covered the body with his weapon, the first man moved in throwing his leather-gloved hand over the sleeper's mouth. Pressing down tight there was no reaction from their target for a few seconds before a slight wriggle turned into a full-blown panic attack. Saucepan eyes locked onto the first operator's face clocking the pistol, silencer fully attached. No loving husband and father holding it, just cold-blooded remorseless killer.

The target was now wide awake and knew enough to stay still and silent.

Motioning their target to remain quiet by taking his hand off his mouth and placing his finger to his lips, their target obeyed, frozen, shaking uncontrollably, not even blinking.

Removing his finger from his lips, the operator lowered his pistol, about to say his first words.

'Hello Conrad Dickinson,' was all that was spoken. A thick Russian accent annunciated the name.

Conrad remained paralysed with shock. His heart pounded as he realised the level of shit he was in.

It was 0237 am.